TEN HAMMERS

LIZ ARCHER

Copyright © 2024 by Liz Archer

All rights reserved.

No part of this book may be reproduced in any form or by any electronic or mechanical means, including information storage and retrieval system, without written permission from the author, except for the use of brief quotations in a book review.

Book Cover & Formatting by Qamber Designs

CONTENTS

Chapter 1: Winnie.........................1
Chapter 2: Winnie.........................10
Chapter 3: Jack...........................18
Chapter 4: Winnie.........................27
Chapter 5: Winnie.........................37
Chapter 6: Winnie.........................45
Chapter 7: Max............................54
Chapter 8: Winnie.........................63
Chapter 9: Winnie.........................72
Chapter 10: Winnie........................80
Chapter 11: Winnie........................94
Chapter 12: Winnie.......................108
Chapter 13: Gavin........................114
Chapter 14: Winnie.......................123
Chapter 15: Gunnar.......................132
Chapter 16: Winnie.......................140
Chapter 17: Winnie.......................147
Chapter 18: Winnie.......................157
Chapter 19: Winnie.......................164
Chapter 20: Winnie.......................172
Chapter 21: Winnie.......................180
Chapter 22: Gavin........................194
Chapter 23: Winnie.......................199
Chapter 24: Theo.........................206
Chapter 25: Winnie.......................215
Chapter 26: Leo..........................224
Chapter 27: Winnie.......................231
Chapter 28: Winnie.......................237
Chapter 29: Diesel.......................245
Chapter 30: Winnie.......................254
Chapter 31: Axel.........................263

Chapter 32: Winnie	271
Chapter 33: Winnie	280
Chapter 34: Winnie	291
Chapter 35: Winnie	301
Chapter 36: Winnie	314
Chapter 37: Mason	325
Chapter 38: Winnie	332
Chapter 39: Winnie	346
Chapter 40: Cruz	352
Chapter 41: Winnie	361
Chapter 42: Winnie	369
Chapter 43: Winnie	375
Chapter 44: Winnie	383
Chapter 45: Winnie	394
Chapter 46: Winnie	402
Chapter 47: Winnie	407
Chapter 48: Winnie	418
Epilogue: Winnie	427
Ten Mountain Men Preview	437

TEN HAMMERS

CHAPTER 1

Winnie

The superpower of any great reality show producer is getting the cast to cry, but Goldie hasn't even asked me a single question yet, and my eyes are leaky faucets. I dab at them discreetly; the last thing I want is for one of the Hammer brothers to notice and tease me for being such a marshmallow. I have fought tooth and nail to convince the entire world–especially them–that I'm tough.

"Do you need a minute?" Goldie studies me over the top of her clipboard. She isn't just any producer, she's my close friend. She understands how hard today is for me.

Behind her, I can see the brothers as they work around the job site, putting the finishing touches on the kitchen cabinets before install time. It's impossible not to stare, and hard not to drool, when each and every one of my favorite guys is chiseled like the statue of a god, and their bare chests glisten with sweat from the morning sun.

"I'm fine," I lie, squeezing my thighs together. It's like she's made sure the camera is positioned in a way to purposely expose me and every single one of my feelings for the guys, just in time for my last confessional. "Let's get this over with."

I don't want to get this over with.

Our last ever reno, I mean. The confessional—that I can happily do without.

"Oh, Win," Goldie says with a sympathetic sigh. "The final episodes are always hard. Everyone gets emotional."

I snort-sob-laugh. "Really? Have any of the guys ugly cried?"

Goldie snort-sobs-laughs back at me. "The Hammer brothers don't ugly anything." She pauses, and drops her voice to a conspiratorial whisper. "But at least one of them has openly wept."

I raise my eyebrows, hoping she'll elaborate.

This is a story I need to hear. I've known Jack, Mason, Max, Theo, Leo, Gunnar, Gavin, Axel, Diesel, and Cruz Hammer for as long as I can remember. Never have I seen *any* of them shed a tear, except for Gavin when he fell from the old apple tree and broke his collarbone at age six. And even that didn't elicit more than a whimper. But to openly WEEP? It makes me wonder–will at least one of the Hammer brothers miss our show, and me, as much as I'll miss them?

Impossible.

"Sooooo…" Goldie prompts. "You're Winnie Wainwright, co-star of the hottest home renovation show on television. 1 Girl, 10 Hammers was not only your brainchild, it's been your entire life for eight years. Now that it's ending, what's up next for you?"

TEN HAMMERS

I don't know what's next, but one thing is certain: I won't see the guys on a daily basis and that thought makes me feel like my soul is being ripped away. The truth is, the show is a hit, even after so many seasons. The network would've kept us going for eight more. But from the get-go we all agreed that if one of us wanted out, all of us were out. And we've come to that point.

"... I have no idea what comes next," I admit.

Goldie gets this twinkle in her eye I know all too well. She's about to say something provocative and I brace myself.

"You could always be the next *Bachelorette*," she says. "I've heard they're interested in having you on as the first plus-sized leading lady in the history of the franchise. That'd be *such* an inspiration to girls that look like us."

There's sarcasm in her last sentence and she rolls her eyes.

I fake gagging. "Yeah, right."

I feel sorry for whoever the first plus-sized Bachelorette will be, but it won't be me. I do have one piece of advice for her: *Don't read the comments sections, girl.* If I had a nickel for every time a stranger made a negative remark about some aspect of my appearance, I would be the world's richest woman.

Besides, I don't need to go on a dating show to find out it's possible to fall in love with two or three or four people at the same time. I myself am currently madly in love with ten men.

"Something to think about," Goldie says. "You'd still get to travel, be surrounded by hot guys. You might have fun. You have come a looooong way from the girl that was dead set against appearing on-camera, you have to admit."

She isn't wrong – though the show was my idea, I never wanted to be on TV myself. The Hammer brothers had to drag me along, initially. They are all built to be in front of the camera, as if each brother was hand-crafted to be as swoon worthy as the *after* reveals of the houses we renovate.

"So, one more time. What is next for you, Winnie–" Goldie begins, but she's interrupted by Jack Hammer, the oldest at 33, calling out in his gruff tone as he approaches us.

"What's next for Winnie is that she gets her cute ass out here and does some damn work."

Jack is smiling at me and it's impossible not to smile back. His smile isn't just something I see. It's something I *feel*.

"Cut, cut," Goldie says with a groan.

I give her a small shrug. "Can we pick this up later?"

Before Goldie can answer, Jack picks *me* up. The first few times one of the guys picked me up, I about died, thinking they'd drop me or groan at my weight or worse yet, pull a muscle in their back. Now it's a semi-regular thing and I'm well aware of their strength, so I just enjoy the ride. I'm over his shoulder, my face pressed upside down against his bare chest. Am I tempted to lick it? Yes. Am I ashamed of myself for even thinking such a thing? Not really.

The guys are always shirtless when we're filming. No joke, it's in their contracts. The whole thing is designed to make every straight woman in America want to lick them.

"You're sweaty," I complain as if there's anything gross about this scenario. From this angle, I can see his six-pack and his happy trail, disappearing into the waist of his jeans.

I have regular fantasies about Jack sweeping me off my feet and carrying me into another room. Hell, I have that fantasy about all of the guys. But in my fantasies, the room always has a bed. In real life, he deposits me in a chair in the almost-finished kitchen. On the table are a variety of tile samples.

"We need you to decide on the backsplash," Jack says, raking a hand through his neatly combed hair, leaving it slightly tousled. "Today."

"But–"

"Why are you putting this off?" He pierces me with his blue eyes, which radiate with both confidence and warmth.

I glance at the samples. Gorgeous Calacatta blue marble, retro subway tile, genuine Italian terrazzo, rustic slate, Moroccan glass, and more… of course there are ten samples, as if choosing between ten of anything is easy for me. But I can't tell Jack the real reason I have been putting off the final touches. I'm not ready for everything we have built together to end. For us to all go our separate ways.

"Winnie," Jack says, tweaking my wild red hair–which refuses to be contained by a messy bun or ponytail–like he did when we were kids. "Come on. The faster we wrap this up, the faster we can all celebrate."

I force a smile. I won't be in the mood to celebrate. It makes me a little sad that he will be. That any of them will be.

"Did you decide whether or not you're going to Italy with Cynthia?" I blurt, running a finger along a vein in the marble, suddenly unable to look at him.

Lately, Jack is on-again off-again with *the* Cynthia Sinclair. Yes, that one. The supermodel socialite makeup mogul. I try not to torture myself thinking about the gorgeous babies they would make because let's be real. Jack never dates anyone for long.

But jealousy twists my stomach when I think about him dating anyone at all. I make myself sick. I should want him to find love. I should want that for them all. It might be a little easier, though, if there was a snowball's chance in hell one of them might find that love with me.

"I haven't," Jack says but I can tell he's lying. His left eye twitches. He's one hundred percent going. I don't know why he doesn't just tell me.

An even more unsettling thought hits–what if he's being evasive because they are getting serious? I don't know how I'd handle one of my guys getting married, settling down, starting a family with someone else.

"But if you go, it's for a few weeks, right?" I ask. Is there a chance he could be considering moving to Italy with Cynthia Sinclair? There's an edge of panic in my voice and I find myself covering the Italian tile with the subway tile, as if that might subconsciously affect his decision.

"Relax, Winnie," he says, taking my hands in his large, callused ones. Butterflies burst from my heart for a moment before he places my hands back on the tile samples. "One thing at a time. And right now, we have a kitchen to finish. Make a choice."

"That one," I gesture vaguely and get up.

"I didn't even see which one you pointed at," Jack protests, but I brush past him.

Without a plan, I end up back in the yard, surrounded by too many cameras, crew members, and shirtless Hammers to think straight. One set of the twins, Theo and Leo, sun-kissed blondes, are carrying a sleek dishwasher between them, their identical muscles bulging though they don't look like they're struggling in the slightest. The only way to tell them apart is their tats. So many tats, probably even ones I haven't seen. All of which I want to trace with my fingertips, my tongue.

Knowing we'll be parting ways in mere days is messing with my head too much. I have to find Goldie.

I spot her by the coffee station getting her third or forth fix of the day, and grab her arm, pulling her behind one of the film crew vans.

"Winnie! What's wrong? I need my caffeine!"

"I'm going to be a real-life 40 year old virgin!"

"Hon, you won't even be 30 for two more years—"

"I'm going to die a virgin!" I sound so cringey as I wail, but I'm unable to stop myself. "I've waited too long to lose my virginity. And why? Because I cannot lose it to someone whose last name is not Hammer. But do they see me as anything other than a friend? No! And who can blame them?"

"Winnie, wait—"

"I know what you're going to say. Do I actually want my first time to be with one of the Hammers? Yes!" I cover my face with my hands. "No, I NEED it. But do I want any of them, in all their physical perfection, to see me and my every flaw NAKED?" I bark out a laugh that sounds more like a cry.

"Winnie, seriously, you need to shut up right now—"

"I know, I know, I'm sweet, I have a cute face, and guys really do like curves, blah blah, but honestly, Goldie, why would any of the Hammer brothers want to have sex with this—" I gesture down at my body, "when they're banging supermodels like Cynthia Sinclair? And yes, I realize I'm acting like a sixteen-year-old."

"Winnie, stop!" Goldie cries, and I finally notice her pointing at a cameraman half-hidden behind the hood of the van. "You're aware that there's a camera trained on us and your mic is hot, right?"

Oh, god. Ohhhhh, god.

I spin around.

"DELETE THAT!" I shriek, barrelling for the cameraman, a tall, wiry guy called Jonesy. He is grinning like he just caught me and Golds having sex. "You have to delete it!"

Now I really do sound like a teenager having a temper tantrum, but I don't care. There's no way intimate information I've managed to keep private forever can be aired now. No. Effing. Way.

But before I reach Jonesy, he dodges, scampering backwards. "Come on, Winnie, that was way too good to delete," he says with a laugh. "It's what the audience wants, baby."

I want to puke. My vision starts to go white. "Please, no! I didn't mean what I said."

Strong arms gather me up, suddenly, cradling me with the scent of leather and warm vanilla, and I know that I'm being held by Max.

There's a calming blast of sandalwood as his twin Mason rushes past us to get in Jonesy's face.

"What the hell, man?" Mason growls. His ice blue eyes flash with protective anger. "Whatever it is you just filmed, delete it."

TEN HAMMERS

"No way. The tea Winnie just spilled is TV gold–" Jonesy starts, but something he sees in their expressions stops him fast. "Yeah, yeah, cool. Consider it deleted."

"If I find out it wasn't–" Mason warns Jonesy, as he scurries away.

Max gives me a squeeze. "You okay, princess?"

I want to melt into him, feel his comforting arms around me forever.

"Yeah, fine. Everything is fine now. Thanks, guys."

"What was that all about, anyway?" Mason questions. "What did you say?"

Like Leo and Theo, Max and Mason are identical twins, only distinguishable by their ink. They both flash me matching curious expressions.

"Oh...I... nothing," I lie, my cheeks growing hot all over again.

They study me a moment longer before heading back to work and I'm relieved they're too busy at the moment to quiz me harder. Ordinarily, Mason would turn this into a full-blown interrogation, endlessly questioning me until he found out what was wrong.

Goldie raises a brow, flashing me a sly smile from behind her clipboard. "Who knows, Winnie. With the way those boys rush to care for your every need... You might find yourself without a v-card sooner than you think. And one of the Hammer bros might be the one to snatch it up."

CHAPTER 2

Winnie

Our show, while unscripted, is heavily edited, because there are things the viewing audience doesn't need to see, like when Samantha, our make-up artist, needs to swoop in with a powder puff. At least these moments never appear in the episode, because I adore her but she never hesitates to loudly announce what she's touching up and why.

"You're so flushed today," she announces, coming at my face for what is probably the sixteenth time since Goldie made that remark earlier about me losing my v-card. "Let's get this decolletage, too, hun. It's practically neon pink."

The never-ending flurry of activity continues on around me as she pats me down. "There. Hopefully that'll hold for a minute. Damn, girl, you are flushed!" she adds, for anyone who didn't hear her the first time. "Are you getting overheated? Do we need to–"

"Have I mentioned that out of all the crew, I'm going to miss you most, Sammie?" I ask, my tone sweet and loaded with sarcasm.

Before she can respond, Max's eyes are on me from across the room, where he's wielding a power drill. "Hey, can somebody grab my water bottle? Win might need a drink." Then to me, he says, "Sammie's right. You may be getting overheated."

He winks at me before returning his attention to the task at hand. His tattooed back is slick with sweat. I have each of those tats memorized. I could trace the lines with my eyes closed, starting with my favorite–the dragon winding up his bicep…

So, yeah, I'm overheated. But it has little to do with the stifling hot air that fills the house. Without the HVAC up and running yet, even with the windows open, it must be at least eighty-five degrees in here. It's July.

But the true problem is that Goldie's comment turned on my imagination, which turned on other parts of me. It's probably pathetic that I have ten vivid, individual fantasy scenarios for how I would lose my virginity to each of the Hammer Brothers. It's more pathetic that I regularly–

"Hellooo? Jackie? Where is my Jack Hammer?" an unmistakable voice calls, breaking into my thoughts, which indeed, had had me getting red-faced again.

"What the fuck is she doing here?" someone hisses.

My thoughts exactly.

Cynthia Sinclair poses in the currently doorless front entrance. She's more stunning in person. I bet she's never gotten flushed in her life. And she is most definitely not going to die a virgin. I push aside any thoughts of her having sex with Jack.

While we're in production, all guests are supposed to be pre-approved before being allowed on set. No woman the guys have ever been involved with has appeared on our show. I'll be damned if even one second of screen time of our final episode will go to a side story about Jack and Cynthia Sinclair.

Though I bet it would make the network execs salivate at the thought of a potential spinoff about their romance. Love equals money, so they loooove love. They've forever been pushing a fabricated romantic storyline between me and one of the Hammers. We all said hell no to that and I said it louder than any of the brothers. I already get enough harassment from internet trolls, who've given me super flattering nicknames like Whiny and Winnebago.

"Hellooooo all." Cynthia waggles her fingers at us. They're perfectly manicured. I glance down at my own chipped nails, which I keep short. It's a necessity of the job. "Does anyone know where Jack is? I didn't see him outside?"

No one answers.

I imagine the guys are all stupefied into silence by her flawless hotness. Even I fight to keep from ogling her long, tan legs which stretch up from gold stiletto sandals.

Do not think about them wrapped around Jack's hips.

A pleated, button-up mini-skirt is slung low around her hips, pulling my envious gaze to her tiny waist and the sparkling diamond stud in her belly button. Her breasts are so small and perky she doesn't even need a bra under her lingerie-style top and she clearly isn't wearing one. Her nipples are hard as rocks against the satin.

Sucking in my stomach, I cross my arms and try not to barrel across the room and shove her out onto the porch with enough force to land her on her ass on the newly installed pavers. Not like that's something I would actually do, but I'm not going to deny that it's fun to visualize. She knows what it's like to be with Jack in a way I never will. I'm jealous as hell and not too proud to admit it.

"Cynthia Sinclair!" I cry with a pasted-on smile, because I'm also apparently two-faced. "How lovely of you to stop by!"

At that exact moment, with timing so perfect a producer had to have sent him down, Jack appears on the staircase, wearing a quizzical expression—and a t-shirt. The lack of bare chest means nothing that's about to happen will ever see the light of day.

He trots down the steps, placing a reassuring hand on my back as he passes me by without speaking, and then marches towards Cynthia. He says something to her in a low voice no one else can hear and the two of them head outside.

"We need to get her to sign a release," a producer says.

So they can use the footage with her in it. My pasted-on smile slips.

"No, we don't," Cruz Hammer, one of the triplets, responds. He sidles up next to me, bumping my hip with his. "The show is called 1 Girl, 10 Hammers, and our girl is right here."

He slings an arm around my shoulder, and my hand moves automatically to touch him— to run my fingers over the small, heart-shaped birth-mark, just a shade darker than his own tan skin, in the center of his muscled forearm. In my Losing My Virginity To Cruz fantasy, he uses a bungee cord to tie my wrists to the door frame of an unfinished reno, and he wraps his arms around me, holding me in place, that little heart flexing as he bounces me up and down and we gasp and moan as one.

I fight to keep my cheeks within the normal range of pink so I don't get attacked with the powder puff again.

"Is that staircase a thing of beauty or what?" Cruz asks me.

I smile. "Well, you may be a little biased since you were the one who carved the detailing on the rails, but yes, it is a thing of beauty."

"What can I say?" He drops his voice into a conspiratorial whisper and gives my shoulder a quickie massage that feels downright salacious. "I'm real good with my hands, Win."

Is he flirting? Yeah, probably. And it's working. But it's Cruz. He probably flirted with the wood while he was carving it.

When it is firmly established that Jack has gone AWOL with Cynthia, all of the other brothers are herded outside to get some B-roll footage of them faux-painting the exterior of the already-painted house.

I walk across the street and sit on the opposite curb to watch and, boy, does the sight take me back. The moment I turned eighteen, I moved out of my so-called family home. I could not live another second under the same roof as my father. I was going to rent a crappy apartment with the meager savings I'd squirreled away working at the movie theater during high school. But the Hammer brothers had been saving, too. They pooled all their money with mine and helped me purchase a fixer-upper in every sense of the word. They turned the small falling-down cottage into my dream home. I was mesmerized as I watched them bring their vision to life, at how their individual flawless bodies became one well-oiled machine of physical perfection and team work. I knew without a doubt that they were doing what they were put on this earth to do. And I also knew that America would love watching them do it.

I smirk. I was soooo freaking right about that.

Except for me, everyone in the country has a favorite Hammer brother. Diesel captured hearts when a cameraman filmed him singing a soulful love song in his deep, soft voice, and leaked it online. The song rose to the top of the charts. Jack, the rough and rugged redhead, listens to classical music to keep focused on his projects, becoming an unexpected champion for those with ADHD. Gavin's piercings started an entire piercing resurgence after he posed for a Sexiest Men in America calendar with nothing but a strategically placed tool belt and his nail gun. Yes, I secretly bought my own copy to lust over and a few backup copies, just in case.

I could go on. Each brother has their own devoted fan club, but I'll never be able to choose a favorite. For me, the Hammer brothers are a package deal. Always have been.

I'm not sure how old I was the first time I was sent off to Gram's house. That was something that happened whenever Dad was in jail–and after my mom died when I was young, that was a fairly frequent occurrence. My life didn't really start, however, until the day when Gram was at work and I was left to my own devices, and I glimpsed from the window, three identical boys about my age, playing on the grass of the house across the street. I was instantly spellbound. Little did I know, they'd already hatched the plan to invite me to play with them, having seen me walking from the social worker's car into Gram's.

We'd played all day, until we were all hungry and the boys were called in for dinner.

"What are you having for dinner?" Axel had asked.

"Instant noodles." I always had instant noodles for dinner.

"We're having pot roast and all the fixings!" Cruz had said, and then he invited me to join them.

"You'll get to meet our brothers. We're all adopted, except Jack," Diesel had added as I followed them inside and my nose was hit by the most delicious scent I'd ever smelled in my life.

I'd had no idea what the word adopted meant, and when I met the rest of the Hammer brothers – sets and sets, of them, like copies of each other, and all within a few years of each other in age – I assumed adopted meant being twins and triplets, something they'll forever tease me about. But I was warmly welcomed to their table that day, and treated like they'd always been my friends.

A welcoming home was something I didn't quite understand until the Hammer family. Gram wasn't nurturing. Dad had a cruel mouth when he wasn't absent. But the Hammers kept a permanent place at the table for me and they have a permanent place in my heart. Instead of always feeling lonely and scared, I grew up with ten best friends who were there to protect me, no matter what.

Ten best friends who grew up into insanely hot men.

A noise behind me draws my attention away from the eye candy display and I glance over my shoulder.

Cynthia Sinclair has Jack backed up against the side of the house I've been sitting out in front of. It's not like there are any residents inside to piss off. We always rent the entire block when we're renovating a house, putting up the families in hotels. Jack's shirt is off again, clenched in Cynthia's talons as she mashes her boobs against his chest.

His hands are tangled in her hair and it looks like they're in a race to see who can swallow the others' face first.

That is *not* how he likes to kiss in my Losing It To Jack fantasy.

I get up quietly and go back across the street.

"Hey," Max approaches me. He's holding his water bottle and hands it to me. "You never got anything to drink, did you?"

I shake my head and in that moment, I make up my mind. I may not have a Happily Ever After with one of the Hammer brothers. Sooner or later, they'll all find their Cynthia Sinclair. But. I have no doubt that even though I'm not girlfriend material for any of them, any of them would do anything I asked them too. They may not love me that way, but they do love me.

Before we wrap, before we go our separate ways, I'm going to ask one of them to have sex with me. And the Hammer brother standing in front of me is the obvious choice.

Reaching out, I place my hand on Max's shoulder, moving close enough to feel the heat from the sun radiating off his skin. "You know, there's actually something I wanted to talk to you about."

"Hey, Winnie!" Goldie calls over from one of the vans before I can say another word. "Someone's blowing up your phone! Looks important!"

I drop my hand, reluctantly moving away. "Later, I guess."

But he grabs my hand. "Anytime, Win," he promises.

Without thinking, I stand on my tiptoes and give him a quick kiss on his cheek, shivering with anticipation as the sensitive skin of my lips brush his rough stubble. Then I turn on my heels and hurry away.

CHAPTER 3

Jack

Cynthia Sinclair kisses as if every kiss is the last she'll ever have. At first, it turned me on. But now, I find keeping up with her frenetic desperation is more of a chore than a turn-on.

When I pull away, she blinks up at me with lust-heavy eyes. "Is that a screwdriver in your pocket or are you just happy to see me?" she purrs.

Okay, I might be *hard* as stone, but it's not like I'm made of stone. No, it's not a screwdriver.

"All of these houses are empty, right? Let's sneak into one and do it," she whispers with a giggle. She grabs for my hand, but I catch her wrist.

"Cynthia, we need to talk."

"We do!" She smooths down her hair. "I forgot to tell you. I pitched my idea to Diane and she adores it. She's already scouting locations for us to move in together. Only when filming, obviously, but it'll be an instant hit. You're a reality TV darling already, and I'm, you know, me. I think we'll call it Cynthia Loves Jack. Or Jack Loves Cynthia? Diane would want me to push for top billing, but I think Jack Loves Cynthia is sweeter."

Last night, on a video call that I tried to keep brief, Cynthia informed me of the five year plan she'd made for her life. Great. I'm all for a life plan.

What made my balls feel like she was tugging at them – and no, not in a pleasurable way – was when she divulged the role she wanted me to play in that plan.

I thought when I'd ended that call we were on the same page about not being on the same page. We're not even in the same book.

"Listen, Cynthia, like I told you last night–"

"So what do you think? Jack Loves Cynthia?" she bulldozes on.

I close my eyes. Diane, her agent, is the sister of Eric, our show's sound engineer. When they set us up I made it clear I wasn't looking for anything serious. How did we get here?

One desperate kiss at a time, I suppose.

"I'm sorry, but the thing is, I don't love you."

Also, as I've told her about a million times, when 1 Girl, 10 Hammers wraps, so does my stint in reality TV.

She swats me playfully on the arm. With an eye roll, she replies, "Duh. And I don't love you. You're not at all what I'm looking for long-term. Don't get me wrong, you're hot as fuck, and one of the best lovers I've ever had– and I do mean that, babe. But you're not soulmate material, you know what I'm saying? At least not for me. You're a bit too rugged, too rough around the edges. Actually that will be a part of your character arc on the show, I think. The extremely hot makeover of a Hammer brother."

I open my mouth.

"Now, Jack Hammer, don't you dare look surprised! You should know better than anyone that reality television is all about the fantasy. It's fiction– *fake*. But doing this will catapult our careers into the stratosphere."

Her career is already in the stratosphere and I'm content with my next career move being: has-been D-list celebrity. Designing and building houses in the country, far from all the lights, cameras, and actions related to a TV show, is my kind of life. I've loved every minute of 1 Girl, 10 Hammers, but I want my privacy back.

"Just say yes, babe. Come on. You know you want to." She shoves my arm playfully, but I recoil from her touch.

"There's nothing fake about our show." Has she even heard a single word I've said? Ever?

My attention strays. Across the street, Winnie has her hand on Max's shoulder. Maybe standing a little closer than *friends* should as she looks up at him. I scowl and run a frustrated hand through my hair, recognizing that I'm actually jealous of my brother. It's just that when I'm talking to Winnie, I always know she's listening, absorbing every word, truly paying attention and valuing what I have to say. I'd give my right nut to trade places with Max right now. Both nuts, even.

TEN HAMMERS

Cynthia snaps her fingers. "For god's sake, Jack, would you stop gawking at Winnebago and–"

"What did you just say?" I cut her off, my hackles rising.

"I said stop gawking over there and pay attention to me!"

"No." A cold fury settles in my chest. "What did you just say about Winnie?"

She waves her hand dismissively. "Oh, you know I didn't mean anything by it. It's just a silly name people call her."

"It's what assholes call her," I growl.

Cynthia looks startled. "Jackie, I didn't mean–"

"I don't care what you meant." I'm bone tired, all of a sudden, drained from interacting with this woman. "I care about what you said. Winnie is my best friend. She's family."

As I'm speaking to Cynthia, my gaze roves over to Win.

"She's everything," I say, mostly to myself.

Rubbing the back of my neck, I manage to tear my eyes away from Winnie. And Max. I can't tear my thoughts away from the fact that she seems to be touching him a lot more than usual. I watch as she gives him a kiss on the cheek before she scurries off, as if someone has summoned her.

"Look, Cynthia. I think… no, I know… you and I are done. Actually, I don't know if we ever really got started."

Cynthia shapes her glossy lips into a pretty pout. "What about Italy?"

"Pasta gives me indigestion. You go and have fun, though."

She stares at me, with one eyebrow arched and both arms folded across her chest. After a moment, she whips out her phone. Typing away, she says, "For the record, the official story is going to be that I dumped *you*."

I nod. "Fine by me. Take care, Cynthia."

I leave her and jog across the street.

Why do I keep wasting my time with women like Cynthia Sinclair, when what I really want is a woman like Winnie?

You don't want a woman like Winnie, that annoying little voice creeps into my head. *A woman* like *Winnie doesn't exist. Winnie is one of a kind.*

I want Winnie. It's not the first time I've had the thought. And it won't be the last, I'm sure. But as far as romance goes, between Winnie and me, that's not an option.

But.

I can't deny how damn much I'm going to miss her when she's not a constant presence in my life. The show has been the glue keeping her with all of my brothers and me. Keeping all of us in the same place at the same time. Suddenly, I want a ninth season more than I want my privacy back.

Could I convince them to go for one more?

Nah. The triplets are done with the show, more so than I am. It wouldn't be fair to try to twist their arms into agreeing to keep going. We agreed it had to be unanimous.

Us and our damn agreements.

I head back into the house, planning to get back upstairs where I was installing the recessed lighting fixtures before

Cynthia showed up. But I hear something in the powder room off the kitchen. I edge closer to the door, and, yep, there are undeniable soft sobs coming from inside.

Rapping lightly with my knuckles, I whisper, "Win? Is that you?"

She doesn't answer immediately, but I know it's her.

It takes a moment for her to open the door. She was trying to gather herself, to hide the fact that she was crying, but her red-rimmed eyes tell the tale and my heart pains from her obvious distress.

Win, you don't have to hide your tears from me. You don't have to hide anything from me.

I don't dare say those words out loud. She'd probably roll her eyes and tell me that after we wrap, I should try my hand at writing romance novels.

"Hey," I gently say, concern lacing my voice. "What's wrong? Why are you crying?"

She takes a shuddering breath, attempting to compose herself. "I'm not," she argues, but a tumult of emotion surges behind her eyes.

I gather her into my arms, breathing in her strawberry-scented hair. She sinks into me, all soft curves and sweetness. I'll never get tired of how it feels to hold her.

Fuck, maybe I *should* try my hand at writing romance novels.

"Winifred," I say, a warning note in my voice. Winnie isn't short for anything.

"Jackhole," she retorts with a snuffly laugh, pressing her forehead against my chest.

"Oof. Not Jackson or Jackmire, even? Straight to Jackhole?" I stroke her back, then add, serious and gentle, "Tell me. I'm here for you."

But she doesn't answer.

It kills me that she won't tell me what's weighing on her heart.

The soft glow of the pendant lights above the sink create a serene ambiance, and I decide to lighten the mood for her.

"This house is turning out really beautiful. What a shame it'll never be as elegant and sophisticated as the first house we ever built."

She tenses just a fraction, and I bite back my smile.

"You remember it, I hope," I continue. "It was the epitome of rustic and you gave it the perfect little kitchen, complete with toy stove to bake mud pies…"

I can feel the pull of her cheeks as she smiles against my chest, remembering the tree house we built for her in our backyard when we were kids. A sanctuary for her and her alone.

"You've come a long way since your infamous treehouse building days," she says.

"Hey, that 'treehouse' was a masterpiece of engineering."

"It barely held up my stuffed animals!"

My brothers and I were full of ambition but without any carpentry skills.

"It was a disaster," I admit

"It was," she agrees with a small laugh. Then she links her arms around me and squeezes. "But it was our disaster."

TEN HAMMERS

She lets out a breath and then says, "I just got a call from the probate lawyer and a real estate agent. Someone wants to buy the house as a tear-down for the land."

Her voice trembles. She's talking about the house where she grew up with her grandmother across the street from us. That is, until her Gram passed away just after she started high school, and her rarely present deadbeat dad settled in for good, treating her like trash and filling her head with garbage thoughts about herself. After he died during his final stint in prison a few years ago, she inherited the house.

"I've just kind of been pretending it doesn't exist and now I have to make a decision."

She isn't kidding when she says she's been pretending it doesn't exist. And we've all been helping her with that. We never go home to celebrate the holidays. Instead, we pick a spot on one of our bucket lists and fly our parents out every year to celebrate Christmas there. And all of us gathering at Winnie's cottage for Thanksgiving has become a can't miss tradition.

"What do you want to do?" I ask her, softly.

"I want to tell them just to do whatever and send me a check when it's done and I'll donate it to charity or something. But…"

"You feel like you need some kind of closure?"

"My mom grew up in that house. It's all I have left of her. How can I just let them bulldoze it?" She nods against me. "But on the other hand, how can I go back there? It would be like stepping into a time capsule of awful feelings." Her voice sounds heavy, as though weighed down by her memories. "I used to dream about living at your house, where it was warm and welcoming, everything Gram's wasn't."

She lifts her head off my chest to glance around the room. "Our show and all of our renovations have always represented a fresh start for me. A chance to leave the wreckage of the past behind and create something beautiful."

"And you've done an amazing job. You've turned so many homes into sanctuaries, proof of your resilience."

She peeks up at me and her eyes are two warm pools of blue in the soft glow of the lights. "You think so?"

I squeeze her tighter in my arms, not wanting to let her go anytime soon.

"It's true. You're incredibly brave, Winnie."

The disbelieving smile she flashes cracks my heart in two. "I don't know. I'm not sure I'm brave enough to face that house again."

"You are. And I hope you know I'll support you every step of the way."

Though I hate to see her hurting, I suddenly have an idea how I can keep us all together for at least a while longer. How we can help her get some closure.

But first I have to talk to my brothers.

No way will I be able to convince Win to go for this by myself. I'm going to need all ten Hammers to get the girl on board.

CHAPTER 4

Winnie

Two days later, it's the final, final day of our show, the day of our grandest reveal, and I thought or well, I hoped the guys and I would spend every second of it together. Instead I'm in the living room alone, and there's nary a Hammer to be found. Where are the guys?

Pretending to be content, I karate-chop a pillow with more force than necessary while Jonesey, who has been assigned the thrilling task of filming me, slowly dies of boredom.

Finally I turn around and break the fourth wall.

"Do you know where the guys are?" I ask him.

He shrugs. Since I lost it on him the other day, his interactions with me have been reduced to silent gestures. Shrugging. Nodding. The occasional lackluster thumbs up.

"Hey, Jonesy, about the other day–"

Before I can apologize, there is a thunderous boom over our heads.

Oh, shit.

The second floor is done. I've done the walk-through of every room, making sure everything is flawless, and no one– absolutely *no one*–is supposed to step foot in any of the areas I've inspected until the reveal. I want to make sure everything stays perfect for the family.

I spin and race up the steps, Jonesy on my heels. He can't risk missing the potential drama of a loose ceiling fan crashing to the floor or a demonic squirrel in the attic.

Please, oh, please, don't let it be the one-of-a-kind chandelier in the main suite. Please, oh, please don't let it be another squirrel–

I stop suddenly on the landing and Jonesy almost smashes the camera into the back of my head. I glance back to see him lose his footing, almost losing his camera. Whoops.

"Sorry!" I exclaim but I immediately turn my attention upward.

There's another boom, but the noise is still above me.

"It's coming from the attic," I mutter, starting towards the end of the hallway, but stop short as the hatch to the attic opens and the ladder drops down.

I start to scream, because what if we've had a squatter living in the attic this whole time and they're now deciding to show themselves?

But, no.

It's… Mason?

And then I stare, confused and dismayed, as one by one, the Hammers descend from the attic. Almost every one of them bumps their head on the way down.

"What in the fresh hell are you boys doing up there?" I demand when they're all together in front of me in a long, delicious, maddening line.

"Making sure there are no bats," Leo answers. Dirty liar.

"What's that sound I hear?" I cup my hand around my ear. "Oh, I think it's my BS detector." I shoot him a look. "It takes all ten of you to check for bats? And what the hell was all that racket? Were you smashing the bats with a sledgehammer?"

Gunnar steps away from the line. He puts his hands on my shoulders, his eyes locking on mine. When he speaks, he uses the sexy and hypnotic voice he always trots out when he wants someone to focus less on the words he's saying and more on how he's saying them.

"We were having a secret meeting," he says.

You are getting very horny, say his eyes. I can't tear my gaze away from their blue depths and his long, dark-as-sin lashes.

"We needed a place where you wouldn't find us," he adds.

You are getting verrrrrrrrry horny. You are–

Wait, what?

I put my hands on my hips. "You were having a secret meeting without me? You were hiding from me?"

Gunnar might as well have punched me. I don't know whether to be shocked, angry, or deeply hurt.

I go with angry. I glare at him through narrowed eyes.

"We're supposed to be a team!" I poke him hard, just above his left nipple, really digging my index finger in. In my fantasy about losing my virginity to Gunnar and then to Gavin, we spend an awful lot of time on each others' nipples. I'm mystified by their nipples – they're the only set of multiples that I wouldn't be able to tell apart by looks alone if it wasn't for Gavin's array of piercings, which started with the sexy silver barbells in his nipples. And Gunnar, though entirely free of metal, has the best pecs of the bunch.

Trying to veer my attention away from their deceit, Gavin sidesteps my question and says, "This moron," he gestures at Gunnar with a nod of his head, "sat his dumb ass on some kiddie chair and it broke. When he got up, he knocked over a stack of boxes."

"We cleaned everything up," Jack cuts in, ever the peacemaker despite his gruff voice.

Shaking Gunnar's hands off my shoulders, I side-step away from him.

"I don't care about any of that," I tell Jack, though I do. I just happen to care more about their secret meetings. "Cruz, can you make a replica of the chair? We need to replace it, obviously."

Cruz's chestnut brown hair flops into his soft brown eyes as he nods.

Ignoring how cute he looks, I return to the more pressing matter. "You guys were having a secret meeting without me?"

I try unsuccessfully to keep the hurt out of my voice. Gav immediately steps up.

"Hey," he says, reaching up to tuck a particularly boingy curl behind my ear, his thumb brushing my sensitive earlobe as he does. "We will tell you everything as soon as we wrap, okay? It's all about a surprise, for you, or we would've looped you in."

I'm skeptical. "You swear?"

"We could never keep anything important from you otherwise, Pooh bear. I promise."

Gavin has a way of instantly making anything better. He could promise me the moon and I'd unquestioningly believe he could deliver.

I relent. "Okay."

"Now give me one of those smiles I love," he says and my face obeys without any input from my brain.

"The Taylor family is ten minutes out!" someone calls.

My smile wavers as reality hits.

"This is it, guys. Everybody, bring it in," Axel says, his voice growing thick.

My eyes begin to mist over as I'm enveloped by all of the brothers.

One last group hug. One last reveal.

It's been all about lasts, lately, and I haven't had a spare second alone with Max to talk to him about that very significant *first* I am still determined to make happen.

To keep myself from dissolving into a puddle of tears at the reality of it all being really and truly over for 1 Girl, 10 Hammers, and this entire chapter of our lives together, I wonder if perhaps the surprise they have for me is the kind where we'll all be naked.

Mmm... They'll line up in front of me so that they're all looking at me, as they've always done, and I'll lose my virginity to them all. Each taking turns thrusting into me, all hands and mouths and hard, hard bodies worshiping mine until I yell "next!" for the Hammer to pass me on and...

"Did you just moan, Win?" Cruz asks.

"I was holding back a sob," I reply, and my voice is shaky enough to be believable.

There are so many muscular arms around me, I don't know which one is connected to the hand that grazes my ass. The graze turns into a playful squeeze.

Please, oh, please, let their surprise be of the sexy variety.

While I had allowed my imagination to go buck wild, cooking up a full-blown orgy, what the guys actually had in store for me wasn't sexy at all.

"No," I say flatly.

We're in a hotel together, taking up the penthouse floor. Production wanted to keep us around a few days to film some extra this-is-the-last-show-ever footage. I'm sitting on one of the beds in the room Theo and Leo are sharing, waiting for room service to bring up the feast we'd ordered to share, family-style. I've never been claustrophobic before, but in this room, with all ten of the Hammer brothers and their way-too-big idea, I feel like the walls are closing in on me.

"Come on, Win," Diesel says. "Just hear us out. You usually love our surprises."

No, I always love their surprises. But then Jack dropped the bomb. And now he's got them all *defending* it!

"*One last renovation – the true 'best one yet.*" I repeat Jack's words, dully. "You seriously want us to renovate Gram's house."

"We do. Before summer ends, before we all go our separate ways." Jack's eyes are earnest, eager, even, as my stomach twists with knots. "Our parents will be leaving for that 40th anniversary tour of Europe we set up for them, so it will be just us. Say yes, Win."

Ten pairs of eyes search mine, and I see in each of them a mix of apprehension and hope. I shake my head, but stop because I've grown dizzy.

"The house is a wreck. It's not worth it."

Mason gives me an encouraging smile. "It's an opportunity to do so much more than rebuild that wreck of a house, Win."

"Really?" I snap. "Like what?"

"We know it's a lot to take in," Max begins, his voice gentle. "We know you've never wanted to go back, that the bad memories have always haunted you. But–" He tries to put a hand on my shoulder, but I can't handle being so close to him. Not when emotions are growing into a tempest in my chest and I don't want to cry.

I pull back. "But?"

"Winnie." He runs a hand through his blond locks. "You know we'll be there every step of the way. We'll help you bury the ghosts."

"*Burying my ghosts* isn't as simple as redecorating outdated rooms or fixing broken windows," I hiss. It makes me tremble, the thought of opening those old wounds. The rotten walls of that house will always hold too much ugliness and pain.

A rap at the door and "Room service!" called out in an enthusiastic voice cuts through the tension.

Axel moves for the door first, sliding his thick black glasses up the bridge of his nose. "I got it."

I'm not hungry anymore. Standing up, I somehow make it to the balcony door on unsteady legs.

"Win–"

It's Jack, and he sounds stricken for some reason. Well, he can join the club.

"I need some air."

A cool breeze hits my face as I step out onto the balcony and try not to break down. Until now, I've managed to dam up my tears, but the river threatens to burst free.

How could they all throw this at me? How could Jack, who only just held me through a breakdown mere days ago, think I'd want this?

I place a hand on the railing to steady myself as I take in the city lights and sounds below. Jack's words continue to echo in my mind. They twist up my conflicted heart.

Their plan means more time with my boys. I'm not ready to let them go. But exorcizing the ghosts of my past isn't a step I've ever planned to take. My whole body sags under the weight of the thought.

"Winnie?"

I'm not ready to turn around. By his voice, I know it's Leo.

And then, "Win?" It's Theo, as well.

"Come here, baby," Leo says softly, and I can feel the space between us shortening as he comes up behind me. Large, strong hands circle my waist, gently tugging me back, hoping I'll let go of the railing, to sink into his rock-hard chest.

Of course, I do, my tight stomach muscles releasing as he gathers me up against him. He kisses my temple, once, twice, and then he rests his cheek against the side of my head.

Theo moves before me, fits himself like a puzzle piece against the front of me, his hands settling higher up my side. He's nearly skimming my breasts, although I don't point it out in fear that he'll move his hands away.

And I don't want Theo or Leo to move an inch. All the tension leaves my body as I'm surrounded by them, enveloped in them, every one of my senses overtaken by two of my favorite boys.

Leo breaks the silence, whispering into my ear, making me shiver. "Six more weeks of this, of us. That's something, isn't it?"

I look up into Theo's eyes, intense green and filled with hope and uncertainty. I know Leo's look will match. Their hope tugs at my heart.

"Of course it's something."

It would be everything.

"Just think," Theo adds, his thumb sliding along my ribs. "It could be 1 Girl, 10 Hammers, but this time without any cameras, without any fans trying to sneak on set. Nothing but us."

Theo's touch moves dangerously closer to my boob and an automatic burst of excitement zaps through me. I have had plenty of Losing My Virginity fantasies related to 1 Girl, 10 Hammers that start just like this.

Spending weeks living in the Hammer house with all the brothers certainly has its allure. Still, trepidation, from the idea of walking through Gram's old house, a place where I never felt a happy moment other than when the boys across the street were calling at my window to take me away, gnaws at me.

Leo slides a hand lower, to the top of my thigh, his fingers splaying. I'm not sure how intentional he's being when it comes to turning me on, but god, it's working. I have to hold my breath and stop myself from shimmying my ass into him, like I'm a cat in heat.

Needing to get a hold of myself before I embarrass myself, I pull away from their twin embrace. "Can I think about it while we eat?"

I'm only buying time. Obviously I'm going to say no.

Leo's fingers begin doing this stroking thing that has me wanting to yell "TAKE ME NOW" for the whole city to hear.

I'm absolutely going to say no.

I have to say no.

Can I say no?

CHAPTER 5

Winnie

Morning sunlight casts a golden glow upon the soft, creamy hue of the Victorian house, highlighting the inviting, wrap-around porch and stretch of large windows adorned with delicate lace curtains that hint at the elegance within. The front door opens.

"Where is she? I need to see my Winnie!"

I hear Anna Hammer, the matriarch of the Hammer family, before I see her.

"Where did she go?" Axel's voice is full of confusion, because two minutes before, I'd been standing right behind him on the porch steps of the brothers' childhood home.

Now I'm on the side of the house, puking into Anna's periwinkle hydrangeas.

I'd been determined not to even look at Gram's, but I caught a glimpse of the small house in my periphery, rundown though unassuming on the outside, and that was enough to bring my breakfast up.

Why the hell did I let them convince me to do this?

Oh yeah, it was me who let my pervy fantasies of losing it to Max in the pool house take over all rational thought.

"Oh Winniefreeeeeeeed," Gunnar sings out. "Where are you, my pretty?"

Your pretty is currently making sure she didn't get cereal bits in her hair, I think.

"Be there in a minute!" I shout. "I wanted to check out the hydrangeas!"

I untie the hoodie I sometimes wear around my waist to make it clear I have a waist and dab around my mouth and chin with the sleeve. Then I stuff it under the bush to retrieve later because nothing says *I'm so happy to see you!* like vomit, right?

I'd hurriedly wrangled my hair into a disaster of a ponytail using the scrunchie on my wrist when the first wave of nausea hit. Now I let it down and shake it loose and free–the way nature intended.

"Win?" It's Cruz that appears around the corner. "Are you really checking out the flowers? Because if you wanted one of us to follow you around here and, y'know, maybe sneak off to the pool house for a little makeout session, I'm all about it."

Cruz waggles his eyebrows and makes a kissy face at me.

He's joking. Obviously he's joking. But I'm surprised my face doesn't erupt into flames.

His eyes still twinkle, but the corners of his mouth turn down. "Hey. You did not come around here to check out the flowers."

"Had to throw up," I admitted.

The cringe is slight. Then he lifts a chin in his patented *I got you* gesture.

Walking towards me, he teases, "Let's say rain check on the makeout sesh, then, but…"

Then I'm wrapped in his arms. He presses his lips against my temple.

"We don't have to do anything you don't want to do. Any time you want to stop, you say stop and you will not get any pushback. I'll make sure of it, alright?"

With a shaky breath, I nod. Letting me go, he holds out his hand and I take it. I manage not to swoon when he entwines his fingers with mine and leads us back around front.

Anna practically tackles me in a hug.

"My Winnie," she says when she finally lets go. She holds my shoulders, taking a step back, and when there's an arm-length between us, she looks me up and down. I'm grinning, full-force, and not a bit insecure. There's not a critical bone in Anna's body.

"You are gorgeous. Do my boys tell you you're gorgeous on a daily basis or did I not raise them right?" she demands. There's so much love in her voice, happy tears fill my eyes.

She's the gorgeous one, elegant and graceful. She's wearing a flowing floral dress, and matches her house so perfectly she could be on the cover of a magazine.

She pulls me close again and then whispers, "My boys are still all smart, aren't they? I don't know why not one of them has swept you off your feet yet. I really don't."

Jack clears his throat. "Ma, the car's here." His voice sounds rougher than usual. "You and Pops need to get to the airport."

As if on cue, Jonathan Hammer, who has always insisted I call him Pops, like one of the family, comes through the front door. His dark hair, shot through with silver, is covered in a wide-brimmed straw hat, and his warm eyes match the soft blue hue behind the bold flowers of his Hawaiian shirt.

"Winnie-bug!" He beelines towards me and sweeps me up into a bear hug.

"Popsy!" I sniffle, settling into his embrace. I can't remember my own dad hugging me. Ever.

I hate to see them go the moment we arrive, but at least I get to hug them now, when I wouldn't ordinarily have gotten the opportunity until Thanksgiving. They're the ones who make the five-hour drive to my cottage each year. When the boys surprised Anna and Popsy with the trip a month ago, I'd been so bummed that I couldn't see them off with Axel, Diesel, and Cruz, who'd planned to house-sit. Back then, I couldn't have imagined coming back here for anything. I'm here now and I still can't believe this is really happening. I've allowed it to happen.

"You all promise not to throw too many wild parties while we're away, alright?" Popsy jokes. "Winnie-bug, you'll keep them in line?"

Despite everything, I laugh. "As much as anyone can!"

"Let's cancel the trip!" Anna cries. "I can't be gone for eight weeks with you all here! I want to stay here and spoil you all rotten."

"Ma," Jack says. "We'll still be here when you get back. You'll have plenty of time to spoil us."

"Yeah, besides, some of us are already pretty rotten," Theo sniffs the air. "Who didn't shower this morning?"

"Oh my gosh. You all behave." Anna wags her finger at them, then gives them each a quick hug. "Winnie, you make them behave."

I promise that I'll try.

Within minutes, it's just me and the guys again.

Me and the guys and the elephant across the street.

I still can't look over there.

"We don't have to start today or even tomorrow," Jack reassures me, as if reading my mind. "Whenever you're ready."

The thing is, I don't know if I'll ever be ready.

After a full day at the Hammer house, caught up in a maelstrom of memories as I went from room to room, focusing all my thoughts on the happy times they always provided me, we ended the day with a BBQ on the back deck, and talked until long after the sun went down. I'm now exhausted and in the coziest bed imaginable, but I still can't sleep.

No. That's not accurate. I can fall asleep. But I wake up immediately, my heart a wild thing in my chest, convinced I've heard my father yelling at me.

I sit up in bed, trying to calm my ragged breath.

Just the memory of his voice makes my entire body tense, every muscle rigid with dread.

He made me hate my own name.

He can't hurt you anymore, I tell myself.

But, oh, he can. He may be dead and gone, but his words live on, immortal. They're scars on my soul.

I slip out of bed and pad downstairs, keeping the lights off so I don't wake anyone. Or blind myself. But there's a dim light coming from the kitchen, and when I enter, I see someone in front of the open refrigerator, shirtless.

He's bending over, digging around the back of the fridge, a very familiar pair of striped pajama pants slung low over his hips, and no boxers in sight. I can see the outline of his ass, and when he straightens, he's all muscled back, and tousled blond hair.

It's Max. Oh hell yeah, this is what I need right now.

What I always need, but especially now.

My mischievous side takes over, and I tip-toe closer, snaking my arms around his waist, whispering, "Hey, Big Max, if you want a midnight snack tonight, I'm available."

Just as I'm about to plant a playful kiss on his tan, muscled shoulder, I realize there is no dragon tattoo on the bicep of this Hammer brother.

Fuck!

"Win?" He turns around, shock painted across his face.

And oh shit. *Shit!*

It isn't Max; it's Mason.

I gasp, my face turning a shade of red that I know clashes with my hair, and blurt out, "Oh! Mason! Hi! I... I was just sleepwalking... I think... you know, having a... uh, sexy dream."

Mason raises an eyebrow, a mischievous smile spreading across his face. "A sexy dream, huh? About Max?"

My mind races, trying to find a fast exit from this hellscape. "Wha—no! It was about Harry Styles! Definitely Harry Styles! Why would you even think—"

Mason is flat-out grinning, now, clearly enjoying my discomfort. "Oh, I don't know, just a hunch."

Dead with embarrassment, I somehow manage to silently stumble my way back to the guest room I'm in, but before I go in, I turn and race to Max's bedroom. I sneak in without thinking, clicking the door softly shut.

"Max!" I try to keep my voice to a whisper. "I messed up! It was Mason in the kitchen, not you!"

Max, still half-asleep, tries to pull me into bed with him. "Why would I be in the kitchen?"

"Max, listen to me! I thought Mason was you and I came on to him."

"It's okay," Max mumbles. "I'm sure he didn't mind."

It's so not okay.

"Are you not hearing me? I called him Big Max! I've blown our cover. I had to pretend I was sleepwalking, and having a sex dream about Harry Styles!"

He opens one eye and smiles. "You what?"

"Don't smile! I've ruined everything!"

"Ruined how?"

"Mason is going to figure out why I was inviting you to have me as a midnight snack! And then everyone will find out," I whisper-wail. "They're all going to know about us!"

CHAPTER 6

Winnie

Thankfully it's dark enough in Max's room that he can't see I'm suddenly flushed as hell.

"I mean, not that there's an us, but you know what I mean."

"There's an us." His voice is coarse with sleep and his words bristle over my skin like an unexpected caress.

"I mean," I clear my throat. "Not like…"

"First," he says, scooting over in his bed and pulling his covers back, "get in here and get warm. You're shivering. And second," he puts his arm around me as I slip into the warmth of his bed, pulling me against him, "there's an us."

"I just meant, it's not like we're a couple or anything," I clarify, because we're not.

My friends-with-benefitsship with Max began quite innocently. I'm affectionate with all the Hammers, obviously.

But then, last Christmas, we were alone in the kitchen of the ski lodge we all rented in Aspen. I'd been trying to put something in the sink, but Max had stood in the way.

"Could you move?"

He'd smirked. "What's it worth to you?"

The wine had been flowing and he was tipsy. I had thought that he was just trying to be difficult. When tipsy, Max tends to get obstinate.

"Max, move."

He'd lifted his chin and tapped his cheek with his fingertip. "Say please and give me a kiss."

"Please." I'd risen on my tiptoes to press my lips against his dimple.

But he'd turned his head.

And everything and nothing changed between us.

Every day since, I've cautioned myself that he did not intentionally brush his mouth across mine. That he did not actually mean for me to kiss him in a romantic way.

But ever since, at least a couple times a month when we can steal a few moments alone, we hook up.

There are two rules of our PG-rated arrangement.

Rule One, mine: Our clothes stay on.

Rule Two, his (though technically, his rule came first, and was the reason for Rule One in the first place): No one ever finds out, especially not his brothers.

Part of me wonders if he wants to keep us a secret because he's ashamed that he's at least somewhat attracted to me. Especially since he's never even nudged the boundaries I set, mostly because I think after all the flawless bodies he's had in bed, he would be mildly repulsed to see me naked.

Well, at least with you gettin' fat I don't have to worry about anyone knocking you up.

My dad's voice, which I've been hearing more and more since we rolled back into Smithville.

"Hey," Max says. "It will be okay. Maybe Mason bought your Harry Styles story. Although, please, dear God, tell me Harry Styles is not actually your type."

I snort. I'd break poor Harry in two.

"Oh, yes. If I ever meet Harry, you and I are done." I bite my lip. "We kind of have to be done, anyway, right?"

He props himself up on one elbow and looks down at me. Then he reaches over me to flick on the bedside lamp.

"You serious? I mean, about us being done. Obviously not about Harry 'cause I'd kick that scrawny punk's ass if he as much as glanced at you."

I sigh. "Max. Come on. Mason, PI is not going to drop this. You know how he is. He'll keep digging until he gets to the truth. Everyone is going to find out."

I love Mason but I also know he is utterly incapable of letting anything go.

"We," he says, pausing to kiss my forehead, the tip of my nose, my lips, "are far from over. I'll tell Mason everything in the morning and I'll swear him to secrecy. It'll all be fine."

"But…" I pause.

"But what?" He's playing with my hair, winding a curl around his fingers, and it's distracting.

"But…" I drop my voice to a whisper. "You didn't want anyone to know we've been hooking up."

"And no one will," he says. "Trust me, I've got some dirt on Mason, that he doesn't want any of the others to know. He'll keep my dirt–"

I recoil. "Your dirt? Is that what I am? Your dirt?"

"Hey, I didn't mean it like that."

But my mouth has gone dry. "Why are you dead set against anyone discovering our little arrangement then?" I choke out.

"It would make things incredibly awkward, don't you think? Besides, I like having something that's just ours. Don't you?"

I can't deny that I do. But if Max Hammer was my man, I would be shouting it from the rooftops. Would he be just as proud? I can't make myself believe he would.

I feel sick all of a sudden, and I want to go back to my own room, but I'm a masochist, clearly, because I want Max's comfort more.

"If this ever turned into anything more than what it is, we would definitely tell everyone," Max says, his hand trailing down to my stomach. I suck in. "But you don't want that. I mean, you don't even want to have sex with me."

I nearly choke on my lung as it dislodges itself from my chest and pushes into my throat. Or at least that's what it feels like.

All I've been thinking about for the past week is having sex with you, Maxwell.

TEN HAMMERS

This is, in fact, the opening I've been waiting for. I open my mouth to say the words. To tell him the truth. My pulse is thrumming in my ears and… other places.

Max, you were my first kiss.

It was during a game of spin the bottle during some party when we were in high school.

It's only fitting that you be my first… everything… right?

"You've never indicated to me that you want that, either," I say quietly. "To have sex." Then like a dork, I add, "With me."

Because obviously he's been having sex with someone. Multiple someones. I don't know. Like with Jack with Cynthia, and the others with their various dalliances, I try not to think about it too much. But certainly what we do isn't enough to scratch his itches.

"You must not have been paying attention," he says, huskily. "But if you're into it, I'll gladly indicate it to you now."

YESSSSS!

Maybe this is the way it should happen. Without talking about it, dissecting it, weighing the pros and cons. Just let it happen naturally.

Usually, we end dry humping until I can't take anymore. He's never seen me come. Instead, I hold out until I can get back to my own bed where I finish myself off with my Max dildo.

Yes, I have a dildo named after each of the brothers. I don't know for sure that the toys are even close to the length or girth of the real things, and it doesn't really matter because I named them after how they make me feel. Though I of course went big with all of them. I know that with Max, the size is accurate. Mason, as well, if they're as identical as they appear.

This time, when we get to the point that I usually end it, I'll whisper, *Don't stop.*

Tonight, it'll be the real thing.

I let Max know I'm definitely in the mood as I reach over to turn the light back off. I do have to swat his hand away when he runs it along my ass, at least until I have hidden all of my dimples – which are not in my cheeks and adorable, like his – under the cover of darkness.

"Hell, yes," he growls, once I slide back under the covers beside him. He pulls me against him, cupping my ass through my pajama shorts, squeezing, as he finds my mouth and claims it with his. This isn't how my Losing My Virginity With Max fantasy starts, but I'll take it.

I reach for him under the covers and my hand brushes along the front of his skin tight boxers. He's hard as a rock under the soft cotton already.

When my touch makes him shudder, and kiss me harder, I grow bolder than I've ever been in my life, and slide my hands under his waistband.

I want him. Now.

But before I can get his boxers down, he has me on my back, and he's kissing me senseless, one thumb tracing circles across the silky fabric of my tank top, sending electrical bursts from my nipples throughout my body. The other thumb traces a long, slow line between my legs.

With a surprised moan, I arch into him. He sits up, hooks his fingers in my waistband, and looks into my eyes.

"Is this okay, Win?"

"More than okay," I whisper.

"Good."

I don't have a chance to be embarrassed that I'm going to be naked – with Max Hammer! – before he peels off my pajama shorts followed by my panties, and replaces them with his gorgeous mouth.

In the last few months, I've had more than my fair share of Max's kisses. Sneaky teaser kisses quickly dropped on my shoulder when no one was looking. Soft, sensual kisses drawn along the line of my throat. Deep, passionate kisses against my lips, full of primal rhythm and plenty of wicked tongue.

But this kiss is by far my favorite. I'm about to tell him so when a long finger drags through my slick folds and I can't speak a single word, I only moan as he slides his finger inside me.

"Fuck, Winnie," he says in a rough voice. "You're so tight." He flutters his tongue over me, swirling it along every single nerve ending as his finger moves in and out, stretching me, making me writhe. "You're so fucking wet." He laps me up, and moans as though I'm a delicious treat and he's eager for more.

I want to stop Max from going any further so I can strip his boxers off and hold him in my hands. I want to touch him. Stroke him. Taste him.

I want–

His hot tongue licks into me, the pleasure so shocking my toes curl. As I gasp, he slides his hands under my ass and grabs me, pulls me closer, licks deeper.

Stroke after stroke after stroke. I can't stop my hips from beginning to rock, joining the thrusts of his tongue.

I slide my fingers through his hair, greedy for the sensations he's giving me. Wanting more. The building pressure winds tighter and I'm not going to last. I'm not ready for these feelings to stop, everything feels too good.

"Max," I cry, and he growls in response.

He plunges his finger into me, pumps until I moan and then he gives me another finger to ride. And I do. Hard. When his mouth returns to my clit, I have to cover my sounds with my hands. I buck off the bed but he only sucks harder.

Too soon, I break apart at the seams. Fireworks burst in my veins, molten coils rushing through me. My entire body shudders and shakes, but he continues lapping at me, drinking me in until the last shockwaves of my orgasm leave my body.

I've never been able to make myself orgasm this intensely. Not a single dildo in my collection ever came close to eliciting the full-body, mind-blowing sensations that Max's tongue drew out of me.

"That was delicious," he says, stretching out alongside me. I can't move, fully boneless, can't even open my eyes. He pulls the covers up around us and kisses me gently. I taste myself on his lips, and finally manage to crack an eye to look at him.

I feel like I'm floating, then I crash back down to earth from the highest of highs.

What if I wasn't delicious? What if he changed his mind and doesn't want to go any further now?

"Max," I whisper.

"Hmm?"

"That was pretty much one of the best things that ever happened to me, but… I want you inside me. I thought… I thought you wanted that too?"

I can feel his eyes on me in the dark.

"I want it now more than ever," he says and for a moment, the entire world stops spinning. The naked sincerity in his voice brings tears to my eyes. He strokes my hair. "But not everything has to happen tonight. It might be cliche, but I want your first time to be special. Romantic."

Yeah, he knows I'm a virgin. I don't know if they all do, but I've told Max. But swoooooooooon.

"Also I really kind of need to clear the air with Mace before you and I take the next step."

I swallow. Okay. I can accept that.

But… when he says take the next step… he is just talking sex, right?

A guy like Max Hammer doesn't want to be your *boyfriend, stupid. He's just interested in getting it wherever he can. I'm the only man that will ever be honest with you. You remember that.*

My dad's voice. Even now.

"Is that okay with you?" Max whispers, sending my father's words scattering to hide.

"Yeah," I whisper back.

The smile he gives me is wicked and satisfied. It's the last thing I see before he pulls me into his arms and holds me tight against his chest and I fall into the deepest, coziest sleep.

CHAPTER 7

Max

It's the familiar jeering of the blue jays in the oak tree outside my childhood bedroom that wake me up, but before I open my eyes, I'm enveloped in the scent of ripe strawberries and the warmth of the girl wrapped in my arms. Everything else ceases to exist for a second.

Winnie Wainwright, hugging my right arm in her sleep, a smile playing on her lips. My morning semi is already eager for attention, especially when she shifts, pushing gently against my cock with her gorgeous naked ass. She sighs softly, and settles back into a serene sleep, her worries from yesterday clearly forgotten.

Dropping the barest kiss on her shoulder, I slide out of bed for my morning piss. I head to my bathroom, though I'm tempted to linger in bed with her - hell, I want to stay in bed with this girl for the rest of my life; make her my breakfast, lunch, dinner, and every snack in between. God, she's incredible. But there will be hell to pay with Mason.

I'm already dreading what's in store for me.

Big Max.

It's hard to worry about the collective wrath from my brothers when I think of my girl in the kitchen after dark, wanting some from me – wanting it all from me – and it makes me feel like a god. Not to mention, the thought that she mistook my twin for me and called him Big Max, makes me laugh my ass off.

My mirth is short-lived, because the conversation with Winnie last night and the knowledge that she actually wants me to fuck her, whips through my filthy mind. I need to take care of a few things before I leave the bathroom… namely my dick, which is in full salute now.

I turn on the shower and drop my boxers into the hamper, letting the real Big Max spring free. With the memory of the taste of her, the feel of her pushing herself down on my fingers, on my tongue… fuck, it doesn't take more than a few pumps into my soapy fist before I'm releasing my load in thick streaks.

Winnie is still fast asleep when I get out, so I throw on a pair of loose-fitting jeans and a t-shirt and head downstairs to make some breakfast. I'm not sure yet what I will say to Mason when I see him. He's bound to bring it up before I can open my mouth. But I need to get to him before the others are awake, explain how Winnie and I are…

Fuck. We didn't exactly define the relationship while my head was buried between her thighs.

The wolfish grin spreads across my face, unstoppable. I feel unstoppable.

I take the steps two at a time and swing into the living room.

The room is stunning, really. My dad was the guy who taught us everything we know, and built Mom the living room of her dreams. It has wall-to-wall bookshelves that stretch long and high enough for a sliding ladder, large and luxurious furniture, big enough for a family of our size to spread out. Everything is perfect, down to the last of my mom's homey details. Perfect except for the small addition of my nine brothers, reclining on the sofa, the love seat, the stool by the fireplace, all glaring at me.

Mason's glare is fiercest of all. Well, shit.

We don't have the kind of twin telepathy you hear about–thank god–but I shoot daggers at his forehead anyway.

You couldn't come to me first, bro?

He's sharing Mom's favorite green armchair with Gunnar, sitting on the arm. Mom would be seriously pissed to see him sitting there, weakening the arm of the chair when there's plenty of space beside Cruz and Theo on the sofa. I don't bother bringing it up right now.

"Uh… hey," I say, just delusional enough after what happened last night to hope that maybe they're collectively pissed at me about something that has nothing to do with Winnie. "Anyone had breakfast yet? I'm making. Waffles, eggs, bacon. Who wants what?"

I start towards the kitchen.

"We're not hungry, *Big Max*," Mason says the second my back is to him. I wince.

"Is she still sleeping?" Jack asks.

I scrub my hands over my face before turning back to face them.

"Is she still sleeping?" Jack repeats. He and Gavin are both on the loveseat, and they might not be blood brothers but the look on their faces as they glower at me from across the room are identical.

Lifting my chin, I say, "Yeah. She's still sleeping."

"Good. Join us. Seems like you have quite a bit to catch us up on." Jack has a mug of coffee. Takes a sip, his steel eyes never breaking contact.

I stay put as I glance at Mace. "You couldn't get my side of the story before you told the world?"

"What is your side of the story then, man?" Gavin interrupts. There's a fire in his eyes I've never seen before. His nostrils flare. I'm surprised lava isn't pouring out of his mouth instead of words.

Raking my hands through my hair, I wonder not what's going to appease my brothers, but what Winnie would want me to say. What she would want me to keep private.

Before I can say anything, Mace speaks up. "After she came onto me in the kitchen... well, came onto *you* in the kitchen, I went up to her room. You know, just to make sure she got back to bed safely, because clearly I'm a fool, because I'd actually believed she was sleepwalking–"

"But she wasn't in her bed," Gunnar takes over.

"Want to tell us where she was?" Gavin leans back, folding his arms across his chest.

God, he's pissed.

"No." Theo, from the sofa, holds up a hand to silence me before I've even had time to begin putting a response together. "You don't have to."

"Because as Mason was coming out of Winnie's room, I was coming out of mine," Leo picks up.

He's leaning against the wall, and I swear my neck is getting a workout as I try to keep up with them all. It's like they've got me surrounded.

Fuck, did they rehearse this?

"What is this?" I say, rolling my eyes. "An intervention?"

"A Wintervention," Jack shoots back dryly.

Diesel, sitting by the fireplace, snorts into his guitar. Some of the other guys have to keep straight faces, too, and I hope Jack's quip will break the tension, as he usually does.

No such luck.

"Mason told me what happened," Leo plows on. "We decided we should look around for her, make sure she didn't sleepwalk into the damn pool to skinny dip with Joe Jonas."

"It was Harry Styles," Mace murmurs.

"What-the-fuck-ever." Leo slams his left fist into his right open hand. "When I walked by your room, it became pretty fucking obvious where Win was." He looks down, diverting his eyes away from me. His voice is thick with betrayal. "I heard some very interesting sounds. Moaning, groaning, her crying out your name."

"Okay, yeah, I'm sorry you found out that way–"

Jack sits up straight. His mug hits the coffee table with a thud, sloshing some of the liquid onto the wood. "We agreed, Max. Every last damn one of us *agreed*."

The triplets have been silent, so I shift my gaze in their direction, hoping one of them will inject some semblance of… reason… into this conversation. Come on, Axel, at least you?

From the looks on their faces, they're ready for a brawl. Never do the triplets look more identical than they do when they're about to lose their tempers.

Well, shit.

"We made a pact," Cruz says. He looks disappointed in me. Even though *he's* the one still in his pajamas, eating sugary cereal. And with bedhead to boot.

I press my lips together. What can I say? I wanted Winnie, she wanted me, deal with it? You snooze, you lose?

Over the years, we've all had more-than-friends feelings for Winnie at one time or another. So it made sense, eight years ago, when we were all in our late teens and early twenties, when we were embarking on a career in reality television where we knew it would be imperative we all stick together and, above all else, stay a team… We made a pact that none of us would get romantically involved with Winnie. Period.

Cruz is now looking down into the cereal in his lap. "We all saw how her father treated her, dude. We vowed to be her army of soldiers, to protect her no matter what, not to ever risk being someone who broke her heart."

I was just about to say that the pact was childish and stupid, but well. That part wasn't childish or stupid.

"We all agreed that romance makes things messy and that none of us ever wanted to do anything to mess up our friendship with her," Diesel adds.

Axel, on the sofa next to Cruz, says nothing, but his knee is bouncing and his jaw is working and that says a lot.

Fuck.

"We agreed that if we all couldn't have her, none of us could," I point out. "But we didn't consider what *she* might want."

No one is looking at me now.

"Are you two official?" Jack gets up from the loveseat and saunters over to me. "Is it a serious relationship?"

I don't know how the fuck to answer that.

"No, it isn't like that, but–"

"So you're just fuck buddies?" Axel finally speaks and I kind of want to punch him in the mouth. He shakes his head. Gets to his feet.

"Axel–" Diesel begins.

Axel holds up his hand, palm out, as if to say *don't, man*. He heads out the door to the back patio, letting it slam behind him.

We all flinch.

"Whatever you are, I assume this has been going on for a while," Jack says after a long minute. "It wasn't right of you to not divulge this information to us when we were offered the spin-off, Max."

Now I really want to punch Jack in the mouth. What a massive load of steaming crap.

I jab a finger at him. "You wanted nothing to do with that spin-off, or being on TV anymore. So don't give me that bullshit."

"This thing between you and Win," Mace begins. "Whatever it is. Which one of you initiated it?"

I remember last Thanksgiving. She had on these shorty-shorts and a pajama top so thin my mouth still waters when I remember. When I saw her in the kitchen, she was the only delectable thing I saw. It was either kiss her or starve.

There's no point in lying now.

"I did."

"Of-fucking-course," he mutters under his breath.

"We unanimously agreed to turn down the spin-off because of the pact, Max," Gavin says, stretching his legs into the empty space Jack left behind on the loveseat. He looks relaxed but his jaw is tight. "Because of all the reasons we made the pact."

"Would it have made a difference, if you had known about me and Winnie? Would you have wanted to do the show, then?"

I wait on them to all say no, that of course they wouldn't have, because that damn spin-off would've torn us apart.

But Jack shocks me when glares at me and fiercely says, "I would have at least wanted to tell Winnie about the opportunity. See what she thought."

I hope that none of my brothers can see how hard his words hit, but I feel like an idiot.

I hadn't ever considered that if given the chance, if I hadn't pursued her first, would Winnie have even picked me at all? Would she have preferred Axel's boy-next-door charm? I already know she likes his glasses because she's complimented them enough times. Or maybe Gavin's piercings are more her thing? Or would she have preferred Jack, because he's always been the one who makes her laugh the most…?

"What opportunity?" a soft voice asks.

We all turn our heads to see Winnie, standing in the doorway, biting her bottom lip and studying each of us with her curious blue eyes.

Well, *shit*.

CHAPTER 8

Winnie

Max wakes me as he tries to creep silently out of his room, but I pretend to still be asleep. I want to give him time to find Mason and sort through things, but more than that, I want to lay in his bed and relish in the euphoric memories of last night. I'm not ready to burst this happy little bubble yet.

I pick up his pillow and press it to my face, squeal into it as a worldly and mature lady of almost thirty does.

Max Hammer went down on me last night.

Max Hammer fingerfucked me last night.

Max Hammer wants to take my v-card… he wants my first time to be romantic!

I squeeze my thighs together. My horny little love button is already pulsing. Normally I wouldn't hesitate to give in to the call, but how will my own hands ever pleasure me after I've felt Max's touch?

I stretch and my yawn turns into a grin so big it actually hurts my face.

Max made me feel sexy. Desired. Alive.

Maybe if every night of the next month and a half is like last night, I can survive the reno from hell.

My mind wanders again to the word romantic. I find myself mindlessly winding a curl around my finger, probably to keep my hands from wandering elsewhere. None of my Losing My Virginity to a Hammer Brother fantasies have been romantic. Imaginative, wild, unrealistic, kinky. Yes, yes, yes, and yes.

But romantic? Never.

There was a moment last night, when my clit was being ravaged by Max's tongue, when my body and brain were overcome with heavenly sensation, and I stared at the dragon tattoo on his muscled arm, I thought that My Losing My Virginity to Max fantasy was well on its way to coming true.

In my fantasy, Max doesn't take his time. He is speed, he's strength, he's precision. He grabs me from behind, his hands gripping tight to my hips as he pulls me up against him, to make me feel how hard he is for me. So hard. And so huge. And in one swift motion, fierce, like his dragon tattoo, he pushes me over his work bench and yanks my panties down. His powerful thrust has me crying out for more.

When Max is concentrating on the final touch wood-working details in a renovation, he wears this expression that turns me liquid. His gorgeous lips curl into a snarl and his brows knit over green eyes that are piercing and possessive. That's the expression he wears as he drills me from behind, over and over, harder and harder, until I scream from ecstasy.

Not romantic.

I wonder what he has in mind for my first time. Us sneaking out together late one night, driving to the middle of nowhere. Maybe a field?

A field. He'll have put a mattress in the bed of his truck and we'll make love under the stars…

I bite my lip. Sliding my hand down my belly, I spread my thighs. I'm so wet. My finger circles my clit. I squirm and I bite harder on my lip to keep from making noises.

A door bangs shut downstairs, causing me to jump and my finger to slip and poke a decidedly non-sexy place. Ow.

I cringe, a wave of dread washing away my pleasure. I hate the sounds of doors slamming more than just about anything.

Hurriedly getting up, I locate my pajamas and get them back on. I probably still have all kinds of bedhead, but I don't bother trying to tame it. I fly down the stairs but there are terse voices coming from the living room, causing me to stop dead in my tracks.

I hold my breath and inch my way toward the voices on my tiptoes.

"I would have at least wanted to tell Winnie about the opportunity. See what she thought."

Jack.

My eyebrows go high.

Opportunity? What opportunity?

I can't stop myself from barging in.

"What opportunity?" I ask, moving closer until I'm standing in the doorway.

Jack and Max are standing in the center of the room, practically nose to nose, looking like two warring angels in the soft morning light.

Jack has already showered, his rusty hair damp and glistening. His beard is thicker today, not trimmed as neat as usual, and I like it.

The other guys are scattered around the room.

Cruz sits on the sofa with a bowl of cereal, still in his pajamas, a colorful and slightly rumpled set with plaid flannel pants and a t-shirt with a matching pocket.

All the others are dressed, although Theo, sitting beside Cruz, is wearing only sweatpants, which might count as pajamas to him.

Unless Theo sleeps naked.

The thought flashes through my mind unbidden and I have to tamp it down before I begin drooling.

Diesel sits on a stool by the fireplace with his guitar, his disheveled hair falling across his forehead as he tunes with nimble fingers.

Leo leans against the wall, Mason perches on the arm of the green velvet armchair chair Gunnar sits in. Gav takes up the whole love seat, his long legs stretched out, and his sock clad feet on the leather arm.

Axel is missing.

He's not one to storm off, slam doors.

"Well? What opportunity?" I repeat.

With my hands on my hips, I wait for an answer, but no answer comes. The vast majority of the Hammer brothers are suddenly very interested in the artwork Anna hung on the walls around the room.

Only Max makes eye contact with me.

I'm sorry, he mouths.

My eyes widen.

They all know? I mouth back.

He nods.

"Everything?" I mouth.

I can't read his lips to decipher what his response is.

Well. Either way, this is not ideal. But it doesn't explain while everyone is acting like I just walked in on them in the middle of a circle jerk.

No one will look at me.

"What's going on?" I ask. "Wait, don't tell me. I've walked in on another secret meeting?"

Several of them shoot me guilty looks, but no one says a word.

"*I said* what's going on and I know every damn one of you heard me. You," I point at Gavin. "You *promised* me you would never keep anything important from me. If whatever you all were discussing caused Axel to storm out of here, slamming the door, it's important to me. One of you better spill. NOW."

My heart is beating fast, but not in the super pleasant way Max made it race last night. It's an angry beat, a scared beat.

"We all found out about you and Max," Gunnar's voice is tight, each word clipped. "So, yeah, I'm not sure you coming at us about keeping stuff from you right now is cool."

Well. The boy does have a point. Also a pretty, pretty pout. I hate myself a bit for wanting to go sit in Gunnar's lap, put my arms around his neck, whisper my apology, my breath against his ear.

I received oral sex for the first time in my life last night. I am not myself.

Focus, horndog, focus.

"You have a point," I agree.

Jack holds up a hand to stop me before I can apologize. He knows me well enough to know that's what I was about to do. "We were offered a spin-off show. The network didn't want to let us go."

My eyes automatically go to Max. Now he's looking out the window.

"The ten of you?" I ask, trying not to feel hurt, because the sadness isn't even from the fact that they kept it from me. It's that 1 Girl, 10 Hammers wouldn't have existed without me, and apparently the network had no issues letting *me* go. Of course, the audience's love for me was never as ubiquitous as it was for the guys. The guys could do no wrong. I was Winnebago.

"The ten of us, yes, but you would've been the star," Max says.

I couldn't have possibly heard him right.

"Wait, what? *I* would've been the star?" I blink. "I would've been the star, and I'm just hearing about it now?"

Jack clears his throat. "Because we turned it down."

Why hadn't they told me? Why wasn't I a part of the decision?

My anger simmers, but underneath it, an insidious whisper of self-doubt creeps in. Am I just not good enough for them to think of me as star material? I know they don't see me as Winnebago… at least I don't think they do. But are they ashamed of me?

"Why?" My stomach twists. "What was the concept for the show?"

Gavin is one of the most sensitive guys I have ever met. His piercings and his raven hair make him look hard, but he's just a sweet cinnamon roll. Which is why it cracks my heart when he says, "Similar to the Bachelorette. It was centered around you, Win. And your journey to finding a connection." He clears his throat, uncomfortable. "With one of us."

"They pitched it to us as 'Winnie's Favorite Hammer,'" Theo says. "You would date us all, eliminating us one by one, until you chose the brother you felt was the one you could fall in love with."

"Or are already in love with," Leo adds, shooting a disgusted look in Max's direction.

You would date us all, eliminating us one by one, until you chose the brother you felt was the one you could fall in love with, Theo's words echo in my ears.

Not only were none of them interested… none of them even wanted me to know about it.

As the weight of all this information settles over me, I hear my father.

Where are you running off to, girl? Another dinner with that fancy family? Hope they still want you 'round after you've eaten them into bankruptcy. People like them don't think girls like you are cute forever, remember. They'll be laughing at you behind your back. Ashamed to be with you. Take my advice: turn down the sweet tea and cakes you stuff your face with over there. Sure, cry now. But you'll thank me one day.

A sickening realization churns in my stomach: maybe my father was right about me all along. Maybe I am just a punchline, a joke for others to laugh at.

My brain can't process any of this. It's just too much.

Winnie's Favorite Hammer. The title alone feels like a blow. How could the producers reduce the amazing legacy we built into some kind of tragic dating parade, and with me being dangled in front of the brothers like a prize pig at a county fair?

My face burns. The idea of being reduced to an object of ridicule makes me furious.

But that isn't what burns the most. It's knowing now, for sure, that despite how much I desire all of them, not one of them desires me back.

Of course they don't, and of course they'd say no. I'd say no to myself if I were offered the same 'opportunity.'

What the hell was last night with Max, then? What has the whole past year with him been? Was my first time with him just going to be a pity fuck?

I can't believe that. I can't believe he'd lie to me, toy with me like that. I won't.

"We're sorry," Jack says, genuine remorse in his eyes. "We should've talked to you about it. We were just caught off guard by the offer."

Max interjects, "We didn't want to put you in an uncomfortable position."

I sigh. I can't believe Goldie hadn't breathed a word of this to me, either. I think about the last time I sat in the 1 Girl, 10 Hammers hot seat. She knew I didn't want to be a plus-sized Bachelorette, but I can easily see that twinkle she gets in her eye, and can imagine her hoping for something she'd find even sexier, and therefore perfect for TV - a Bachelorette starring all of America's official favorite brothers.

"Goldie knew I didn't want to star in a plus-sized Bachelorette," I say through gritted teeth.

Jack winces, guilt etched across his face. "We were taken aback by the offer. But we ultimately turned it down because we knew it wasn't right for you, or any of us."

"That's why we didn't tell you about it," Gav says quietly. "Because it was a non-starter, since none of us were into it. It wasn't worth bringing it up to you. And as far as I know, Goldie didn't know a thing about it."

"It was a stupid idea."

It was Axel who spoke and we all pivot to see he's slipped back in through the back door and closed it behind him so quietly we didn't even hear him return.

"Of course it was," I agree, swallowing the lump in my throat.

"I mean," he goes on. "You've already chosen your favorite Hammer, after all, right?"

CHAPTER 9

Winnie

Before I can respond, Axel goes on, "The rest of us didn't even have a chance to toss our hats into the ring."

My mouth drops open slightly as I try to process his words.

What hats? What ring?

And why the actual hell does he sound *sad?*

I want to go to him, hug him, comfort him, because that's what my boys have always done for me when I need it, and that's what I do for them.

Max's eyes are on me, and his expression stops me. He's expectant, like he's waiting for me to fix everything but I don't know what to do. My mind is boggled.

I glance down at my hands, twisting my fingers. Bad time to realize I didn't bother putting on a bra and it's chilly in the house. My nipples are standing at attention.

Not now, girls.

I turn my attention back to Axel. Max. Axel. Max.

"*Have* you chosen Max, baby?" Jack's voice is low.

"Um," I hesitate.

Max's hands are fisted in his lap. My eyes flit to Axel. His jaw is clenched.

"Max and I have… an arrangement," I stammer. "It… I mean. We didn't tell anyone because…" I remember the reasoning Max gave me last night and use it. "It would have been incredibly awkward. I mean, people, as a rule, don't announce *'Hey, your brother and I are… something! But we haven't defined the relationship or anything!'*" Shit. I said *relationship*. I shoot a furtive look at Max and his hands have relaxed. I begin again, "People don't just shout out their personal business. Especially not to the siblings of the guy they kiss. Right?"

"I don't mean to sound crass," Leo says. "But the thing between you and Max has been *just* kissing?"

"Are you asking how far we've gone?" I wrinkle my nose trying to stave off the thought of Max Hammer's head buried between my thighs. "Because that is kind of crass, Leo."

He has the decency to look a little ashamed. But just a little.

I wait for Max to back me up on this. But it's Mason who speaks from where he sits on the arm of Gunnar's armchair. "Was it your idea to keep it a secret or was it Max's?"

"Hey…" Max cuts in, the word sounding an awful lot like a warning.

I glance around the room at all my boys. The way they look at me, the hurt I can see they're barely holding in… it's all so confusing. I don't know what to do, to say. Why are they this upset about me kissing Max? What the hell is this all about?

I shrug helplessly at Mason. "Initially? It was Max who wanted to keep it between the two of us. And he was right. It is the sort of thing you keep private. I agree with him on that one hundred percent, especially now that I see how you're all reacting to us having this tiny little—"

Mason draws in a deep breath, then lets it out in a huff. "Max wanted to keep it private," he spits out *private* like it's a swear, "because we all have… or *had*, I guess…" he shoots a blistering glare at Max before returning his gaze to me, his eyes softening. "Because we all had a pact."

"A pact?" I echo, confused.

From the armchair, Gunnar nods. "We all agreed to the terms before 1 Girl, 10 Hammers started filming. It was not a decision any of us made lightly."

"A pact," I repeat, flatly this time. "I don't understand what the hell you mean. A pact to do what?"

Leo pushes off the wall, his eyes gentle as he strides to my side, tucking a strand of his tousled beach blond hair behind his ear.

"A pact to never get involved with you in a romantic way." His hands are on my shoulders, sliding gently down my arms. "That's why we said no to the spin-off. Not because *none* of us wanted to pursue you as a love interest. But because we *all* wanted to."

"It's why we made the pact in the first place. If all of us can't have you, none of us can have you," Diesel mutters with a delicate strum of his guitar, his fingers rippling expertly across the strings. He shoots daggers at Max. "Apparently someone didn't understand the assignment."

I'm flabbergasted, like… one part of my brain is screaming at me to say something because I hate it when the boys argue, but the other part of my brain is like *What the fresh hell are words and how do I make any come out of my mouth?*

Pulling away from Leo, I jam my eyes shut. My head is whirling and I need to breathe. *In, out, you can do it, girl. In, out.*

As my eyes reopen, Mason stands up from his perch on the arm of the chair, and our eyes lock. There's a subtle arch to his brow, as slight but as fully captivating as his smile. I'm struck by the look he gives me. There isn't a speck of denial in his expression, only playful tenderness. Leo's words, Diesel's words, *nothing* is being refuted.

Instead, Mason stands straighter and his smile slides into something a lot more secretive as his gaze drops to my mouth. Suddenly, his tantalizing lips are the most interesting puzzle I didn't even know I was waiting to solve.

Gunnar snags my attention next as he rises from the chair and stands beside Mason. His hypnotic blue eyes catch mine, momentarily stealing my breath. *Fortune favors the bold.* His favorite quote by Virgil is tattooed on his left forearm, and the way he looks at me now, with bold determination in his gaze, is almost like *I'm* the fortune to be won.

What in the world is happening right now?

Leo steals my attention back when he takes a few steps forward, moving to Mason's other side, tucking that stubborn gold strand behind his ear again.

It's not because none of us wanted to pursue you as a love interest, but because we all wanted to.

The memory of his deep voice and his earnest eyes as Leo said those words will forever have their own place in heart and head, something I'll be drawing on for my own pleasure-time inspiration long after my boys have come to their senses or I wake up from this because it has to be a dream. Has. To. Be.

The way Leo smiles at me now is almost too much and I have to tear my gaze away to keep my eyes from welling up.

But the line is growing longer. Gavin no longer reclines on the love seat, but is next to Gunnar. His intense expression makes my insides melt. Not to mention his body is a work of art. His jeans are slung low, showing his deeply cut v-lines. His shirt is off, and I forget to not stare at the barbells in his nipples. They're like shiny toys I want to play with, and I can already feel them against my tongue.

As if he can read my mind, Gavin's smile turns wicked. He holds my gaze and licks his lips, and his tongue ring teases me as it glints and then is hidden again behind his smirk. I shiver, imagining what he could do to me with his mouth.

Theo is next to Gavin, and his green eyes light up when our eyes connect. The sudden pull I have toward him is magnetic. He looks at me with an alluring grin, as if he sees all of this as an adventure. I grin back at him. How can I help myself, baffled as I might be by this entire situation?

If all of us can't have you, none of us can have you.

I turn to Jack, the voice of reason, because surely he doesn't feel this way. He doesn't want me. He's holding back laughter at the very idea. What about his hot models and socialites, like Cynthia Sinclair?

But when I see Jack standing tall beside Leo, there isn't laughter in his eyes, only stark desire.

I squeeze my thighs together as warmth floods through me, something I have to do a hell of a lot with the Hammers around.

And it really doesn't help that Cruz is looking at me with a sly smile on his sexy mouth. He's in pajamas, and his brown hair is rumpled, slightly, but all that does is make him look like he's had a long and wild night in bed. And the way he bites his lip and shakes his head at me, his eyes sliding over my body, lingering on what are clearly his two favorite parts, I get the feeling *back to bed* is exactly where he wants to go.

I must have died and ended up in the sweetest heaven. There's no other explanation that makes sense.

Certainly none to explain the way Axel looks at me from behind his glasses, serious and fascinated, like I'm one of his rare rose bushes that he grafts himself and cherishes.

Or how Diesel, without his guitar now, so I can easily see the tattoo on his arm, in the pattern of his favorite constellation, looks as if I'm the star he's been waiting to find.

I can hardly bear it, any of it.

My gaze slides to Max. Somewhere deep down, I register that I should be furious with him for never telling me about this fucking *ridiculous* pact. On one hand, what are they, twelve? But on the other hand, if they made a pact, then Max was betraying all of his brothers every single time we…

I shake my head.

Then I burst out laughing. I laugh so hard I think I'm going to pee myself.

Every single set of their gorgeous eyes are on me now.

Every single set of their gorgeous eyes are alarmed.

"Win…?" Cruz asks. "Are you… alright?"

Tears stream down my face. I'm laughing that hard. I can't stop laughing.

"Okay. Okay," I say, trying to calm myself down, but another giggle escapes. "Come on. It's hilarious. I'm actually supposed to believe that if it wasn't for this pact… You all would've wanted to go on national television and compete for my love?"

"It would've had to be unanimous, like 1 Girl, 10 Hammers was," Axel says. "We would have all had to… be very, *very* open and honest with each other and agree that no matter what the outcome… there would be no hard feelings." And the corner of his mouth tips up. "But hell yeah."

My knees actually go weak.

"We'd all love to be your favorite Hammer," Jack says, his gruff voice rougher than usual. He swallows, like he has a lump in his throat and I'm overwhelmed by his emotion.

My eyes swim with tears. "Is that true? You would *all* want to date me, if given the chance?"

"No," Jack says and once again, I'm thrown for a loop. "We don't all want to *date* you, Win. We all want to be your man."

Max presses his lips together, silent, but every single one of the others responds, agreeing with Jack.

Yep, I've definitely died and gone to heaven.

"Would you have done the show?" asks Mason. Probably because he never wanted to quit with 1 Girl, 10 Hammers. He loved being on television. Relished the low-key fame, and the perks of being a semi-celebrity.

I shake my head. "No. For starters, what we all have is way too special. I would never want to exploit our friendships like that. But… also… I'd never be able to eliminate any of you. Are you kidding me? I don't have a favorite Hammer. I never have. Never will."

I stare at Max until he meets my gaze.

"I love you all. All of you. As individuals, of course, but also as a whole." I speak my truth to them in a way I'd never ever dream of in a room filled with anyone else. They make me brave. "I'd never do anything to damage the relationship we have. Obviously, Max is very special to me. But you all are."

"Let's say it wasn't going to be televised," Jack says suddenly. "Winnie's Favorite Hammer."

And then he blows away the last of my mind when he adds. "Is it an experiment you'd be interested in participating in if we kept it private?"

CHAPTER 10

Winnie

s it an experiment you'd be interested in…

Is it…?

My mind needs a moment to recover but my ladyparts urge me to scream *hell yeah, I would!* An opportunity to be pounded for real by all the Hammers?

Thankfully, my heart and gut both respond with a resounding and unanimous NO, and that's what stops me from running to Jack, jumping into his arms, wrapping my entire body around him until the tune from a phone alarm goes off, and then Leo says, *Time's up, Jackie boy, it's my turn…*

Oh my God, I want it, all of it. All of them, but I can't imagine the havoc that would wreak on our friendships. I mean, if this morning has taught me anything, it was that Max and I have been playing with fire and it burned us all.

Dearest Virginity, my old friend, I suppose I won't be losing you anytime soon after all, I think.

TEN HAMMERS

What a colossal bummer to realize I'll be living in Dildo City, Population 1 for the foreseeable future after getting so damn close.

I shake my head. "No," I say, though I might've whimpered just a little when I said it.

"No," I add, more forcefully. "Like Axel said, it's a stupid idea. Each and every one of you knows that. I mean, the network wasn't motivated to do *Winnie's Favorite Hammer*," I scoff at the ridiculous title, "just so America could root for *me* to find true love with one of *you*."

My chest starts to tighten even though I've spent plenty of time thickening my skin against the judgments of people who don't even know me.

I laugh, trying to clear away my emotion, "They wanted everyone in America to root for *their* favorite Hammer brother to be eliminated, not chosen. Save their favorite for themselves, of course. But then PLOT TWIST! The brother I choose will turn me down in the end, leaving me brokenhearted and humiliated!"

Even as I laugh, I'm crossing my arms over my chest defensively again.

"Win, with all due respect, what the actual fucking *fuck* are you talking about?" Gavin cuts in.

The semicircle of brothers around me has lost some of its order as I rant. They're all wearing matching expressions of disbelief, as though they truly have no clue what the fucking fuck I'm talking about.

"Come on, guys. They were looking for trash TV and ratings, not for me to have a happily ever after with one of *you*, because no one—least of all me—would buy that."

"Buy what?" Cruz genuinely looks confused.

They are the smartest guys I know, my boys, and yet they still need me to spell it out for them?

"That not one, but *all* of the Hammer brothers were genuinely competing for *my* love."

They're all staring at me like I've just sprouted wings and told them I'm a fairy princess.

"WHAT?" I demand.

Theo breaks away from the row of brothers, and comes over to me. I probably shouldn't let him get too close. His green eyes are a trap I fall into all too often. They make me forget what I'm doing. How to think rationally.

"First," Theo says. "Do you seriously not know how much everyone who has ever had *anything* to do with 1 Girl, 10 Hammers adores you?" He touches my cheek. "Angel." His eyes ensnare mine and I fall. "Trust me, they absolutely want to see you get your happily ever after. You've helped so many people get theirs."

I shake my head, still not buying it.

His hand drops from my cheeks but he's not defeated yet. "You were the soul of our show, Win. Yeah, it was about us showing off our bodies, but it was so much more than that. Because of you."

I can't deny that what he is saying is true. Yeah, the original idea for the show was all about them making America drool as they renovated houses. But once I was brought on board and the concept morphed from 10 Hammers into 1 Girl, 10 Hammers, it became so much more. I handpicked every family whose house we renovated. Those I chose were kindred spirits, people like myself, who'd never had a home that was truly a sanctuary. I wanted to give them not only safe spaces, but beautiful spaces. So, yeah, the show had a lot of skin, but it had a lot of heart.

"Still," I say. "Look at yourselves. You each put so much time and work into keeping your bodies perfect. Why would you possibly want someone who looks like me?"

Don't get me wrong. I don't think I'm some kind of Sasquatch or anything like that. It's not like I don't take care of myself. I make sure to exercise. I try to eat right. I care about being healthy. But I am never going to have visible abs. I was built with big boobs and thick thighs. My ass has always filled my jeans, and I'm never going to have the type of physique you'd expect a lady on any Hammer brother's arm to have.

"At the risk of being unoriginal, what the fucking fuck are you talking about?" Diesel asks. "We would want someone who looks like *you* because each and every one of us think you're hot as hell."

"And," Axel adds, "we'd never compete for anything else with the same intensity and determination that we'd compete with if the prize was *your* love."

Gram used to watch old episodes of the Twilight Zone like that show held the secret to world peace and I honestly wouldn't be surprised at, if this moment, Rod Serling rose from the dead and walked in to narrate.

What the fucking fuck indeed.

I laugh. "Sorry. I just… What you're asking me to believe is… kind of… farfetched."

"Then let us help make it a bit more realistic." Jack says it with a flirty smile, but I know behind his teasing, a part of him is very, very serious.

I swallow hard. "What do you mean?"

"You aren't interested in Winnie's Favorite Hammer–televised or not–and we all respect that," he says. "But I can't let you leave this room until you believe, with your whole heart, that if you were in, every damn one of us would be in."

"You can all talk 'til you're blue in the face, Jack Hammer, but you're never going to–"

"Oh, none of us will be talking, baby, because I firmly believe that actions speak louder than words," he says, his piercing blue eyes pinning me in place. "Give us each five minutes to persuade you?"

My heart hammers–no pun intended–in my chest.

"What about your pact?" I stammer.

"Well, *Big Max* obviously made that null and void," Mason says. "If you give us the same opportunity he had, we'll show you just how much we all want you."

"Five minutes each…?" The idea was enough to make me faint. That's almost an *hour* of kissing. I'd need a whole pot of lip balm to recover. "There's no way that–"

"One minute," Cruz rushes in. "I won't need more than that to convince you." He shoots Jack a smirk. "Unlike Jack, apparently."

Everyone laughs, even Jack.

Everyone except for Max, who stands apart from the rest of us. He watches his brothers solemnly, and when our eyes connect, hurt quickly flashes across his face and I want to run to him, comfort him.

But then Jack walks toward me, wrapping his large, callused hands over mine and squeezing reassuringly. His eyes alight on mine playfully. I wonder how his beard will feel against my skin…

Uh oh, I'm a goner already.

He tugs me gently toward him, unintentionally blocking Max from my view, but before I can do anything about that, my senses are flooded with Jack's zesty, woodsy scent. Something with ginger in it, and so delicious I want to lick him.

With a soft sigh, I melt against him, and that's when I feel how hard he is for me through his jeans. Shyness overtakes me even as I want to rub myself against him.

My cheeks burn and I'm aware of everyone else in the room. Some are watching, some trying excruciatingly hard not to.

"Win, relax," Jack whispers. He bends his head down toward me and my heartbeat ratchets up ten notches.

He's going to kiss me. Oh my God, Jack Hammer is going to kiss me!

I've wanted this my entire life, so why am I suddenly terrified?

"Relax, Winifred," he whispers again. "I don't bite. Not unless you want me to." He says it with a joking wink, and when he bends toward me, the tip of his nose touches mine and he rubs our noses together like we're bunnies.

I'm so startled I smile, and that's when he brings his lips to mine.

Jack's hand skims my side with a touch that is gentle for only a moment, just long enough for me to brush the silk of his beard with my fingertips and return his kiss with soft kisses of my own. The next thing I know, his mouth is ravenous, our kiss is devouring, and he's lifting me up as if I weigh nothing. He settles me against his solid abs, so I can wrap my legs around his waist. His hands slide under me, squeezing as he pushes me closer to him. The world around us is long gone as his mouth possesses mine, and then–

Jack pulls away so abruptly I lean forward and try to claim him again, but he shakes his head. "Times up," he says.

My gaze flies to Leo, who'd been beside Jack, but there are hands circling my waist from behind me, and in one swift movement, I'm shifted around in Diesel's arms.

"My turn, now," he says, settling my legs around his waist. "I've been the next-to-last choice in just about everything for twenty-eight years." He touches my lips, tracing them gently with his thumb. "I'm not waiting around to be the penultimate kiss."

I don't want him to wait even a second. I lean forward to close the space between us and Diesel makes the sexiest growl of approval as he grips the underside of my thighs. My hands go to his shirt, bunching the soft cotton fabric in my fists.

Pleasure sweeps through me when his lips close over mine. His kisses are long and lingering, and the pulse between my legs begins to ache.

Diesel presses into me. *Oh my*. Our bodies rock together, like we're dancing to our own secret music, and–

I need more of him but he's sliding me to the ground, suddenly. I can barely stand, because my legs have softened to jelly, and I want to protest.

Until Gavin pulls me back against his chest and drops a gentle peck on my cheek.

"You're *my* girl, now," he says.

His sensual amber and musk scent is so familiar, I can't help my automatic response to breathe him in long and slow. But I want to *look* at him, not waste our precious minute with my back to him.

I spin around, taking him off guard for a second as I link my arms around his neck. He smiles warmly as his hands rove along my back.

"Hey, Pooh Bear."

I smile as he tucks my boingy curl behind my ear. My eyes move to his mouth. *I get to kiss his lips.*

With his lip ring–!

"Hey, Gav," I whisper back. My voice is thick with desire. I lick my lips. He grins.

"What are you thinking?" His hands slide around my sides again, his fingers feathering across my skin, making me tremble.

He's torturing me. It isn't fair.

"I'm thinking you better kiss me right freaking now."

The predatory look he gives me is enough to send shivers along my spine. My arousal has fully soaked my panties, and when his mouth crashes over mine, another wave gushes between my thighs. I press my palms against his pecs, my fingers twitching to play with his nipple rings. I'm desperate to feel his hard body against mine. He smiles against my mouth when I whimper.

"Is this what you want?" He hooks one of my legs up over his hip and swivels his body, grinding into me.

I'm seeing stars. I try to answer, but I can't make a sound, not even to moan my approval. He doesn't mind. He parts my lips, deepening our kiss. My tongue slides over his, finding that tantalizing metal stud. His tongue twists, caressing mine as his hips roll.

Oh! *Ohhh*. I could spend entire days doing this, not just a single minute that ends much too soon–

But suddenly it's Theo's turn, and he grins mischievously as he pulls me away from Gav, his lips finding mine without hesitation. His tongue is teasing and inviting, so different from my last kiss, but so delicious he pulls small hums of desire out of me instantly. He tastes like mint, and smells like citrus, and his kisses are sensual and sweet.

But I need his hands on me.

More, I want to beg.

With a smirk, he touches my face, then his hands move to my ribs, skimming the underside of my breasts with his thumbs. Another pair of hands on my waist causes me to jerk back in surprise, but I relax into his touch when I breathe in all of the familiarity of Leo.

"If we share, that means our time with you is twice as long, right?" Leo's lips dance across my shoulder.

Theo claims my mouth again before I can answer Leo, but I don't need to even say a word. Leo slots himself behind me and Theo takes the front, and their bodies and mouths move over and around me like yin and yang, nipping here and tasting there, until I'm writhing in ecstasy.

More, I want to cry. I want all of it. All of them. Everything my boys have to give me–

Too abruptly, they pull apart, and I feel bereft for a split second until I realize it's Axel's hard body that my backside now presses against.

"I was hoping you'd want to go for five minutes," he says as his lips drop to the crook of my neck. He pauses just before touching my skin, leaving me wanting. One of his hands is in my hair, tightening his fist around a handful of curls.

I lean my head back against his shoulder, giving him access to my mouth.

But he doesn't kiss me yet. His free hand touches my belly, his fingers splaying. He isn't gentle with his touch; it isn't tickly. His hand is strong, *possessive*, just like the one in my hair.

He turns my head for better access to my throat in this position and drops a hot kiss, accompanied by a tiny lick, on my neck.

"I guess I better wow you," he says, and then he smiles against my neck as his hand creeps lower.

My eyes jam closed as every nerve in my body springs to attention, following his touch, and a fresh cascade of warmth releases between my legs.

"I mean, that's a tough act to follow." Axel's mouth vibrates my skin. "Not sure I'll be able to compete–"

"Shut up," I pant. "I don't want this to be a competition."

"Oh?" he says. "Isn't that exactly what this is?"

"Not right now. I just want a kiss."

"Ah. So that's all you want, sweetheart." He says it in a voice that sounds resigned to a sad fate, sad like he was a short while ago, but this time his sadness is just a ruse. As his hand slips lower down my belly, his fingertips deliberately stroke the front of my pajama shorts *exactly* where I want them, and his smile against my neck becomes a grin as my eyes fly wide open. "Or do you want more?"

I squeeze my thighs together. His grip on my hair releases and his hand slides down my body, his firm fingers landing on my hip.

"Spread your legs," he commands quietly in my ear. "Let me touch you."

I can't believe how bold he's being right now. I've seen the bossy side of Axel here and there during our years on the show, when we were in a time crunch and his gardens and planters needed attending one way or another before a big reveal. That's why, in my How I Lose My Virginity to Axel fantasy, as he instructs me on how repot his favorite roses (his glasses giving me Hot For Teacher vibes, naturally), my fantasy-Axel is bossy and bold. And when fantasy-Axel demands that I unbuckle his belt, slide down his jeans, and take him in my mouth, get him lubed up before he fucks me, I'm more than willing. I love this side of Axel, just as much as his gentle, sensitive side.

The real Axel is even bolder than in my fantasy, and I do as he commands, widening my stance, and gasping when his fingers find me again, this time passing under my waistband and touching me without the barrier of my sleep shorts.

"Is this okay, sweetheart?"

As I nod, he traces a line across the drenched fabric of my panties, feeling all of my desire. My face heats, and I'm glad for a second that my back is to him so he can't see my embarrassment. My face is on fire. Hell, my entire body is on fire. Then his body rolls into mine and he groans softly, a sound sexy and filled with pleasure as he presses me against him, that it causes me to melt once more.

"Fuck, Win. You want this as much as we do, don't you?" he growls. "Are you wet for me or is this all for my brothers?"

"Not a competition," I push through gritted teeth.

Again he traces the line between my thighs, but this time, he hooks my panties aside, enough for the tips of his fingers to stroke through my folds without a barrier.

I moan so loudly I have to bite my lip to control myself.

"Damn it, Ax, are you going to kiss her or what?" Mason calls, and thank God none of them can see what he's doing to me, because the next thing I know, Axel is on his knees before me, both of his hands on my thighs.

How the hell I manage to stand on my own is a mystery, especially when he looks up at me, his glasses slightly steamed up from the heat coming off of us, and says, "Do you have any boundaries regarding *where* I kiss you, sweetheart?"

Oh, God, he wants to–

His thumb creeps closer to my horny little love button, starting his agonizing tease all over again. But this time he only uses his thumb to draw my shorts to the side. As he licks his lips and draws closer, he raises a brow at me, his chestnut hair flopping across his forehead.

Too breathless to speak, I shake my head. No boundaries. None. Not for my boys.

My eyes glaze over as Axel's mouth hits the exact spot over my panties, so expertly its like he can see through the cotton–

"*Time*, you fucker," Mason growls.

Axel stands, and I'm miraculously put back together before Mason closes in on us. Sleep shorts in order, curls swept back behind my ears.

Inside, however, I'm fully shattered.

When Mason takes me in his arms, he has to lower me to the ground so I can regain control. My breath is coming rapidly, my chest rising and falling so hard it's like I've been running laps around the house, not standing still.

"Do you need to cool down for a minute, cupcake?" he says, dropping a kiss on my forehead.

I'm sure I do, but Mason's brushing the tops of my thighs with his fingers and as I dig into his hard, hard pecs, he presses closer to me and I feel other things are very hard, too…

God, so very hard.

I wasn't too wrong when I mistook Mason for *Big Max*, either. He really is just as huge as...

And with that thought, Max's beautiful face flashes through my mind, and a coil of guilt twists in my heart, sharp enough to reverberate through my body. My ecstasy and joy fizzles away as I'm snapped back to reality, and I scan the living room for him.

But Max is gone. I shouldn't be so bothered but I am.

I look at Mason and he smiles gently. "You okay, Win?"

I start to nod, but end up shaking my head.

"I need to talk to Max," I say, stumbling as I jump to my feet. I feel terrible, *amazing*, rotten, absolutely *glorious*, too many things all at the same time. "I'm sorry."

And I am sorry. God, I am SO damn sorry. As I back away from them and rush off to find Max, I'm so sorry I'm not finishing what they started. But I'm more sorry for not pulling Max aside and making sure he was okay with any of this *before* we started.

CHAPTER 11

Winnie

I know Max Hammer well enough to guess he'll be in the home gym, so the first place I head is to the stairs leading down to the basement.

I have to grip the stair railing for dear life to steady myself as I walk down so that I don't break my neck. If it wasn't for my weak knees, breathlessness, and the desperate, carnal need for more of my boys still pulsing between my thighs, I would swear I was dreaming.

Did that just happen? What is my life!

But as mind-blowing as the last half hour was – holy shit, is that really all it's been since I followed their voices out of bed? – I need to *not* think about the others for five minutes and talk to Max.

Somehow I push aside thoughts of Theo and Leo sandwiching my body between theirs… the feel of Gavin's stud against my tongue… Axel's breath ghosting along my neck as he curled his fingers into my….

TEN HAMMERS

Whoa, girl, get it together.

I pause to squeeze my thighs together when I reach the door at the bottom of the stairs. There's a lot of *thunking* and *clunking, clinking* and *clanking* coming from the other side of the door. When I ease it open, the subtle aroma of cleaning spray hangs in the air, softening the tangy scent of sweat leftover from whichever Hammer worked out earlier this morning. There must be an intense amount of lingering pheromones, or else I really am so freaking horny that the smell of the Hammer brother's sweat makes me want to race back to the living room at once, flinging my pajamas off as I run…

Focus. On. MAX!

There's another round of *thunking* and *clunking* to distract me. I want to call out and ask if he's lifting weights or throwing them around, because that's more what it sounds like. But I catch sight of him in one of the full-length mirrors, and my mouth goes dry.

Max doesn't seem to notice me from where he's doing bicep curls with astonishingly large dumbbells. Or if he does, he doesn't show it. He's too deeply focused on his workout routine. His bulging muscles are the epitome of grace and strength.

Popsy and the boys put this gym together several years ago, between seasons of the show. He let the boys buy the latest everything, to their absolute delight. The tall windows and back door are at ground level to the patio and Anna's vegetable garden. Sunlight bathes the entire basement with a soft morning glow. It's beautiful down here.

This is my first time seeing it in person and it's hard to believe that this was ever an actual basement, dark and packed full with long-forgotten boxes of toddler clothes and building blocks. We used to play hide and seek in the darkness, but now everywhere I look is bright and open.

Hidden speakers around the room soften the space with light music. Wait, is that…? Yeah, it *is* Adele, her voice drenched in sorrow and pain.

Thunk. Clunk.

Clink. Clank.

"Sounds like a poltergeist down here." I call as I head over to him.

Sweat glistens on his skin, evidence of his exertion even though he doesn't show any exertion whatsoever.

Max shoots me a wry look as he sets the barbells down. "Well, I'm happy to see your lips haven't fallen off." His voice is light, joking as he grabs his towel and dries the sweat on his face and shoulders. "I wasn't quite sure my brothers would leave you in one piece."

He puts down the towel and looks at me. First in the eyes, then along all of the places his brothers touched me, his expression impossible to decipher.

Is he mad?

That I can't tell bugs me. I can always tell with Max.

I close the gap between us. "Hey."

When I reach out to touch him, he turns his head away and says, "Don't, okay?"

Oh, boy.

"Max," I begin.

"It's okay, Win."

He grabs his phone from the floor beside the workout bench. Staring hard at the screen, he flicks his thumb enough times that I wonder for a fraction of a second if this is how he's dismissing me, and the hurt cuts through me almost as hard as when I learned about the pact and his stupid lies.

The music shuts off. Max drops his phone, though he still doesn't look my way.

"Max, I–"

"Really," he interrupts. "It's okay."

But it doesn't feel okay. It feels like I've severed some connection between us. I try again. Because it's Max. I have to try until I get through to him. "I probably should've at least talked to you first, though. I mean, before…"

"Before you let every one of my brothers rub you all over themselves, one after the other, like they were some kind of kinky assembly line, with a saliva-cleansing machine and–"

"Eww, Max, *stop*. What, are you writing car wash erotica, now? We made out. That's all."

Okay, even I know that while I'm being technical, I'm still lying a little. None of those felt like just *making out*.

I want to call him out for not telling me about the pact, about how they all felt, but that little voice in my gut tells me I need to tread lightly here.

"Anyway," I say, "it was a one-time thing."

"Don't you mean a nine-time thing?" he mutters, and I want to grab his sweat rag and swat him in the ego.

"Six, but you can shut up. I was going to say that, even though I have been convinced that you all… feel things for me, too, there's no way.

He raises a brow. "No way for what, specifically?"

"This," I try to explain. "Us. Them. Me. You."

Now both of his brows are up.

I let out a sigh. "What I'm trying to say is that I can never choose one of you over the others. I know that now more than ever."

My words settle into the space between us, heavy enough that I have to check the corners of my eyes

There is a long pause before he answers. "What does this mean for you and me?" he asks, finally, but he's not making eye contact.

"We're going to need to, you know. Stop."

But if it makes you feel any better, I'd rather cut off my right ear.

"Alright."

I shift my weight from foot to foot, waiting on him to say more. He doesn't.

"Max–"

He reaches for his weights, turning further away from me. "I just need some space, alright? Please, Win?"

I take a deep breath and let it out slowly. "Okay."

"Hey, Win?" he calls and hope surges through me.

"Yeah?"

"Why only six?"

"I cut it short when I realized you'd left. Checking on you was more important to me than—"

"Sorry to have ruined the fun," he says.

"Max—"

"Just give me some space," he says again.

And I do.

I am well over my recommended daily allowance of testosterone and I haven't even had breakfast yet. Usually stress makes me hungry, but at the moment, I'm still too twisted up to eat. I need some perspective, and I need it now.

I need Goldie.

As I wander back through the house, and upstairs to my room, I try not to be seen by anyone. It's an easy feat. Too easy of a feat. Where did everyone go? The Hammer home is ginormous, but it's still usually impossible to take a step without tripping over a Hammer.

I linger on the stairs and allow myself to be distracted by all of the family photos that dot the wall. The love and joy is palpable from the still images of long-gone moments. I normally hate seeing pictures of myself, but my inclusion on this wall brings on happy tears. With them, I was always smiling, always taken care of, always watched out for. Always treated as if I mattered. As if I was wanted. Those feelings, those memories—the only good parts of my past in Smithville—are captured within these frames.

I will never do anything to jeopardize what I have with my boys.

I continue on, pausing here and there. I love every single part of this house, every nook and cranny. Everything except for the rare view of the house across the street. Anna often shut the curtains so that I wouldn't have to see it. Will it be possible to exorcize my ghosts, even with all ten of the Hammer brothers by my side? I can't imagine it, but I can't imagine them ever letting me down, either.

Once in my room, I grab my phone from the bedside table, and sink onto the bed. Goldie answers on the first ring.

"I MISS YOU SO MUCH!" she wails. "I have no idea what I'm doing with my life. I feel adrift! Totally adrift! Do you think I've peaked already? I think I may've peaked already."

Okay, so perhaps Goldie wasn't the right person to turn to for perspective. But she's clearly spiraling and it's my duty as her friend to save her from herself, rescue from her funk, and distract her by completely and utterly blowing her mind.

"I made out with all the Hammer brothers!" I say in a rush. "Well, not all," I frown. "Six. Well, seven, if we're getting technical, but that's a different story."

There's silence and of course, my first thought is that she doesn't believe me.

But then she screeches, "OH MY GOD. Why did you never tell me this! I would have kept it off the record! Like when? Over the course of the show? Over the course of your life?"

"Over the course of… since like almost an hour ago?"

Technically that's not true since I haven't made out with Max since last night. There's a vase of fresh, colorful flowers that Anna left in a milk pitcher on the bedside table, and I run my finger over the delicate petals as it sinks in that I will never make out with Max Hammer again. For a moment, I, too, feel totally adrift.

"WHAT! Tell me everything. Tell me everything right now. Wait. I have to know. Who's the best kisser? I bet it's Gav with the hardware, holy smokes."

"Goldie," I say to her. "Producer mode off, best girl friend mode on, please."

"Okay, okay. Sorry. I am so happy for you! Tell me everything!" she squeals.

"Everything? You asked for it."

Flopping backward onto the bed, and scooting myself around so that I'm nestled into the generous helping of pillows, I start with the story of my friends-with-benefitship with Max.

She's stunned into silence – I know this because she tells me.

Next, I tell her how the guys found out about it. I only pause when I get to the part about the spin-off.

"Tell me you didn't know about Winnie's Favorite Hammer," I say. "Golds."

"Winnie's Favorite Hammer?"

I can tell without seeing her that her brows are knitted together and she's pursing her lips. Her I-have-no-clue-what-you're-talking-about face.

Trying hard to keep my voice from shaking, I explain.

"Holy shit!" she cries. "Girl. If I would've known about that, you would've known about that. I can't believe the guys didn't tell you. *Why?*"

I resume my story, keeping some details to myself, of course, and get all the way up to the part with Max in the basement before I pause again.

My pause makes Goldie impatient because she says, "Girl, why the silence? You better not be slapping the clam over there! Although, I would *totally* be slapping the clam if I were you. In fact, if you give me a quick little minute to take off my pants, we can slap our clams in unison while you tell me – with painstakingly lurid descriptions, obviously– which Hammer bro is the best kisser and why!"

I burst out laughing. Only Goldie.

"I miss you too," I tell her. "But there will be no mutual clam slappage here, okay? And I couldn't tell you who the best kisser is. They're all…"

My voice trails off as playful shouts from the yard below my window remind me that the Hammer brothers are always somewhere near. From the sounds of splashing water and joyful laughter, I can guess at least most of them are poolside.

"Okay, okay," Goldie says as I climb off of the bed. "You refuse to reveal some secrets. Changing the subject. Now, tell me, who has the biggest schlong?"

Sunlight seeps through the sheer, billowy curtains, which I move aside so that I can catch a better sight of the guys at the pool, knowing the light will obscure me from their view. Tan biceps flex, tattoos waver under water, hair drips with water onto washboard abs... as always, I try not to drool.

Voyeuristic, sure, but hey, they're all in swim shorts, from what I can see. It's good, clean, family fun.

Unfortunately.

"I said we made out, not that we made out after they all did stripteases for me and got out their measuring tapes."

The deep azure of the pool catches the sunlight and sparkles like stars, accentuating the chiseled bodies of Gavin and Gunnar, both waist-deep in the water. The sight releases a new wave of warmth between my legs.

"So what you're telling me is that all those *fine* pieces of Hammer meat want you, and you're *turning them* down?" she asks bluntly. "*All* of them?"

"Well, yeah."

I can hear Goldie wagging her head at me in the pause before she says, "You know, silly girl, it's actually no surprise to me that you turned them all down. I know your doubt about whether or not you're worthy of being... that is to say *hammered* by a Hammer, is rearing its nasty little head right now–"

"Golds, I just want love!"

Goldie laughs softly. "I know you do, babe. But you've always been so preoccupied by how the show's audience sees you that you're oblivious to the way all your boys watch you. You may have a hard–no pun intended–time believing it, but I would not be surprised at all if every single one of them wants to give you that love. All that hot, hot, hot love."

She drops it like it's not an emotional bomb and then carries on cheerfully.

"If I were you, I would do it. And by 'it', I'm strictly referring to the Winnie's Favorite Hammer but not-televised thing this time. No eliminations, obviously... but just because they can't *all* have you doesn't mean you shouldn't have *one* of them. Go on, my big-hearted, vibrant, sexy-as-hell best friend. Make me sickeningly jealous by dating *all* of them, at least until you figure out which one is Mr. Perfect For You. Go get that happily ever after, girl."

She says it like it's easy. But what if they're *all* Mr. Perfect For Me?

My attention is drawn to Gavin as his piercings catch a sunbeam.

The intricate celtic knot on Jack's upper back wavers underwater as he tries to swim past Diesel.

Diesel grins as he splashes Jack, and my heart squeezes.

"I could never choose."

"Yes, you could, dear naive little one. If you keep an open mind."

I shake my head, even though she can't see me. "It's not my mind that's the problem, Golds. It's my heart. My heart wants them all."

She snorts. "Wins. Despite what our industry–"

"Former industry," I correct. "At least for me."

"Despite what the reality television industry is selling us, you cannot be *in love* with multiple people at the same time. You just can't. Eventually, you'll discover for yourself that though you may love them all, you're only really, and I mean truly, in love with one of them."

She doesn't have the same view right now as I have, clearly.

"We're going to have to agree to disagree here."

"Deal, but… I still say you're nuts if you don't go for it."

"You're not thinking through the consequences."

"The only consequences I see are you having only very sore—"

"Good talk, Goldie. I have to go now!"

She laughs. "They make creams for that, though! GO FOR IT. Keep me up to date."

Rolling my eyes, I head straight for the pool. I think over what I'm going to say to the guys as the breeze carries the faint scent of chlorine, mixing it with the hint of coconut. It's a combo which brings back all the best memories from childhood summers and stirs up all the conflicting emotions within me again.

"Hey, sweetheart," Axel calls from the side of the pool. "Want me to apply your sunscreen?"

He wears a happy smile and a flirty wink. Tears threaten suddenly, but I swallow them back as I shake my head.

"Hey everyone," I call from the edge of the porch, unable to make it all the way over to them lest their faces and muscles change my mind. "I've been doing a lot of thinking."

In a flash, all eyes are on me. Nine pairs lit up, eager, happy, waiting…

Shit, I have to swallow the tears back again.

"I've got to go," I choke out. "Back to my cottage. For a while. I need time to sort some things out in my head."

I swallow harder than ever but my throat is too dry.

"Babe. What's wrong?" Gunnar calls. He's in the water next to Gav, but he's making his way out, and that's the last thing I want.

"Nothing, I'm fine. I'm just going to drive up for the day. I need time—"

I break off when the tears win and pause to discreetly wipe my face.

"You all know how impossible this trip down memory lane is for me. This upcoming renovation, and being at Gram's, it's going to be too emotionally difficult. I know it. So, I can't add any more upheaval in my life. I need you. I need us. Our team. But I need us without any romantic drama."

"You have our word, Pooh Bear," Gav says, his expression soft and earnest. "We're friends first and foremost, you know that."

I shake my head. "Not friends first and foremost. Friends, period."

"Absolutely," Gunnar jumps in. "We support you, no matter what. But… you will come back, right?"

"I said for the day, and I meant it. Just a little time to get my head on straight is all I need."

"But—" one of the triplets protests.

"See you tomorrow!" I cut him off, turning back to the house to grab my keys, even though walking away—no, *running* away—feels so wrong. A part of me wants to yell at myself for doing something so stupid… but my father did enough of that to last me a lifetime.

And because I know my thoughts and emotions are too far from steady around my boys to make rational decisions, no matter what Goldie thinks, I do the only thing I can and that's jump in my car, drive far from Smithville, fast as I can, and don't look back.

CHAPTER 12

Winnie

For my eighteenth birthday, the boys gave me a check. A check that made my eyes bulge out of my head. I immediately said, "No way," put it back in the card they'd all signed, and thrust it back at Jack.

My mind is still boggled and my eyes well with tears when I think of the amount of money they'd saved up for me.

"I'm not a charity case." I'd jutted my chin. "I'm not taking a dime from your parents."

I'd been convinced that it was all from Anna. I have self-esteem issues now, but back then? The fact that these guys could do something so thoughtful with no strings attached, for me? It was too much for my brain to process.

"None of this is from Mom or Dad," Jack said. "It's all from us. It's all for you. It's a gift. It's not charity."

It didn't make sense. They had always been a hard-working family, each brother taking on part-time jobs around their homework and various school activities. But they should be using that money towards their own futures, towards college.

"Why?" I think I said, I might have been too emotional to manage actual words, though.

"We're going to use it to buy you your own place."

Gavin had a lot less piercings then, but his lip ring always made me pay extra attention when he spoke. "It won't be a palace, but we'll fix it up however you want."

Back then, like now, we were on the precipice of a new chapter of our lives, all or most of us going our separate ways.

Jack had already been living in California, majoring in Architectural Engineering at UCLA. Renovating the disaster of a house he bought dirt cheap at an auction in his freshman year became his focus outside of earning his degree.

"Jackie's distracting himself from the loneliness of being so far away from home," Anna had said.

But that house paved the way. It became the place where Max and Mason eventually joined him, pursuing screenwriting and film production. Over spring breaks and summer vacations, the other boys went out to visit, but my dad firmly rejected all of my invitations for me.

I knew Gunnar and Diesel wanted to move into the remaining spare room and pursue their music, and I panicked sometimes, that they'd all leave me. Forget the chubby girl next door, easily replaced by the hot girls of California.

It went without saying that I did not want to live in Smithville once I no longer had to. But the boys didn't want me putting down roots too far away, either. Their roots would always be in Smithville, no matter how far away they scattered, they would always return to their homebase with Anna and Popsy. And even if I planned to never go back there, the boys wanted me to be close enough that their parents were within a day's driving distance of wherever I was, in case I ever needed them to come to me.

When they showed me the cottage in Whispering Glen, I was sold. Not because of the cottage itself–that was a hot mess–but because of the name of the quaint little town the cottage was in. Whispering Glen. It might as well have been called Heaven. I hated screaming more than anything–still do–so Whispering Glen sounded like a dream.

I pull into the driveway and smile.

My cottage is snug. Quaint. It's cozy and idyllic. It boasts a layout meticulously planned to conserve space. Those are a few of my favorite design biz descriptions to use for my tiny one bedroom, one bath, with a kitchen, and a single living/dining space.

But the size hasn't mattered to me. The boys asked me for a wishlist and then they proceeded to fulfill every item on it, like Santa's most overachieving team of elves.

I wanted a home, and I got the most adorable house imaginable, with a white picket fence, a scarlet red door, and a porch swing that looks out over a lush garden. Inside, there's a reading nook tucked into one of the windows, even.

But the house is better than all that, because the wreath on the door was lovingly handmade by Anna. The swing was a surprise put in by Jack because I had wanted one as a kid. Every plant in the garden was one I'd called a favorite while tagging along with Axel on his weekend gardening jobs back in high-school. The reading nook was designed by Gav. It was all made just for me. A cottage built with love by my best friends. My found family. It's my sanctuary.

"Home sweet home," I whisper, and I wish the words didn't feel so incomplete. Because this is the thing that has never made sense: it's my perfect house… but it has never quite felt like home.

Don't get me wrong—I adore my cottage and I will be forever grateful for what the boys did for me. This place will always hold a special place in my heart. But the concept of home will forever be a slippery one for me. Odd for someone who spent almost the last decade of her life co-starring in a home renovation show, but to me, maybe home isn't about the walls and the roof and the rooms. Maybe it's about who shares it with you.

Once inside, I open up all the windows to let fresh air in.

The long drive here gave me a lot of time to think, but my mind kept getting snagged on something Goldie had said about me worrying too much about how the audience watched me to notice how my boys were watching me.

I have never, not once, watched any of our shows. Not even the premiere. When Anna and Popsy threw a watch party in the ballroom of a hotel near where we were filmed, I slipped out once the lights dimmed. Cruz noticed and followed me and we played cards up in my room, sneaking back in before the end credits rolled. He didn't ask a single question. He just… accepted what I needed and was there without a discussion about it.

I'm stronger now. I can handle watching myself—seeing my body, each and every one of my insecurities out on display for the world's mean, hungry eyes. I have to, because maybe watching our journey will give me the perspective I need.

Curling up on the couch with my phone, I queue up that first episode. I don't have time to watch them all, but I decide to choose one from each season.

The opening to the show is a montage of tan abs and tools. It's awful. But I recognize my boys, chest by chest, and I drool like every viewer in the world probably has, which is shameful, I know. And worse, I'm instantly ready to run to my bedroom, grab my dildos, and give myself ten glorious hammerings.

But then there I am beside Max as he introduces the renovation we're about to undertake. It's weird being on the outside, watching myself. I cringe at my awkward smile, my thighs, ugh. I'm not a whale, not exactly. But with my pale skin, the name baby beluga pops into my mind.

Baby beluga. It's my dad's voice in my head. That was one of his names for me.

Stop, I tell myself. *Focus on something else.*

My hair looks cute.

And Max? He's shirtless, as always, and seeing his younger body, younger face, that shorter haircut, makes me smile so much it's hard not to enjoy the show.

Watching all the guys on screen, listening to their interviews about me, seeing what the camera chose to show of our camaraderie, our laughter, our happiness as a group, makes the episodes sail by. My transformation from awkward and uncertain to relaxed and spontaneous is obvious.

And the reason why is clear – I'm never without my boys. Axel is always available to lend a helping hand and a listening ear whenever I am struggling on a project. Gav and Gunnar bring joy and spontaneity into each project, Max encourages me to be gentle with myself when things aren't going to plan… nearly every scene has at least one of them either praising me to the camera – which makes my face burn and my smile grow – or it shows us hard at work, playing around during down times, and working as an amazing team.

I remember so much about our demolitions, renovations, and grand reveals. The laughter and disasters, and great successes, and yet this view is like watching an entirely different side of my life. I'm absorbed for hours, only stopping for necessary pee breaks. And by the time my phone battery is at 1% and I need to head back to Smithville, I know two things for certain. No man will ever love me like the Hammer brothers love me. And no, I can't keep them all with me forever.

But there's no way I can just let them all go at the end of the summer, either. Basically, I'm more confused than ever.

CHAPTER 13

Gavin

I've taken three cold showers over the course of the day. Jerked off six times. I'm not proud to admit it, but the count would be higher if I hadn't lost control the last time and maybe broken my dick.

I mean, it still functions, thank God. I'm hard again just thinking about this morning. But as I blew my load, I found myself wondering for the first time if it's anatomically possible to pull it off.

I grab my phone. It's well after midnight. Winnie hasn't responded to any of my messages, though she has seen them. I pull up the group chat I have with my brothers. At one point, she was in it too, but then she was like *I can't with you guys talking about roof shingles and farts*. And that was that.

Any of you heard from Win? I ask.

Jack replies immediately: She said she needs space. Leave her alone.

Prick.

Gunnar responds after a couple minutes: Don't tell us what to do, douchebag.

> That was for Jack.
>
> Nothing from her, G.

No one else reads our exchange or chimes in. So either they're all asleep or choking the chicken. Otherwise, they, too, would be semi-obsessively checking for any word from Win.

I smirk. Jack is probably pacing his room, checking the time on his phone obsessively, and my twin is definitely off with Deez, writing her a love song.

I can stare up at the ceiling, testing my self-control. Try to keep myself from winding up in one of those if-you-have-an-erection-that-lasts-four-hours scenarios that'll result in an ER visit because Winnie Wainwright is walking Viagra. Or I can go for a run and try to burn off some of this pent-up energy.

Deciding on the latter, I throw on some clothes and head downstairs. I grab my water bottle from the fridge on my way to the front door.

Slipping out into the night, I begin stretching on the porch. After letting loose so many times, you'd think my body would be nice and relaxed, but nope. My neck and left arm are particularly tense.

A throat clears nearby.

The instant flood of warmth through my body at the realization of her presence hits my heart harder than my dick. But it definitely hits my dick.

I glance around and squint. There's no moon. It's dark as fuck out. But I can make out her silhouette, in one of the rocking chairs further down the porch.

At least I think the dark lump is Win, with her knees pulled up and her arms locked around them.

"I didn't know you were back," I say.

The lump moves. Definitely her. I want to go to her, but I know my lower half isn't ready, so I move into another stretch position, one that will hide the bulge in case the sliver of moon is shining too generously upon me.

"How long have you been sitting out here?"

"A while."

I don't hear tears in her voice, so I don't think she's been crying. "You alright?"

"Mm-hmm. What are you doing up so late?"

"I'm heading out for a run to try and stop myself from masturbating to death." I shift positions, and this time my bulge isn't quite as hidden as before.

She bursts out laughing, the sound ringing out through the silent night, and making me grin. I love making her laugh.

"You asked," I tell her.

"That I did."

"Want some company?"

"I mean, not if it's going to end with you masturbating to death in one of Anna's beloved rocking chairs."

A soft breeze carries that damn intoxicating strawberry scent of hers over to me and I have to force myself to push away the new wave of thoughts in my mind that are a hell of a lot more interesting than masturbating alone in one of those rocking chairs.

Mom does love these chairs. Cruz built them for her a couple of birthdays ago. I focus on this, on my mom and brother, and push the remaining thoughts out of my head.

"I'll control myself."

I mean, if she wants me to…

But as I walk over, I swear I can sense the heavy mood around her. I pick up the rocking chair nearest to her and place it even closer to hers.

Now I can see her better and a hollowness to her eyes. Shit.

"Hey," I say softly, rocking forward.

She doesn't look at me, doesn't say a word, and as I force myself to relax into the chair, or at least appear relaxed, she chews her lip and wrings her hands, and I can't stand it. I wish I could drain that nervousness and all the negative feelings from her, just kind of absorb them and shoulder them myself.

Reaching over, I touch her arm, walk my fingers down to her elbow, and tug her toward me just enough to give the hint that I want her hand in mine and she can take it if she wants it.

She does, thank God, pressing her thumb into my hand, a tiny thank you gesture that feels immense.

"I'm trying to work up the courage to go over there," she says, after a minute.

"Oh?"

I hear her exhale. "I'm super anxious about tomorrow."

"Totally natural for you to feel that way. But we're all going to be with you."

"That's part of the problem. I don't know if I'm going to be able to handle it and I don't want to go inside and fall apart in front of you all. You guys *see* me," she says.

I don't know what she means with that last part because of course we do, but my heart aches for her, and I squeeze her hand a little tighter.

"So I was going to kind of do a trial run," she continues. "Go inside by myself. See if it's as bad as I think it's gonna be." She sighs. "I kind of just want to forget the sledgehammers and just bulldoze the whole damn place to dust."

She looks so sad, and I want to tell her anything that will make the pain leave her expression. I want to promise her we'll burn it to the ground tomorrow if that's what she wants. She can light the match and we'll all bring gasoline.

But no. Over the years, seeing what that fucking house and everything it represents, even now, has done to her, I know we are right in at least trying to heal her wounds rather than adding another Band-Aid to the pile.

Even if it would feel really fucking good to watch it go up in flames.

"Winnie, you deserve all the love and happiness in the entire world. I can't erase the past, but–" I'm making myself cringe – "This sounds so damn cliché, I know, but I can promise you, that I'll be right by your side, now and always, as long as you want me there. Want us there. I know every single one of my brothers feels the same."

Jealousy still simmers in me over her thing with Max, but I swallow it down. Winnie's needs will always matter more to me than anything else. "You're running the show here, Pooh Bear."

I don't just mean in the reno, but now's not the time to bring up the other stuff. Though I do want her to know none of us are going to push her to do anything she doesn't want to do.

She sniffles, freeing her hand from mine to swipe at her eyes. "I don't want to go in for the first time with all of you. But I'm not certain anymore that I want to do it all by myself, either."

"Is *one* of us a good number? I'll come with you, if that's what you want," I offer. Yeah, I'm not gonna push but I'm never going to make this woman beg, or even ask twice, for anything she wants, ever.

"Yes, oh my God, please, yes. Do you mind?"

The light is back in her eyes, and the sight of it ratchets up my heart rate.

"Do I mind? Winnie Wainwright, do you still not understand?" I get up. "I'd walk a mile over shards of glass if you needed me to."

"I'll try to never need that," she promises with a laugh. She pulls her phone from the back pocket of her jeans and turns on the flashlight. Then she stands. She grabs my hand, which I hadn't even realized I'd fisted, and it unfurls in her palm. She intertwines her fingers with mine.

Winnie's grip on my hand tightens with every step we take as we walk across the street. I can feel her unease growing as the moment stretches longer and longer, but she never takes her eyes off the house.

"Shouldn't the lawn be a jungle, all grown up and weedy?"

She's visibly confused, with a cute little eyebrow wrinkle. It was that way the last time she saw it, probably. That's how her dad tended to keep it.

"Pops has been mowing it, trimming the hedges."

"Your parents are… something else." Her voice grows thick with unshed tears. "I should pay Popsy something, I should–"

She breaks off and her breath is ragged as she turns her face away from me. She tries to rip her fingers from mine, as well, but I tighten my fist just enough to let her know I want her hand to stay.

"I am going to fall apart in there," she chokes out.

"Do you want me to stay on the porch? Give you some privacy?"

"No!" she cries. "No. I want you with me. And I think I need you to go first, too."

"Of course."

I lead her inside, the musty, stagnant air enveloping us instantly, and we cough together. The worn floorboards groan. Every surface is coated in a layer of fine, powdery dust and decay, and hints of long abandoned lives cling to every corner with the spider webs. Cracked windows allow shards of feeble moonlight to pierce the darkness, casting long, ghostly shapes across the floor. It's fucking grim.

I glance at Winnie and my heart wrenches. Her eyes are once again hollow. In the dim light, shadows play tricks in the corners of my eyes, but the shadows in her eyes are very much real.

"Win," I say softly.

Her gaze flies to mine, but I'm not sure she's seeing me fully. A single tear runs down her cheek.

"He's right, though," she says, with a sad, bitter laugh. "How you look at me doesn't matter, because the curb appeal doesn't mean crap if the house is a teardown."

She can hear him, her piece-of-shit deadbeat dad. I know she can. As though his raised voice and sharp words linger in the walls. Peeling out of the wallpaper. Tormenting her everywhere she looks.

"Winnie, no," I start, pulling her close to me for a hug, but she shakes her head and pulls her hands from mine.

"None of you deserve this–"

"You're right. Not a damn one of us does. You're too good for each and every one of us."

"Gav! That's not what I mean and you know it. None of you deserve to have to put up with my baggage, or the emotional scars left behind by my father. You'll never be able to heal them. They're a fucking part of me." She crosses her arms over her chest and turns away from me again but this time she walks too far away for me to reach for her hand to reel her back to me without chasing her.

"They were lies, Win," I tell her, though I don't really know the specifics. What I do know breaks my heart. I once heard Pops call Win's father a verbally abusive bastard and

Pops would not say that lightly. But all Winnie would ever say was that her dad yelled a lot. We made her swear he never touched her. Had he laid a hand on her, we would've–

"It doesn't matter," she says, and I stop to listen. "I hate feeling this way. But his lies became my truth. They're not just shackles you all can help me break free from. I'll take everything he ever said to me with me wherever I go." Her voice rises. "They're a part of me," she finishes on a hollow sob, void of tears. "He's dead and gone, and no matter what we do with this place, that is my inheritance. It's pathetic. I know."

"Win–"

"Please," she whispers. "Please don't try right now."

She doesn't turn back to me and I ache to pull her into my arms and take her to my old bedroom. Not even to my bed, necessarily, but to sit together in the same place where, as kids, we'd whispered and laughed together. Where we sat side by side, reading from her favorite of the books on my shelf.

My best friend, my Pooh Bear. I wish I could give Winnie all the comfort she deserves. But even if I could, she's not in a place to accept it and that tears me up like nothing fucking else.

CHAPTER 14

Winnie

For ten years I vowed to never step foot inside Gram's house again, and yet here I stand. Barely past the threshold and already I'm hearing my dad's voice louder than ever. Taunting as I bring a Hammer into the house for the first time, another thing I vowed never, ever to do.

What do you think that boy really wants from you, girlie? We all know it ain't true love and it sure as hell ain't gonna be a salad! Ha! Ha!

I realized it on the drive back from Whispering Glen: my father made me feel like my appearance, my body and its inadequacies, was the only thing about me that meant anything. And in the process, he damaged what really mattered. My soul. My heart. My ability to believe, *really* believe, with 100% faith, that someone could love me. Because he and Gram, the people who were supposed to love me unconditionally, couldn't.

The Hammer brothers are attracted to me. Mind-blown, but so what? Watching the shows made me think they might all even have romantic feelings for me. Again, mind-blown, but so what? At the end of the day, when it comes to a life partner, a soul mate, a 'til-death-do-us part, they all deserve someone who won't forever question their hearts. Someone whose doubts in herself won't leave her constantly wondering why, second guessing their words and actions.

I sniffle, and tell myself it's okay. I may never end up with the kind of love I yearn for with any of them, but they'll always love me as a best friend. I will never doubt that. And I will not destroy that. Just because 1 Girl, 10 Hammers ended, just because the summer will eventually end, doesn't mean my friendship with any of the boys will end. I won't let it.

Maybe the only reason I've been unable to envision my happily ever after with anyone other than a Hammer brother is because I thought my boys were a pipedream. Never going to happen, and therefore, safe. Maybe I just need to stay away from romantic relationships, period. I've survived almost thirty years of being single. What's thirty more?

I'm going to need a bigger cottage, though, I warn myself. *Because I'm going to seriously need to expand my collection of toys.*

Gav watches me warily and I suspect the way my eyes glaze over from my thoughts of new dildos are concerning.

I glance at my phone. My battery charged in the car, but it's getting low again. "Is there electricity?"

"We called the power company as soon as you said yes," he confirms. "You want me to…?"

"Yeah," I whisper and brace myself. A second later, the lights flicker on.

He whistles under his breath. There's still a litter box in one corner, but from the scent I can suddenly name, the carpet was the preferred place to pee.

"Who would let that man have a cat?" I shake my head and put away my phone.

Gavin sniffs and clearly catches a whiff of the same smell I had. Even his gross-I-smell-piss face is adorable. "I think it was more than one."

"Damn."

I glance around the room, finally. Tears flood my eyes as they land on it. The recliner.

What the fuck do you think you're wearing? You ain't leavin' the house in that. My God.

Bile rises in my throat and I cover my mouth.

"I'm here," Gavin says. "We can leave anytime you want to."

I take a moment to make sure everything threatening to come up stays down.

"You know how girls wear short skirts and their parents are like, you can't wear that out, it's not appropriate, it shows too much and might tempt the boys? Or it's against the school dress code. Whatever."

"... I guess?"

I raise my finger and point at the recliner.

"My dad sat right there on the first day of middle school. I got a cute skirt from the mall. Your mom took me to buy it, actually."

"I don't remember you ever wearing a skirt, other than your prom dress."

That dress was floor-length. With sleeves. Gavin went with his girlfriend, the most popular girl in our grade. I went with my lab partner, a guy named Bert who told me, after we got there, he didn't dance.

"You don't remember me ever wearing a skirt, because the one I got for the first day of middle school was the last. My dad told me I couldn't wear it."

He frowns, genuinely puzzled. "Because it would tempt the boys or was against the dress code?"

I shake my head. I can't bear to look at him as I say, "Because my thunder thighs would gross people out."

It's extra humiliating to say, because, well, my dad probably did save me from a lot of teasing that day.

"If he was still alive I would kill him," Gav says, matter-of-factly. I look at him again and see the rage etched on his face.

But he's not going to let it out. He's going to restrain whatever he's feeling, keep the anger under the surface and under control, because that's what I need him to do.

"What a piece of shit. Him, not you. I'm so sorry, Win. I'm sorry he spoke to you that way and I'm sorry your own grandmother let him."

I don't tell him that not only did Gram let him, she often laughed.

"Everyone at school felt so bad for me when dad went to jail, again, but it was a reprieve for me. Gram would at least leave me alone. To dad, I was like some scab he couldn't resist picking at. For a long time, I hoped she would die. I had this fantasy that if she did, your parents would adopt me, the way they did all of you."

"I think Mom had the same fantasy," he says.

I take a deep breath and try to steady myself. "Come on. Let's do the grand tour. Say hello to all the ghosts."

He's by my side in the blink of an eye. But this time, he doesn't hold my hand. He puts an arm around my shoulder and pulls me close. Together, we walk from room to room. It's like a museum of misery and I'm so grateful he doesn't let me go, not even for a minute.

Haunted as I am by the rooms, which are more wrecked than the house was in my memories, and that's saying a lot, I manage to open up to Gav. I tell him things I could never say before. I show him where Gram sat, eating her snacks – the ones she never shared with me because *"more snacks are the last thing you need,"* and as I share the pain with him, he hugs me tight.

Last, I lead Gavin into my childhood room, and I brace myself for the horrible slam of memories. It surprises me when it's not as overwhelming as I expected. Maybe because at this point, I've shared enough of the horror to make it bearable. Or maybe because Gav is the greatest shoulder to lean on, somehow passing his strength on to me. My room is a trash heap, and smells like an entire family of cats had been locked up in here at one point. But the purple crayon-drawn window with a view of a family of 12 stick figures, all grinning, is still hidden behind my bedroom door. I actually manage a real smile as I show him, crude as it is.

"I desperately wished I could see you, your brothers, and Anna and Popsy from my bedroom window. Since I couldn't, I drew my own version of you."

It's a dumb, childish scribble, but it was the only thing about my room I ever liked. This old drawing of the Hammers is how I see them all, still. A beautiful sea of smiling faces, always happy to see me.

When we finally turn off the lights and shut the front door behind us, I'm still holding on to Gavin but not with the tight grip of dread which I held onto him with before. Now I just don't want to let him go. Not yet. Not while I feel light in a way I never have before. Buoyant. My stomach is fizzy from the elation of having tackled the most dreaded moment of my life. My heart still races.

"That was intense," I say, and I'm glad when Gav doesn't move away from the doorstep but pulls me closer.

"You are the bravest person I have ever met, Win." I can't see his face but I hear the emotion.

"I'm not brave," I say with a small laugh. "I ran away from the internet trolls for how many years? I only just managed to pull on the big girl pants necessary to watch 1 Girl, 10 Hammers."

"You finally watched it? That's huge! What did you think?"

"I think I'm more grateful than ever that you turned down the network's stupid spin-off. I've already dealt with my bullshit excuse for a family and countless internet trolls, scrutinizing every aspect of my appearance. I can't fathom the scrutiny that would come with a dating show."

Before I can tell him the rest, that watching the show made me more confused than ever, he says my name in a way that make chills shoot down my spine.

He looks down at me, frowning. "Pooh Bear. If we were doing a dating show right now, I'd look straight into the camera filming us." His dark eyes flash with determination. "I'd tell those trolls to go screw themselves, and then..." His voice softens as his fingers skim down my cheek, and he adds, "I'd kiss you, and I'd probably never stop."

I stare at him in the dark, and my heart rate jumps into high gear. It's his lip ring. Moonlight shines on it, and my senses flood with memories of his mouth on mine. And his tongue ring...

I shiver, even as my entire body floods with warmth.

"Are you cold?"

"No. I'm remembering what happened this morning," I admit.

He nods his understanding, and the air changes between us, grows heavier. He pulls me closer to him.

"That minute was the most incredible minute of my life, Win," he says, his voice growing more emotional. "I'd give anything to have whatever it is that Max has had with you. Anything. My left nut, even."

He's joking, but I can't manage to laugh. Not as I stare at him, unable to tear my gaze from the intensity in his eyes. I could drown in it.

"I was so fucking jealous when I found out."

I'm still trying...I *have* to break away, or else I'll do something stupid, like blurt out that I'm in love with him. No. Way. Because then I'd have to clarify that I'm not choosing him as my favorite, that I'm in love with them all.

So I do the only thing I can think to do before I drown myself in my own verbal embarrassment, and that's to stand on my toes, circle my arms around the back of his neck, same as I did earlier, so that I can run my hands through his gorgeous midnight hair. But now, I waste no time, and pull his mouth to mine and kiss him. I run my tongue along his lip ring, drawing it gently between my teeth. When I kiss him again, softly, he moans against my mouth and my pussy clenches.

And then he grabs my ass and fits me up against him, kisses me hard, scraping his barbell against my tongue in a way that has me bucking closer, so I can feel *all* of him.

There he goes again, making me soak my panties. Not to mention destroying all of my rational thought. How can I think when he's as hard as this, and I'm melting into a puddle of warm goo?

But thinking be damned. My instinct take over, rocking my hips into his, allowing the pleasure to wash over my body until I break my mouth from his to gasp his name.

My cry does all sorts of things to turn Gavin on even more and I lose track of all time and space after that, my only dimension being his kiss. The softness of his lips mixed with the hard lines of his body, his nipples with their barbells, which I would suck on if his shirt weren't in the way…

Does his shirt need to be in the way? No. His hands rove over my body and I decide that my shirt doesn't need to be in the way either—

Do you really think he wants to see that blubber, baby beluga?

And just like that, I come crashing back down. It's like cold water thrown on me all of a sudden, and I pull away.

"You okay, Pooh Bear?"

"Oh my God." I'm gasping as I untangle myself from him and take a few steps backwards as it hits me my dad's voice,

Gram's voice, the ghosts that haunt me… they're not in that damn house. They're inside me. I'll never escape them.

What the hell am I doing?

"Sorry, I'm so sorry," I say to Gavin. He calls after me as I turn and run, but I don't stop. I don't stop as his voice gets closer. I don't stop when his footsteps echo behind mine. I only stop when he catches up to me and pulls me back into his arms, when I'm sobbing against his chest.

It all comes pouring out as he strokes my back.

"I'm so damn conflicted," I admit into his chest, the fabric of his shirt clutched in my fingers. "I want you," I sob. "I want you all, but–"

"No buts, Pooh Bear," he whispers into my hair. "You're allowed to want everything you want."

"But–"

"No buts," he kisses me on the forehead. "You're allowed to have everything you want."

"But I literally told you all we can only be friends. I ended my friends with benefits thing with Max. I don't want to hurt any of you. I don't want any of you to hurt me. But I want you. But I can't keep changing my mind. I can't…"

I trail off and take a breath and inhale the intoxicating and familiar scent of him. "It's like my worst nightmares," I gesture back at Gram's, "and my wildest, best fantasies are both coming true at the same time and I don't know what to do!"

"Hey," he says firmly. "You can do whatever you need to do. Except run from us. I'm not going to let you do that."

CHAPTER 15

Gunnar

I don't have many regrets in my life - there's no point to regret, you know. Just gotta learn from your mistakes and move on.

But barely twenty-four hours after that scorching hot kiss-a-thon with Winnie – the one I didn't get in on before she pulled a runner – and I'm desperately regretting not kicking Jack aside and being the first to shoot my shot. Or Diesel. Second in on the love train would have been great. Or third, even. I would have been thrilled to knock Gav on his ass and take her in my arms and kiss her instead of my twin.

I'm trying not to be bitter, but I haven't even had my chance to kiss Winnie yet, and one of my rat bastard brothers spent half the night fucking her.

And now I'm feeling actual pain as I think of my missed chance, and my betrayer of a brother. Song lyrics keep rolling through my wounded soul and head.

TEN HAMMERS

Win - the one I dream of / Win - the one I need / Yet he's the one who holds her / Now my heart bleeds

Fine, bad song lyrics. Very bad song lyrics.

I don't actually know which of my brothers was keeping her bed springs squeaking, but they made damn sure she stayed satisfied.

See, my room shares a wall with Winnie's, and even with a pillow over my ears, I could hear her sexy-as-fuck little whimpery moans of ecstasy as she came.

I couldn't hear *him* at all, though, which annoys me to no end. A blessing and a curse. How can I punch that dickhead traitor in their traitorous dick, if I don't know which of my brothers committed the crime?

I had been betting it was Max. So much for "just friends," right? But then, I swear I heard her moan Axel's name.

I wanted to bust in and punch that bastard in the face, naturally. Her fucking bed wouldn't stop squeaking.

But just as I was getting all worked up to holler at Axel to shut the fuck up in there, I swear I hear her panting out *my* name, and I decided must be fucking delusional and hearing things. I'm not sure. After her fifth orgasm, I moved downstairs to the couch where I tossed and turned for a number of reasons.

His kiss on her lips / A knife in my chest / Promises broken / My dick left bereft....

Uh… *Promises broken*…

Shit, usually back-stabbings and broken hearts inspire the best lyrics. Blame my exhaustion.

I move from the couch to the kitchen breakfast bar to drown myself in OJ and cereal instead of self-pity and woe. I sit in peace for a half hour or so before Jack enters the kitchen.

He's whistling. Something's made that bastard happy.

"Why the hell are you so fucking chipper?" I demand.

"Why the hell are you so fucking grumpy?" he counters without skipping a beat. "Where's the coffee?"

"Make your own coffee, douchecanoe."

"First one up makes the coffee. House rule."

"Mom's rule, and Mom's not here."

He skips a retort in favor of opening and closing the cabinets in search of God knows what with way more noise than necessary.

Elbows on the table, I drop my head into my hands. Jack goes back to whistling.

"Speaking of Mom. Did you see the pics she put on Insta though?" he says with a chuckle. "They are having a blast. Her ridiculous overuse of hashtags cracks my shit up."

Holy hell. Would you shut up, Mr. Happy?

"You sleep good last night, though?" I ask, sarcastically. I'm wondering if he slept at all. I'm wondering if he was the one who—

"Who pissed in your cornflakes, bro?" He glances over his shoulder at me, then immediately goes back to whatever the hell it is he's searching for to make so much goddamn racket.

"*I* didn't get much sleep," I tell him.

"Then you definitely need some coffee, my man. Black as your mood."

I roll my eyes. I'm not in the mood for Jack's dad jokes.

"Winnie kept me up most of the night," I say, and that gets his full attention, as well as the attention of Cruz, who has just wandered in, with wet hair and a towel wrapped around his waist.

"The fuck is this, a locker room?" I say. I'm tired, sure. I'm grumpy, obviously. But I *hate* the fire of jealousy that roars through me when I imagine it was Cruz who broke the pact and made Winnie come so much last night, and that he'd just been showering away the scent of her…

"What do you mean, Winnie kept you up most of the night?" Jack asks.

My eyes narrow on him again. As the oldest, Jack got the apartment over the garage, so he wouldn't have heard what I heard unless he was the one eliciting the sounds.

Those blissed out, glorious sounds. My cock twitches at the memory of her moans.

"Uh… what'd I miss?" Mason has joined us.

I point up at the ceiling. "Somebody broke our pact, again, and was keeping her in a *very* good mood for hours."

Somebody with mind boggling staying power. It would stop and just as I started to drift off, thinking it was over again, there they went at it again.

"No fucking way," Jack growls. Then, "You can stop shooting daggers this way. Wasn't me."

"Me either," Cruz says and there's enough envy in his voice for me to believe him.

"It was probably fucking Max," Mason rolls his eyes. "Had to shoot his shot before she cut him off. What a shitbag! Where's the coffee?"

"You bitches talking about me?" Max demands, rolling in. He definitely has the bedhead of a dude who spent the night getting laid. Over and over. And over.

"Winnie had company last night," Jack fills him in.

"Oh," Max says. But he looks disappointed.

"Wasn't him," Jack mouths at me.

One at a time, the others spill in. We'd agreed to meet across the street and get started at seven. It's a quarter 'til now. Everyone denies that they were the culprit, with varying degrees of vehemence.

But when Winnie comes down, she is fucking glowing and there's no doubt that there's a liar amongst us.

I immediately perk up–in more ways than one–at the sight of her. She's still in her teeny tiny sleep shorts that give hints of her ass when they ride up as she walks, and a matching satiny tank top that can barely contain her tits. Nothing has ever lifted my mood quite like Win.

"Well, there's our little noisemaker," I tease, before realizing it might embarrass her.

She indeed flushes, her cheeks turning an adorable shade of pink, but then she laughs. She looks so relaxed, so carefree.

Regret slashes through me again, and I want to kiss her so fucking badly. Take her face in my hands and push her up against the pantry door and kiss her until the end of time.

She is so relaxed / So carefree / Why didn't I show her better / How much she means to me?

"Oops. Was I loud?" she asks. Then she scrunches up her face in a way that makes me want to sweep her off her feet and take her upstairs to my room. Take her volume to a whole 'nother level.

"I was the only one that heard you. Well. Me and whichever one of these bastards," I gesture at all my brothers, "is lying about being the one with you."

"Lying, huh?" Winnie makes a face then laughs again. She comes over and massages my shoulders. "Is someone jealous?" she asks, kissing the top of my head.

And then I feel her breath on the back of my neck and she bends down to tease my ear with her lips as she says, "If you must know, I was indulging in a little – well, a *lot* – of self-care."

"Self-care," I repeat, and my voice practically cracks like a horny teenager.

She blows on my earlobe gently and I shiver. "To word it as a lady would."

Oh. Ohhh.

I can't move, frozen in my seat with the burn of her smile against my skin as Winnie floats off and around to the other side of the breakfast bar. She grabs a box of cereal and a bowl.

My brothers, all shades of red, are very busy doing breakfast-y things, as well. But we are all trying not to stare at the smirk that is growing on her face.

Then she says, "I'm no lady, as you know. So yeah, I got myself off, multiple times. Hard not to keep going while fantasizing about having a big ol' orgy with all of you."

It's as if someone has yelled FREEZE OR DIE, because we all freeze.

For a second, even Winnie looks shocked by her own admittance. But then she bursts out laughing. "Your faces. Oh, my. Oh come on. It's not like I'm the only female on the planet who has Hammer Bros gang bang fantasies. You were all very, very good by the way."

I can't resist. "I know how good we were. I heard, remember?"

And she winks at me.

Holy shit.

Then she looks like she swallowed a live goldfish.

"Oh my God," she whispers and then, with her head down, she beelines back towards the door she euphorically entered just moments earlier.

Gavin intercepts her. Both hands on her shoulders, holding her in place.

"No running, remember? Not from us."

What the hell is that all about?

"I'm not running." She wriggles away from him. "I just need a moment to collect myself and…"

"I don't know." I get up. "I kind of like you uncollected."

She glances over at me, her face beet red. "I cannot believe I just admitted… My filter hasn't had a chance to kick in this morning and…"

I stride over and all but hip check Gav to get him to move the hell out of my way. Taking the spot he reluctantly gives up, I pull her into a tight embrace, so that her body is fully against mine.

"You have an erection," she whispers and I laugh.

"Around you, pretty much constantly, yeah," I confess, gazing down into her pretty blue eyes. For a split second, we're alone in the room. I take her face in my hands and say to her, as seriously as I've ever said anything, "You do realize you never, ever have to get yourself off again, right?"

Her pupils are dilated. She parts her lips.

I grab her hand, take it in mine and head towards the door, pulling her with me. "We need a few minutes of privacy," I tell the others, without looking at any of them or waiting for their responses, which they toss at my back.

"We agreed to just friends, Gunnar," one of them–don't know who, don't give a damn–reminds me. "We promised her–"

"Yeah, well, I don't think that's working for Win and it sure as hell isn't working for me," I say as I tug her behind me into the hallway.

CHAPTER 16

Winnie

Gunnar pretty much has to drag me. But to be fair, the only reason I don't go skipping along enthusiastically on my own is because I've lost all feeling in my legs.

I never knew being aroused could have this effect on a girl, but when his hypnotic blue eyes with their midnight black lashes hooked mine, and his you're-getting-very-horny voice said, *"You do realize you never, ever have to get yourself off again, right?,"* low and so husky and so… so… so damn lust-filled… I lost all feeling from the waist down, except in one certain area, which is now insistently pulsing as all the blood in my body rushes to fill that one tiny…

I gasp as Gunnar backs me up against the coat closet door the second we're out of sight from the others.

No, don't back me up against a closed door, my horny little heart cries. *Open the door, pull me inside, close it behind us, and fuck me right now.*

TEN HAMMERS

You'd think my pussy would need a break after taking ten dildos last night, but I had to have them all.

"You know, Winnie," Gunnar says. He plants one hand on the door frame to the left of my head, and uses the other hand to lift my chin. "I never got my kiss yesterday."

"Grievous oversight on my part," I whisper as he traces my lower lip with the pad of his thumb.

He drops his hand, the one that was on the door, and his fingers graze the side of my breast, the touch featherlight but no doubt intentional. He lowers it further to grab my hip.

I stare up at him, too overwhelmed by emotion to move. My hands are shaking. I just confessed to my ten best friends, the hottest men on the planet, that I masturbated while fantasizing about gang banged by the whole lot of them. I should be ashamed of myself. I should be mortified.

But all I feel... other than horny as fuck... is... safe. So incredibly safe.

That's your problem, girlie. No damn self-control. This is just another all-you-can-eat buffet for you to put out of business. You'll break their backs. You'll–

"Oh, shut the fuck up," I mutter.

Gunnar's brows raise. "You talkin' to me?"

I shake my head. "Nah. And you're right. I owe you and I always pay my debts."

Reaching behind me for the handle to the closet door, I pull it open. "Fortune favors the bold, after all," I add mischievously, grabbing his bicep with my free hand and squeezing the muscles under his inked skin. "So here we go, Gunnar Hammer."

My plan is to heave him inside the closet with me and kiss him and more until my lips are sore as... other areas of my body, but a vacuum, several shelves overflowing with cold weather clutter, and more coats than I expected are in the way.

When I turn back to Gunnar, his brows are higher than before. "You need something from the coat closet?"

"No. I just..." Smiling awkwardly, I shut the door and lean back against it, assuming the same position as before. "Ah, that's better."

He grins, shaking his head like he doesn't know what to make of me but he likes what he sees, and my heart squeezes. Then his hands are curling up into my hair and his mouth is on mine.

I've fantasized about kissing Gunnar so many times, naturally, but my imagination has always gotten it wrong, starting hot and fast instead of the soft, sweet, languid kisses he's giving me now as he finds my hands, laces his fingers with mine, palm to palm.

"Mmm..." His kisses travel down my neck, nipping a gentle line from the back of my ear down to my collarbone. Pulling a moan from me as he lowers his head, his mouth dipping to the tops of my breasts.

He's using our linked hands to brace himself against the door, caging me in as his lips grow more demanding. I thought heaving bosoms was just a phrase used by romance novelists but... it's an accurate description. I hadn't realized just how insubstantial and thin my pajama top was, but as his tongue swipes my nipple, it doesn't feel like there is any fabric at all between his touch and my sensitive skin. I arch my back, wanting more.

"Better than I imagined," he says. His voice is deep and gritty, and the sound of it tickles every nerve between my legs. "You taste so fucking good."

He straightens, and as he does, his hips push forward, pinning my body against the door. All humor dies as he captures my gaze with his hypnotic ocean-blue eyes, and lets go of my hand to hoist my thigh up over his hip.

Again, a moan escapes me, which makes his lips tip into a sultry smile.

"This okay, Win?" he asks, his voice rougher than before. His eyes darken into a tempest as he grinds against me.

I can't reply; I can only pant. Sweet God, he's so hard. His baggy sweatpants hide nothing from me. I can feel the ridges of him, and the way he stares down at me, the way I automatically surrender to him, rakes desire through me so hard I shudder.

My shudder is just enough movement to rub his cock against me again, exactly where I want him. This time my moan is louder.

"Shhh, baby," he says with a laugh. "I'd love nothing more than to make you scream my name, you realize that, right? But I don't want to give anyone a reason to interrupt this." He captures my mouth with his, but I don't know if I can keep quiet. Not when he's kissing me and kissing me and kissing me…

Ten minutes, hours, maybe even days later, it's me who finally pulls us back to reality. Somehow we manage to untangle, but the only way I can wrench my body out from under him is by promising myself that this moment between us isn't done. Far from it.

All the guys are still in the kitchen when we arrive back. My cheeks flame, because I know how I must look - as wanton and desired as I feel after being thoroughly ravished by Gunnar Hammer. It's written on Mason's face, the way his eyes dim as he glances out the window. It's written in the tightness in Axel's jaw as he stirs his coffee. Max won't even look at me.

"I made pancakes," Jack says, and it's there in his voice, too, the way it sounds just the slightest bit dejected.

I glance at the plates of pancakes dotted around the kitchen where the others sit, surprised. Somehow I'd been so lost in Gunnar that I hadn't even noticed the uncomparable scent of Popsy's Famous Pancakes, but it hits me now and my stomach growls.

"That sounds amazing, but while we eat… I need to talk to you all about something."

Ten pairs of eyes land on me as I say the words, and the vulnerability I see in all of them chokes me up.

But I say it, clearly and confidently. "I want us all to do it."

All ten pairs of eyebrows raise.

Bad choice of words, okay, but accurate. I laugh at myself and then carry on quickly, "I want to do Winnie's Favorite Hammer. NOT as a show, I mean. No cameras, no crew, and for the love of God, no eliminations. Just us."

The thought of choosing a favorite from among my ten favorite men, each selfless, generous, respectful, and caring in their own special way. Each too beautiful to put into words, seems impossible. But although I want to believe what Gavin said as he kissed me good night, that I can have everything I want, it's not like I can have ten boyfriends. That's absurd.

But at least I can give them all a shot – no, give *myself* a shot – to find out if I can have at least one of them as my boyfriend.

I have to.

Because if Goldie is right, if it is impossible to be genuinely head-over-heels for ten men at a time, I can at least try to find that kind of love with one of them. Maybe that love will grow into something bigger than the love I feel for all of them together now?

And what if I can find a Hammer brother who will feel that much love for me?

The thought, as impossible as it seems, warms me more than anything else. As much as I want all of my boys for myself, what I truly want is for each of them to be insanely happy.

I know they want nothing less for me. So… if two of us can be insanely happy together?

Then screw what my father would have said. Screw what the internet trolls would say. Screw what my own self-doubt says.

My gaze sweeps the room, taking in each and every beautiful face. I can't imagine choosing one of them. But choosing none of them seems just as unfathomable.

I know they'll all be careful with my heart–and I with theirs. I know that none of them would ever lie to me. If they say they want me, they do. If my soulmate exists, he's in this room…

"Love, you seem to be in a trance," Leo says, shaking me out of my thoughts.

"I want to do it," I say again, and laugh at my choice of words again. "That is… if all of you still want to do it with me."

I expect silence, for them to weigh the pros and cons, and question what an insane idea it is. I'm overwhelmed by an instant, enthusiastic chorus of LET'S DO IT!, as if they'd rehearsed it, as if they've all been waiting for it. Even Max is grinning.

I'm swept into a Hammer group hug so fast I don't know who started it. Their hugs are the best thing ever. I close my eyes and am enveloped by each and every one of them, all muscles and squeezes and kisses on my brow. A kiss drops on my lips, now and again, as they surround me with their warmth and love.

Then I wake up.

No, then Jack says, "We're gonna need rules."

Everyone groans. But we all acknowledge that he's right. Set rules are the only way to keep things friendly and fair and, hopefully, drama-free

CHAPTER 17

Winnie

Before my announcement, Jack had apparently been urging the others to eat fast so that they could get the reno started without any further delay. But after my announcement, the others teased Jack to no end while he, reno be damned, frantically dug through the garage in search of Anna's old whiteboard, which probably hasn't seen sunlight since she used to organize their activities as kids.

With an enthusiasm that makes my heart warm and my thighs clench with flared desire, the Hammer brothers immediately start making up rules as if this is going to be an actual dating competition. I roll my eyes, but I can't stop smiling.

The final result is an agreed-upon list that Jack writes out and places on the top of the breakfast bar.

> *1. Everyone gets uninterrupted alone time for a weekly date they will plan for Win.*
>
> *2. Numbers will be drawn to keep things fair.*

3. No sabotage or undermining anyone else's chance with Win.

4. STFU, you filthy braggart. Keep your time with Win private.

5. After the renovation is done, Win will choose her boyfriend, and there will be no hard feelings.

How will I choose? How will this end without any hard feelings? I really don't know. But if the boys think I'm worth the risk, I can put my heart on the line for them.

Below the rules, a grid with each brother's name across the top has been drawn, to record the dates they'll have with me.

Dates with me so I can figure out which one of them will be my boyfriend. As they eagerly draw their numbers and fill in the grid, I have to pinch myself repeatedly.

"Well," Jack finally says, grinning from ear to ear. Project planning has always been his happy place. Or it could be a grin because he used sleight of hand to steal the first date, and no one but me noticed. "Now that that's sorted, who's ready for one last reno?"

They all look at me.

"You ready, Pooh Bear?" Gav asks.

I nod. With all my boys… I feel ready for anything.

I clear my throat. "Just one thing first… if most of you guys don't mind heading over to Gram's… I need Mason and Cruz to stay here with me for a few minutes."

For a moment I wonder if they might be concerned that my hesitation is about the reno, that I'm just dragging my feet, but I guess I overestimate them, because they all know why I am asking. Mason and Cruz are bombarded with nudges and winks and wolf-whistles. My face heats.

"Give me the pen," I say to Jack, grabbing the marker, and I add one more rule to the list.

6. No bro-slapping!

I raise my brows, daring anyone to cross me. No one does.

Cruz is grinning at me bashfully, his cheeks a shade of pink I've never seen on him before, which is adorable because Cruz is anything but bashful. But he's in a *towel*. He has it tied in a way that keeps it in place while his hands are crossed over his chest, but it's still *just a towel*. Good Lord. That V-line, which disappears just below the edge of the fluffy cotton fabric…

Mason smiles at me, too, nodding as his icy blue eyes sparkle.

My lips begin tingling with anticipation, more than eager to finally kiss the last two of my guys.

"So…" I start, but my voice is rough and I have to clear my throat. "Everyone else ready to get a move on with that reno?"

They catch my drift, and it doesn't take long for the guys to dump their dishes in the sink and clear out of the kitchen, some heading off to other parts of the house, some going out through the kitchen side door, leaving me, Mason, and Cruz, alone in sudden silence.

Sudden *awkward* silence.

Crap. It's never awkward with my boys, but now I stand with my back against the counter and look at them both, feeling a million percent out of my element.

They're so hot. I'm so… me. Who makes the first move, anyway? Me? Am I supposed to choose who I want to kiss first out of two ridiculously hot Hammers? It's hard enough not to combust just because of the fact that Cruz is in that towel…

"You're overthinking it, babe," Mason says, because like all of them, he knows me well. He sweeps me up and places me on the counter. His sandalwood scent wraps me up like a hug as he stands between my thighs, holding me so close that my nipples brush against his chest, surely growing hard through my sleep tank.

There's a raw heat flashing in his eyes that matches the warmth radiating through his body and pouring into me.

"You're finally mine, cupcake," he says, his voice rough. But oh so gently, he touches my cheek with his thumb and kisses my forehead. I smile as he presses his forehead to mine and drops his hands to the tops of my thighs.

Thunder thighs.

I swallow hard, conflicted, feeling both turned on and embarrassed as Mason looks down at all the places where our bodies touch. There is so much of me, and it's all soft and pale and lumpy, and he's so sculpted and sharp and delicious.

"I'm trying to savor this moment," Mason says with a small laugh. "But fuck, I'm too excited to take it slow."

His mouth crashes over mine, and I don't care anymore about being too much for him or too big or too anything. I don't care about anything other than the feel of his kiss deepening, tongue seeking out mine, the gentle nips at my bottom lip from his teeth. The pleasure that courses downward as he strokes and squeezes my thighs digging his thumb into my skin, so damn close to where I ache for him already…

Mason tears his lips from mine with a groan, and I cry out in protest as I try to get his mouth back. At least we are still connected – I still feel the heat from his hands, from his gorgeous abs warming my thighs, and his chest against my breasts. Then even his warmth is gone as he steps to the side, leaving me sitting on the counter top, alone.

No.

I slide off the counter, but before my feet can even touch the floor, I'm in Cruz's arms.

"Baby," he says with a smile. His gentle brown eyes and that sweet, sweet smile are deceiving. Before I know it, his eyes turn molten and he growls "*fuck*," grabbing my ass and backing me into the counter. His kiss is devouring, so hot and plundering that I gasp for breath when he pulls away to kiss my jaw, down to my neck, his teeth scraping my skin, trailing lower, and pulling shivers out of me.

My shivers intensify as he nips a little too hard at my neck and I moan. "Don't leave marks. Rule seven."

At least that's what I try to say. I'm mostly moaning because Cruz's rough hands squeeze my ass again, and they are cupping and curling under me so that a finger from each hand skims the inseam of my shorts.

He licks my neck gently and drops a kiss on top. "Sorry, baby."

When he lifts his head to look me in the eyes, all I can do is stare at his lips, swollen and delicious. I hope this isn't over. I'm not ready for either of their kisses to be over.

"I've wanted to kiss you for so long," Cruz says. "But you wanted to save the best for last, huh?" he teases in that flirty Cruz way. "I've been planning for it to be slow, baby. Sweet and sensual and perfect for you. I didn't mind going last of all my brothers as long as I could at least have a chance to show you how much you mean to me. Treat you like a queen." His eyes blaze as he squeezes my ass again. "But these ridiculous shorts? Fuck, Win. They completely destroyed my willpower."

His mouth falls back on mine and I'm hoping to feel his fingers creep along the inseam of my shorts again, but instead he moves his hands up, one hand to grip my waist, the other to hike my leg up. His hips press into me and I feel the bulge of him through the towel for a bare second.

What is my life!?

I want to feel more of him, but he's back to kissing a line down my neck, lower and lower. And he's moving my thigh up and up… I'm trying to brace myself, leaning back with my elbows against the counter top so I don't fall sideways as he lifts my leg higher. His mouth reaches my cleavage and he darts a tongue inside my tank top. Sliding his rough palm along my leg, he places my foot on the counter.

"Cruz!" I gasp. "I'm going to fall over!"

But I'm not.

"I've got you, cupcake," Mason says from the other side of me, bracing my shoulders with his hands. He slides between me and the counter so that I can lean back against his chest, and balance myself easily while Cruz carries on kissing the top of my breasts. "You can relax if you want. I got you."

They have me spread wide open, only my tiny pajamas keeping me hidden from their eyes, and yet I'm comfortable enough to sink into Mason, allowing my head to fall against his shoulder. I close my eyes, breathing him. God, I love that scent of him. Sandalwood, yeah, but with a sexy layer of musk and sweat and something entirely, sweetly Mason. It drives me crazy. If I could bottle his scent up and sell it, I'd be a billionaire in a week.

I feel Cruz's hands slide along my skin until he's palming my ass again. I wiggle, shimmy, wanting his fingers back where he had them before.

He chuckles as his mouth captures my nipple over my tank top, his breath and the glorious pinch of his lips pulling out a low, long moan from me as I give over to the incredible sensations.

"God, you're so fucking beautiful, Win," Mason says in a growl against my neck, and he tilts my head into the perfect position to reach my mouth with his.

I latch onto Mason's lips, probably looking like a starfish, but his kiss is perfect timing. I need him to swallow my sounds, the glass-shattering moans, as Cruz's searching fingers finally land between my thighs.

Mason kisses me with matching fervor, his arms keeping me steady as I writhe under Cruz's touch.

I'm so wet. I know Cruz feels me dripping, but I can't even be embarrassed by myself, because as he slowly drags his finger along the center seam of my shorts, a low groan of satisfaction comes from deep in his throat.

"Best kiss of my life, Win," he says as he nips at my nipple.

His finger circles my clit once and I squirm until he does it again, whimpering. When he doesn't stop circling after that, I begin to squirm for another reason, and my whimpering grows louder. With Mason's tongue tangled with mine, and Cruz's touch teasing just right, I lose all ability to think rationally. I'm too lost in ecstasy to even realize that I've slid one of my hands into Cruz's hair, raking through his silky brown waves, and the other hand is behind me, brushing across the bulging front of Mason's jeans.

I might not have a lot of experience with men, my eyes might be closed, now, and my mouth might be preoccupied with Mason's lips, but buttons are a cinch, and it doesn't take more than a second before I'm tugging his jeans down, slipping past his boxers and pulling his cock free.

It springs into my waiting hand and when my fingers wrap around him, test the thickness, the weight, and the length of him, Mason groans against my mouth. I stroke my thumb over the head, and now he's the one whimpering.

"Oh, fuck. Winnie, cupcake. Ohhh, *fuck*."

I smile with unparalleled delight to pull these kinds of sounds from Mason, but then Cruz scrapes my nipple with his teeth and a rough finger slides past the fabric of my shorts, hitting my pulsating flesh. My smile turns into an expression that I'm sure is of pure ecstasy. The burst of electricity that jolts through me is more intense than anything I've ever felt in my life.

"Come up here," I plead, tugging Cruz's hair so that he looks up at me. He straightens and my hand slips from his hair to trail down the flat planes of his body.

I stroke Mason harder behind me. I want Cruz too; I'm desperate to see him, and touch him like he's touching me. Look at him the way he looks at me. He licks his lips as his eyes rove over my body, lingering where he has me spread. He steps closer and his hands find even better leverage than before and as he runs his fingers over me again, I restlessly tug at his towel.

The towel drops and I can't breathe, I can only stare at the glorious sight of him. My mouth begins to water, as though my brain is sure the glistening drop I see at the tip of his cock tastes like donuts. I grab him and I can't believe what I'm doing, holding two of my boys, stroking them, but as I do, Cruz eases the barrier of my shorts aside again, and I can't believe that either.

I have to be dreaming.

"Are you sure you're not blood-related, because I definitely see some family resemblance." I'm talking about the sheer size of them, that has me light-headed in the best possible way. My dildos are big, sure, but… they have nothing on the real things.

"Baby, look at me," he says, and I do, my heart squeezing from the pure lust in his eyes as he slowly fills my aching body with his finger.

Everything happens too fast after that. I don't even get enough time to hold both of my boys, or run my fingers over every long, hard, velvety inch of their cocks until they're as imprinted into my memory as the rest of their bodies. Or taste them. Oh how badly I want to taste them, to feel the weight of them on my tongue. But it's Mason's fault. He reaches around to squeeze the boob that Cruz had previously ignored. The sparks fly off of me, and as he thrusts up into my hand and squeezes my nipple hard, Cruz strokes his finger deeper, and rubs my clit with this thumb.

I come undone. I pull my mouth from Cruz's in order to whimper and hiss. I pump both cocks, both slippery with precome, trying to make my boys feel the same delicious licks of desire that are coiling inside me.

"Cupcake, you have to stop," Mason growls, his forehead against my shoulder. "Stop now, or I'll come right here."

"Good, come with me," I growl back.

"Mom will kill me if I spurt all over her kitchen," he pushes the words through clenched teeth.

"I'll kill you if you don't," I murmur.

Apparently the threat does the trick. Mason's cock grows thicker, throbs harder, and he lets loose a thick stream and a cry, which he tries to smother against my shoulder.

That cry, the sound of his pure pleasure, tips me over the edge, and I lose myself completely. I buck hard into Cruz's hand and then pulsate around him, exploding into fireworks. Wave after wave of bursting tingles and flaming heat, and Cruz strokes me through them all.

I lose my balance, finally, as my knees buckle. I fall backward, but Mason catches me.

But he's loose-limbed, too, and as he gathers me up, he falls, pulling me on top of him.

The last thing I see before I fully collapse, is Cruz's sexy-as-sin expression – the way his eyes darken into the richest chocolate as he stares at me. I've never seen him look so damn beautiful as his mouth drops open and, with a strangled groan that melts into a contented sigh, he shudders his release.

"Fuuuck that was good," he says after a minute, still breathless. He falls beside me in a satisfied heap.

"Was that good for you, too, Winnie?" Mason whispers against my neck.

I nod. I'm so damn happy, so damn spent I can't even wipe the tear that forms at the corner of my eye, I can only smile.

CHAPTER 18

Winnie

I'm haloed by an after-orgasm glow that still has me grinning, blushing, and feeling sexier than I've ever felt in my entire life long after I've showered, braided my curls into pigtails, slid on a fresh tank top, overalls, and work boots, and gallop back downstairs to find a spotless kitchen.

Waiting for me at the table are Mason and Cruz, with damp hair and huge happy grins to match my own.

"Ready, cupcake?" Mason asks as they stand.

I nod, hoping my glow will be enough to keep me from running away in tears when I see the house in the daylight, and I'm hit by memories and voices all over again.

"Look at you!" Cruz says, appreciatively, tugging one of my braids. "These cute little things make me want to bend you over the counter and *kiss* you again."

He throws me a flirty wink and I laugh, but suddenly my father's voice is there in my head, choking me into silence. *"Shame you're not pretty enough to be a real girlfriend. You're the kind of girl those guys only want to practice with, you just better not be the whore who takes it."*

Deep breath.

I force the voice away, and head for the door, refusing to let myself be haunted. I'm taking the bull by the horns – or the ghost by the ectoplasm – and facing it head on.

"Hey, look who's come to join us!" I hear Diesel call from an upstairs window as we walk across the lawn.

My heart starts thundering as I approach the house, but seeing the house doesn't put me in the same shut down panic as before. And knowing all of my guys are here for me together is the best medicine.

Hearing Diesel, everyone heads to the entryway, assembling around us as we enter the house. I catch Gav's eye and he smiles, holding me steady as my senses acclimate to the house in the daylight.

"So, what's the verdict?" Mason asks the group.

"Mr. Man with the Plan," Gunnar says, using one of Jack's many nicknames, "thinks we should gut it."

Jack slides a glance at me. It's almost sheepish. "I think a fresh start would be nice, is all."

"Well." I move over to stand next to him, surveying the room, trying to see it through his eyes. Then I lean my head against his shoulder, just because I can. I can touch them whenever I want to and however I want to. "There's no such thing as a fresh start for me, when it comes to this place. But a blank slate would be nice."

He wraps an arm around me and gives me a squeeze.

Diesel raps his knuckles on one wall. "Old girl's got such good bones, though."

"Yes, she does." Axel's eyes take a long, romantic stroll down the length of my body and back up to meet my eyes with a flirty wink. "And I can't wait to jump them."

I laugh-groan-whimper. "Uh, excuse me, he was talking about the house, not me, and if you think referring to me as 'Old girl' is the way to my heart that would be incorrect, buddy." I walk over and poke him playfully in the stomach. "Just thought you should be aware of that little life hack now that we're…"

"Dating," Axel says helpfully.

"Dating," I confirm. Honestly, what is my life right now?

Jack clears his throat and claps his hands together. He has the infamous clipboard. There are grown women who have seriously and publicly stated that if they had one wish, it would be to spend a day as Jack's clipboard. Not world peace, not a cure for cancer. And I mean… he does hold that thing with such a firm yet careful grip.

"So what we were thinking is you can make a wishlist for us, like you did with the cottage and…" his voice trails off as I shake my head. "No?"

"That is very thoughtful and sweet and wonderful and Hammer-ish of you all, but this place is never going to be my dream house. I'm sure it will be amazing, because all of your renos are—"

"Our renos," Leo corrects.

I flash him a grateful smile. I'll never take for granted how he always, always takes that extra step to make me feel included, especially when I'm leaving myself out.

"Right. Okay. All of our renos are amazing. But I am never going to love every nook and cranny of this house the way I love the cottage and no one better make the phrase 'nook and cranny' dirty for me."

This is met with several chuckles, and a devious gleam in Cruz's eyes.

They're all listening, so I go on. "I want to see the vision you guys have for this place. I want to see all of your fingerprints on it. I'll help choose the colors and finishes and everything, obviously, but as far as the layout and all the special features… I want this to be your brainchild."

I've actually thought about this quite a bit. We'll dismantle this place, rid it of every rotten board, even if we can't do the same for all the rotten memories. Then I want them to rebuild it with love. With all of our other renos, we let the families have wishlists, the way they had done with me and the cottage. But this one, I want to be all them.

That's the only thing that keeps me from wanting to just swing into the place on a wrecking ball, ala Miley circa 2013, knocking it all down, until nothing is left but a pile of rubble that can be swept away.

"If that's how you want it, you got it, princess," Max says.

"We'll add so much value, you'll be able to sell it for whatever price you want," Gav promises.

"I'll give it so much curb appeal, Mom and Pops will want to buy it from you," Axel jokes.

I'd been thinking about that, as well. I scrunch up my nose. "I might not want to sell it actually," I rush on despite their expressions, which run the gamut from a quizzical to confounded to perplexed to flirty as hell. "I might want to give it away. If I could pick the perfect family for it… a deserving family, a family that needs it… I don't know. Despite how it was for me, maybe this place can be a happy home. Someone's dream home. A home they'd never get to have otherwise."

All my boys are looking at me, beaming with pride.

"How very Win of you," Gavin says.

"Well, you know what they say, a demo a day keeps the doctor away," Gunnar.

"Absolutely no one says that, dude." Gav rolls his eyes. "But let's do this."

"What room do you want to start in, Win?" Theo asks.

"Actually," Jack jumps in quickly, his eyes finding mine. "Winnie, will you go on a date with me?"

"Right now?" I ask.

"There's no time like the present, Winifred."

"You can't hurry love, Jackman," I retort, but I'm grinning. God, it's a big goofy grin, I can feel it stretching my cheeks.

"You guys mind?" Jack asks his brothers.

No one grumbles but no one jumps up and down cheering, either.

Finally Diesel says, "Go. We got this. Win, is there anything you want us to save for you to…"

"Let my wounded inner child knock the shit out of?" I finish, half-joking. "Yeah, save the recliner for me. Thanks." I turn to Jack. "Do I need to change?"

"Not a damn thing," he says.

I roll my eyes, but my insides are both ooey and gooey. "I meant, do I need to put on another outfit?"

"Nah, but if you want to take what you're wearing off and y'know, not put anything else–"

"It's Jack's turn, Cruz," I wag my finger at him.

SERIOUSLY. WHAT IS MY LIFE RIGHT NOW?

"You know he's going to be incorrigible now that he knows there's a chance you might flirt back with him, right?" Jack asks, amused.

Before I can reply, Jack swoops me up, then, slinging me over his shoulder as he always does around our renos. It feels so familiar but new. He's wearing a shirt for once. I might need to adjust our list of rules to add necessary shirtlessness because this shoulder ride is not nearly as fun as it could be. I've fantasized about him swooping me up and off to the bedroom so many times over the years, but this is the first time it actually could happen because we are officially dating.

"Have her back by curfew or you're both grounded!" Gunnar calls as Jack carries me out the front door.

Oh my God, is he going to take me across the street, up to his room, toss me on his mattress, and have his way with me?

How am I already this incredibly turned on again? Surely I must have some kind of Horny-for-the-Hammers disorder.

TEN HAMMERS

As soon as we reach the curb, Jack swerves off toward his truck, and when he puts me down, it's so that he can open the passenger side door.

"Soooo… where are we going?" I ask as I slide in. It's odd for him to want to do this so spontaneously. After all, he is Mr. Man with the Plan.

"The hardware store," he says.

I glance at him, looking for any trace that he might be kidding, but his expression is dead serious.

"That okay?" he asks.

I mean, my guys all love tools, but the hardware store isn't exactly the place for top-tier romance. Does Jack really see me as a woman he can be with romantically or does he just see me as the friend with an eye for picking out tile?

But his smile is warm, and with enough heat in his eyes to have me answering, "Well, I am fond of hammers."

CHAPTER 19

Winnie

Jack held my hand as we strode briskly through the aisles of the hardware store. Well, he strode briskly, dragging me along. But his legs are much longer than mine, so to keep up, I was doing the kind of run-walk scampering you do when a car stops to let you walk across the street. He was on a mission.

"Is there a BOGO sale on screws ending in the next sixty seconds or something?" I pant, tugging on his hand. "Slow down. You're going to detach my arm from its socket."

"Oh shit," he said, halting in his tracks. "I'm sorry, Winifred. You know how I get when I'm on a mission."

"I do," I said. "I'm assuming whatever your mission is you want to accomplish it with all of my limbs still attached though, so…"

"Definitely want all your limbs still attached," he said, squeezing my hand and slowing down the pace. "Sorry about that."

"It's okay," I say. I can feel his excitement, and it's contagious.

"Aha," he says, finally.

The sign above our heads reads Outdoor Recreation.

"Are we going to *rec*-reate outdoors?" I ask, wrapping my free hand around his forearm. There's something about Jack that makes me want to hold onto him in every way I can. Always has been.

He laughs. "We are."

"Are we going camping? Because I kind of don't want the first time we have sex to be in a tent," I say and feel my face flush.

He stops in his tracks again, giving me serious side-eye. "The first time we do what now?"

I stand up on my tiptoes and whisper, my lips against his ear, "Have s-e-x."

"Good God," he says, with a groan. "If you want to see a tent, just check out the front of my pants right now."

I giggle. "Never change, Jack Hammer. Never change."

He's really looking at me now and there's so much affection in his expression. "You're blushing."

"So are you."

"Well, anyway. You're being awfully presumptuous about the s-e-x thing," he says, as he starts walking again. "Because I am not that kind of guy, Winifred."

I snort. "Ohhhkay, Jackalope. If you say so."

He tugs me down a row and I draw in a little breath. Picnic baskets. So many picnic baskets.

"Are we going on a picnic?" I ask, my smile so wide my blushing cheeks ache.

"You missed breakfast, so I thought brunch might be in order," he nods, while scanning the selection. He keeps flicking his eyes at me, I guess wanting to see if there's any one in particular I want, but I can't take my eyes off him.

It's so natural, so easy, with Jack.

"Is the heart-shaped one too cheesy?" he asks.

"If you were asking one of your brothers, they'd definitely say yes. But I love it."

Jack pulls the heart-shaped wicker basket down off the shelf and examines the tag attached. At first I think he's checking for the price–*should I offer to pay half?*–but then he reads, "A service for two, including hand-blown wine glasses, porcelain plates, stainless steel flatware, cloth napkins and a corkscrew. Sounds like everything we need, except… let's see…"

A few rows over, we find sleeping bags and blankets.

"Hmm, teddy bears or smiley faces?" Jack muses, eyeing the blankets. "Or should we get both? Yeah, we might want both. One to sit on, one to wrap around us if we get cold."

I raise an eyebrow. "There are other ways we can warm up if we get cold."

He winks at me. "On second thought, let's go with the plaid. I can't make out with an audience of teddy bears or smiley faces watching me. But we'll get an extra, just in case."

He grabs two of the plaid blankets and sets them on top of the picnic basket. My chest feels like he's taken a piece of my heart and laid it down on the basket, too, nestling it in the cozy warmth of the blankets.

Okay, that's kind of a gross image, but I'm not able to think rationally when he's leading me to the register, carrying the basket and blankets he plans to make out with me on.

We get in line for the register and are deciding whether we should add a bag of M&M's, a bag of Skittles, or both, when the woman behind the counter suddenly exclaims, "You're Jack Hammer!"

We both whip our heads in her direction, wearing our automatic, professional smiles. He disentangles his fingers from mine, letting go of my hand.

Okay, well. You're going to be dating all ten of them. Probably shouldn't be seen holding hands with any of them in public until you've chosen one…

"I used to see you come into this place when you were just a young little guy," the cashier goes on, beaming. "You probably don't even remember an old woman like me. And now here you are, all grown-up and so famous. And so handsome, all of you Hammer boys! Isn't this something!"

She doesn't seem to notice me at all, or if she does, she doesn't care enough to even let my presence register.

In fact, she tries to peer around me, frowning as though I'm in her way. "Where's Cynthia Sinclair?"

Jack's demeanor shifts, a flicker of embarrassment in his eyes as he glances at me and then answers, "We're not together anymore."

"Oh that's terrible! She is such a lovely girl. Just such a beautiful girl! And you two made such a gorgeous couple! The babies you would've had!"

"Well, we've gone our separate ways," Jack says, his voice terse.

The woman behind the counter doesn't seem to notice. Instead, she continues to gush about Cynthia.

Then she notices the basket. Not me. The basket.

"A heart shaped basket! You must've moved right on then!" Her eyes flick to me. "Oh my soul! You're Winnie Wainwright. I didn't recognize you at first."

I hold my breath, waiting for her to say I look bigger on television, or I look smaller on television, or something to that effect, because it's happened enough times I can predict it coming.

"So sweet of you to help Jack pick out a picnic basket for his new lady," she says. Which is somehow worse than commenting on my size. It's like it doesn't even occur to her as a possibility I might be that new lady.

Will people feel sorry for Jack if they knew about our deal, knowing he went from someone like Cynthia to someone like me? I'm certainly not a rebound or practice girl, but "girlfriend" doesn't quite feel right either. Not when I can't shout our relationship from the rooftops, or dance around the shop singing about it. Not that I would ever actually do that, but still. Keeping it a secret is kind of a bummer.

"I wish I could've told her," Jack says, as soon as we're in the parking lot. "That *you're* my lady."

And that's all that matters.

Jack continues to surprise me as he stops at Tino's Bistro, my favorite restaurant.

"I don't think they're open," I tell him. In the past they didn't open until lunch, but it's been so long since I've been here. My mouth waters thinking about their homemade croissants.

He flashes me a grin that I feel in my knees. "Be right back."

He takes the picnic basket inside while I wait in his truck.

When he returns with the basket, the smells of bacon and pastry wafting out are so incredible I nearly moan.

"Damn, I should've bought a blindfold," he says as soon as we're back on the road.

I laugh. "Oh, so you are *that* kind of guy."

"I mean so you won't be able to see where I'm taking you."

"I could just close my eyes?" I offer.

"Can I trust you not to peek?"

I think it over. "In this particular circumstance, yes."

"Alright then. Close'em. No peeking."

I obey. With my eyes closed and the soothing instrumental piano music Jack has on, I feel sleepiness setting in. I hadn't realized how tired I was after my late night solo activities and my morning very much not solo activities, but I doze off.

"Final stop," Jack says, waking me. Without thinking, I open my eyes and spoil the surprise.

We're at Sienna Park.

"Jack," I breathe.

"I thought you would've guessed when I told you we were doing a picnic," he said.

"I didn't."

He comes around and opens my door for me, which is something he's always done. I know exactly where we're going, or I hope I do. But I let him lead the way. It's a bit of a walk, but he's holding my hand again so I treasure every step.

"Here we are," he says finally.

Nestled beneath the shade of a weeping willow, beside a tranquil pond, there's the perfect grassy spot for a picnic. He sets the basket down.

I remember the spot well despite being away so long. The water reflects the emerald leaves above. It's secluded, intimate.

It's the perfect place to lay down our blankets so I can stretch out beside him and kiss him with my entire being which I'd be doing already but I'm getting too choked up. Good thing he stands a few steps behind me now, because if I was to look in his eyes right this second, I'd burst into tears. I have actual chills and it's not because I'm cold.

"Do you remember when we came here to celebrate your birthday?" As he asks the question, he closes the space between us to gather me back up against his chest, his hands resting on my waist.

Of course I remember. How can I forget? It was the location of the first birthday party that had ever been thrown for me. Jack had planned it all. He was determined to make my birthday party fit for a fairy princess. Princess Winifred. The party started after the sun had gone down, and we knew Gram would be asleep. It was one of the many times Dad was in jail so it was easy to sneak away after Gram had gone to bed. Jack had ringed the clearing with fairy lights, draping them around the tree. The boys had bought me a cake covered in pink roses and presents, small ones Gram wouldn't notice and question or try to sell like sparkly butterfly hair clips. The Hammer boys were always giving me tiny treasures like that.

"I would never be able to forget this place," I say, and my voice is thick. "I would never want to." I turn in his arms to link my hands behind his neck, on my tiptoes to reach his lips better. "I love it here, Jackrabbit."

The nickname makes him grin and the gleam in his eye is suddenly heating me quicker than his embrace. "That's a new one. Jackrabbit is kind of cute, though. You don't mean Jackson? Or Jackass?"

I pull his face closer to mine. "I definitely don't mean Jackass," I say. I brush my lips against his which instantly part. The kiss is gentle, hesitant at first. The tips of our tongues teasing, our mouths pushing forward, then pulling away in a slow sensual dance that's like falling into a dream. It's almost impossible to kiss and smile at the same time, but my face wants to do both. Meanwhile, his hands are all over me, and mine all over him.

"You seem to really like my butt," I say when we pause for a moment to stare into each other's eyes. His big hands are still splayed across it, his fingers bending and flexing like he wants to dig them into the flesh…

"I have been a longtime admirer of your ass," he murmurs, dropping a kiss on my forehead. "Do you want to eat?"

"Yeah," I say. "As long as we can make out some more after."

"I think that can be arranged, Winifred."

CHAPTER 20

Winnie

My picnic with Jack is long and luxurious, and I don't fully realize how exhausted I am, physically and emotionally, until I find myself waking in my bed, morning light streaming through the window. After a moment of confusion, I realize I must have fallen asleep in the truck, again, and Jack carried me inside, tucking me into bed without waking me. This thought is so sweet that it sets off a flurry of butterflies in my chest, which carry on flapping throughout the day, keeping me feeling fluttery and light even after I join the others at Gram's house for the demolition.

While Jack and I had been picnicking, the others worked hard, removing fixtures and gutting all the cabinetry. I'm not one to be left out. Grabbing my tool belt and a sledgehammer, I pitch in, memories of my turbulent childhood hitting hard. But the guys are never far from my side, ready with a hug or another swing of the sledgehammer, keeping me from falling apart.

Once I begin knocking down walls, it's hard to stop, and the next couple of days pass in a blur of hard work, sweat, and pure focus.

By the time the sun has dropped, I drop, too. My muscles are too sore, and my body and brain are too drained to do anything after dinner other than pile up with my boys on the couch. They take turns preparing the meals and cleaning up after, a practice from Anna's family organization days that they slip into so easily it's as if they've never been away. Then we watch movies until we fall asleep, exactly like the old days.

After having a chance to kiss each of them, the fire in my belly and the need between my legs has only intensified, but this is all uncharted territory, and I'm eager to see where everything will go next. The atmosphere in the house since we came to our new agreement hasn't been awkward at all, as I'd originally expected. Instead, there's a mixture of nostalgia and anticipation, familiarity and trust.

How do couples who have been best friends for their entire lives start relationships in their thirties without jeopardizing their friendship? I don't have a clue, especially not when it comes to couples with our circumstances. And yet somehow, perhaps because of all of our years of friendship, it's working.

By the late afternoon on our third day, the demolition phase is nearly complete. I'm covered in a light layer of dust. I walked face-first into at least two spiderwebs. I either forgot to put on deodorant or it stopped working hours ago.

"What are you still doing over here?" Gavin asks when I come downstairs from where I've been pulling out the last of the socket fixtures before taking a sledgehammer to the walls.

"Well, gee, Gavin, I'm so happy to see you, too!" I reply.

"No, I just mean–"

Then I blink real hard and say, "Whoa."

Gavin is wearing a sharp, tailored suit and tie, which accentuates his height and that ridiculously sexy muscular physique of his.

"Fuck me, you're gorgeous," I blurt out in a too-loud whisper, before clapping my hand over my mouth to keep my internal thoughts in check.

Get a grip, girl. I've seen him in a suit countless times…

But tonight he looks like never before. He exudes effortless elegance. His chiseled features and piercings are doing things to me that they've never done before. I'm drooling. I feel my panties dampening.

And he's mine!

"Prince Charming has come to sweep you off your feet," Gunnar says. "He made reservations at La Douche Baguette, over in Ashbourne. I think you two were going to dine on escargot while discussing the finer things in life and–"

"Bite me, you pleb," Gavin said. "The restaurant's actual name is Chez Margeaux and you're going to love it, Pooh Bear. But I think Gun's planning on taking you to the Gas n' Go for their three dollar hot dog lunch special or–"

I clear my throat to interrupt him before someone makes some inevitable comment about weiners.

"BOYS! I think this," I wave my hand back and forth between them, "breaks some sort of rule. Also it's not endearing. Also… why are you ready and I'm… not?"

I'm so very not.

"Cruz was supposed to tell you to go to your room at our house an hour ago," Gavin says.

"Oh, shit!" There's a thud and Cruz, who is knocking down cabinets in the bathroom, peeks out looking sheepish, and rubbing the top of his head. "Bro, I swear I legit forgot. I wasn't trying to salt your game."

"How long do I have before we have to leave?" I ask Gavin.

"Twenty minutes?"

"Oh, my God!"

"Twenty-five if I speed a little."

I drop the sledgehammer I'm holding with a resounding thud and take off running out the front door and across the street.

I don't have anything to wear to Chez Margeaux.

"Excuse me, coming through, out of my way, girl in crisis," I cry, pushing past Mason and Max who are sitting on the porch steps of the Hammer house. I squeeze between them, because pole vaulting over their shoulders wouldn't be within my physical capabilities, even if I had a pole.

Shit shit shit.

Where's Goldie when I need her? Ugh, and Sam and her magical powder puff?

I race up to my room, fling open the door, and flick on the lights. I suck in a sharp breath, my eyes immediately filling with tears.

My feet are rooted to the spot even though I want to run to the bed and pick up the dress that's been carefully laid out across the duvet and hold it up to myself and spin around with it like a six year old who has just been given her first fairy princess costume.

The steps I do take, finally, are small. Timid.

It's probably the most gorgeous dress I've ever seen, a soft, floaty wrap dress in deep blue, adorned with glittering sequins.

There's a piece of paper laying on top of it. A note. I pick it up.

I know you don't usually wear dresses, but I hope you'll make an exception this time. I'll pick you up at 5:30. ~ Gav

Gavin Hammer bought me a dress.

The lump in my throat is immense. I want to sit down on the edge of the bed and cry from the emotion filling me all the way through.

But then I remember I don't have even a second to waste.

I get ready as quickly as possible, and when I'm done, I somehow manage to feel like a sensuous goddess. The dress clings to all the right places, the sequins catching the light with every step, highlighting every one of my curves. The flared sleeves add elegance but the plunging neckline adds pure sex appeal. Gavin is going to lose his mind. Hell, I almost lose my own mind when I see my cleavage.

The girls look fabulous.

When I descend the stairs, hoots, hollers, and wolf-whistles fill the house in a sudden burst. My cheeks warm, but the way my boys are all staring at me, adoration and lust radiating off them all, has me engulfed by flames.

Gavin's eyes are shining, full of appreciation as he pulls me into his arms, drops a soft kiss on my lips.

TEN HAMMERS

"You're stunning," he says, his voice so husky he has to clear his throat. It's impossible to keep restraining myself from dragging him up the stairs to my room and stripping his suit straight off him.

As if he can read my thoughts, he takes my arm. "Let's go, Pooh Bear." And then he adds, low in my ear, making me shiver, "I promise we'll play later."

The rain doesn't make its presence known until we're nearly at the restaurant. The day has been clear, the sun blasting at our backs all day, but now ominous clouds have gathered, releasing a steady drizzle that soon turns into a relentless downpour.

We arrive at Chez Margeaux, and a valet takes over, his umbrella large enough to keep me fully dry, thankfully. Despite the storm raging outside, Chez Margeaux envelopes us in warm, golden light, which spills from delicate chandeliers overhead. The enticing scent of fresh herbs and rich sauces wafts around us.

"It's incredible," I say, wishing I could give him a kiss to thank him right now.

Instead, we follow the hostess (Maria) to our table. The soft hum of hushed conversations mingles with a clinking of silverware on fine china, and a cascading waterfall wall at the back of the room, but no one makes a fuss over Gav as we pass.

"Here you go," Maria says. "Your server tonight is Henri, and he will be here to take your drinks order shortly. Bon appétit!"

The moment we sit, Gavin reaches across the table and takes my hands in his. "Let's leave all the work stuff behind for now and focus on only us tonight."

I nod, and a smile tugs at the corner of my lips.

As we wait for our food, we dunk bread in herbed oil and balsamic vinegar, and share stories from our school days, laughing and getting to know each other all over again. The best of friends for all our lives, but now he's telling me secrets, about all the times he wished he could have acted on his feelings for me. He even confesses that he got his first piercing because he wanted to make sure every time I looked at him, he knew I was seeing him, never, ever mistaking him for Gunnar.

As we savor each spoonful of our French Onion Soup, I'm sure that I have never had such a warming and delicious night out before, and I don't want our date to end. By the time we're done with our plates of Coq au Vin, I almost dread going back to the house, where we will surely be accosted by the others. Not maliciously, but all of our true alone time will come to an end, nonetheless.

Our phones light up in unison as we're sharing the last bites of a sumptuous Crème Brûlée.

Gavin checks his phone and frowns. "It's Jack. The storm's getting worse. Roads are flooded. He says if we don't leave soon we might not make it. "

I read the text on my phone, from Max, and it echoes the same news.

"A bridge washed out nearby. We'll have to leave via the north side, if the roads are still open."

But Gav shakes his head. "We can't risk driving back in this weather. It's too dangerous. We're stuck in Ashbourne."

I flash him a worried look but Gavin's expression doesn't match. In fact, there's the hint of a smile at the corner of his mouth.

"It's almost like you planned this." I say, narrowing my eyes.

He laughs. "I did. I thought a freak flood washing a bridge away would be a nice touch, so I hired the storm."

CHAPTER 21

Winnie

"Uh," I say as Gavin pulls into the parking lot of the nearest available inn and our headlights illuminate the building. "Are we sure this is the right place?"

I squint as though that'll help me see better, through the darkness and steady rain sluicing over the windshield. The scene in front of me is blurred and distorted, so maybe it's not as bad as it looks. Still, it does not match the charming pictures I googled. Perhaps it did twenty years ago...?

Gav whistles under his breath. "Pooh Bear, I think our rom-com might be turning into a horror flick."

I laugh, even though he might not be joking. "This does look like the kind of place people go to get chopped up."

Paint peels from all sides of the compact Victorian house. The wooden boards of the porch look termite-chewed. Inside, soft warm lights radiate a welcoming glow, but even from the car, I can see the curtains in the windows are faded and ragged.

He reaches over and pushes some hair behind my ear, his fingertips grazing my earlobe. The gesture is innocent but I still shiver. "I solemnly swear I'll protect you from the ax murderers."

"Very chivalrous, but what if they chop you up first?" I joke.

"We could just ride the storm out in the car, I guess?"

That would work if I didn't have to pee. And the steady downpour is not helping.

"Um, I think I drank too much wine with dinner to do that."

"Gotcha." He pulls into a space as close to the door as he can get and shuts off the engine. There are plenty of other cars around, at least.

"Okay." He twists, reaching between his seat and mine, rummaging in the back seat. "Fuck. I know I don't have an umbrella but I was hoping there was something you could put over your head so you won't get wet."

I giggle. "Gav. This won't be the first time a Hammer brother has gotten me wet, I promise. Hell, this won't be the first time *you've* gotten me wet."

He closes his eyes for a second, ruefully shakes his head. "Damn, woman, forget ax murderers. *You're* going to kill me, looking at me like that… saying things like *that*." Then he looks at me again. "So… you still wanna get a room?"

"Definitely."

We decide to make a run for the covered porch, and hope we don't fall through the wood before we reach the door. He comes around to my side of the car, which means he's drenched by the time I get out, and together we race to the porch.

I'm soaked to the bone and my teeth are already chattering.

Thank God the door is unlocked. He ushers me inside.

A wave of warmth envelopes us, emanating from the crackling fireplace, but it isn't particularly cozy, not when all the furniture is frayed and the smell of the room reminds me of a carpeted diner that still has a smoking section.

I finally noticed the strange woman staring at us from behind the front desk. She has mismatched eyes and a weird blend of Victorian and modern attire, with a frilly collared button up shirt under a zip-up hoodie.

"Welcome to the Creekside Inn," she says in a weathered voice.

"Thanks," Gav says. "Please tell me there's room for us."

She laughs. "Yeah, storm's driving a lot of people our way, but I do have something. Only thing is… Did you two recently get married?"

Gav glances back at me, quizzical. "No," he tells her. "But I hope one day I'll be that lucky. Why?"

She laughs again. "All we have available is the honeymoon suite. It's… something else."

The honeymoon suite.

"We'll take it," Gavin says, pulling out his wallet and handing her a credit card.

"We dripped water all over the floor," I say apologetically.

"Won't be the first," she says. "I've got a mop. No worries. But let me get y'all some extra towels."

"She seems nice," I whisper.

TEN HAMMERS

"So, definitely an ax murderer?" Gavin jokes in a low voice. I nod and laugh.

But when we're in the room, my laughter dies.

"Is it just me or do you feel like you've walked inside a box of Valentine's Day candy?" Gav asks.

I feel like I am literally in a room designed for people to lose their v-cards. In the 70s, maybe, but still.

Everything is red. The wallpaper. The carpeting. The bed.

"Um. The bed is heart-shaped."

"I see that," Gavin says. "Wonder if it vibrates."

Oh my God.

"Here. You're trembling." He wraps a towel around my shoulders.

We begin drying off. I'm wondering exactly what to do because my gorgeous dress is soaked but it's not like I have a change of clothing.

Gavin is stripping down with zero reservations. Off goes his shirt. Off come his pants. He's wearing skin tight gray boxer briefs, and he's so big he fills the entire front pouch.

I excuse myself and go into the bathroom where I discover that, thankfully, my panties and bra have barely been damped by the rain.

I spot a hairdryer. I'm not going to dry my hair–that would take forever. But it's fine if that's what Gav thinks I'm doing.

Taking off my panties and bra, I quickly dry them, before putting them back on. Then I wrap a towel around myself.

Of course, it doesn't go all the way around. If I tried to dry the dress with a hairdryer, it would ruin it. I'm not going to take that chance. But I can't put it back on wet either.

The Hammer brothers haven't even seen me in a bathing suit since high school. Am I ready to have sex with one of them? All of them? Yes and yes. Am I ready for any of them to see me naked or even mostly naked yet? No.

What if he sees all of me and is turned off?

There's a light knock on the door.

Shit.

"Hey," Gav's voice says. "There are some very fluffy robes out here. They're red, of course, but they're super warm. Do you want—"

I open the door a crack and hold out my hand. "Yes, please."

After I'm fully covered, I go back out.

"Well," I say.

He's wearing one of the robes, too, but where I have mine firmly tied shut, his falls open, revealing a hell of a lot of sexy.

"I think I'm supposed to volunteer the sleep on the floor—"

I'm still cold from being soaked to the bone.

"Shut up and get in the bed, Hammer." I'm already pulling back the blankets—velvet—and crawling underneath.

Gavin laughs. "Well. When you put it that way."

He sheds his robe completely and slides in next to me.

A rush of nerves flutters through me. "So… wanna watch some TV?"

"First," he replies, and his eyelids are heavy, his pupils dilated as he props himself up on one elbow on his side, gazing down at me. "I don't think there is a television, and second, even if there was… no."

He lowers his head, his eyes drifting closed as his mouth finds mine. He pries my lips open with the tip of his tongue.

The second I feel his tongue ring, I'm lost. I have no idea how long we make out for, but when I finally stop things, Gavin is fully on top of me. My knees are bent, thighs spread, and he's been between them, working his hips, pressing against me in slow, languid strokes as our tongues dance.

I should've known my panties didn't have a snowflake's chance in hell of staying dry.

But my robe has come untied and fallen open and his hands are roaming, exploring and it's not that I don't like it. I do. It's just that… I feel the deep, burning need to apologize for my rolls.

Fuck.

"Everything okay?" he asks.

I want him–and all of my boys–to see all of me. To love all of me. I don't want to feel like I have to hide my parts.

And for once, it's not my dad's voice I hear. It's Gavin's. He hasn't spoken aloud, but I hear his words from the other night, telling me I'm the bravest person he knows.

Am I brave if I can't even show one of the men I love my body?

We're in the freaking Honeymoon Suite.

It's tonight, I decide. Tonight I will get naked. With Gavin Hammer.

And if he doesn't run away screaming when he sees me, maybe tonight I will finally, finally have sex, too.

I feel like I'm going to have a heart attack, possibly keel over and die right here amidst all this red and velvet, but I stand up. And I slip off my robe off my shoulders, letting it fall to the floor, and stand before him in only my underwear.

His eyes rove over my body, taking in every dimple and curve. I force myself not to think about how many there are, try not to think about him seeing what I see whenever I look in the mirror.

"Fucking hell, Winnie," he murmurs. He moves over to the edge of the bed. Reaching out, he pulls me closer. My heart is a thousand horses racing around a track. His gaze is hungry as he takes in every inch, then his hands join in, running up and down my waist, my arms, my thighs. "You're so fucking gorgeous."

His hands find my hips and he urges me closer, planting a kiss against my belly as his hand goes between my thighs.

As his fingers push the thin fabric of my panties aside, I take a deep breath and reach around to unhook my bra, tossing it... who cares where.

"Goddamn. These tits, Pooh Bear." He sounds anguished and I smile.

"A phrase never uttered in the history of time–" I begin but he stands up, cutting me off with another kiss, before he drops his head to said tits and latches on. His tongue ring finds my sensitive nipple immediately. I buck into him, moan. I'm holding onto his shoulders, my nails digging in, barely standing up.

"Gavin. Gav. I want you inside me."

"Fuck, Win. I need to *be* inside you." His voice is raw, rasping. He sweeps me off my feet and puts me back in the bed. "I need to tell you something first, though."

Reality pulls me out of the lust-induced stupor. What could he possibly need to tell me first?

Then I giggle. "Gav, I know it's big. Everyone heard the prom night story."

He was dating Brie Courtland, the most popular girl in school. Rumor has it they got a hotel room for after, where they planned to do it for the first time… until she saw his cock, and ran into the hall crying, terrified by its sheer girth.

"That was made up," he laughs. "But, seriously."

He perches on the edge of the bed. "You know what a Prince Albert piercing is, right?"

My mouth falls open a little and a little urch noise escapes from the back of my throat. "Are you trying to say…"

"I have one piercing you've never seen, yeah."

My face has never been so flushed. Blood is pounding in my ears… and… other places.

"I can take it out if it makes you uncomfortable–"

"It doesn't!" I burst out, moving so that I'm on my knees. "I want to see."

He smiles as I sit beside him. He leans to kiss me again, but I place a hand on his chest, stopping him.

Oh my God, his nipple rings. I want to swipe them with my lips…

Don't get distracted by his nipples rings.

"I have to tell you something, too," I say. I don't know why but it feels important for him to know.

"Do you have a piercing I haven't seen?" His hand is on my knee, gently stroking.

I shake my head. "It's not that. And it's really not a big deal. I don't want to make it a big deal, but… I'm a virgin."

His eyebrows go up a little, but his fingers keep dancing across my skin. "Oh." He pauses. "Mind if I ask why?"

I shrug. "I mean I haven't actually dated much, as you know. Does it… make a difference?"

He shakes his head. "Not at all. But… don't you want to wait and decide which one of us is… you know. Your favorite?"

"Nope." I shake my head. "No. Not at all. I want it to be *you*, Gavin Hammer. Right here, right now. In the Honeymoon suite of the Creepside Inn."

He laughs, but his eyes are very, very serious.

"You're the one who told me I could have whatever I want," I remind him.

He swallows hard and I have never seen such desire in my life as I see in his eyes.

"I did say that, didn't I?"

And then we're kissing again. He pushes me back against the pillows, but instead of joining me, he stands, hooks his thumbs in his waistband and strips out of his underwear. His cock springs free.

Oh my. Everything about him is impressive. He climbs into bed, his mouth on my nipple, pulling my sensitive skin with his teeth as he moves on top of me. I reach between his legs so I can hold him, and he groans when my thumb brushes the barbell glinting from his tip.

He's so big – bigger than my Gavin dildo, which I was sure had him beat. I want to stroke him, find out what he tastes like, but before I can, he sits up on his knees so he can strip off my panties and then he settles himself between my legs, taking a hungry lick.

"Mmm, juicy girl. The best dessert," he says with a growl, as if I truly taste better than our Creme Brûlée.

All I can do is moan. And that's before he adds one finger, then two. He pumps into me as he licks, and I want to cry for him to take me now, but I can't even manage a word, only encouraging babbling.

"I have condoms made especially for my kind of piercing, in case you're worried about it breaking," he says against my clit, in between licks and kisses, "but you should also know I was tested a few weeks ago. All clean, of course."

I blink down at him, but he doesn't seem to notice the wheels working in my head as I process his words.

"I'm on the pill," I announce.

He stops abruptly and looks at me. I don't want to tell him why I'm on the pill – my crystal clear skin is my only vanity, and it's too embarrassing. But I do add, "I mean, if you don't want to use a condom. Obviously I'm all clean, too."

His eyes fill with pure fire, and he crawls his way along my body, his hands touching and stroking my skin, making me writhe with matching desire as he nestles his cock between my legs.

He rocks his hips and a zap of pleasure strikes as his pierced crown rubs against my clit. We moan together and when he looks into my eyes, the arousal I see in his face is overpowering.

I roll my body up into him, pressing the rock hard length of him against me. I need him so badly.

"Ready, baby?" He whispers, kissing me.

I nod, enthusiastically.

"Good. I promise I'll be gentle–"

"*No*," I say, grinding against him. "I don't want gentle. I want you to take me hard and fast."

His forehead creases. "For your first time?

"Gav. It's not like I have a cherry to pop. The dildos, remember? Lots of dildos. You're not going to hurt me."

"But I want your first time to be–"

"Special?" I shimmy against him, equal parts horny and frustrated.

We are perfectly lined up. I'm so wet that the tip of him slips in, just enough to remind him I'm ready. Wanting. Desperate.

He groans again, equally desperate.

"Please, Gav. My first time *will* be special. It's with *you*. Now let me be clear. I want you to fuck me like you desire me, so wildly–"

With one hard thrust, he's inside me. He feels so good that I lose the ability to speak, my eyes filling with tears, overwhelmed with emotion.

"Oh, yesss, just like this…" I breathe. I want to move against him, fuck him back, but I'm too full to move.

As I gaze up into his eyes, I'm not expecting to see laughter mixed in with the lust.

"I'm only halfway in, Pooh Bear."

He's only…?

With another hard thrust, I'm speared by pure pleasure, so deep I can hardly breathe. It ripples through me, fizzing every one of my nerves. He moans a stream of worshipful words as he gazes down at me.

When he pulls out, the sensation is so much more than anything I've ever felt before. I need him back, every inch of that luxurious thickness.

"This how you want it, baby?"

I cry out his name as he plows into me again, his eyes black with passion. So good. He feels *so* good–

Then he pulls out and in a quick flash, flips me over, onto my stomach.

"Let me see it all baby," he says, pulling me onto my knees, my ass up in the air. He runs a hand over me, squeezing and giving me gentle slaps, trailing his fingers through my wetness.

With my ass on full display, I start to feel embarrassed, but as I glance back at him, I see him on his knees behind me, licking his lips as he stares at me. Deftly, he removes his piercing. Then he lines himself up at my entrance again.

"Ready to fly to the stars, Win?" he asks, voice thick as he drives into me.

From this angle, he hits so much deeper. The pleasure is so good, even as it borders on pain, that it makes me cry out, loud and long. My breasts bounce, and he bends over me to run his hands up and down my back, and around to palm them. He touches me everywhere, but he doesn't stop pumping his hips. Driving into me again and again, plunging into me so deep it feels like he's piercing through to my soul. He pushes me past sensory limits so high I didn't know they were possible.

I feel it, then, an intensity building deep in my belly. I'm going to come and it's going to be explosive.

I whimper, arching my back, spreading my legs wider.

"Let go, baby, come on," he coaxes. "Come for me."

I've had orgasms plenty, but this one is next-level. With Gavin's cock to ride through it, fucking me harder and faster than ever, the build up is too much, too delicious to handle. The sounds that I make as the first wave hits me is like that of a drowning creature, I'm sure. I'm keening and babbling and crying, pushing my ass back against him to stroke him harder, have even more of him, every gorgeous bit of him, as I tip over the edge.

"Fuck, baby." He's panting hard, slicked with sweat. "You feel so fucking good, milking my dick like this. I never want it to end."

But then he groans, and curses, grinding me hard one last time before his body shudders around me with his release.

We collapse together. I've never felt so fulfilled. Neither one of us can even talk as he manages to wiggle his body higher up the bed, next to me.

He looks as sated as I am, his eyelids droopy, his smile soft.

"That was…" he starts to say, too blown away to even finish the sentence.

"Yeah," I agree, as he pulls me to his chest, wrapping his arms around me. I'm too drained to say more. Too drained to move. Too drained to think.

As I close my eyes, drifting away on a cloud of satisfaction, there's only one thing I know with full conviction:

I can't wait to have more.

CHAPTER 22

Gavin

In the morning, the room, with its porn flick decor, is even more garish. I kind of like it. But that might be based more on my current emotional state.

I lie awake, Winnie nestled against me, her soft, even breaths providing a soothing backdrop to my thoughts as I play back our night together. Not just the way she felt, tasted, and teased, but the way she stood up for herself, unapologetically asking for what she wanted.

More. Harder. Again. Now.

Christ, what a turn on. It spoke volumes about her newfound self-assuredness, as if she's finally realizing her worth. I already know damn well that Winnie deserves the entire fucking world, but last night, I couldn't help but believe she wants *me* to be the one to give it to her.

I yearn to be the one to give it to her.

Careful not to wake her, I swallow the lump building in my throat and gently disentangle myself from our cozy little love nest as I slide out of bed.

A smile curls her lips, and her eyelids flutter as she dreams. The strawberry scent of her shampoo, mixing with the warmth of her skin, feels more like home than any home does. Her warm copper hair is a vivid contrast to the drab, dark crimson room. She radiates.

As I move away toward the bathroom, she murmurs in her sleep, and I take in her flushed cheeks. The sight alone stirs my desire even further.

Shutting the door behind me, I lean my back against it. I need to get a fucking grip. Now. I can't let this absurdist reality we're all suddenly playing at, twist up my heart.

But I know it already is. At the end of the day, my Pooh Bear, my favorite girl, will have to make a choice, and if it's not me she wants, I'll long for her for the rest of my damn life.

I turn on the shower, and when the water is next to scalding, I get in, pull the curtain closed and let the spray wash over me.

I wish to hell that I could be bolder, ask her to cast aside my brothers and just be with *me.*

But I'll never ask that of her. I'll do whatever it takes to make her happy. Cherish any moment with her, regardless of the role I play in her life. I want Winnie, I love her, and I'm prepared to support her, even if she chooses a path without me.

Shit, was that a tear?

I duck my head under the stream, removing all trace of it. I'm not one to look down on dudes who cry. But me? I don't do it a lot. Once, when I broke my collarbone as a kid, falling out of a tree. The other time was during one of our last stupid chats with Goldie, when she wouldn't stop pushing her questions on me about what I'm going to do without Winnie. Two tears that time, because honestly, Goldie is *good* at triggering the waterworks. And she had the audacity to ask if I was weeping. *Weeping*.

Fine, maybe on the inside.

"Gav?"

I clear my throat. "Hey! Morning. Want to come in?"

The shower has steamed up the room and I turn the heat down enough to keep from burning her as she pulls the curtain back.

There's a playful smile gracing Winnie's lips as she peers at me. All of me.

Up he goes, I think as I feel my dick on the rise.

She takes my hand and I help her over the tub edge. Fuuuuuck, those tits. By the time she's under the shower with me, moaning as the hot water sluices over her skin, my dick is fully awake and ready to play.

I grab the soap and suds up my hands, eager to rub all over her.

"Better idea," she says, taking the soap from me. "I'll get you clean."

But instead of lathering me, she lathers her own smooth skin, her eyes locked with mine. She suds up her tits, her belly, the flare of her hips, then reaches for me.

Yes, please. I close the space between us, pull her exactly where she wants to be. She wiggles her hips, sexy, teasing, totally adorable as she rubs her soapy body against mine.

"See? I'm your soap."

The warm water rinses away the suds, spilling between her tits, and I bend down to lick her skin, tasting pure Winnie. Delicious.

I grab her ass, pulling her tighter against me, and slip my fingers between her legs. Her delight is evident. Her wet, warm body invites me in. Fucking *delicious*.

"Gav. The point of a shower is to get clean. I don't think what you have in mind is going to get us very clean…"

She steps back from me, and my fingers slide out. She splashes water playfully at me as I lick them clean.

She raises a brow.

I grin.

"Put your foot here," I say, guiding her thigh up so she can balance with her foot on the side of the tub.

She does. No questions, only trust as she opens her body to me. I drool at the sight of her. Pink and ready.

"This is kind of embarrassing, " she says, softly. "Being so exposed."

I touch her clit and her eyes shut, throat exposed as her head goes back. I slide two fingers into her, using my thumb to circle her hard little nub.

Her eyes are wild when she eventually opens them to look at me.

She fucks me good after that. There's a space at the back of the tub with room for me to sit, and even though she's a little shy, I coax her to turn around and sit on my lap. The cry she lets out as I slam up into her is like a siren song that I need to hear, over and over, and thank God she gives it to me. At least until she moans when I twist her nipples a little too roughly as I squeeze her tits. Can those things bounce… They're heavy in my greedy hands, and I'd really love to turn her around so I can see them again, kiss those rosy buds and lose my tongue in her cleavage. But I'm too riveted by the sight of her ass bouncing in my lap as I hammer into her.

We come together, loud and loose. I have to hold her hips tight to keep her from bucking off me she's coming so hard.

"Oops, guess I have to wash you again," she says with a laugh, pulling me back under the stream.

Not a problem, Pooh Bear. I'll follow you anywhere.

CHAPTER 23

Winnie

Gavin drives with one hand on the steering wheel and holds my hand with the other, all the way back to Smithville. We go to the Hammer House first, to change into work clothes. The place is quiet so things across the street must already be in full swing. I'm tempted to take a moment to text Goldie *I've lost it!*, just to see if she gets it right away or if she texts back and says *Lost what?* But I want to keep this to myself for a while.

"I'm headed over," Gavin calls. It took him like two minutes to change.

"Be there in a few!" I call back. I'm not ready because choosing underwear has gotten way more complicated, now that I know the possibility is very real he could be seeing me in them. Taking them off. I think of the way he looked at me last night, looked at me naked, like he'd just unwrapped the world's best Christmas present.

Part of me hadn't wanted to leave the Creepside Inn this morning. To just stay there forever, having sex with Gavin in that heart-shaped bed. I wonder if the owners would be interested in selling. We could buy it and fix it up–except the Honeymoon suite. Wouldn't change a damn thing about that particular room.

Every time I think about how it felt to have his weight on top of me, his cock inside me, I have to blink away tears. I never thought it was possible to feel that desired. That chosen. That loved.

I make a mental note to go on an online shopping spree that night, to get some sexy underthings and maybe some actual lingerie, but for now, I settle for what what I have, which is more function than fashion, but I do choose a bra and panties that match.

Then I trot downstairs. Gavin and I didn't stop for breakfast along the way and I'm suddenly ravenous.

Well, we did burn plenty of calories, I think.

I stop in the kitchen to make a couple of smoothies to take over and am surprised to find Max in the kitchen.

"Oh," I say. "I didn't know anyone was here."

"I left my water bottle," he says.

I can feel him watching me as I move about the room, gathering a couple of bananas, and some peanut butter.

I glance at him. His head is tilted. He's looking at me thoughtfully. Studying me. "What?"

"Can I ask you something?"

"Sure," I reply, heading to the freezer for ice. "Want a smoothie?"

"Did you fuck Gavin last night?"

It's a good thing I'd put everything I'd been holding down on the island. I would've dropped it.

I whip around and blink at Max. "I beg your pardon?"

"I mean... you spent the night with him. So. I was just assuming..."

"You know what they say about assuming, Maxwell," I say. Maxwell isn't a cute nickname thing like what I do with Jack. It's his actual full name, what Max is short for, and I hope my usage of it tells him he's crossed a line.

"So... you two didn't...?"

"Max!" I point at the list of rules. "Number four, buddy."

> *4. STFU, you filthy braggart. Keep your time with Win private.*

"I'm asking *you*, I'm not asking Gav. You can tell me whatever you want."

I square my shoulders and stare him down. Then I go over and pick up the dry erase marker and underneath the original list, I write:

> *Win's Rules*
>
> *1. All relationships are separate but equal, until I make a choice.*
>
> *2. I'm not choosing until the reno is over.*
>
> *3. I don't kiss and tell.*

I cap the marker and gesture at the board, then tap number three. But the look that boy is giving me. I wonder if he can read my thoughts. All I can think about is the sex with Gavin. And I don't regret my decision to be with him at all. I *won't* regret my decision at all.

I sigh. "Max."

"I'm just going to point out, that this whole Winnie's Favorite Hammer thing wouldn't even be happening if my brothers hadn't gotten all in their feels and demanded to know what was going on between you and me. I wasn't allowed to keep our private business private, so it's a little bit hypocritical that they want that respect themselves now."

He has a point. Also we both know if Gavin and I hadn't had sex, I would just tell him Gavin and I hadn't had sex. If it was any of the other Hammers, I would probably gently reiterate that it's not any of their business. But this is Max.

Max, who'd been the one who introduced me to both the wonderful words of dry humping *and* getting eaten out. Max, who I'd actually discussed losing my virginity to. Max, who'd wanted my first time to be special… and with him.

I feel a surge of affection for him. I press my lips together for a second and then say, quietly, "Yeah, Max, Gav and I had sex."

He gives me a wordless nod. Then after a minute, he says, "Well. Work to do."

"Max," I close the distance between us, "are you mad?"

He shakes his head, but his Adam's apple is working, his jaw is clenched. I move in to hug him and he *flinches*.

"Max, it's obvious you're mad. Just say so. You're allowed to feel what you feel, but you have to be honest with me about it, okay? I can't stand you being upset and not telling me."

I can't stand the thought of this coming between me and Max. Or me and any of the guys. Or any of the guys and each other.

Tears prick my eyes and Max looks at me, his gaze going soft.

"Hey," he reaches out and touches my elbow. "I just always thought it would be you and me, you know? That we were going to take things to the next level. That it was going to be us. But as long as you're happy, I'll get over it."

Impulsively, I say, "Max, if you want me to call the whole thing off, I will."

WHAT??!

But it's Max. I say what I say. Do I mean it? I don't know.

He leans forward and presses his lips to mine, sweetly, almost chaste.

"I don't," he says. "It was just a moment of petty jealousy, I swear. I thought I was going to be your first. But I mean, hey, I still might be the last, right?" He gives me a wink and I honestly can't tell if he's still bothered or truly shaking it off that quickly. "If I'm the right guy, you'll choose me in the end, no matter how many other guys are vying for your attention. But your happiness is the most important thing, Win."

I could tell him that now that I've had it, I'm 100% pro-sex and will definitely be wanting more, but… I have a feeling gushing about how great Gav is in bed would not make this situation any better. So instead, I forget the smoothie-making, grab the bananas, and go across the street with Max to 'round up the fellas and have a little heart-to-heart-to-heart-to-heart-to… oh, fuck it.

"Hey," I call upon entering. "Can I get everybody in the living room for a minute?"

When everyone is assembled, I say, "Raise your hand if you're wondering if I had sex with Gavin last night."

It takes a minute, but all the hands go up except Gavin's. He looks like he might want to back slowly out of the room.

I nod. Then I look at Gav. "Do you mind if I tell them what did–or didn't–happen?"

"Can you give me a couple minutes to hide all the sledgehammers first?" he says, half-jokingly. Then he says, "Whatever you want to do, Pooh Bear."

"Winnie," Jack begins. "You do not have to–"

"I had sex with Gavin last night," I tuck some hair behind my ear.

"Well, okay then," Jack says. "Now that everybody's aware, can we get back to work?"

Unlike Max, he doesn't seem bothered. Just... not shocked. Maybe it's because he's the oldest and therefore most mature. Or maybe because he's the natural peacemaker and if he lets on that he's bothered, the others will follow suit?

"No," I say. "You may not." I glance at Max. "You mind if I tell them what spurred me to call this team meeting?"

He shakes his head.

"So... last night was my first time. And Max knew I was a virgin and so..." My voice trails off. I didn't think this through and all of a sudden, it's like I've had a bucket-full of awkwardness dumped over my head.

"I was jealous as fuck for half a minute because I knew Win was a virgin and that her first time was with Gav and not me and yes, Gunnar, I am a douche and realize that, thanks for not saying it."

I give him a grateful smile. "So, I'm bringing this up, not because I want you all to do a Winnie's-open-for-business-now dance of joy, but because I don't want any bad blood brewing silently. Yes, in order to foster our individual relationships, we need to keep some things private. But at the same time, it is super duper important to me that we air any resentments and concerns when they arise and keep the lines of communication open. Okay?"

I look around at my boys, having another *what is my life?* moment. This is so fucking surreal.

"Until we figure out how to clone you and each have a Winnie of our own, we're going to get jealous," Jack says. "But we'll get over it. The most important thing is for you to be happy."

"Even if what makes you happy is having dinner at La Douche Baguette and boning that bonehead," Gunnar says with a nod at Gavin. Then he stage-whispers. "Even though we all know I'm the better-looking one."

Gavin rolls his eyes. Except for Gav's piercings–which I have a whole new appreciation for this morning–and different tats, they're identical right down to the number of eyelashes they have, I think.

"So everybody's good?" I ask. I look from face to face. They all nod. "And if at any point you're not, you'll tell me?" Again, I look from face to face. Again, they all nod.

And all I can do is trust them. And I can trust them. I don't doubt that for a second.

CHAPTER 24

Theo

Back when we were in school, Winnie loved dancing. And I mean, *loved* dancing. Put on a song with a good beat and her body would begin moving, hips gyrating, sweet glorious God. It was hard not to stare. Hard not to crave her when I was as horny as a teen boy can be, and she filled out her clothes like no other.

And the way she could sway those beloved breasts of hers back and forth like a hypnotist's watch…

So I've never been more excited about anything than I am about our date tonight. And nervous. See, since Winnie agreed to give us a chance, I've been going over how to wow her most, how to woo her best. I want my angel to choose me so damn much I ache. And every time I think about what she might want to do most, I see her shaking her hips on the dance floor, head thrown back, smile wide. She was born to twirl in the center of that dance floor, under the spotlight.

Not to mention, dancing is the perfect way to get my hands on her at the start of the night and never let go.

Leo found this club in the city, Rebel, and we booked the three of us a private room. Keeping dates low-key, when the whole damn world knows your face, isn't easy. But what's a night out dancing with your twin and best friend? Just a night of innocent fun, as far as everyone there will be concerned. It'll be loud, dark, and easy to be anonymous in the crowd. But if we get stared at too hard on the dance floor, we can move to the private room and hang out, just the three of us.

I'm outside cutting and measuring plywood when Winnie sidles up, looking like a whole-ass snack. Except for when we catch glimpses of her in those heaven-sent pjs, I can't remember the last time I've seen those shapely bare legs. But her typical job-site overalls are now cut off shorts instead of full-length pants, and *damnnnnnn.*

Can I drop what I'm doing and pull her across the street and into the pool house for a few minutes of privacy? Is that allowed?

"Hey, Theo," she says. Is it the sun getting to me or does she say my name differently now? Like she's tasting something delicious.

"What's up, Angel?" I ask, flipping the lock switch on my jigsaw before setting it down to give her my full attention. "You're looking extra beautiful this morning. And no, I'm not telling you anything about my secret project."

We all agreed we'd do one really big thing for the house that she won't know about 'til the very end. Yeah, she said this isn't going to ever be her dream house and that's fine. She wants it to be our brainchild and have our fingerprints all over it, and that's fine, too. But we're not *Us* without Win, so we're each putting a feature she'd love into the house, too.

Not to mention, since she's going to be giving it away, whoever wins it will want pieces of the wonderful Winnie Wainwright in it.

Her cheeks are pink as she grins at me. "Oh, I don't want to talk about the reno. I wanted to talk about tonight."

I pull off my safety goggles and cock an eyebrow. "You're not canceling on us, are you?"

Now it's her eyebrow that goes up. "Us?"

Well, fuck a duck. Guess I'm shit at keeping surprises.

"Weeeeelll, Leo and I thought we'd keep the whole sharing-to-get-double-time thing with you going," I say. "If it's okay with you, that is."

"Ohhhh," she says and my Angel has a devilish gleam in her bright blues.

I feel a smirk tugging at my lips. "That okay with you, then?"

She breathes in deeply and my eyes are drawn to the rise and fall of her breasts. I feel tugging elsewhere.

I don't want to be a pig because Winnie means far more to me than the physical stuff, but… it's fucking amazing that the lust I feel for her doesn't have to come with an aftertaste of guilt anymore.

"Of course *I'm* okay with that. A night out with the two of you sounds amazing. As long as it's okay with *you*," she says. "Technically you guys are supposed to get uninterrupted alone time with me on your dates. Per the rules. I don't want to deprive you of that."

I nod seriously, crossing my arms. "Jack would lose his shit if we didn't stick to the rules, so we're factoring that in."

It'll be her, me, and Leo for a while… then his punk ass has got to go so I can have some one-on-one time with my girl. Vice versa when it's his turn for a date, because fair's fair.

"Trust me," I add, "I want as much alone time with you as you'll give me, Win. You have to know that."

Her cheeks turn the sweetest shade of pink.

"Sooooooo," she says, tucking a stray curl behind her ear. "Without me asking outright where we're going or what we're doing… what should I wear?"

My eyes travel down her body, slow and deliberate, taking in every gorgeous inch, before finding her gaze again. "I like what you've got on."

"*Theo.*"

Her nose is crinkling up so cute.

"Wear whatever goes with your dancing shoes, Angel," I tell her with a wink.

Her eyes light up and her smile is *giddy*.

I must be hungry 'cause those are not damn butterflies in my stomach as she places her hand on my shoulder and leans in to press a kiss against my cheek.

I turn my head and her sweet lips are on mine.

"*Theo,*" she says again, but this time it's a sigh against my mouth that I can feel all the way in my balls.

I skim my fingertips over the tops of her thighs, even as I will my dick to settle down. A futile thought, of course. I want to sink into this girl, make her say my name again and again. Pant it, moan it, cry it, scream it.

The project to-do list Jack pushed on me can wait, surely?

"Theo," she says again, but with a regretful tone. "I have work to do. *We* have work to do."

Her lips are plumped up. She pouts as she looks up at me, but when I groan with pure lust and frustration, she smiles, just a little, knowing what she's doing to me.

"Oh, you like making me crazy, do you?"

With a flirty wink, she trails a finger down my chest. "Only as payback for how you make *me* feel."

As she walks away, all I can do is stare at her ass, those legs, the tempting sway of her hips. Such a tease, my angel.

I put my safety glasses back on, but I have to wait for my rock solid dick to lower before I pick up the jigsaw.

The private room Leo booked is on the second floor, away from the crowd. It's a lounge space with swanky chairs, and a private bar on the balcony that extends over the dance floor. If someone tried hard enough they might catch a glimpse of us up here, but for the most part, we're hidden from view by a strobing screen of lights.

The club pulses with a bass that reverberates throughout the building. Its fucking perfect. Neon lights cast an electric glow around the room, giving the atmosphere a retro vibe. Sexy as fuck. It's the perfect place to be out with my angel who, speaking of sexy, is a knock-out tonight. We've only just arrived and Winnie is already on the balcony, gyrating to the music, hypnotizing me in that ass-sculpting black leather skirt. It has a side slit up her thigh that I can't wait to slide my hands into…

"Here," Leo shouts, to be heard over the music as he pushes a shot glass into my hand.

He heads off to give one to Winnie, and I follow, looking into the glass. It's a layer of piss-yellow topped with a layer of jizz-white. Rank.

Smells delicious, though.

"What is this shit?" I mutter.

Leo lifts his glass.

"To you, love," he shouts to Winnie. "Here's to an unforgettable night, where every beat feels like a heartbeat and every dance move brings us closer."

I snort at his pathetic poetry, but Winnie beams as we clink our glasses together and all knock the drink back.

Sweet. Like… butterscotch schnapps and Irish cream.

I check Winnie's reaction, but find Leo is talking to her. It's too loud in here to hear what he is saying.

Irritating. I want her to myself.

"A Buttery Nipple?" she exclaims with a laugh. "Is that really what it's called?"

Those words out of her mouth, mixed with the sexy warmth of the drink, hit me hard. Without wasting another second, I take Winnie's hand.

"Dance with me?"

My breath hitches when colorful lights play across her face, revealing the joy in her eyes.

As the DJ mixes a rising tempo, the dance floor below us becomes a sea of movement. Winnie joins in, her eyes flashing as her excitement builds along with the music. I slide up close to her, and she bumps and grinds herself into me. The slit of her skirt allows me to pull her leg up so that I can touch the exposed bare skin of her thigh.

So, so soft. I groan, and her lips curve knowingly. I don't know if she can hear me, or if she felt the vibrations of my desire, but as she gazes up at me, the need in her eyes mirrors mine.

I want to kiss her badly. I hate that I can't right now. The bartender will know we're semi-celebrities. He'll have to keep things under wraps. But until Winnie chooses her Hammer, I don't want to risk a potential photo leak that could jeopardize her in any way.

From the corner of my eye, I see Leo head to the bar. He'll refresh our drinks, but I know he'll have the bartender pull a round of water, too. Neither of us wants to cloud a single moment tonight with drink-dulled senses.

"Theo?"

Winnie has her sweet hands on my chest and she's looking at me like she's thinking hard.

"What is it, baby?"

She chews her lip for a sexy little second, and then she's got her arms around my neck, stretching on her toes, to speak directly and loudly into my ear.

Her sweet breath is hot against my face. But there's no way she just said what I think she just said.

Did Winnie Wainwright practically yell in my ear that she wants to fuck me?

From the look in her eyes… yes?

Holy shit. How fast can I get my girl into the lounge, out of her skirt, and onto my dick?

I glance back at the bar to catch Leo's eye as I lead Winnie to the open door. He takes a sip of his drink, raises his brows. He's cool. He'll watch the door for us.

The moment we're inside, Winnie has her hands all over me, tugging me toward a chair, pushing me into it so that she can climb into my lap.

My hands slide up her thighs, under her skirt. Her mouth is greedy and I love it. I feed her my tongue and she sucks sucks, sucks, and my dick is so fucking jealous, even as the rest of me thrills at the sensation of her sweet mouth devouring mine.

She wiggles and gyrates on top of me like she's still on the dance floor and the movement is making it impossible for me to go slow. I slide my hands higher, squeezing her soft skin as I go.

I finally reach her panties and she's so wet my finger nearly slips inside.

"Leo," she moans.

I pause, my stomach dropping lower than my balls. She doesn't think I'm Leo, does she?

But then she adds, "I feel bad that he's out there by himself."

I mean, he has the bartender to keep him company.

I don't say that. Instead I say, "Do you want me to switch with him so you… can have a few minutes with him?"

Emphasis on a few *minutes*. I'm deeply regretting the whole let's-share-a-date thing at the thought of standing on the other side of that door when her panties are so fucking damp.

"No." It comes out as a little mewl and my balls might just explode. "I still want you. Can… can he join us?"

CHAPTER 25

Winnie

The request slips from between my thoroughly kissed lips, unbidden. Instantly the air between the two of us changes as Theo's hand slides out from under my skirt. For a split second, I'm terrified, because he pulls back from me.

But the way Theo is grinning at me says yes. Or at least maybe.

"That's what you want, Angel? I'll get him."

He shifts us both, as if I weigh nothing, so that I'm the one sitting in the sumptuous wingback chair and he's standing over me, hands braced on the chair arms. He kisses me again, slow, his tongue making me shiver with delight.

Then he's gone, and I blink in surprise. I'm dreaming. I touch my lips, plumped up and sensitive. Is this really happening?

A moment later, it's all three of us in the lounge. I hear the click of the door as Theo locks it. Leo slides me a wicked smile and my stomach flutters with anticipation.

Somehow I manage to rise from the chair, and stand. My legs are shaky. My whole body is trembling with desire as my two boys close in on me.

They slot themselves around me, Theo in front, Leo behind. As if they've choreographed it, they each put a hand on one of my shoulders and one of my hips, in perfect mirroring movements.

Holy fuck. The sensations their hard bodies pull from mine are so intense I need to shut my eyes to keep from being overwhelmed.

Leo pushes my hair aside and kisses a trail from the top of my spine, down, down, down my back. I'm infinitely grateful I picked an almost backless top. I don't know where the fuck I got the confidence to actually wear it, but my back is one part of my body I'm okay with.

Theo slides his hand from my hip down the side of my skirt until I feel his fingertips graze the side slit. He seems totally obsessed with the slit in my skirt tonight, and I make a solemn vow to wear this outfit often.

I lift my chin as Theo's lips settle on the sensitive skin along the edge of my jaw. He gently but insistently licks and sucks one side of my neck before switching to the other. His mouth finally lands back on mine, as his hand slips under my skirt.

Leo licks a line back up my spine, and as he does, he slides a hand around the front of me. He skims my ribs, the underside of my boob.

Blood rushes in my ears. I have no idea what to do with my hands in this situation. I slink one arm around Theo's waist and reach back with my other hand, intending to grope Leo's thigh.

I miss.

Oh my God.

When I moan into Theo's kiss, too excited by the feel of Leo's cock straining against his pants to contain myself, Leo tilts his hips forward, pushing himself further into my open palm. He groans softly against my spine, which shoots electricity straight through my core.

Theo's mouth is back at the edge of my jaw, his hand is as far up my skirt as my skirt will allow in this position. His hand wraps around my thigh, skimming back and forth along my skin, igniting every previously untouched nerve.

I'm afraid if I open my eyes and catch a glimpse of even a hair on either of their heads, I'll lose myself completely and rip my clothes straight off. Rip off theirs, too.

None of my vast experience with dildos had prepared me for Gavin, my whole body utterly and completely claimed by him... Am I ready for my first threesome, when I've barely had my first twosome?

Would Theo and Leo even be down for...

"Have you two had lots of threesomes?" I blurt. "I mean, the two of you with one woman?"

They laugh in unison, low rumbles I feel vibrating against my skin.

"Why do you ask, love?" Leo questions. He turns my head, holding my face in his hands, forcing eye contact. "Are you ready for double trouble?"

There's a smile in the glittering green of his eyes, but he's seriously asking.

"I…"

Can't speak.

"We've had quite a few offers for that scenario," Leo's voice is low and seductive. He pauses, nipping my earlobe.

My panties are flooding now. He might make me come just by talking to me.

But then he says, "We've never taken anyone up on it."

"Oh." My face already felt hot… my entire body feels hot… but it gets even hotter. Embarrassed. Of course they wouldn't want to… with me…

"But if *you* were to ask, love," Leo continues. He turns me around so that I'm facing him now. "My answer would be *yes*."

Theo slides his hands up my thighs, which he appears to have claimed, then pulls me back against his chest. He drops his mouth into the hollow of my neck, which he also seems to have claimed, kissing my skin.

I can feel how hard he is through my skirt. "My answer would also be yes," he says.

The new gush of warmth inside my pussy compensates for the dryness in my throat. The thought of them both, wanting me… at once…

"How long do we have this room for?" I rasp.

One side of Leo's mouth quirks up. "As long as we want it."

I nod. "Okay. Um. Can we just play around and see where it goes? I don't know if… I know this isn't sexy but I don't have a lot of experience and…"

I'm talking too fast. I'm breathless.

"We'll take care of you, love." Leo's reassuring promise is pressed against my temple.

His other promise, the hard one, is pressed into the front of my skirt.

Theo's is pressed into my ass.

The image of the three of us naked, of their hard bodies and harder cocks pressed against me, and into me, makes my stomach flip.

"Um, wait," I blurt out. "I'm not ready for…"

The inexperience is really showing itself, now. I can't even say the word *anal*. My cheeks are heating up.

"Winnie," Theo says, turning me back around so that I face him again. His gorgeous green eyes are shining with affection. "Don't be afraid to tell us what you want *and* what you don't. We want to know. We need to know."

"I'm not ready for anal."

"Noted," Theo says and then his mouth captures mine in the most sensuous and sweet kiss in the history of time. Without words, it tells me he's not going to push but he wants anything and everything I'm willing to give. "You tell us when you want to stop."

"Let's take some clothes off, shall we?" Leo asks, his palm pressed against the small of my back.

I nod, automatically reaching for the buttons of Theo's shirt. As I work the buttons down, Leo finds the zipper of my skirt and works it down, matching my pace, which feels agonizingly slow.

My skirt comes loose and Leo tugs it down over my hips, his hand grazing my ass. As my skirt pools around my feet, he slides a finger into the top part of my thong, making an obscene noise in his throat, before gripping my hips and pulling me against him.

I yank at the last of Theo's buttons, yank off his shirt, and strip him out of his undershirt, too. Run my hands over his pecs. Bite my lip.

"You can use those teeth on me if you want to," he says.

I press a few kisses to Theo's chest and then suck one of his nipples into my mouth, ever-so-lightly grazing the skin around it with my teeth. He lets out a low moan, his hand curving the base of my skull, his fingers tangling in my hair.

Leo's hand is skimming down the front of my panties, teasing along the edges. "Mmmm, soaked through. I wonder if you're as wet as I am hard. I'm so fucking hard for you, Win."

He takes one of my hands pressing it against the bulge in his pants. Indeed, rock hard. Harder than before, somehow.

"How are you doing, Angel?" Theo asks, pulling my attention back to him.

I undo his belt, then the front of his pants.

Holy fuck, he's not wearing any underwear.

Holy fuck, he's bigger than Gav. Not that it's a competition, but…

"Win?" he prompts.

My basement is flooded and needs your immediate attention, sir.

"I'm okay."

Theo slides his pants down and steps out of them and then stands in front of me completely buck-ass naked and so fucking gorgeous, I can't even.

He spins me around so I'm facing Leo. He pulls my shirt over my head and drops a kiss into my neck.

Leo is baldly staring at me in my peach lace bra and panties, looking like a kid in a candy shop. "Well, I just got even harder. Damn girl."

Not possible for him to be even harder, surely.

"You're wearing too many clothes, Leo," I try to say, but I'm babbling.

I am nearly coming undone at the way Theo fingers slip past the waistband of my panties, his lips on my shoulders, his cock grazing my back.

Leo takes a few steps back, locking eyes with mine. He undresses himself with agonizing slowness, starting with his shirt.

Theo's very skillful fingers find my clit. "This okay?"

I nod, very aware of Leo's eyes watching my face.

I can barely keep my eyes open and my knees feel like they're going to give out as he works me.

Leo's gaze drops, watching my hips as they begin to rock back and forth, grinding myself against Theo's touch. He unbuckles his belt.

My head falls back as Theo discovers a spot I wasn't even sure I knew was there and the sensation sends a jolt through me, causing me to cry out in surprise. When my gaze finds Leo again, he's naked, too, and my brain short circuits.

"You have tattoos on your cock," I babble, stupidly. I'm five seconds from coming all over Theo's hand. He has an arm around my waist now, holding me against him, his cock pressing against my back.

Leo glances down at himself with a lopsided smile and says, "Damn, how'd this get here?"

I can't stop looking at the bold design, something Celtic or Viking, in the shape of...

"Thor's Hammer. Want to see if you're strong enough to wield it, love?"

I laugh, but it quickly turns into a moan as he comes back to me and takes my face in his hands. He kisses me and I reach for his cock. I have to hold him.

His cock is so thick, the silky soft, yet solid skin rippling as my fingers go around him.

Theo's finger slides past my panties, slipping inside me. I'm on sensory overload, moaning into Leo's mouth as Theo rapidly brings me to the precipice.

Leo pulls back and says, "Come for us, love."

At his request, I go crashing over the edge and damn, I hope this room is soundproof. Waves hit me and by the time they stop, I'm boneless.

"Now," Theo says, "the fun begins."

"That *was* fun," I murmur. I wouldn't still be standing if they weren't holding me up.

I yelp when Theo takes his hand away. But he kisses my shoulder as he gently tugs my panties down.

Leo takes off my bra, his hands instantly replacing it.

"Maybe so, but that," he says, "was the opening act."

CHAPTER 26

Leo

Winnie's eyes are luminous as she stares at me, her mouth parted sinfully as her breast heaves in my hands. "The opening act…"

She's crazy adorable right now, wobbly legs, her hair all mussed up, and lips begging for more. I rub her peachy pink nipple with the pad of my thumb, and slide my other hand around to grab her ass.

I pull her against me hard. The bass from the dance floor reverberates through my chest. If I dip my hips just right, I can… ahhhh. *Yes.* My cockhead brushes over her sweet pussy, warm and wet.

With a sweet cry, she thrusts her hips up, looking surprised by herself, like it was an involuntary reaction to the feel of me.

"Yes, love," I encourage, struggling to keep my voice even. I need her so damn badly. I ache to angle her just right so I can push inside. "That's right, just like that."

My hand, squeezing her bare ass, has never felt paradise quite like this. I don't want to intimidate Winnie tonight with my own personal double trouble dream, so I promise myself not to touch her where I want to stick my cock most.

Fuck, I'm not greedy. I'm over the moon just getting to see and touch her sumptuous round ass. It's the perfect ripe peach. The ass that has had me entranced since I used to jerk off to thoughts of her backside in high school.

My fingers graze the soft hills of her crack and my cock twitches against her pussy. I need to pull back or I really will push my cock inside her. Maybe sex with me is what she wants, but until she asks, I won't take that step.

Theo and I have had a pact of our own. It was something we cooked up long before this wild dream come true started. Long before we knew about Max, even. Before Winnie made it clear that she wanted us, too, Theo and I agreed that if ever the moment arose, he'd shoot his shot with her first. If she rejected him, I could try.

Our agreement gave me the permission to fantasize that I'd sought.

Truthfully, I didn't think a night like tonight would ever be something to hope for, so the promise I made him wasn't a big deal. But still my persistent sweet dreams about her had grown filthy over the years as I often pictured her ass in my hands, my dick being sandwiched between her cheeks. I catch Theo's eye now. He knows I want her.

He knows it's his turn. Ah, well.

"Angel," Theo says as I take a step back.

She starts to protest my absence, but I don't go far. I drop my t-shirt onto the armed chair that Winnie had vacated as I'd come into the lounge. I sit on it, and her eyes are back on my tattoo.

Her appreciative eyes on my cock are making it weep. I'm bobbing heavily, my balls aching to be emptied. With her staring down at me, licking her lips, I'll be exploding stupid soon.

"I want…" she starts, then her words drop away and she shakes her head fretfully. I smile, because she's staring so hard at me spreading my legs wide for her that she can't even speak.

"Tell me, love," I tease as I circle the head of my cock with my fist. "What do you want?"

Theo is behind her, touching her thighs, her hip, and gently guiding her closer to me.

"What do you want, Angel?" he says. He kisses her shoulder, strums his fingers over her belly. "Do you want us both at the same time? Or do you want us to take turns?"

"At the same…?" Her eyes are glazing over, and it doesn't take much encouragement for Theo to guide her onto her hands and knees in front of me.

Her breath is hot, coming out rapidly. My balls tighten and my cock twitches at the feel of it, and when she takes me in her warm hands, I have to grit my teeth and not think about how her tongue will feel.

Her cheeks are pink and her lips are full and wet.

"Leo," she says with a whimper, looking at me like she's begging. Holding me like she's praying. "I don't know what to do…"

Even as she says it, she pumps her hand down over me, squeezing just right, and her tongue flicks out to lap at the bead that drips from the tip of my dick.

She glances up at me, her large eyes wide, looking so fucking sexy as she gauges my reaction.

"You're perfect, love," I have to clear my throat. It's thick with the feelings she's pulling from me. "Just do whatever feels okay with you. We'll stop if you're uncomfortable."

She rocks her body as she shifts her position, spreads her thighs wider. I catch a quick hot look of her tantalizing pussy as she braces herself to bend forward. Then all I see is the top of her head as she slips me past her warm lips and into her fiery hot mouth.

Fuck, yeahhh.

She sucks me hard, making slurping sounds that I will be remembering for the rest of my life.

Theo's got a hand pumping his cock, and a view that is surely as sexy as mine. He watches her ass bob up as her head goes down. I close my eyes when he gets down on his knees behind her. I hear the sound of the condom foil rip. I'm happy for my brother and all, I guess, but I don't need to see it.

As it turns out, even with my eyes closed, I know when he touches her. Slides his fingers into her. Her mouth starts to go fucking crazy on me, sucking me like a lollipop.

I know when he begins to fuck her, too, because she's suddenly digging her fingers into my thigh as she swallows my entire cock down her throat.

I can hear Theo pounding a rhythm into her. Her beautiful mouth dances up and down, sucking me in deeper. She's making whimpering moans and gurgling noises so loud I feel them everywhere. Sooo fucking good.

I open my eyes to make sure she's okay, and find that she's looking at me, her eyes shiny with tears. Alarmed, I start to pull out, but before I can, she slides her mouth off me and grips me in her fist. "Is this okay, baby?" she pants.

There's a strand of her saliva trailing from her mouth to my throbbing cockhead. She licks her lips and eagerly waits for my response.

I nod. I have never been speechless before, but my love, making sure *I'm* the one who is okay as her sweet mouth fucks me, calling me baby in that sexed up voice of hers, is enough to kick me right over the edge.

She smiles, and I reach for her bouncing tits, holding, squeezing, before she drops her mouth back on me. She hums her satisfaction before going back to swirling her tongue up and down my shaft.

"Hey, Lee," Theo says, catching my eye. "Hold her arms a sec. I want to try something…" And to Winnie, he says, "Let me just ease your legs back a little – don't worry, angel, I've got you. There, now, you won't slip. But you'll be able to take him in as deep as you want. And I'm going to–"

He thrusts into her and Winnie cries out so loud it shocks me for a second but as I hold her upper body steady to keep her from sliding off me as Theo pulls her back onto him, holding her thighs, spreading her legs around him and fucking her hard, she drops her mouth back onto my cock and lets gravity take me in.

I have to rock my hips and fully fuck her face in this position, and her eyelids flutter closed as she opens her mouth wider. Wanting more of me. Jesus fuck.

I feed her every inked-up inch of me, and instead of finding my long, fat cock too much and pushing me away, she flips her arms over so that she can grip onto my forearms tight as she opens herself further to the both of us.

My heart is racing and my brain is on fire as I watch what looks like unfiltered heaven on her face.

"Oh, fuck," I pant, and her eyes open to find mine.

That's it. I'm gone. The look of joy in her eyes has me bubbling up. My cock pulses and jumps as exquisite pleasure rolls through my entire body. She holds on to me tighter and doesn't move her mouth from my cock. And then I explode so hard my vision goes black.

I never expected her to swallow, or to moan as she does. When I can see again, I watch her ease off me, smiling as she licks her lips, and I'm struck by how beautiful she is.

Then Theo curses and thrusts into her so hard her fingers clench, holding on to my forearm tighter. Her head goes back as ecstasy crosses her face.

"I'm going to… oh, God, I'm coming," she groans.

Her voice is so sultry my cock wants to wake up and play again, but there's nothing left. Winnie sucked me dry.

Mostly dry. My eyes start to water as her face flushes and she begins to keen. Her lashes flutter, she pants hard. The sights and sounds of her orgasm hit me so hard I feel a twist in my belly. Damn, I don't want her to think I'm crying. I blink to remove the blur, to watch as she falls off the edge of the world.

"Fuck me, Angel, you feel so good—"

And then it's Theo shouting out his release.

For a long moment, there's only our heavy breathing and the club's pulsing music beating along with my pounding heart.

Winnie lets out the most gloriously obscene moan I've ever heard and I glance away, realizing it's Theo, that lucky bastard, pulling out of her that elicits that sound. Since Theo and I are identical through and through, except for our tattoos, will my cock be anticlimactic for her after she's had his?

She just gave you the best damn blow job of your life, loser, get the fuck over yourself.

I look at my girl. Our girl.

More than ever, I want her to choose me.

But I have the most ridiculous thought:

As long as I get to be with her, I wouldn't mind sharing her forever.

CHAPTER 27

Winnie

Holy fuck, I just had a threesome.

In an insanely cool nightclub.

With *Theo and Leo Hammer!*

Who am I and where has the real Winnie Wainwright gone?

I feel like I'm *strutting* through the club as we head out to leave. My whole body feels weaker and stronger than ever at the same time. I'm stretched and sore, satisfied, and yet there's a small flame of need in my core that I'm not sure is fully extinguished.

Just before we reach the door, the opening notes of a techno song from our college days blast like a sign from the damn universe. It's my favorite ass-shaking song, ever.

"One more dance before we go?" I shout.

"Anything for you, love," Leo says, his hand on the small of my back as we weave through the crowd to a spot on the dance floor.

He pulls me in close, the front of his body pressed against mine, while Theo moves in behind me.

My body is so sensitive from what we just did together that it wouldn't take much to make me come again, and the secret of it pulls my cheeks into a grin that I try to hide in Leo's chest.

We move to the beat as one. A piece of paper couldn't fit between either of their bodies and mine.

Sweet heaven, they're both hard again.

Gazing up at Leo, I lick my lips, remembering the velvety soft skin of his dick, the sweet and salty taste of him. I get why people call them a *snack*. He tasted better than a candy bar. And having Leo in my mouth while Theo was opening me wide and banging me hard, in an angle that perfectly hit my g-spot…

I shudder, remembering.

The song ends too soon, but though I never want this night to end, I'm ready to go home. I want to be cuddled up in bed with one, or both, of them.

The ride back to the house isn't at all awkward, which is both surprising and not. It's Leo's truck we're in, a fully restored classic Ford, with a bench seat for three. I sit in the middle and lean back against the headrest, happy, sleepy.

Theo's jacket covers my lap like a blanket and his fingers trace the skin along my skirt's slit. Leo holds my hand. I snuggle into the warmth of their bodies against mine.

I fall asleep before we reach the house, but not before Theo tugs my skirt up, reaches under, his jacket which hides his hand as he slides his fingers into my panties.

I gaze up into his eyes as he fills me with a long finger. They're dark and glittering green under the streetlights, watching my face.

"You're extra tight, angel. Is this okay"

I nod as my eyes jam shut, and I bite my lip to keep back my sounds of pleasure as he expertly urges me to come into his hand again.

When I next open my eyes, we're home. After coming, I'd snuggled into Theo's side for the rest of the ride. Theo has gone to sleep too, and is snoring softly.

I nudge him. "Wake up, Theo. We're home. Though sleeping out here doesn't seem like a bad idea since it means not having to move."

"I've got you, love," Leo says as Theo stirs awake. Before I can protest, Leo's scooping me into his arms. He carries me from the truck to the door, then inside before setting me down.

The house is dark. It looks like everyone else is asleep.

With an arms-wide stretch, Theo yawns. "Early morning tomorrow, and you wore me out." He drops a kiss on my lips and then says, though there is regret in his voice, "I'm headed to bed. Thanks for the perfect night, angel."

He gives Leo a nod and then hops the steps to his room two at a time.

I'm snuggled up against Leo's side as he walks me to my room. He kisses me at my door, but before he pulls away, his eyes fill with a regretful look that matches Theo's.

"I don't want any of this to end, Win." He lets out a breath. "Can I hold you in my arms tonight? I promise that's all I'll do, if you want. I hate the thought of letting you go."

I wonder how Theo will feel if I sleep with Leo tonight, but then Leo kisses my forehead and says, "Theo's given us his blessing, if that's what you're worried about. But if it's something else causing this brow to wrinkle, please, love, tell me."

"I don't have the energy to do more than cuddle," I admit.

"I can't wait."

He follows me inside with a smile and we get ready for bed. For several long, lazy minutes, we kiss. When he looks tired, I roll over, and he pulls me into his chest, his arms around me.

I try drifting back to sleep, but it's suddenly impossible. By the instant and easy breaths Leo makes, I know he's having no problem falling to sleep.

Then the music begins from the other side of the wall. First a few notes being played on Gunnar's keyboard, then his husky vocals.

That old Sophie B. Hawkins song, "Damn, I Wish I Was Your Lover".

"Well, someone's not at all subtle," Leo groans, then presses a kiss on my shoulder before reaching up to bang on the wall. "Rule three, Romeo!"

No sabotage or undermining anyone else's chance with Win.

There's a moment of dead silence.

"Rule four, douchenozzle!" Gunnar throws back. "I didn't know you were in there with her."

STFU, you filthy braggart. Keep your time with Win private.

Leo nuzzles my neck. "Yeah, right. I call intentional sabotage."

I smile. "He's probably telling the truth. He does this most nights."

"Gunnar serenades you most nights?"

"Yeah," I say, quietly. It's a Gunnar and me thing that goes way back to high school. On the hardest days, he'd always call me after we'd both gone to bed and sing me to sleep. Never did he express any wish to be my lover back then, though.

"Well," Leo says. "Can't compete with that. Everyone knows I'm tone deaf."

"You have other talents," I tell him. Then, because I can't not ask. "Speaking of talents, was the blow job I gave you okay?"

He chuckles into my shoulder. "No it wasn't okay. It was phenomenal."

"You better not be just blowing smoke up my ass, Lee."

He groans and rocks his hips into me. "I want to do many things to this ass, Win, but blowing smoke up it… not one of them."

My face grows hot.

"No pressure, love. I know you said you're not ready for that."

He scoops me against him and we try to sleep again, but I can't relax anymore. Not when I feel Leo's dick growing hard yet again, bumping at my entrance from behind over my thin silk panties. I try to muffle my sounds.

He clears his throat. "Can't sleep?"

I shake my head.

"I can help, if you want. Or try, at least."

There's a big grin in his voice. I roll over and look at him, even though it's too dark to see him.

He finds my mouth and kisses me.

"You tasted me earlier," he whispers against my lips. "All I can think about now is tasting *you*."

I'm fully awake now, but that's not a problem at all as he kisses his way down my body, landing tongue-first between my legs.

We eventually do fall asleep, our boneless limbs tangled together, but it takes several orgasms apiece first.

CHAPTER 28

Winnie

As the days and nights pass, the anxiety I had felt about spending so much time in my childhood home drains away, thanks to my ten gorgeous men. In the span of a few days, my life has shifted and widened in unexpected ways. The relentless rhythm of hammers striking wood, and the sweet symphony of the brothers' laughter, fills my world like never before.

By day, my boys are the architects of the house's transformation. By night, they're the architects of *my* transformation. If I were to sit down and write my memoir today, I'd call it *From Virgin to Vixen: Renovating Winnie Wainwright*. This has all happened so fast. I still can't believe it is happening at all. The time before I started dating my boys, in some ways, seems like a distant memory already.

As I walk out of the Hammer house, I can't help singing about myself in third person—as sexually and emotionally satisfied women obviously do.

"Winnie has work to do, Winnie has work to do!"

I have the silly, giddy urge to stop in the middle of the street and yell at the top of my lungs, "My name is Winnie Wainwright and I love my life!"

I waltz into the reno house—which is how I've started thinking about it to keep myself from getting dragged back into the mire of emotions from the past every time I walk through the door. I expect one of the boys to shout at me about what zones I'm forbidden from entering, as they usually do upon my entry. They're so adorbs with their secret projects.

Though, I can't lie. I'm a little nervous about what's going on in the room that used to be my dad's. I haven't been allowed in there at all. One of them even put a padlock on the door.

Today, the house is still and silent.

"Hello?"

I'm earlier than usual, but some of the brothers have to be over here already? I didn't see anyone in the Hammer house as I left, but sometimes the guys go on breakfast runs.

Not all at once, though.

"Hello?"

I walk through the house. Movement outside a window catches my eye. Taking another look, I see that Gunnar and Cruz are in the backyard. They're both looking at a phone.

Cruz's expression is hard to read. Gunnar looks *pissed*.

Unease prickles through me.

The second I open the back door, they fumble the phone like I'm Anna and they're twelve and I just discovered them googling *big naked boobs*. Gunnar jostles Cruz, who drops the phone.

Gunnar catches it mid-fall. He hands it back to Cruz who shoves it in his back pocket.

"Good morning, baby," Cruz flashes me a grin. "You were up late last night."

"Um, we were all up late last night." Binge-watching episodes of some new zombie show, but Jack's not going to let any of us use that as an excuse to sleep in.

"Still, why don't you go back to bed for a while? And by bed, I mean my bed. I'll come with you. We can get it on."

He rocks his hips back and forth, comically thrusting. His energy is frenetic, awkward. He's talking too fast, trying to flirt, which tips me off even more that something is up. Cruz doesn't have to try.

"Morning, Win," Gunnar says. "Ignore this doucheface." He elbows Cruz in the side hard enough to make him wince. "Told you putting coffee beans and an energy drink in your smoothie was a fucking stupid idea."

Gunnar's stormy blue eyes avoid my gaze.

I march over to Cruz and hold out my hand. "Give me your phone."

"I–"

I cut him off. "Show me what you two were looking at on your phone."

"It was a new card game app I found, alright?" Cruz says. "I was going to buy it and surprise you. No big deal and we've got to get back up to–"

My eyebrows rise like an elevator zooming to the top floor. "A card game app, huh? What's it called, Liar Liar Pants

On Fire? What is going on? We agreed to open and honest communication, remember?"

Gunnar's stormy eyes are close to thunderous. "We're not showing you the phone. Period."

Which makes me more scared than mad, frankly.

"What is it?" I ask, my voice rising with the panic I feel. "Is it something about us? You know I can just google on my own phone and likely find whatever it is in two point five seconds, right? You might as well show me."

They exchange a glance and Gunnar, lips pressed together. He gives Cruz an almost imperceptible shrug.

Cruz sighs and pulls out his phone. He unlocks it, but as I go to take it, he seems to change his mind and we have mini tug-of-war with it for a few seconds before he relinquishes it with another sigh.

I blink at the screen.

It's a post on c-list celebrity scandals. Some blog devoted to people who are famous for being famous; has-beens and reality TV stars. Puzzled, I stare at a picture of a fat girl between two gorgeous guys.

It takes a moment for me to realize it's *me* in the photo, between Theo and Leo.

The image blurs before I can stop the tears that well up. That night, I felt so sexy and desirable.

Sexy and adorable is *not* how I look in the photo. In the split-second captured for all time, it looks like I have three chins. The skirt I bought years ago and dared to wear for the first time, thinking I looked hot, looks like it's a size too small for my ass.

My ass that Leo was obsessed with.

My ass that Leo and Theo both saw naked.

I blink away the tears. The worst part of the photo is that my face is flooded with pure pleasure. My unadulterated joy. But in a stunning case of bad timing, both Theo and Leo are grimacing like they just smelled a particularly rank fart.

My insides have shriveled into a painful knot. I'd had a brief moment last night, where I'd worried that my boys might be comparing me to the other women they've been with. How could I not think that, at least once?

But at least that moment, and the wrenching doubt it gave me, was fleeting. I believe with my whole heart they aren't thinking of anyone but me when they're with me.

But just because *they* aren't making that comparison doesn't mean the internet isn't.

"Win," Cruz says, making the grabby motion with his hand. "Give me my phone back. Now."

"C'mon, Winifred. That's long enough," Gunnar echoes.

They don't want me to read the comments.

> *A lot of meat in that sandwich hahaha!!!!*
>
> *Guess Theo and Leo couldn't get real dates!*
>
> *The bros have always liked fixing hot messes… hopefully this will lead to a serious makeover on that house!*

The comments get more and more brutal from there.

Nauseous, I pass the phone back to Cruz. I do not look at him or Gunnar because I don't care to see how they're looking at me.

"Win–" Cruz begins.

I hold up a hand. "Don't. It's fine. I'm fine. I'm used to the online trolls. Let's get back to work."

"But–"

"Cruz, please."

"Alright…" he says, but the hesitancy in his voice is real.

My face is crumpling, and I hurry back into the reno house before either of them see me ugly-cry. At least here I can pretend that a piece of sawdust in my eye is the cause of my tears.

But the door I close behind me opens a split second later, and Gunnar follows me inside.

I meet his gaze, expecting to see pity, but there's only fire.

"Don't you believe that bullshit, Winnie Olivia Wainwright."

"Oh, you don't want me to believe I'm overweight?" I roll my eyes. "Because I know I'm overweight, Gun. They are not saying anything that's not a fact–"

"Bullfuckingshit. You're perfect just the way you are, and that's what I want you to believe, dammit." His jaw works as he stares at me. The anger in his eyes is unlike anything I've ever seen from Gunnar before. "How fucking dare anyone on this goddamn planet make you feel otherwise."

He strides towards me. He takes my face in his hands. I flinch.

My chins in his perfect hands.

Ugh. But still, from the way he's holding me, I'm expecting the world's most passionate kiss. Yet, he just looks at me.

TEN HAMMERS

And looks and looks. It's like he's trying to form a telepathic connection so that I won't just hear his spoken words, but his thoughts as well.

So I'll know he's telling the truth.

"It was an unflattering picture," he says. "It was deliberately chosen by the paparazzi *scum* because it looks like Theo and Leo were miserable with you while you were obviously having an amazing time. It's a bullshit money-making ploy designed and executed by parasites. And people are pouncing on it, and being cruel, because people can be shits. But do you think Theo and Leo were miserable, Win?"

I'm suddenly exhausted. Even my tears are dripping from my eyes slowly, as if they don't have the energy to go at it whole-heartedly. "Look, Gun, I just need to be by myself for a while. I'll get over this, okay?"

"Nope." He lets go of my face to take my hands. He lifts them to his mouth, kissing my knuckles. "You're hurting and I'm not going to leave you alone. Sorry not sorry."

"Gunnar–"

"Theo and Leo were with you because they wanted to be with you, Winnie. I will keep telling you this until hell freezes over or it sinks in, whichever comes first, but we all want you. *Want* you, Winnie. You have a beautiful soul, and it's wrapped up in an equally beautiful body and I want you so damn bad."

I swallow hard, my cheeks flushing from his words and his gaze, as he stares at me.

"I want you right this second." His voice is growing huskier the longer he stares. "I want to show you how much I want you."

I shiver and he then nods, as if he's been having a silent conversation with himself. "Let me show you, Win."

He dries my tears with his fingertips and kisses me. Then he unbuckles one strap of my overalls. "May I?"

"Um…"

He raises his eyebrows. "That a no, sweet girl?"

"Um…" I look around. "Here?"

His eyes twinkle mischievously. "Well, unless you want to wait until my secret project is done. I'm turning the basement into a sex dungeon complete with shackles on the wall and–"

Despite myself, I laugh. "Gunnar. You are not."

He unbuckles my other strap and I shimmy out of the overalls. I'm down to my tank top and panties, and he shakes his head, as if he's in actual awe.

"How do you know I'm not building you a sex dungeon?" His voice sounds like it belongs to a man who would be building his lover a sex dungeon as he leans in close. I can feel his mouth move against mine as he speaks.

I laugh again. "Because this house doesn't have a basement."

"Fucking hell." His fingertips skin my jawline. "Lay down, Win," he says, his voice somehow deeper, thicker and sexier.

Fucking hell indeed.

"Right here?" I squeeze my thighs together as my panties dampen.

"Right here."

CHAPTER 29

Diesel

I'm supposed to be searching for Gunnar, who is the only damn one of us with the full certifications for the kind of delicate electric rewiring that needs to be done, according to Jack, Right. This. Second. Naturally Jack is in the garage, losing his shit because Gunnar is nowhere to be found, and Jack can't stop being a micromanager, waving that damn clipboard around.

And now I keep hearing sounds echoing through the entryway. I'm thinking it's a lost kitten, probably stuck in a closet or box of tools or something. Poor thing.

I need to go looking for it, especially when the mewling grows louder and louder. I can't just leave a kitten to suffer. What kind of sadistic fucker would I be if I didn't go and search for it?

It sounds like a very insistent and very, very hungry kitten.

Well, well, well. Imagine my utter shock and delight when I follow the mewling down the hall and look over to the stairwell and find a certain vixen laying backward against the stairs, arms up over her head, gripping the banister as if for dear life.

One hundred percent naked.

Her tits are stretched as she grips the banister, and her perky nipples bounce as her breath heaves.

And her legs. Sweet, merciful Lord, her *legs*. Bare and spread, positioned so that her knees are bent, her feet on one step, and her lacy yellow panties hooked around one ankle.

The only crappy part of the view of her spread legs is Gunnar's big, stupid head right there in the middle of them, blocking the best part. Guess he found the pussy cat first.

I'm struck with instant jealousy, sure, but I gotta give Gunnar credit where credit is due: he's clearly got an expert mouth because Winnie's hungry little kitten mews have become full blown tigress moans, now. She's not holding back. She's so loud neither of them even hear me approach.

Gunnar is making his usual *oh yum, you taste like honey, smack, smack* sounds. Same as I used to hear coming from his room when we were roommates back in our college days, trying to get a music career going. Personally, I think he sounds stupid but Winnie is making cute little answering sounds back, and adding in some whimpers.

Fuck me, my cock is hard as a rock. I want to be the guy making her whimper and mew like that, though, and I try not to wonder what my odds are with Winnie. Why would she choose me, anyway? I'm the only one among all of my brothers who has never even been in a serious relationship. Who knows whether or not I could be faithful to one woman?

Well, sure, if it's Winnie, I could. That is one thing I do know without a doubt. But I don't have any kind of track record to prove it to her.

I hate to ruin their fun – I do, honestly – but Winnie doesn't even appear close to coming, because Gunnar looks like he's using his tongue to recite long, languorous love poems into her clit, rather than giving her a quick and dirty lashing.

Like, Gunnar knows we're on a schedule, right? Jack's schedule, which is tighter than the Marines, probably.

"Aren't you afraid of getting sawdust in your coochie?" I say.

Gunnar lifts his head and Winnie's knees knock together as she tries to hide herself, but because they're both sex-drunk, their movements are slow.

"That's exactly what I told him," Winnie says with a laugh.

Gunnar blinks at me, irritated. "She's on my shirt." His frowning mouth drips with her juices, and he wipes his face with the back of his arm.

And Winnie, sweet Lord, even with her knees together, I can see her pussy glistening at me like a beacon.

The underside of her sweet ass cheeks peek out. They are rubbed pink from Gunnar's shirt, or the stairs, I don't know, but the sight makes my mouth water. My cock is straining toward her.

"What the fuck do you want, Diesel? You can't see we're busy?" Gunnar growls.

"Take it up with Jack. Today is rewiring day, in case you've forgotten."

Gunnar groans, curses, and then returns to Winnie, spreading her wide again. She tries to hide herself but he hugs her legs, and I ache to be in his place, holding her bare body open to me.

"Oh, no you don't," he says with a mischievous laugh. "You're not finished yet. I want to hear you come."

"But what about Diesel–" she protests.

"Diesel thinks the view is fantastic from here, thanks," I reply with a wink. "Please don't change it."

She laughs. "But what about Jack?"

That works. With a final aggravated groan, Gunnar lets go, and Winnie closes her legs tight.

Well, as tight as she can when the stairs allow for her cute pink ass and that beckoning pussy of hers to remain on display if I stare enough.

And I do.

Gunnar kisses her. "Have you at least forgotten the bullshit internet comments yet?"

She shakes her head and leans back on her elbows, looking at Gunnar with wide, fuck-me eyes and a pretty pout.

"Is there anything I can do to help?" I ask.

They turn to me in unison.

Winnie stare is sultry, feverish, her teeth caught on her bottom lip. "Yes, please."

The resignation in Gunnar's eyes as he looks at me and nods once does make me feel a little bad for the guy. But holy shit. He drops one last kiss on Winnie, this time over her nipple, and she moans, her legs falling open again.

"You'll probably want to take off your tool belt," Gunnar snarls at me as he walks away.

Leaving me with my dirtiest fantasy, spread out in front of me. Wanting me. Primed for me. That's enough to nearly blow my load at the thought.

Ordinarily I love long and extended foreplay, but we are on Jack's schedule, after all, and my balls are ready to burst.

I strip off my belt and shirt, standing over her, taking her in up close. "You're really upset about those comments, baby?"

"I know it's stupid, and I know better than to read the comments, but I'm just sick of all the scrutiny over my fat ass—"

"Whoa, show me this so-called fat ass. I need to judge for myself."

She rolls her eyes, but she's smiling, and as I strip off my jeans, she turns her body around, her knees on the stair, her elbows resting a couple steps up.

With her ass on display, and the way she gazes back at me over her shoulder, I can't wait anymore.

"Mmm." I grab her ass cheeks, spreading them before me while she blinks her sinful eyes at me and blushes. "I love this ass."

I pop my thumb into my mouth, and then brush it across the tight ring of her asshole.

Her eyes widen and her body bucks automatically. I don't remove my thumb from her tight entrance and she makes a sexy squealing sound deep in her throat.

"That okay?"

She nods, and I love the mix of surprise and excitement in her eyes. I do it again, this time rubbing a circle around her hole. The new sound she lets out is a cross between a squeal and a moan, and so fucking hot I can't wait anymore.

Her pussy is slick and I slide right in. With her ass in the air, she's at the perfect angle to be fucked hard, and it doesn't take more than a few frantic thrusts before we're both coming together. Our shouts of pleasure are probably loud enough for the others to hear, even at the other side of the house.

"I want to stay inside you forever." My voice is low and raspy now.

Hers is, too, when she replies, "Then do. Let's stay like this. They can finish the reno around us." She sighs deeply. "Screw the hater paparazzi and their stupid photos. God, I feel amazing."

The smirk tugs at my lips, refusing to be denied. My girl was sex-drunk with Gun, but it seems I've taken it to a whole 'nother level.

I straighten and run my hands over that perfect ass before pulling out. We both shudder when I do. Then I lower my head and press one kiss to each of those voluptuous cheeks.

"Deez!" She sounds embarrassed.

I do it again. "I'm in love with your ass because it is *your* ass, Winnie Wainwright, and I'm in love with you."

I give her ass another nibble and expect her to laugh or groan or anything. "Fuck, Win, I want to spread these sweet cheeks and run my tongue along–"

I realize suddenly that she's completely silent. Frozen.

It was the L word, wasn't it? Well, shit. I didn't mean to say I *loved* her like that. Or at all.

Everyone knows right after you fuck is the wrong time to tell a girl you love her for the first time. Especially when you're doing it for the first time.

She doesn't say anything back.

Fuck.

She clears her throat. "Well. We should probably get dressed before…you know. This becomes a show with a live audience."

"Probably a good idea," I agree. Mostly to put any other words between us than my ill-fated *I love you*.

I help her up. Pick up and pass back her sexy-as-fuck yellow panties. Then, with our backs turned to each other by unspoken agreement, we each put our own clothes on.

"I'm starting to feel like a bit of a nympho," she admits with an embarrassed chuckle. There's the sound of fabric against skin. "But I really, really, really like having sex."

Obviously I'm thrilled that she's a fan of sex, but I'm not sure what to say now.

I said I was in love with her and she says back something is basically telling me I'm one of ten guys that she really, really likes having sex with?

She's definitely not choosing me.

"Well." I pause to swallow the ridiculous emotion I don't want her to hear in my voice. "You've got a lot of ready and willing bodies to give you all the sex you want, peach. So… any time you get an itch, all you've gotta do is ask."

I'm so glad she can't see my face right now. I probably look like I've swallowed one of Cruz's nasty work boots.

"I know," she says. "I just don't want it to seem like I'm in this just to cock-hop. It's not just about the sex."

"Too bad," I tease. "Because if it was just about the sex, I'd automatically be your favorite Hammer. I'm pretty sure I'm the best in bed."

Should I add that I usually have more staying power?

I sneak a peek over my shoulder. She's dressed and fixing her overall straps now.

"Well, I've never had you in a bed, so I can't comment on that," she says, and her tone is teasing too.

She turns around and our eyes meet. And I can't stop my fucking mouth, again.

"Winnie, I didn't tell you I'm in love with you just because we had sex."

She looks down quickly, adjusting a strap on her overalls.

"I loved you before the sex, I mean. I've said it hundreds of times in my head. I just couldn't hold it back anymore."

She looks up at me with those big eyes. And unless she's just seen the ghost of Gram, floating around my head, I think it's safe to say my words are putting an expression of extreme terror on her face.

She doesn't love me back, clearly.

Well, fuckity-fuck.

"So…" I say hoping to change the subject. "This doesn't count as my date, does it? Because I was looking forward to tonight."

To my extreme dismay, she looks more panicked than before.

Fuck, how did I manage to make this worse?

"Do you hear Jack calling us?" she exclaims, suddenly. "I think I hear him. We should go."

"No–" I start to answer.

Don't go! I want to finish.

But what I say instead is, "Sounds good, bud."

I don't know why I said that, to be honest, but now she's paying attention instead of walking away.

Her expression is incredulous. "Did… you just call me *bud?*"

With a sheepish grin, I shrug.

And then, because I don't want things to stay weird between us, but I am so out of my element here, I resort to childish antics and give her perfect butt cheeks a two-palm squeeze before dashing off ahead of her.

"Hurry up, peach! We've got work to do."

CHAPTER 30

Winnie

I hadn't actually heard Jack calling us, and I'm pretty sure Diesel could see right through my lame excuse to beeline away from emotion. But *bud?* What the hell was *that?*

More importantly, I LOVE YOU? What the hell was *that?!*

I think there needs to be a new rule, possibly the most important one: *No one tells Winnie that they love her. Not while her heart is fully cracked into ten even pieces.*

Just the thought of Diesel's words makes me panic. And forget where I'm going or what I'm doing, which is why, as I round the corner, I smash face-first into Jack's chest. Possibly breaking my nose on his rock hard pecs.

My nose smarts, my eyes prick with tears, and I howl, which summons the whole crew instantly.

"Are you okay?" Jack asks, holding me by the shoulders. He tilts his head this way and that, examining me, as the others gather around, all of them concerned.

TEN HAMMERS

I groan, but more from embarrassment than pain.

"Well, you're not bleeding," Doctor Jack says with a nod. "That's good. Still, maybe we should go across the street and get an ice pack to–"

"No way, Mr. We've Got To Stay On Schedule." Gunnar shakes his head with a glare. "You're not getting any alone time with her today. Not after you interrupted *mine*."

I can still feel Gunnar's head between my thighs when I look at him. A hot flush creeps up my neck.

Then I catch Diesel watching me.

I'm in love with you.

I can hear his voice when I look at him. I swear I can see that love in his eyes now. Has he always looked at me like that?

My brain is still short circuiting, because holy fuck, Diesel Hammer literally just kissed my ass.

And I liked it.

"I can get my own ice pack," I say because I'm overcome by the need to have Diesel Hammer not look at me like he wants to spread my sweet cheeks and do God only knows what to me.

All things I'd scream *yes, please!* to without thinking twice.

I call out, "I'll be right back," before beelining across the street. I head first to the kitchen for a bag of frozen peas, then up to my room. I lock the door behind me and sag against it. Try to control my breathing and my heart, because they're both all over the damn place.

Maybe the frozen peas will shock me back to my senses?

No, although they do feel good on my nose, and will hopefully keep me from looking like I'm ready to lead Santa's sleigh through the dark of night, just in time for my date with Diesel.

A date that hopefully won't get photographed and gossiped about all over the Internet.

Oh God, what is my life?

My chest hurts. And I suspect that the cause of the pain is less because of the awful comments online and more the realization tightening its grip on me that this journey is leading to a moment where I *must* choose one of the Hammer brothers.

And I must choose *one* of the Hammer Brothers.

How on earth can I make such a choice? The mere thought leaves me frozen, and my mind auto-rejects the idea of choosing any of them as my one and only. I've experienced incredible chemistry with each brother, and they all treat me like their queen.

And what happens to the others when I choose? I can't bear to imagine it.

When I'm utterly unsuccessful at getting myself under any kind of control, I pull my phone out of my back pocket.

I'm reluctant to open it after keeping it silent and ignoring it all morning, but when I do, I see that Goldie has sent me fifteen texts and I've had four missed calls, and the same amount of voice messages from her, too—I'm assuming she's seen the photo.

"Well, it's about damn time!" Goldie's familiar voice bubbles forth as soon as she answers, and there's nothing in it but enthusiasm. "That picture!"

Sorry I didn't pick up. Gunnar was going down on me on the stairs, and then I had sex with Diesel…

Obviously, I can't tell what I was doing, because I need to ease her into this crazy new journey of mine. I already failed to ease myself into this crazy new journey of mine, and I can't have her brain short-circuiting, too.

"So you've seen the picture?" I say.

"Hell yeah, I've seen it! Obviously, I'm going to need you to spill the tea. Because girl, things looked hot and heavy."

"Emphasis on the heavy, I guess," I say with a cringe.

"Hey," she says. "You know I get you, right?"

Goldie and I are about the same size, but she doesn't have the same self-doubts her appearance as I do mine.

"I know. But you read the comments, right?"

"Win. I mean, I scrolled but we don't care about them, remember? Well, except for the ones from people wishing they were you. What the clueless idiots have to say doesn't matter."

I nod even though she can't see it.

"But I also know for a fact," she marches on, "that it doesn't matter what you weigh. You could be physically flawless and the vultures would still find something to pick apart. Jealous fuckers."

"I don't recall Cynthia Sinclair getting this treatment."

"Well, but yeah. I mean, is Cynthia Sinclair actually mortal, Win? She defies all criticism."

"What you mean is that *she's* the kind of girl that people expect the Hammer brothers to have on their arm."

"What I mean is that *you* need to stop hating on yourself. And also, I'm sorry, but no. You were not on a Hammer brother's arm. You were pretty much in the prequel to Theo & Leo Have A Threesome. *That's* what got tongues wagging. Now spill the tea, girl!"

I draw in a deep breath and let it out slowly. "We decided to try dating. All of us, like the whole Winnie's Favorite Hammer idea. Obviously I date them all one-by-one. Or, I guess two-by-one, sometimes."

"Ah, so you're saying the picture actually was taken before the threesome?" she jokes.

"After," I confess.

There's a moment of silence just before it sounds like she's inhaled an entire pizza and is choking on it.

I wait.

Finally, the hacking subsides and she sputters, "Are you *serious?* Am I talking to a non-virgin right now? If you had your first time with Theo and Leo, I am going to–"

Despite everything, I laugh. "My first time was with Gav."

"Hell yeah it was! WINNIE OLIVIA WAINWRIGHT. Tell me *everything*."

I tell her *almost* everything. There are some things I do need to keep to myself.

"So…" she says when I'm done. "Have you gotten any clarity?" There's a reality television dating show buzzword for you. "Do you have any inkling at all about which one might be The One?"

I sigh. "I want them all, Golds. Even more than I did before they let me out of the friend zone."

I told Diesel this wasn't all about the sex for me, but maybe that's what it has become.

"Ughh, Golds, I'm being such a freaking cockhopper. And why? I'm still no closer to choosing."

She goes wild, insisting I'm living the dream, not being a cockhopper.

"Golds," I interrupt. "Diesel just told me he's in love with me."

The sudden silence rings loudly through the phone line.

"Okay, you really should've told me to sit down before dropping a bomb like that!" she finally says. "Easy Deezy! Oh my God, Winnie, I am so happy for you!"

I'm silent, but she happily carries on

"This is so romantic! He never could settle down and then, boom, he discovers that it was because Miss Right, or rather, Miss Wainwright, was there in front of him all along. Swooooooooon!"

I chew my lip.

"Okay," she says. "I know it's been a minute but when I say *Swoooooooooooooon!* you say *Swoooooooooooooon!*"

It's kind of a thing we do when talking about grand romantic gestures performed by book boyfriends on the page and Hollywood hunks on the screen.

"Why are you not *swooooooooooooon!*-ing with me? You're in love with Diesel, Diesel's in love with you. You should be sending me pictures of maid of honor dresses to approve by now."

"It's not that simple," I tell her.

"Oh, yeah? To me, it sounds pretty damn easy peasy Deezy squeezy! It's exactly what you've always wanted! Love! With a Hammer brother!"

I draw in a deep breath and it comes out as a laugh. A possibly slightly deranged laugh.

"Okay, so you're doing the whole Winnie's Favorite Hammer thing..."

She's drifting into producer mode on me.

"Do not ask me an open ended question," I warn her.

"First, I have to say, I bow down to you, Winnie Wainwright. You are my queen forever. I am so freaking glad you went for it. Second, since you sound conflicted… I'm assuming that A) Diesel is the only one who has told you he's in love with you and B) he's not the one you're going to choose? Those are both yes or no questions, by the way."

This isn't something I'm proud to admit, even to myself, much less out loud to someone else.

"I've been so enraptured by the journey I kind of… well, I won't say forgot… but… definitely have not been giving much thought, if any, to the final destination. Then Diesel said those words and I am officially shaken to the core. He didn't follow the telling-someone-you-love-them rules."

Okay, even I know what I'm saying sounds ridiculous.

"The rules?"

"Golds. You're a reality TV producer. You know the rules. They say *I think I'm falling in love with you*. Then, at a later time, they say, *I'm falling in love with you*. Then, after that comes *I'm in love with you*. Diesel just blew past the first two stages. I had no warning, no…"

"Ahhh. You've just realized you have the power to break their hearts and it *terrifies* you," Goldie says.

Just hearing her say it clenches my chest up again. When we started this experiment, I only worried about myself getting hurt. I felt lucky just to discover they're interested in me, so to think I could have one Hammer love me the way I loved him was too good to be true.

Now, I see the darker side. I know they said there would be no hard feelings, but there will be broken hearts… and why the fuck didn't I even consider that my heart might not be the only one?

"I'm a selfish cow," I wail to Goldie. "Should I just end the whole thing now? Save all our hearts before any more feelings are out in the open?"

"Winnie Olivia Wainwright, I know you don't think that just because Easy Deezs said it, he's the only one who has caught the feels. If these boys all want to line up and date you one by one, there's a chance feelings are already at play. And why not. You're hot, you're sweet, you have great taste in best friends…"

"So what do I do?"

"You probably know what I'm going to say.

"It better not be *follow your heart*, Goldie."

She sighs. I was right.

"Alright," I say. "You want me to follow my heart? That's impossible, Goldie. Because following my heart means I have all of them. Seriously. All ten of the Hammer brothers all to myself forever and always. That is what I want."

Greedy as it sounds, it's the truth.

CHAPTER 31

Axel

I don't mean to listen in on Winnie's conversation with Goldie, I swear on my life.

Not at first, at least. I woke up to a barrage of online bullshit regarding a picture of Winnie dancing, got sucked in, and spent far too long anonymously battering trolls with my wit. I know, I know, useless past time, as they weren't even bright enough to realize they were being outwitted. But before I realized, half the morning was gone.

That's when Winnie came bursting into her room. Her room and mine share a wall, and this house has walls that are a bit thin.

So when that girl throws around words like *cockhopper* and *love* and *all ten of the Hammer brothers*... Well, a guy would have to physically and forcefully cover his ears in order to stop listening.

Like hell I'm doing that.

Especially when I'm fully engrossed in the story of Diesel telling Winnie that he loves her (shit, Deez, seriously? Rookie mistake, brother). I'm only hearing one side of the conversation, yeah, but I can imagine Goldie reacting to it well enough.

And I'm laughing at Diesel, quietly, but then Winnie says, "Should I just end the whole thing now? Save all our hearts before any more feelings are out in the open?" and my heart sinks down into the pit of my stomach.

No no no, that is the last thing I want. The last thing any of us will want. Except Max, maybe.

But I know that sound in Winnie's voice all too well. She's more guarded than Fort Knox. She wants to run, as if running away from us will make anything easier.

For her, maybe it will, but it won't be easy for me. I have been deeply in love with that girl for too much of my life for feelings to be easy. Since long before the family pact to not date her. And now that I have kissed her, and placed my mouth in the perfect spot to pull the sweetest sounds out of her, I will fight to keep her.

"I'm a selfish cow," she says, and it sounds like she is in tears.

My heart twists at the anguish in her voice.

"So what do I do?" she asks. "It better not be *follow your heart*, Goldie."

And then I'm not sure I'm hearing things right. I can't be.

Holy shit, did Winnie Wainwright just say that she wants *all* of us. All to herself? *Forever and always?*

Weirdly, no matter how I picture it, I'm fine with it. I'm grinning, even.

Even though she sounds close to devastated by the impossibility of the idea, if there is any girl capable of taking on me and each and every one of my brothers, it's the incomparable Winnie Wainwright. She's all heart, laughter, and quick thinking, and won't let any of us piss her off without saying so.

I vow here and now to seek our girl out as soon as her conversation with Goldie ends, and put an end to any doubt or worry weighing over her about us. I'll have to be careful not to let her know I've overheard her, naturally. Hopefully I can get her to talk to me willingly.

At least that's my plan until she laughs and says, "Oh my God, Golds! All three holes at the same time?"

She's not talking about…?

"Obviously I'm new to all this," she says with another laugh. "Would that even be possible? They're all so huge. I told Leo and Theo I wasn't ready for anal but… if three of them want to try…what you just suggested…with me, I don't think it would be possible for me to say no."

Am I dead? Did Jack realize I haven't yet shown up to work and has somehow murdered me? Because this has to be Heaven. There are too many words coming from that girl's sweet cupid mouth that have my dick jumping to attention and my heart rate ramping up. The thought that she'd be up for what is basically my wildest fantasy has me losing my mind.

Also, wait, did Theo and Leo come right out and ask her for an invite to come in the backdoor? Brass balls on those two. You wait on a woman to offer that access like the goddamn gift it is.

I need to get out of my room or else I'll wind up jacking off to thoughts of Winnie and whichever hole she might want me inside for the rest of the afternoon. Tempting, but also tempting fate a little too much when it comes to pissing off Jack.

I put on my glasses and sneak out of my room quietly enough that Winnie won't hear me and know I've been eavesdropping. I'm in the hall when I hear her winding up her conversation with Goldie, so I race down the stairs and into the kitchen. I lean against the counter casually, grab an apple from the fruit basket and take a bite.

A minute later, I hear her footsteps at the bottom of the stairs.

"Hey, you," I say as she comes into the kitchen.

"Axel. Hey. I thought everyone was across the street."

"I was. But then I got hungry so…" I hold up the apple, nearly finished now. "Have you eaten yet?"

She shakes her head.

"Think Jack would kill us if we played hooky until after I made us some French toast and we fueled up properly?" I toss the core into the garbage can.

"Yes, I do, actually," she says, walking over to the counter and grabbing a couple of granola bars. She tosses me one. "Let's go."

"Wait a sec," I say. "I have something to run by you."

My date with her is tomorrow night, and with the photo of Winnie dancing with Theo and Leo circulating as rapidly as it is, I doubt she'll want to be out and about where more cameras will find her. I was going to take her roller skating, at the rink we used to go to in middle school. I thought she'd love the nostalgia of it all. But now, I have an even better idea. It's brilliant if I do say so myself.

"What do you think about Diesel and Cruz tagging along with us on our date?"

No, I'm not just thinking I need two extra cocks for the three holes thing. But I mean. If they're there and she wants to…

I have to fight to keep the grin from sliding back on my face at the thought. But her expression is serious. Too serious.

She's tilted her head, contemplatively, and is chewing on her bottom lip. "Well. I'm not sure. The dates are supposed to give us, y'know, alone time. To help me choose."

I close the distance between us, settling my hands on her shoulders. Gently massaging the crook of her neck with my fingertips, I say, "I don't want my date to be about choosing, sweetheart. I want it to be about making sure you're enjoying every moment of this time we all have together without worrying about choosing."

She cocks an eyebrow at me. "How much of my conversation with Goldie did you overhear?"

Well, so much for keeping her from finding out about my foray into eavesdropping. Maybe subtlety is not my strong suit. But at least I'm not dropping any L-bombs on her and making her more confused about her feelings.

"A little," I admit. "But I'm glad I did." I run the pad of my thumb along her lower lip. "We're supposed to be open and honest with each other, remember? I can't speak for all of my brothers, Win, but if you're not ready to choose one of us when the reno is done, I don't see why you should have to. You should have as much time as you need. It's not a decision that you should have to rush. And I'm personally fine with things staying just the way they are until you're comfortable with changing the situation."

She raises her eyebrows. "Isn't that just putting off the inevitable, though? Prolonging it is only going to make things harder."

I push her curls out of her face. I need her to stop thinking about what happens in a couple of weeks or a couple of months or whenever and just enjoy now.

All of a sudden, her cheeks flush bright pink. "Oh, my goodness. Did you hear the part about–"

I raise my eyebrows. "The part about what?" I ask, innocently.

"Oh, no, you heard. You *heard*."

She goes to cover her face with her hands and I capture them with my own before she can. I kiss one flushed cheeks, then the other, and whisper, "Winnie. I don't ever – and I mean *ever* – want you to be ashamed or embarrassed about any fantasy you have. Okay? If you don't promise me anything else, promise me that no matter who you end up with, it'll be a man who moves heaven and earth to make every one of your fantasies come true, and never *ever* makes you feel any damn kind of way for having those fantasies."

Her beautiful, thoughtful eyes are wide.

"So…" She twists my fingers with hers. "You're saying if I wanted to… do what Goldie and I were talking about…"

"You just say the word."

She scrunches up her nose. "Is that why you want Cruz and Deez to come with us tomorrow night?"

I shake my head and drop kisses onto her knuckles. "Nope. No pressure on that front. Or rear, as it were." I grin at her. "I just want to remind you that we are very, very, *very* good at sharing, so you understand that none of us are going to pressure you into making any kind of decision before you're good and ready. We never should've given you a deadline."

Will everyone else agree with this? I don't know. But they sure as hell better.

I study her face as she considers my words. She's deep in thought, and I've wished I could read minds for the first time since we were kids and picking super powers.

"So where are we going on our date?" she finally asks.

"It's a surprise," I tell her.

"Because I really don't know if I want to be out in public with the three of you after… You saw the picture, right?"

"I might've, you know, spent my morning baiting some trolls."

She rolls her eyes and wags a finger at me. "You'll never learn."

"I'll never stop defending your honor, Miss Wainwright. Even if I have to do it as *RandoGuy75121*."

She doesn't have to worry about any cameras tomorrow.

It'll just be me, Cruz, Diesel, a helluva lot of trees, and maybe a squirrel or two.

I tell her so, and then, even though Jack might try to kill me for making us even later, I pull her to me, and drop a kiss on her lips.

I might not be able to read minds, but I know, as she starts to pull away, that she doesn't want us to be even later… so I deepen the kiss. She sighs sweetly and I know I've got her.

My hands tangle in her curls as she surrenders her mouth to mine. It's hard not to test how long she'll let me kiss her, or if she'll let me touch her, too.

This girl. I want to kiss her forever. But with every moan she makes, I can't help but picture Jack lurking by to catch us.

"Come on," I finally growl as I reluctantly pull away. "Let's get this day over with so that we can be closer to our date, and pick this up without the fear of Jack lurking over our shoulders."

She laughs. "You keep picturing him jumping out and catching us, too, don't you?"

"Waving a hammer at us, yeah."

She grabs my hand, lacing our fingers together. "Terrifying, now let's go," she says with a mock-shiver as she pulls me toward the door.

CHAPTER 32

Winnie

"How much longer 'til we get there?" I ask.

It's the next night and I'm sitting between Axel and Diesel in the front of Axe's extended cab pickup as he drives us to what he's reassured me is a remote and perfect date destination. Diesel's arm is slung around my shoulders and I've been idly playing with his fingers during the drive. Cruz, in the backseat, curls my hair around his finger. It would be perfect except the blindfold I'm wearing is making me too antsy. I want to see everything there is to see on this date with my favorite triplets.

"Do not answer her," Axel warns his brothers as he drops a hand from the steering wheel to the top of my thigh. "I don't want to give her any hints about where we're going."

Diesel laughs and drops his mouth to the top of my shoulder. "You could give Win thirty hints and she'd never guess," he says, his lips skimming across my skin.

Okay, perhaps the blindfold isn't too bad an idea, not when it heightens every single touch.

"You could've at least gotten road trip snacks, bro," Cruz grumbles.

"We'll have plenty to eat when we get there," Axel says.

"If you're bored, Win, blame it on Axe." Cruz says, and I can practically see the adorable pout on his mouth. "He shot down my idea to liven up the drive."

"Which was?" I ask, cocking my head in Cruz's direction. "Also, not to be Cathy Complainer, but this blindfold is making my eyeballs sweat."

Diesel laughs again. "He wanted to put a mattress in the back so the two of you could spend the ride stargazing." The hand I'm holding moves and he emphasizes the word *stargazing* like he's put air quotes around it.

"Oh, I'd be seeing stars, alright," Cruz comments, making me smile. I don't have to be able to see to know he's waggling his eyebrows.

"And I told him I'm not his chauffeur and my truck is not his fuckmobile," Axel states.

There's a smile in Axel's voice and he gently kneads my thigh, his glorious hand slipping higher up my leg.

"Aww, poor Cruz," I say, unable to hide my giddy smile. "Cruzie, if it makes you feel any better, any time you want, we can drive your truck somewhere and park it and I'll lie in the back with you and stargaze."

I reach my free hand behind me and Cruz grabs it, pulling it gently so that he can nibble my fingertips.

"You doing anything tonight, darlin'?" he jokes.

"I don't know. You tell me," I shoot back.

Cruz makes an appreciative sound, and both Axel and Diesel squeeze where they touch me, hand and thigh, and I feel all of their touches in every fiber of my being.

After talking with Axel yesterday, after my call with Goldie, the anticipation I have had for our date has had me feeling like a kid waiting for their birthday party. The permission Axe gave me to embrace my fantasies unlocked a freedom I've never felt before.

Last night, I told my boys that I wanted to have a night to myself, a long bubble bath and my own bed. I insisted I needed to give my body time to recover, but really, I pulled out my dildo collection and experimented some more.

I've fucked each of my "boys" plenty, but last night it felt different. I didn't have any lube, but with the memory in my mind of Gunnar on the stairs, lapping me up, and then Diesel turning me around, his thumb touching my ass as he fucked me, I was slippery and ready.

Pushing the first dildo inside my ass didn't feel like I thought it would. I picked my smallest, mightiest one, and after fucking my pussy to get it slick, I moved to my knees and circled my ass with the tip. There was resistance when I pushed inside, and my muscles clenched tight at the strange feeling. I winced as I stretched and had to remember to breathe and go slow in order to relax enough for my body to adjust. I nearly gave up. But the thought of Diesel behind me, his hands gripping my hips renewed my excitement. And when I touched my clit, the jolt of electricity that hit me was nearly as powerful as the feeling

Diesel's touch had given me when he fucked me on the stairs.

It took biting my lip hard to keep from gasping and moaning loudly at the surprisingly sweet sensations that washed over me as I allowed my body to take a bigger dildo. And by the time I came, muffling my cries into my pillow, I was no longer afraid of how much anal sex would hurt. I was wetter than ever just imagining it.

In the confines of Axel's truck, breathing in Diesel's familiar scent, I grow wet all over again. I'm tempted to turn my head and seek out his lips.

Then I hear the distinct sound of Axel putting on the blinker and we're making a left-hand turn. And slowing down.

The blinker again. A right-hand turn. Slowing down more.

The road turns into gravel, crunching under the wheels as the truck coasts forward. Axel's pulling into a parking space.

"Are we here?" I ask.

"We are here," he announces. "But do not take the blindfold off."

Diesel helps me out, and he keeps a steady arm around me as leads me away from the truck. The air is heavy with the rich scent of earth and pine. The gravel gives way to leaves crunching beneath my feet as I'm guided into what I'm sure is a forest, or at least a heavily wooded area.

"We're camping," I say, glad the blindfold covers up my tears as memories of my childhood camping trips with the Hammer family flood my mind.

TEN HAMMERS

The aroma of wood smoke and roasted marshmallows, the crackling sound of the campfire, and the laughter echoing through the trees, were all core memories for me. Not to mention Anna's makeshift kitchen, with the stunning view of a babbling brook, and the array of culinary delights prepared by the brothers as they scrambled to impress me with their cooking prowess. The taste of charred hot dogs and extra-gooey s'mores still lingers on my tongue.

And after our campfire dinner always came the games. They changed over the years as we grew from kids into teenagers, the raucous rounds of hide-and-seek giving way to intense poker games and Truth or Dare. Their playful competitiveness never failed to make me laugh.

Cuddled up under the stars together, watching the campfire snap and flicker until we were falling asleep in our blankets…

I used to live for camping weekends with the Hammers.

Sure, Gram had said the first time I asked her permission to go camping with them. *With you gone at suppertime, I might actually get a bite.*

After that, I rarely ate in front of Gram or my dad if I could avoid it, but it was like they competed to see who could tell the meanest weight-related joke sometimes.

I push thoughts of Gram and my father away. Thankfully, they haunt me less frequently, and when they do, their embarrassing criticisms grow easier to ignore.

Axel's voice brings me back to the present. "Ready, Win?"

His fingers are where the blindfold is tied at the back of my head. I nod.

As Axel unveils the campsite, my eyes widen in awe. Inside a wide ring of trees, edged with glowing golden orbs and flickering lanterns, is a billowing white tent. It's more Taj Mahal than traditional camping gear, and it sparkles inside and out with fairy lights.

Plush rugs lead to a circle of benches around the fire pit.

"What is this place?" I wonder aloud as curiosity pulls me toward the tent's entrance. As I peek inside, my breath catches. The interior is a haven—a vast mattress, adorned with luxurious blankets and plush pillows. Soft, ambient lighting from star-shaped lanterns wash the space in a warm romantic aura. The thought of this intimate bedroom under the stars fills me with a warmth that spreads through my entire body. I'm ready to strip off my clothes and dive in, it looks so cozy.

And I might. There's not a single other person, or camera in sight. My boys turned camping into a secret romantic fairy tale, and I feel more cherished than ever before.

I practically skip back toward them, and they all watch me with identical grins.

"Is this okay?" Axel asks.

"It's better than okay," I reply, my voice catching with emotion. "It's perfect."

"We just have to be back by noon tomorrow," he tells me. "But we've got all night to do whatever you want."

I glance at the tent entrance again, and shiver thinking about doing whatever I want inside it with three of my boys.

"Who's up for a little skinny-dipping in the lake?" Cruz asks, starting to take off этот shirt.

I catch a flash of abs. My mouth instantly waters.

Diesel, who is already unpacking things, tosses a bag of marshmallows at Cruz. "And I thought you were hungry."

"Before we do anything else, we build a campfire," Axel says.,

The triplets all seem to go caveman at that plan – the invention of fire still excites them – and not twenty minutes later, we're sitting around the firepit, all of us gazing into the dancing flames.

Cruz and Diesel are manning the weenie-roasting skewers and I have my head on Axel's shoulder. We're holding hands.

"This is perfect," I whisper to Axel and when he drops a kiss on my temple I marvel over the fact that I've managed to find perfect, when I didn't even believe perfect existed.

"This one is yours, Peach," Diesel says, handing the skewer to Cruz who passes it to me.

It looks delicious, smells even better… and I don't know why but I'm suddenly shy about eating such a phallic shaped object in front of them.

Maybe I'll wait on the s'mores.

"Don't worry," Cruz says. "I solemnly swear not one of us is going to watch you eat a hot dog and think about what you look like giving a BJ."

"I don't solemnly swear shit," Diesel says with a chuckle. He winks at me.

I blush, and blow on the weenie to cool it down. Then I say, "Hey, Deez," and when he glances at me, I chomp down on it, taking a huge bite.

"Nothing you can do will turn me off, baby," he promises, winking at me again. "That I will solemnly swear."

Axel nods. "Ditto."

Goodness, but they look even more gorgeous in the firelight.

As is Hammer tradition, the games begin after we eat. Axel proposes we play Truth or Dare, which I'm eager to try now that we're adults.

The rules to our relationship have changed since we last played, so the rules of the game should change, too, right? There are bound to be plenty more truths and dares for us than ever before, and I can't wait.

Unfortunately, we're too stuffed with s'mores to do anything that requires us to move, so our game ends up being more *truth* than *dare*. And it's surprisingly more PG than not.

"What was your favorite memory from one of our renos?" Diesel asks.

"Oh, that one is easy," Cruz replies, even though technically it was Axel's turn to answer. "The Lennon house."

Cruz remembers every reno we ever did and can tell you not only what season it was but what episode, and the first names of each family member and the ages of the kids when we redid their house. He still keeps in touch with many of them.

"That was the first time I saw Winnie look comfortable on camera," he explains.

The smile he gives me is sweet and genuine and I get goosebumps.

The truth portion of our game goes on like this a while longer, and I find I don't mind. I'm wrapped up in nostalgia and Axel's strong arms, both warmer than a blanket. And I'd be happy to keep the night just this sweet and cozy.

That is until Axel raises my hand up to his mouth and brushes my knuckles with his lips. "This has been nice… now, who's up for some dares?"

And the mischievous gaze he gives me is enough to take my body from cozy-warm to too-hot and flushed.

I *definitely* am.

CHAPTER 33

Winnie

It's Diesel who speaks up first.

"Let's make it Dare or Dare," he suggests.

"Dare or Dare?" I ask, raising a brow.

Diesel grins. "It goes like this. You offer up two dares, and the person you're daring has to take one of them. Then they offer up two dares to the next person. But here's the catch—one of their dares has to be the dare they didn't take for themselves. And this goes on."

Cruz snickers. "You just made that up, didn't you?"

"Well, yeah," Diesel admits.

"No, wait," I jump in. "It sounds like fun. But there are four of us, so why don't we make it Dare or Dare or Dare or Dare?"

They all look at me like I've inhaled too much smoke, but I'm really liking this idea, now.

I hold up a hand. "Hear me out. I'll give Diesel four dares. He takes one, and the next three pass along to Cruz. Then the next two pass along to Axe. Then the dare none of you took becomes the dare I *have* to take."

"All I want to know is… does this game end with us naked in the lake?" Cruz asks. "Because I'm fine with that."

I laugh. "Maybe." I wiggle my brows.

"I'm in."

Axel winds a finger around one of my curls and gives it a tug. "Go ahead, Win."

"Okay. Diesel, here are your dares." I hold up a finger as I think about it for a moment. "Dare one, strip down to your undies and don't put your clothes back on for the rest of the night."

"Wait, hold on," Cruz cuts in. "Deez, skip that one. If either of you keep Winnie from having to take it, or your body's gonna be found at the bottom of the lake in a couple weeks when they drag it."

I can't help my grin, and when Axel sees it and grins back at me, the twinkle in his eye tells me he knows I have something more up my sleeve.

"Dare two," I say sweetly. "Take off your shirt and don't put it back on for the rest of the night. Dare three, give any one of us a lap dance for a full minute. And dare four, put on the blindfold and kiss everyone here, to see if you can tell who is who."

"Wait, hold on," Cruz cuts in again, and the other guys groan. "No seriously, I change my mind. Leave the last one for Win. I don't give a shit about kissing you two losers, but the thought of Winnie's luscious mouth on me is too much. It trumps anything."

My cheeks warm up with the look he gives me.

"Does it trump skinny-dipping?" Axel says.

Cruz gives him a serious look. "Winnie's mouth, though."

They all three murmur in agreement while looking at me like they want to devour me. Diesel rips off his shirt.

I'm glad I won't have to strip down to my panties right now. I'm not ready for them to see how wet they're making me already, and I don't think the peach cotton thong I picked out for tonight will hide it.

After Axel gives me the world's most hilarious, yet arousing, fully-clothed lap dance, Cruz peels his clothes down to his tight black boxers, his eyes on mine so intense I feel like it's me he's undressing. When his near-naked body glows like a god's in the firelight, the blindfold comes back out.

"Your turn. Get on over here Winnie," Cruz says, dangling the blindfold toward me.

"But there's just one little thing," I say with a smile as I make my way over to him. Diesel and Axel follow me, and I give them a sassy wink.

"I guess for this to work, you two boys will have to strip down to match Cruzie. Otherwise when I get handsy, your clothes will be a dead giveaway as to who is who."

I give them all a satisfied smirk. Like I didn't design the game to have this exact result. I'm a boss at campfire games.

"Oh no, you don't," Axel says.

My brows pull together.

"As much as I love the thought of you getting handsy with me, baby, *we're* kissing you, don't forget," Cruz says with a wicked grin as he saunters up behind me, and takes my hands, pinning them behind my back. His breath is warm on my neck when he runs his lips along my skin

My heart squeezes. Before I can even gather my wits about me, he has a bungee cord out and he's tying my hands at the wrist behind my back.

Well, shit, now my panties are wetter than ever. I've never even told Cruz that being tied up in his bungee cords makes the very top tier of my top sex fantasies list.

After he has my wrists tied, he covers my eyes with the bandana. His lips skim my neck again, and this time my senses are doubly heightened.

"Ready?" he says.

I nod, and there is a long moment where they force me to wait. And wait, the bastards. The anticipation has my body quivering with need.

The atmosphere shifts suddenly and then lips touch mine. Softly at first, and then fingers touch my chin, holding me steady as his mouth opens, and the touch of his tongue against mine ignites me.

It's Diesel, of course. I've known it since that moment before our lips even touched. But I kiss him and kiss him, until his hands are raking through my hair and my tongue is tangled with his. I'm already desperate to pull my hands free and touch him. Run my hands along the hard planes of his chest. His nipples.

Oh, God, it's not fair.

As if he can read my thoughts, he palms my breast, and his fingers caress my nipple. I moan, and he pulls away, leaving me whimpering as the space between us grows empty and cold.

"Diesel," I whine.

Three laughs surround me.

"Wow," I hear, and I know it's Diesel.

The next kiss is Axel. It's strong from the get-go, his lips commanding mine. He's the sweetest guy in the world but I suspect he's bold and commanding in bed. It's a place I've never been with him, and as his hands grip my hips, his thumbs stroking my belly, I'm so aware of how close the giant bed is. And how much I want to be in it with Axel. And Diesel. And Cruz.

I push my mouth into his, wanting more, and my cheek bumps his glasses. When Axel pulls away, I'm practically panting. "Axel."

The next kiss is a trick. They really are adorable for thinking this would be a challenge. I know my boys. I don't need to see them to tell them apart. Even under a sugary layer of melted marshmallows and chocolate on their tongues, the scents of them before we even touched are as distinct to my senses as the taste of them when our mouths meet.

But I play. I let Axel – this time with his glasses off – kiss me, again. I let his hands skim my tits, squeezing. I let his tongue steal every last sense in my head, other than the ability to kiss for dear life, and rock my hips into him.

"Axel, that wasn't very nice of you. It was Cruzie's turn," I say when he pulls away.

He laughs, and then it's Cruz in front of me for real this time.

When Cruz kisses me, he brushes his lips across mine with just the barest hint of contact. I smile against his mouth.

"Hi, Cruz," I say, biting back a laugh.

He takes my face in his hands, his thumbs caressing my cheeks. "Damn you're good, Win."

He whispers the words into my hair, his breath hot against my ear. Then his tongue teases my earlobe. He gives it a playful little nip as he moves his hands down to my breasts. Running a thumb over the tight bud of my nipple, he says, "Will one of you please dare me to motorboat Win?"

Diesel snorts but Axel groans. "Good God, Cruz."

"Good God is right," Cruz says, kissing my hair, and squeezing my tits. "Because I'm pretty sure I've got the sweetest heaven in my hands."

"I beg to differ," Diesel says.

I perk up at the feel of movement behind me. An arm wraps around my waist from behind and then Diesel's murmurs, "The sweetest heaven is right about… here."

One of his hands parts my thighs, slipping between them, while his other hand palms my ass. "And this is a close second."

Diesel's expert fingers rub against me through my pants while Cruz gently kneads my tits. I moan. My knees are weak. And of course, I'm wet as hell.

And then a hand takes my jaw, and it's Axel turning my face toward him. His mouth covers mine just as Diesel brushes my clit with his thumb, just right, and Cruz grazes my nipple with his teeth.

My brain suddenly can't deal with the number of hands or something because all thoughts in my head other than *holy shit!* And *ohh my God, more, more, more!* are long gone.

"Okay, Win," Cruz says, his voice huskier than I've ever heard it before. "I dare you to take off all my clothes and fuck me right here, darlin'."

I laugh against Axel's lips, but it's not like I'm not tempted to take Cruz up on the offer.

"Wait," Diesel says "Let's slow things down a little, shall we?"

"Easy for you to say, Alice," Cruz growls. "You've already been to Wonderland." Then he says, "Fine. I dare you to play Seven Minutes in the Tent with me, Win."

Axel frowns against me before pulling away and suddenly I'm alone again, and I hate that I can't see them, or touch them.

"Seven minutes is all you'll need, buddy?" Diesel teases, and his tone sounds good natured enough, but I suddenly don't want to lose three pairs of hands on my body. Or three pairs of lips against my skin.

Oh my, God, am I really thinking about that?

"Untie me now, please," I ask, and within a breath the blindfold is off and my hands are free.

I blink at them all as the firelight flickers behind them, and I'm suddenly nervous as fuck because I know what I want.

How sturdy is the bed in that tent, I wonder.

"It's okay if you want to go into the tent with Cruz, Winnie," Axel says. "Go. Have fun." Then he adds, to Cruz, "Just bring her back in one piece, alright?"

Cruz looks surprised, and turns to me, brow raised.

I glance at the tent as waves of desire wash over me. Still, I hesitate.

Then I meet Axel's eyes and hope he correctly interprets the meaningful look I give him as I say, "Actually, could we... could we go...?"

My heart is starting to race so hard that I can't get the words out right at all. Cruz and Diesel wear matching expressions of confusion as they try to figure out what I want.

"Give us a second, guys," Axel says.

Diesel is still confused, but Cruz looks positively deflated as Axel takes my hand and leads me away from the fire pit, behind one of the trees ringing the campsite.

I lean against the tree, reminding myself to breathe. My heart is... no pun intended... hammering in my chest. Axel looks down at me, his eyebrows raised slightly. The expression on his face is so gentle, so serious.

"Are you okay, Win?" he asks. "Are you trying to say you're ready for...?"

I nod, my face growing hot. "Did you bring lube?" I whisper, practically choking on the words.

Axel reaches up, his fingertips skimming the side of my face. "Yes, sweetheart, I brought lube," he whispers back. "And remember what I said. There's nothing for you to be embarrassed about."

I reach up on my toes and kiss him. "I'm ready."

"Okay," he says. "But just because you want to experiment with this doesn't mean everything has to happen tonight, alright? You can have fun with all of us without having to take all of our cocks at once, if you're not ready for that."

Oh. My. God. I am going to spontaneously combust. Did Axel Hammer really just say that to me?

"I googled positions," I confess. "It's kind of like human Tetris and I am not as bendy as women in porn. But I'm ready."

The corner of his mouth quirks up. "Well, damn. But you know, googling positions could've been an activity we did as a couple."

"The thought of looking at the naked perfect bodies of other women with you does *not* appeal to me."

"Oh, Win. I wouldn't have been looking at the screen. I would've been watching your face while *you* looked at the screen."

He sounds so sincere, I know his words are true. Yep. Definitely going to spontaneously combust.

Suddenly we're locked in the most passionate kiss of my life and that's saying a lot. Before I know what's happening, Axel has literally swept me off my feet. My back rests against the tree and my legs are around his waist and he's grinding his cock into me.

"Hey! You two get eaten by a bear or something?" Cruz calls.

Axel and I break apart.

"Do you regret not being on a one-on-one date?" I ask him, breathless.

He shakes his head. "Not a bit. Are you ready?"

I chew my lip. "I don't really know what to say to them. How do I even start? Should I just tell them I want to have sex with all of you at the same time?"

My nerves are beginning to fill my head with doubts again.

"You can," he says. "Or I can get things started for you. It'll be fine, I promise." He puts me down and takes my hand and we walk back to Diesel and Cruz, who wait expectantly.

"There must be a breeze behind that tree we're not gettin' over here," Diesel teases, "because your hair has gotten all mussed up, dollface."

I smooth down my curls and Diesel cracks, "I was talking to Axe."

I glance at Axel, and I suppose he does look like he's stuck his head in a salad spinner. His glasses are slightly crooked, too, and somehow all it does is make him look hotter than ever. I let go of his hand to comb through his locks with my fingers, taming them a bit. I straighten his glasses before dropping a kiss onto his gorgeous lips.

"Do you want to tell them or do you want me to?" Axel takes my wrist, giving me a reassuring squeeze.

For the millionth time since we've started dating, I find myself thinking: What is my life?

I clear my throat. I can't do it if I can't even say it, can I?

And I want it badly, so I blurt out, "I've been thinking about having sex with all three of you. Tonight. At the same time."

Diesel and Cruz's eyes both go real wide for a split second before they get their expressions under control.

Axel squeezes my waist.

"Shit, babe. Don't make proclamations like that around an open flame," Cruz says with a laugh. "I might pass out and fall into the campfire."

"Did Axel dare you to tell us to mess with us?" Diesel says.

"This isn't a dare. I'm not messing with you," I tell them. "It's something I really want.

"Seriously," Cruz says again. "I might pass out and fall into the fire."

"I mean," I twist my hands together. "If you are both… into the idea, that is."

"We're into the idea," Diesel and Cruz say together, without another beat.

CHAPTER 34

Winnie

The campfire might be dimming, but the fire that burns in all three of my triplets' eyes is enough to keep me warm all night. I grin at their enthusiastic response to my desires.

Still, I'm nervous. And I know why...

Chewing my lip, I look at Diesel. "First, um... Diesel... Can I talk to you for a minute?"

I gesture back in the direction of the trees where Axel and I had just been.

"Why, yes, Miss Wainwright," Diesel rakes a hand through his hair, "I'll gladly let you pull me behind a tree any day of the week."

He lopes over and I pull myself away from Axel to take Diesel's hand. I give Axel a smile. He responds with a wink.

Poor Cruz pouts again as he watches us walk away.

But I blow him a kiss and call out, "Don't worry. You'll get plenty of my time tonight, Cruzie."

My promise gets me a genuine grin, complete with dimples.

Once we're around the tree, I back Diesel up against it and stand in front of him, shifting from foot to foot.

"I need to clear the air with you," I say. "When you told me you were in love with me–"

"Shit, Win." He winces. "Can we pretend that didn't happen? It was the first time I've ever told a woman I'm in love with her, and I obviously did it wrong, and… fuck a duck, I probably just made it worse, maybe."

What's that feeling in my chest? My heart growing bigger? Seeing such a big, strong, tatted man being so sweetly vulnerable and awkward makes me swoooooooooooon.

"I've never been in love with anyone else, though, Peach," he clarifies, and his blue eyes are an ocean of sincerity. "It's only ever been you."

I cannot put into words how much I don't want to hurt this man. But Goldie was right. I can't choose based on who loves me the most or who I think I should choose. I have to follow my blasted heart.

"Deez." I squeeze his fingers in my hands. "I need you to understand why I didn't say it back. It's not because I don't feel the same way." I take a deep breath and summon all my bravery. "I am very much in love with you. But I'm very much in love with all of you."

I say it in a rush so the first part doesn't sink in before I can get the second part out. "I didn't want to tell you that your feelings are whole-heartedly reciprocated because I didn't want you to think that…well…"

"That it means you're going to choose me," he finishes for me, matter-of-fact. Whatever he's feeling, he's keeping it well-concealed. "I get it, Win. We should probably get back before—"

"I'm not done," I tell him. "I am nowhere near ready to make a final choice yet. But Diesel," I take another deep breath, hoping to inhale some courage with the fresh night air, "I do choose you to be the man I want to–well, to use your own words–spread these sweet cheeks and go where no man has gone before." I touch my butt, in case he doesn't remember. Bite my lip and add, in case I'm still not clear. "Um. Tonight. If you want."

He stares at me for what feels like forever, and then he whispers, "Holy shit, please merciful Lord, don't let me be hallucinating right now."

I laugh. "I am not really up to date on how the whole prayer thing works but I'm not sure asking to be blessed with ass sex probably isn't, you know, kosher. But you're not hallucinating and Axel has lube." And I say again, "If you want."

"I want. Oh, I want. Christ on a cracker do I want to claim your gorgeous ass tonight, Winnie Wainwright."

I laugh and Diesel laughs, too, grinning as giddily as me.

"So that's a yes."

"It's a fuck-yes. Shall we go to the tent now?"

I want to do that so much my whole body quivers at the thought. But the memory of Cruz's face as he watched his brothers go behind the tree with me has me thinking it's only fair if I pull him over here, too.

"One more thing first… can you send Cruz over here?"

Diesel lopes off, and a minute later Cruz and I are alone behind the tree.

He smiles at me curiously as I put my hands on his shoulder and rise up on my toes to drop a kiss on his lips.

"To be honest," I say, "I pulled them over here because I had confessions to make. Like, with Axel, I confessed that I secretly crave all three of you. With Diesel, I confessed that I'm hoping he'll be the one to…"

I break off, blushing.

Cruz's eyes twinkle as he says, "You're hoping he'll be the one to claim your sweet ass?"

As I nod, he scoops me up by my butt so that our mouths are in line, and pulls me against him in a kiss.

In only his boxers, I can feel he's rock solid, and I push myself closer, kiss him deeper.

"So tell me, then. Where do you want my cock, darlin'?" he says against my lips.

"In my mouth Cruzie," I whisper.

I look up at him, into fathomless blue eyes, and add, "Because, well, I suppose I have a secret confession for you after all."

His brows rise. "Yeah?"

I nod and then tell him about the How I Lose My Virginity to Cruz Hammer fantasy that I've fantasized about for years. About his bungee cords tying my wrists up to the door frame and his hands on my hips as I bounce on his cock… "So you see, if you claim my mouth tonight, maybe another night we can…"

His mouth swallows up the last of my words as he kisses me again. And then, before I can say another word, he scoops me up and we are on our way across the campsite, and toward the entrance to the tent.

Diesel is pouring water over the campfire to put it out. Smoke is billowing around him as it sizzles, giving him the appearance of a mighty god.

Axel is nowhere to be found when I search the campsite, but the tent flaps, which were rolled and pinned up, have now been closed.

As Cruz brings me into the tent, I catch sight of Axel and my heart squeezes. He's still fully dressed, but his shirt has been unbuttoned and the glow from the warm white fairy lights gives his chiseled chest a golden glow. He's placing water bottles, towels, and a bottle of lube beside the bed.

He's getting us ready for sex. The thought sends my lustful thoughts into a frenzy. I have to cross my legs when Cruz places me on the edge of the bed. I've never been so turned on in my life.

The bed itself is a colossal mattress, adorned with layers of sumptuous blankets, and piled high with plump pillows. I run my fingers over the silky sheets and close my eyes, imagining my boys naked in the bed beside me, their hard bodies against the silky fabric.

The mattress shifts as Cruz sits beside me and begins kissing me again. His mouth is soft and I sink into him, trying not to feel nervous, especially when the bed dips on the other side of me, and I don't even have to open my eyes to know that it's Diesel. When I pull back from Cruz and turn my face toward him, Diesel captures my mouth with his, tasting of wood smoke and chocolate.

Diesel cups my face, Cruz's twists my hair so he can move it aside and kiss my neck. And then I'm being ripped away from them both, abruptly.

Opening my eyes, I blink, dazed, as Axel swoops in and pulls me to a stand. I'm already growing breathless and this has only begun. Then he's kissing me, too, and Diesel and Cruz move in around me. Axel in front, Cruz and Diesel at my sides.

When the three of them each have their mouths on me, and three sets of hands roam my body, the pleasure that rockets through me feels so good that I moan and writhe. I feel so incredibly sexy with each one of their touches.

But you felt sexy on the dance floor, too, when the photograph was taken. Look how THAT turned out? I hear in my head.

A knife of ice trails along my spine and I stop kissing Axel, momentarily freaked. He doesn't seem to notice. His lips work down my neck.

I glance to one side, at Cruz. His gaze is in the direction of my stomach as his hand skims my side.

Diesel's eyes are closed and he's making just about the hottest face of ecstasy as his mouth hovers close to my nipple.

Then Cruz's mouth roves down to nuzzle my belly and his eyes are actually open as my body quivers under his lips.

I jump away from all of them. "I'm not sure I can do this, actually. Maybe in the dark—"

"Fuck no!" Cruz says. "What if Easy Deezy pokes the wrong hole? Light on."

"Sweetheart, what's the matter?"

When it comes to them exploring all of me with the lights off, I have no worries. I can only feel it, enjoy it, yearn to have my boys take me in every possible way they can. It's shocking how the only anxiety I have is about how I'll look to them. The photograph of me dancing with Theo and Leo haunts me every time I think about losing control and having fun, letting my face show my ecstasy.

My stomach twists as a wave of nausea fills me.

"What's really wrong, darlin'?" Cruz asks. "Are we that ugly?"

My eyes fill with tears, even as I start to laugh. "The opposite. That's what makes this so hard."

I'm not sure how I do it, but I manage to explain my thoughts about myself, about the photograph. About how they'll see me.

It's Axel who says he has the perfect solution. He produces the blindfold and waves it in front of me.

"But there's one blindfold and three of you–" I point out.

"It's for you, Win," Axel says.

I raise a brow. "But you'll still see me."

"And thank fuck for that," Diesel says as he closes the space between us again, and slips his hand under my shirt.

"Diesel! I'm serious!"

"I'm serious, too. You think I'm gonna be looking at my brothers?"

They all laugh while making faces of disgust.

"No," Diesel continues. "The sight of your body puts me in a drugged-up high, Winnie Wainwright, and I want to see myself inside you. I want to see your thighs wrapping around me, and your pussy stretching around me." His tongue grazes my ear. "Your mouth and your ass, each welcoming me in as I fuck you. I want to see all of you, Peach. And when it's your turn to do any of those things with my brothers, tonight, I hope to watch your face, or hear your cries, and know my girl is being fully satisfied."

Diesel growls, then. Actually growls and I grow even wetter.

"Come on, sweetheart," Axel says. "We are *all* desperate to strip you down and hear the pretty sounds you make when you feel so good."

Cruz snatches the blindfold from Axel and waves it toward me as he smirks. "Bet you can't guess whose cock belongs to who, like you can with our mouths."

I roll my eyes. "I definitely can," I say with confidence.

"Prove it, then, darlin'."

His challenging smirk is adorable, and the twinkle in his eyes is slowly melting the icicle of anxiety spearing my body.

Diesel and Axel smirk, too, as they wait for my reply. I roll my eyes again. I can give them something to smirk about...

"First," I say, "You have to let me undress each of you down to nothing."

"Fine," Diesel says as he steps forward, and pulls me into his arms. "But we'll be undressing you, too. And you'll be blindfolded."

Before I can say another word, Diesel kisses me deeply on the mouth. As he does, Cruz ties the blindfold around my head again.

The three of them immediately resume kissing me, but this time they're peeling off my clothes as they do, and kissing every swath of my skin they expose. My shoulders, my breasts, my stomach, my thighs, my knees, and right down to my ankles get attention from their talented lips.

I follow their lead as I strip them naked, using my hands and mouth to guide me. I kiss Axel's pecs as I peel off his shirt. I lick Cruz's abs and then a line down to the tops of his thighs as I slide his pants and then his boxers down.

His cock springs free, and I grab it. Imprint the feel of him into my memory before he moves away and I'm being undressed some more. My bra is pulled off and they each take turns kissing my nipples.

Axel's boxers come down next and last is Diesel. I touch each of them but only long enough to make them moan once before Diesel's saying, "Ready, Win?"

"I think you forgot my panties," I murmur against his mouth when he returns to kiss my lips again.

"Mm-hmm," he whispers back, huskily. "Let's leave those on for now."

The three of them guide me to my knees and I realize I'm shaking. Not from nerves, but anticipation.

It's Axel who goes first. Like with the kiss, I guess the moment his cock brushes against my lips, but I carry on as long as possible. Without my sight, I am one hundred percent focused on the feel of him, the taste of him. I love it. When I have to stop sucking him and guess, he kneels before me and kisses me hard and tells me I'm amazing.

As I go through the same with Cruz, my pussy begins to throb, desperate to be touched as well.

Luckily they don't try to trick me. It's Diesel who goes last, and his cock is rock hard. I swipe up a drop of pre-cum from the tip with my tongue. He groans, and I'm going to take him in my mouth when he pulls his cock away and holds my face in his hands.

"Diesel," I say with a whine. "*Please.*"

"Glad you know it's me," he says, "but *uh-unh*. This erection is for one place, Peach, and it's not those pretty lips of yours."

My stomach flips over and I rip the blindfold off my eyes.

A shudder of lust passes through me when I see that his eyes are as passion-filled as his voice.

"I'm ready," I whisper. "Tell me what to do."

CHAPTER 35

Winnie

Diesel pulls me up from where I kneel on the floor, and kisses me hard. "Get your fine ass on that bed. On your hands and knees, at the very end."

The directive rolls off his tongue, smooth and sexy as hell, and I do as he says.

"Good girl," he growls, and my body trembles at his praise.

His hand cups my ass, a finger dipping into the fabric of my panties and giving it a gentle tug. He lets out a low whistle. "This is a sight I never want to forget. But now these panties come down."

He indeed pulls them down, but not off. He presses a kiss into the small of my back as my panties stretch around the middle of my thighs, keeping my legs locked together. I whimper.

"Any time you want to stop, you say so, okay? Let me know what feels good and what doesn't, okay, Win?"

I nod, even though I know for a fact I won't be telling any of them to stop. I can't see what Diesel is doing and my anticipation is through the roof. I jump a bit when his hands splay across my ass.

"Relax, baby, okay?"

Then Diesel Hammer fucking spreads my ass cheeks with his thumbs and I feel his hot breath between them. My pussy quivers. I'm so turned on. Yet it's impossible not to tense up.

"I've got you, Peach," he murmurs against my sensitive skin. "You want me to stop?"

"Hell no," I say confidently. Maybe I am a selfish cow but I want all of them to have all of me.

Diesel drops kisses all around my crack as he teases my skin with his fingertips. I glance behind me, and see the expression of ecstasy on his face.

Axel and Cruz, looking like bronze statues of the gods as they flank Diesel, are rock-solid ready and staring at me with lust-filled eyes. I'm about to call them over to the bed, but then I feel the warm, wet swipe of Diesel's tongue against my asshole and anything I planned to say flies straight out of my head as I moan.

I can't believe what he's doing. My face has ever been so hot.

"Deez…"

"I just had to have a taste, Peach," he says.

Axel smirks at me, knowing I liked it despite my embarrassment. My gaze slides over to Cruz to see he is gripping his cock now, licking his lips like he wants to dive into my ass, too.

Oh, my God. The heat in their eyes is so intense, the flames will surely consume me. If I keep staring at them over my shoulder as Diesel caresses and kisses the nerves around my asshole any longer, I'll come.

I'm not ready to come yet. and, thankfully, Diesel straightens, placing his hands on my hips. The tip of his cock teases my pussy.

"Wrong hole, Hammer," I say, or maybe I moan. That's pretty much all I can do right now.

He laughs. "I know what I'm doing, Win."

He moves, tracing me from my pussy to the top of my crack with the tip of his cock. I don't think my heart has ever beat so fast.

Then he rubs his cock against my ass. I close my eyes, ready myself, but then the pressure of him moves away.

Pouting, I open my eyes, but it's Axel coming around the side of the bed and crawling over to me that has my heart speeding up again.

My body's natural inclination to spread my legs wide keeps hitting, but my panties are still locked around my thighs. I'm not sure exactly how I'll be positioned for Axel, but Diesel holds my hips in place, so I follow their lead.

As Axel kneels in front of me, his cock bobs, the tip glistening. I want to suck him, but as I open my mouth for him, he cups my face in his palm.

"Not yet," he whispers before he kisses me deeply, his tongue stroking mine.

Closing my eyes, I melt into him, relishing the feel of his demanding kisses and his hand sliding across my body, teasing each of my nipples.

The mattress dips on the other side of me, and then Axel pulls his mouth away from mine. As his hands trail across my belly, and down between my legs, he shifts to the side, allowing Cruz to move into the space he vacated.

"Hi, Cruzie," I whisper.

Cruz cups my face in both of his hands, but instead of kissing me, he strokes my eager mouth with his thumb. "Feeling good, darlin'?"

I nod, and he smiles, holding my gaze as Axel rubs my clit and slides his fingers through my folds, and Diesel dances his fingers across my hole again, teasing as he puts pressure on me and then takes his hand away.

I'm glad I practiced with my dildos because instead of being scared when I hear the lid to the bottle of lube pop open and the squirting sound of it behind me, I'm so turned on that my hips buck against Axel's hand.

Cruz grins down at me, and I wait for him to kiss me, or feed me his cock, but instead he slides his thumb into my mouth, placing it between my teeth. As his gaze breaks from mine, he looks first to Axel, and then to Diesel, signaling them with a nod.

I gasp as Diesel yanks the fabric of my panties and the waistband snaps.

"You'll pay for that, Hammer," I growl, teeth on Cruz's thumb, but before I can say anything else, Diesel parts my legs, and then he and Axel slide their fingers into me.

My brain short circuits, or I've died and gone to heaven, because the sensation as they fill me at the same time, is more than anything I've felt before.

Cruz says, "You can bite down on my thumb if you need to, Win."

I lock eyes with him and see how sincere he is, giving himself up to pain in case I react to the pressure of their push inside with the need to sink my teeth into him. Instead, I give Cruz's thumb a lick before wrapping my tongue around him and sucking hard. I love the way his eyes glaze over.

I breathe slowly as their fingers stretch and fill me. Diesel moves much slower than Axel, and the sensation has me writhing and moaning for more.

"You're so fucking hot, Peach. You think you can take more? We're barely to my knuckle."

I nod, and look at Cruz. "Kiss me, Cruzie," I beg.

He grins and bends forward, capturing my mouth and swallowing my cries of pleasure as Axel begins to finger-fuck me.

And I love kissing Cruz's sweet, soft mouth, but as Diesel's finger pushes all the way in, and joins Axel's pace, and Axel flicks my clit, I want more. So much more. I want their cocks. All of them.

But the need that hits me is so much more than just the craving my body has for all of theirs to possess mine and let me possess theirs back. It's the need to let them all love me this way forever. With their hearts as well as their bodies. The desire to let them protect me, and care for me, and let me do the same for them.

God, how I love these boys.

"Fuck, Peach. I am losing my shit here."

Diesel and I groan in unison as he pulls his finger slowly out.

Without his finger, I feel so empty, and rear against him, letting him know I'm not happy about it.

Axel laughs at my neediness and adds another finger to my pussy. But he only fucks me long enough to make me moan a few times before, after a shared look between the others, Axel pulls his fingers out.

"Ready for this, Peach?"

Diesel shifts me so that he's holding me upright in his arms. He kisses my neck and I feel his cock pushing against my crack.

I nod, shudder. I can't even speak as he parts my legs, spreading me wide.

Cruz sits back on his heels, his gaze roving over every inch of me. I'm too turned on by the naked desire in his eyes to be self-conscious about how I look right now, something I never would have believed possible.

Axel scoots into the space in front of me, kissing my lips quickly, and teasing my nipples with his magical fingers before laying back. He rests on one elbow and gazes at me with a sexy grin. "You're so beautiful, Winnie. Come here, sweetheart."

Diesel and Cruz settle me over Axel's cock, but they won't let me slide onto him the way I want. I squirm and try again, reaching between us so I can place him where I want him.

"Be still, sweetheart. It's not time yet."

I'm ready to protest when Axel pulls me against him in a kiss and as he does, his arms wrap around me and his hands grip my ass. And as I hear the lube bottle snap open again, Axel spreads my cheeks for Diesel.

"Fuck," Diesel growls as he coats himself in the gel. "I don't think I'm going to last long, you know. Not when I'm living my life-long fantasy."

Cruz and Axel chuckle, but as Diesel's cock settles against my ass again, and I push against him, feeling suddenly desperate, they murmur in agreement.

"I would ask you to be still," Diesel says, flexing his hips, testing me out. "but I like how it looks when you wriggle that ass at me. Ready, Peach? I'll go nice and slow."

True to his word, he pushes into me slowly, but *nice* isn't how I'd describe the feel of it once he gets the cockhead past my tight ring. Electrifying. Heady. *Blissful*. I let out a little gasp when he pushes further in, and though my body wants to resist the forbidden sensation, I relax, embracing the thrill that he's actually taking me, stretching me, making room for himself inside me.

Diesel lets out a groan. "Do you know how goddamn good this feels, baby?"

I don't know how it feels for him but as Axel moves under me, kissing my jaw and rotating his hips so that his hard cock rubs against my pussy, my eyes fill with tears at how full I feel already, how delicious the sensation.

"Do you know how goddamn hot this *looks*, baby?" Cruz says echoing Diesel, and I realize I've closed my eyes.

When I open them, Cruz is kneeling beside me, rubbing the tip of his cock with the palm of his hand.

I lick my lips and our eyes connect. The jolt that goes through me is exhilarating. I've never felt so close to my triplets before.

"How... do... you... feel?" Diesel pushes the words out around labored breaths as he inches further in.

Surging pleasure floods my body as my need to orgasm hits.

"Stop," I gasp. "Oh, My God, stop."

Both Diesel and Axel freeze.

"Sorry, Peach," Diesel says, starting to pull out. "Does it hurt badly?"

"No, I love it," I glance back at him, at his worried expression, and the sheen of sweat on his brow. "I want more. So much more. I want *all* of you." I'm babbling and moaning the words as his cock continues to slide out. "But I'm going to come if you keep going and it's too soon—"

With a groan, his hips thrust forward, and his cock slides its way back inside me, deeper this time. So deep I can't speak anymore. It's too good. Holy fuck.

"Sorry, baby," he says. "Your words made me go a little feral, there."

I murmur something unintelligible, but I want him to know it's all okay, so I do the only thing I can think of, and capture Axel's mouth in a kiss.

"I think she's ready for more," Cruz says.

"Yeah?" Diesel asks.

"Ready for me, Sweetheart?" Axel whispers against my lips.

My senses are in overload already so I can't manage an answer. But whatever they see in my expression has Cruz and Axel grinning.

They help me rise up so my hands are braced against Axel's chest. Then, as Diesel holds my hips in place, keeping his cock buried inside me, and Cruz holds my upper body steady, kissing my shoulders, neck, and sliding his hand into my hair, Axel guides his cock inside me.

My breath hitches.

"Breathe, Darlin'," Cruz says, kissing my jaw.

Axel's breathing grows labored as soon as the tip of his cock slides into me. "Holy shit, that's tight. Does it feel good, sweetheart?"

I open my mouth to answer, but as Diesel's hips flex and Axel pushes deeper, I have to look to Cruz, knowing he'll tell them.

"Yeah, it feels good," he says. "Give her more."

They do. They both at once give all of themselves to me. My eyes fly wide open, and I stare at Cruz, my lips parted in a silent cry of pain so delicious my brain doesn't know how to handle it.

"Ready for me to thrust a little?" Diesel says.

"Yes," I manage to gasp. "Thrust. Thrust a lot."

Axel laughs, but I mean it. I push back against Diesel's cock and hear his hiss of surprise.

"Fuuuuuck," Axel says. I glance down at him, and there's a look I have never seen before in his eyes. His pupils are fully dilated, his lips parted. Sweat glistens all over him.

He's enjoying his date.

It's a silly thought at the moment, but it makes me deliriously happy as it strikes me. And my body reacts as wildly as my heart does.

I fuck them. Axel's eyes slam shut so I lock eyes with Cruz as I work my hips. Axel and Diesel are both making sounds that can only be described as desperate whimpering.

It's so sexy. But I want more.

I can't speak, all sound is caught in my chest, but I can convey my desire through my eyes.

I want more, Cruzie. Please.

Cruz's gaze is heavy-lidded as he places his plump-as-a-ripe-cherry cockhead against my lips. I lap up the pre-cum before slurping him into my ready mouth, and he groans in appreciation.

His sounds mingling with his brothers' sets me off into a new frenzy. If I let myself think about the sensations roaring through me, for even a second, I'll come. I don't want that yet, so I don't think, only fuck. Harder, faster.

"Slow down, baby," Axel groans with a small chuckle.

"We want you to be able to sit down tomorrow, Peach," Diesel adds, his voice strained.

But I can't stop fucking them. I roll my mouth down Cruz's cock, sliding Axel and Diesel out, and then push them back inside me as I slide Cruz's cock out.

"Fuck, Peach, I'm gone," Diesel says, and then suddenly he's coming hard into my ass. I can feel him pulsing and stretching. He grips my hips and shouts and then he slides out and my nerves are suddenly heightened as only Axel and Cruz are left inside me.

Axel grips my hips, and pumps himself into me, making it easier for me to me fuck and suck at the same time.

I close my eyes and give them both all I have to give them. Axel's arms tighten around my hips, Cruz fists my hair.

I think I actually come first, but it's hard to know when Axel and Cruz are both shouting out, and two cocks are pulsing in me. My own release is basically an out-of-body experience as Axel's hips grind my clit and I swallow Cruz's cum, lapping up every drop.

Finally, I drop onto Axel, fully boneless. He wraps his arms around me, squeezing me tight.

As I lay in Axel's arms, spent and deliriously giddy, Diesel and Cruz clean me up. With warm, wet washcloths, they gently wash my body, kissing my cooling skin as they clean me. I feel so cherished, and I want to tell them how good it felt for me, how amazing I feel now, but all I can do is cuddle Axel.

Finally Cruz and Diesel collapsed on the floor on either side of us, and they each skim their hands along various parts of my body.

"I just had an orgy with the Hammer triplets," I say.

Really? The first thing I manage to say is that? But I giggle.

Because oh, my GOD, I just had an orgy with the Hammer triplets!

"Only woman on the planet who can make that claim," Cruz says, with a grin in his voice.

"C'mon, Cruzie," Diesel gets to his feet. "This is technically supposed to be Axel's date, so let's give them some alone time."

"You don't have to," Axel says, half-heartedly, sounding as happy as I feel.

"Nah, we've got sleeping bags out there with our names on them," Cruz says. He stands, too, and drops a kiss onto my forehead. "Thank you for a night I'll never forget, Winnie."

"Oh, the pleasure was all mine," I say.

"Not all yours. I promise it wasn't all yours," Diesel says emphatically, and Axel laughs.

We say our good nights and then it's just me and Axel.

I inch even closer to him, nuzzling my face against the crook of his neck, breathing him in.

"You smell like sex, Axel Hammer."

"Mmm. Have no idea why." His fingers idly stroke my naked back. "Maybe because I just had the best sex of my life? You are something else, Win."

I smile. "Please promise me we can do this again before I have to choose."

He shakes his head. "Shhh. We're not talking about choosing tonight. Or tomorrow."

"Okay, but–"

"You enjoyed tonight?"

I roll my eyes. "Of course I did."

"And you want to do it again?"

"Well, not immediately because I think I'm going to be a very, very sore Winnie tomorrow, but... soon? Absolutely."

He kisses me, and smooths a satiny sheet over my warm skin. "Then I promise you, we'll do it again."

CHAPTER 36

Winnie

"Where exactly do you think you're going, Winifred?"

Jack's voice startles me, and I turn to find him standing there, clad in faded jeans that mold to the contours of his sculpted legs. Yum.

But his eyes betray his lack of sleep, and I can't help but notice the weariness etched on his face.

Oops. Totally my fault.

It's been four days since my camping trip, and going by the original plan drawn up, it's meant to be Max's turn for the next date. But for some reason, Max hasn't brought up our date – or lack thereof – yet. And I haven't pressed the matter, hoping it's just because everything has been full steam ahead with the reno.

I don't know, but I'm trying to go with the flow and enjoy every moment. Thankfully that hasn't been a difficult plan to follow when a different Hammer has been in my bed each night.

Last night, as Jack and I stretched out in my bed, he held me in his arms and we chatted for hours. It was a throwback to childhood, thick with memories of our best times together. At one point, we made each other laugh so loudly the guys in the rooms surrounding mine banged on their walls multiple times to shut us up. Naturally, that only made our laughter worse.

I know how it sounds, having a different guy in my bed every night. But it hasn't been a nonstop fuck-frenzy. Far from it. We talk and we cuddle and there's plenty of kissing and affection, but that's as far as it's gone. After taking Cruz, Axel, and Diesel all in one night, my body really, really needed a break.

Maybe that's why Max hasn't mentioned the date? To give me a chance to rest?

Or maybe Max is just taking extra time to plan a special date for me?

Whatever it is, I'm so excited for it. Just the thought of being alone with Max makes me giddy. I miss our private time together.

"Winnie, I mean it. Where exactly do you think you're going?" Jack repeats, this time with a frown. "You're not even supposed to be over here today."

"Hey, Jackalope," I grin.

He closes the gap between us, lifting my chin so my mouth meets his in a sweet kiss. Then he spins me around, so I'm facing the front door I've just come through.

"Go."

I turn right back around. "I'm only here for a second. I just…"

I glance around. This renovation has been unorthodox in a lot of ways. For starters, you know, sex on the stairs. That's new and different. But also the guys have been pretty much treating the upstairs and downstairs as completely different job sites.

Not to mention, they won't allow me upstairs at all anymore. When the triplets and I returned from our date, an elaborate scaffolding had been erected in front of the house, with tarps completely shielding everything behind it from my view.

I peek into the living/dining area, which has been pretty much completely neglected until now, and see that the insulation has been installed and a bunch of the guys are putting up drywall.

"Which one of you douchenozzles took my measuring tape?" Gunnar demands.

He sounds incredibly grumpy and I smile. It's around this point of every job that Gunnar gets impatient.

"Why?" Cruz calls back. "Checking to see if your microweenie has had a growth spurt?"

"I can assure you, Cruzie," I pipe up, "there is *nothing* micro about Gun's weenie."

Cruz glances over his shoulder and sees me. He grins, nods. Then he stops and frowns. "Hey, what are you doing here? You're not allowed to be here."

I place my hands on my hips, and put on a fake pout. I know I've been banned from the reno house because there's stuff happening that they don't want me to see, and I live for their surprises. But. It doesn't mean I can't give them a hard time about it.

"Y'all need me here," I say, matter-of-fact. "Stop pretending you don't."

"Y'all?" Gunnar crosses his arms as he looks at me with both eyebrows raised.

I lift a shoulder. "I got bored and started binge-watching a show called Designing Women. That southern twang is contagious."

"Oh, no." Leo peers around the corner from where he's in the kitchen. He's overheard what I said, and his nose scrunches adorably. "No, love. You weren't watching that gross show where inbred meatheads are given a budget to turn their lady into their idea of physical perfection, were you?"

"The fucking *what* kind of show?" Jack says, staring at me.

"Yeah," Leo says. "Complete makeover, including plastic surgery. Totally fucked up."

"Um, *no*," I say. "What the hell? I wasn't even aware such a show exists."

How gross, indeed. And now I'm especially overwhelmed with gratitude that I've somehow found not one but *ten* incredible men who wouldn't change a freckle on my face.

I blush, thinking about how Gavin likes to play connect the dots with the freckles on my body… using that pierced tongue of his.

"Gun," I say, before I start up with my fantasies and spin myself out of control again, "your tape measure is on the stairs."

I point over to the stairs just as Max appears at the top of them. He sees me and stops.

"Oh, I thought I heard your voice," he says. "I was just coming to get you."

And suddenly anxiety strikes me. Max doesn't seem particularly excited to see me, does he?

But then again, he doesn't look *un*excited to see me, either...

"I'm not supposed to be over here today," I remind him.

My heart sinks when he frowns, and says to the other guys, "We're done." But then he holds out a hand to me. "Come on up, Win. Gav and I have something to show you."

"She's already seen Gav's and was clearly not impressed," Cruz teases. "Better luck to you, bro!"

I don't miss the look Max shoots him. "Ignore him, please. This is about our secret projects for you."

Secret projects?

I practically skip up the stairs to take his hand and I'm relieved when he smiles genuinely into my eyes. He squeezes my hand, tugging me toward the hall.

"Close your eyes, princess," he says and I oblige, following as he leads me down what feels like smooth wood floors.

I wish I didn't have to close my eyes, because I want to see all the changes I can sense. And to be honest, if I'm not meant to see, I wish he'd brought the blindfold. I kind of love that thing, and I've never been blindfolded with Max...

My stomach tenses up, an instinctual reaction, when I realize he's leading me into my old room. I swallow hard, but I don't open my eyes until Max tells me to.

When I'm finally instructed to open my eyes, I draw in a breath. For a long moment, I'm speechless. I cover my mouth with my hand as tears fill my eyes. Max stands behind me, kneading my shoulders while Gavin grins.

"What do you think, Pooh Bear?"

When this was my room, the walls were a dark shade of tobacco-stained white. Now they're a sweet and calming shade of lavender.

The dingy brown shag carpet has been replaced by shining antique-washed oak floors. They're in a herringbone pattern, stylish and sophisticated, exactly the same as one of my favorite floors done for 1 Girl, 10 Hammers.

The two small windows, which always seemed to be grimy and clouded no matter how hard I cleaned them, have been replaced by a ginormous bay window and a huge window seat, flanked on either side with built-in bookshelves.

"Look," Gavin says, pointing to a rod above the window, waiting for the drapery. "It'll be a cozy nook to hide away and read in. You get to pick out the fabric for the curtains, obviously."

The longer I look at the window, the more beautiful details I take in. The glass sparkles and gleams, letting in so much light. Stained glass flowers along the top of the windows throw a rainbow garden onto the floor. Under the window is the most elaborate window seat I've ever seen, with storage drawers below.

"It's stunning," I whisper. "Absolutely incredible."

I glance around the room, and a frown forms as I notice the absence of the closet.

Well, damn. The renovation was perfect until now.

"This isn't up to code as a bedroom without a closet, is it?"

Max grins at me, his eyes glinting with a secret. "Oh, there's a closet."

As my eyes follow his gesture, surprise replaces my initial worry. The closet has transformed into a hidden door, seamlessly integrated into the room's design. Another clever hiding spot, a testament to the Hammer brothers' ingenuity.

"How epic will the games of hide-and-seek be here?" I murmur.

"Right?" Gav touches my arm. "Look, Pooh Bear."

Like Max, there's a mischievous glint in his eye. He directs my attention to the back of the door.

It's my silly little crayon picture of the Hammer family, me included, only now it's adorned with an ornate gold frame.

"You didn't paint over it," I say, trying to swallow away the tears in my voice.

Gav chuckles. "It deserved a frame."

"You guys, this is truly amazing. We have to choose a family with a little girl to have this house, to have this room. It's everything I wish I would've had growing up."

"You're already mentally picking out the furniture and decor, right?" Gavin asks.

I nod, picturing a big bean bag chair in one corner, a canopy bed in the center of the room, fairy lights every freaking where…

I hug Gavin, and then Max. Is it my imagination or does Gav squeeze me a little tighter, hold me a few seconds longer than Max does?

Go with the flow. Enjoy every moment. Stop looking for drama where there isn't any.

We head downstairs, and the guys are all there at the bottom, waiting together. When I babble on to them about how much I loved the first surprises, they cheer.

And cheer again when I promise to stay away so I don't spoil anything.

"But wait," I say as I head out the door. "I came over to say that if you guys need anything from the store, let me know. I'm running out in a minute. Because," I give them my sauciest wink, "I'm making a fabulous meal for *you* tonight. All of you. A surprise of my own."

They've all done so much for me, and I want to show them how much I love them— via a pot roast with *all* the fixings… their favorite.

"Whoa, hold on," Mason says. "The Hammer family dinner will have to be another night, Cupcake. Tonight, it's just you and me. Date night and I have something epic planned, if I do say so myself."

Wait, *what?*

I can feel the confusion written all over my face as I say, "But it's Max's turn for a date next."

Behind me, Max clears his throat. "About that…"

My heart flies into my throat as I turn around and catch sight of his wary expression.

"What's going on?"

Max winces. "Win, can we talk for a sec?"

So much for going with the flow and enjoying every moment. I am freaking the fuck out. Fully panicked.

As I follow Max outside, following his lead as he sits on the porch, trepidation rushes through me. Is it possible that he's decided he doesn't want to be a part of this?

Has he decided he doesn't want me?

My hands are shaking embarrassingly hard, so I sit on them. "What's wrong, Max?"

His frown deepens. "I should've told you this earlier—"

"Are you self-eliminating?" I jump in, as if trying to prepare my heart by getting the terrible truth over with.

He blinks at me. "What?"

My heart is showing no signs of being prepared. "Are you taking yourself out of the running to be my favorite Hammer?"

God, it sounds so silly saying it, and yet tears are springing into my eyes, because it matters to me. More than I ever imagined it would.

"No," he says. "Of course not." He smiles at me, but it doesn't quite reach his eyes. "Of course not, Win."

"Okay," I say, trying to get my heart to stop freaking out. "Okay. Good. Then…" I'm more confused than ever. "Why am I going out with Mason tonight? It's *your* turn and I haven't gotten to spend any time with you since we started this whole thing. I really miss you, Big Max."

He scratches the back of his neck, something he knows I love. "I miss you, too. More than you'll ever know, Win."

For a split-second, his voice snags, emotion creeping in.

He misses me. He really does. This has to be the reason he's acting weird. Is he upset with me because I haven't spent any more-than-friends time with him, just the two of us, since we started this whole thing?

"We're still okay, right?" I ask him. Point blank, because I honestly can't tell.

Dammit. Before we started this, I could always tell with Max. Always. But I have to admit that while I've been getting closer with all of the others, Max and I have backslid from our starting point as friends-with-benefits. A sad truth, but how could we not have? I've now had sex with almost all of his brothers.

But shouldn't that make him more eager to have his chance with me? Doesn't he want me?

Or did he only want my virginity?

I shake that stupid thought from my head, because it's beyond ridiculous.

He holds out his hand and I intertwine my fingers with his. "Are you happy, Winnie? Truly happy?"

I nod emphatically.

And he smiles. "Then we're okay."

"But I want you to be happy too, Max. I want everyone to be happy. And I really, really want my date with you."

"You'll get it, Princess." He takes a deep breath, lets it out. "I promise you nothing is wrong. Actually Mason asked me to switch. He wants to take you somewhere very specific and they've been booked solid. Except for tonight."

I look at him, study every inch of his face. "You swear?"

"I solemnly swear."

I let out a sigh of relief. "Okay, good. Can we just sit here and hold hands for a bit?"

I've found I love holding hands almost as much as I love the naked stuff.

Almost.

He gives my hand a squeeze. "There's nothing I would rather do."

I squeeze back, and I'm smiling again. Feeling so much better, we sit there on the porch together, until Jack barks an order at him to come in. We are silent and still, with the exception of his thumb gently and lovingly running along the top of my hand.

CHAPTER 37

Mason

She isn't going to choose me.

I glance over at Winnie as we head off on our date. Her hair is wild, her grin is wide, her cheeks are pink from the wind. She's gorgeous.

When I suggested we take my 1972 Jaguar XK-E convertible, she beamed. When I suggested she drive—no one even sits behind the wheel of that car but me—her eyes lit up like nothing I've ever seen and she tackled me with a hug.

Now, from the driver's seat, every few seconds she lets out a delighted whoop and laughs. And her laugh makes me laugh, despite the fact I can't get out of my own damn head.

She isn't going to choose me.

It's a thought I can't shake. I've been unable to shake it since she ran out after Gav, when it was my turn to bat, that first day in the living room, during the kisses. I hoped, back then, I'd hit a home run, but instead I'd struck the fuck out.

No. I take that back. I did shake that thought, once. For a few minutes, when she and Cruz and I were in the kitchen, I believed all my bases were loaded. But that's only because I wasn't thinking about anything, then, my brain completely shut down. My bases weren't loaded, they were *overloaded*, with lust and joy and foolishness.

I'm in a different position than most of my brothers, because of Winnie's thing with Max. Yeah, our personalities are night and day, but physically, Max and I are identical.

When she decided to be friends-with-benefits with one of us, who did she pick? My *identical twin*. Which means, even if you took the others out of the equation and it was a head-to-head competition between me and the guy with my exact DNA...

He'd take the W.

The win.

The Winnie.

The One and Only.

Good God, would you listen to me? Pathetic, I know.

But it doesn't matter. She isn't going to choose me.

If she was attracted to the look of me, even if only on a strictly superficial level, she would've just stuck with Max, anyway. Why not? She already had something going with him. Something good, apparently.

Or at least, that's Max's theory, which he reminds me of at least once a day.

She had me, he's whined to me over and over. Which might actually be more intolerable if he was being cocky about it, but he's just despondent. It's horrific.

I was a sure thing, Mace. And still, she needs to date and fuck all of you guys before appreciating what she had? She is not choosing me. And she's not choosing you, either. You know it deep down, too, don't you?

I shove Max's voice away. I've got to get him out of my head.

I've got to get out of my own head.

Because right now, my body is *exactly* where I have been dreaming of being. Maybe not the passenger seat of my car part, but that's surprisingly okay. I just mean I am on a date with Winnie Wainwright.

Sure, it's the only date we'll ever have together, but that only furthers my desire to enjoy everything. Tonight, I'm going to live in the moment and I'm not going to give any thought to what comes tomorrow or the next day or the day after that. For tonight, even if only for tonight, Winnie Wainwright is my girl.

Mine. And I'm going to live for every single second of it.

What I've planned for us is pretty epic, if I do say so myself.

Winnie is taking her driving cues from the GPS, where I'd already input our destination before we hit the road. She's completely in the dark about where we're going.

When the GPS voice announces, "Make a left turn. You have now arrived at your destination," Winnie turns into the parking lot. Only when we're fully stopped in a space, does she glance over at me.

"Are we going to smash, Mason Hammer?" she jokes, gesturing to the sign on the building in front of us. *The Smithville Smash Zone.* She waggles her eyebrows at me.

No, Winnie. We are not going to smash. Because the word smash *implies casual sex, and if I ever have sex with you, there will not be a single damn casual thing about it, Cupcake.*

But I grin. "We're going to smash *things.*"

"A demolition place, though?" She looks perplexed and I know what she's thinking.

"I promise you, Win, this is going to be way different than just taking a sledgehammer to falling apart cabinets on demo days."

"Okay," she says, flashing me a full-fledged smile.

I send up a quick prayer that I've done something brilliant here and not something shit. You can't shine a shit, after all.

We walk inside. I want to hold her hand, but this is kind of in public, so I resist the urge.

"Mace!" the girl behind the counter cries as we enter. "When Devon told me you were coming, I didn't believe it."

"Hey, Linds," I say to her. Then I explain to Winnie, "Lindsey's brother Devon is a good buddy of mine. He owns this place. Lindsey, this is–"

Lindsey holds up a hand. "Mason. This amazing woman needs no introduction. I don't want to make things awkward, but since the first season of 1 Girl, 10 Hammers, I have had the *biggest* girl crush on you! You are a force to be reckoned with, lady. I want your autograph before you leave."

Winnie lets out a surprised laugh. "Why, thank you."

"Actually," Lindsey says, "I need both of your autographs now. You didn't e-sign the waivers in advance, and we need to take care of that real quick."

After we do, Lindsey hands me a stack of gear. "Your room is that way. Devon has everything set up around back when you're done."

Winnie slides a curious glance at me.

Pressing a hand to the small of her back, I guide her in the direction Lindsey indicated. I sincerely hope this goes over well. My plan seemed fucking impeccable as it rolled out in my head, but now I'm wondering if maybe I should've asked one of my brothers their opinion before steamrolling ahead.

We stop at the door that has a sign on it reading Hammer - Party of 2. I think about what's on the other side of that door and wonder if maybe I should warn her about it first.

"We have to suit up before we go in," I stall, handing her one of the two gray jumpsuits Lindsey gave me.

Once we have those and our safety goggles on, I take a deep breath and open the door.

"Damnnnnn," she says, as we cross the threshold.

I reserved the biggest space they have, which has a huge garage door on the exterior wall. Winnie's gaze is the wall to our right, that holds everything from pickaxes to baseball bats on hooks.

"What's your poison, Hammer? I think I'm going to go with the…"

Her voice trails off as she glances to the left and I can see her facial expression change as she starts noticing things. It would be pretty fucking hard not to notice the car in the middle of the room.

"Is that Gram's Ford Escort?" she asks. Then her gaze travels the space and I watch her expression change as she takes in the things–most of it pretty trashed, already– we removed from her grandmother's house.

Belongings of her grandmother's and her father's, which we were supposed to take straight to the dump.

The vehicle in question had been on cement blocks in the Wainwright backyard as long as we'd known Winnie.

"Yeah," I say. "It is."

She whips around and faces me, her eyes glassy. "Mason."

She's starting to cry. Shit. I really hope I haven't fucked up. I've seen such a change in her since we began the renovation. She practically trembled with fear when we first began, but now she marches in boldly.

I thought she was ready for this, and I'm about to apologize for being such a dense bastard, when she rushes at me.

And then I have to steady us both as she jumps into my arms, so we don't fall over sideways because she's caught me completely off guard.

She's good at that, her unpredictability. And her brand of unpredictability is always fun, especially when she's planting her sweet, smiling mouth on mine in a kiss that will rival even our kitchen kiss.

"When you and your brothers first pitched the idea of renovating Gram's house," she says, "it was you who said this reno would be an opportunity to do so much more than rebuild that wreck of a house. And you were right."

She takes both of my hands in hers. "I really don't think any of us could have fathomed just what kind of opportunity we would turn it into." She giggles, rosy cheeks growing rosier.

"And it was because of *you*, Mason, because I mistook you for Max, that this opportunity for me to be with all of you opened up. This is a perfect date for you and me."

"Yeah?" God, I'm so relieved.

She nods. "Because sometimes ghosts don't need to be buried. They need to be fucking obliterated."

When she kisses me again, there's even more fervor behind it. Then I watch her, a smile spreading across my face, as she goes to the table with her grandmother's china on it.

One piece at a time, she picks up the china and hurls it against the wall.

"Come help me, Mason!" she shouts.

"Always, Winnie," I call, and race over.

With every cup, saucer, and plate that shatters, I can see on my girl's face that the pieces of her heart have definitely healed throughout the process of the reno… and, miraculously, from dating us.

I'm overjoyed to see that there's peace in her expression, not fear or anxiety or rage, even if they're all justified.

Fuck. I desperately don't want this to end between us.

I grab two sledgehammers, hoping that the sounds of us wrecking her terrible grandmother's terrible clunker of a car will drown out Max's voice in my head.

She isn't going to choose us.

CHAPTER 38

Winnie

An hour later, there's nothing left to break and as Mason and I leave behind the rubble we've created, I'm panting and sweaty and feeling *fantastic*.

We're back in the hall, and are silent as we pull off our goggles and strip out of the jumpsuits and drop them into the waiting basket.

"How was that?" Mason touches my face, wiping away my tears. Cathartic tears. "Are you okay?"

I laugh. "Better than ever. I just… *really* needed that." I let out a deep, satisfied sigh that shakes my whole body. "Would you think I was totally twisted if I said that that was some of the most fun I've ever had in my life?"

He grins, but I mean it. It really was.

"I just wish that," I add wistfully, "that *godawful* recliner would've been here so I could take the pickaxe to it."

"Actually," Mason says, trailing his fingers down the side of my face. "That's Part Two of your surprise. Devin has it set up out back. In the Burn Zone. I thought you might want to douse it with gasoline and throw a match on it. Watch that fucker burn."

I grin. "Oh, Mason Hammer. You say the most romantic things."

But I realize, then… I don't give a shit about the recliner anymore. This has been so much fun, but… now I want another kind of fun for Part Two.

I shake my head. "I really, really appreciate it, Mace. I have had a freaking blast. But… tell Devin to let someone else take their trauma out on it, okay?"

Mason gives me a quizzical look. "You sure?"

"Yeah." I stand on my tiptoes, stretching, stretching, to press my forehead against his. "I'm in the mood for another kind of smashing," I add with a giggle.

Yep, we don't need to light any matches. There's pure fire in Mason's eyes. He grabs my hand and practically drags me into the hall.

"Lindsey, we're headed to our decompression lounge, now."

"Sounds good, kids!" her voice floats back. "All the drinks and snacks in the basket on the table are yours, but if you need anything else, give us a shout!"

Mason squeezes my hand and leads me down the hall and through another door to the decompression lounge.

Our lounge is just as cool as the smash room was, but an entirely different vibe. Calming, with soft music;

comforting, with large plush couches; and surprisingly cool, with a sleek red and black pool table as the centerpiece.

The door latches behind us with a thud and a satisfying click, and the sounds of the public world vanish, leaving only the soft hum of the lights above us.

Alone together at last. It feels like the silence is amplifying my anticipation as Mason's eyes lock on mine. His gaze is so intense, as if he is trying to drink up the sight of me before I disappear, like I'm a mirage.

I waggle my brows. "Ever made out on a pool table, Hammer?"

He bursts out laughing, breaking the intensity of his gaze, and heads over to one of the low tables, and the gift basket on top.

"What?" I ask, following. "Is that, like, your speciality or something?"

"No, but… that is my pool table." He grabs an energy drink and cracks it open, passing it to me before doing the same for himself. "Devin's keeping it for me until I figure out where I'm going to land eventually."

He clinks our cans together before chugging at least half of his in one go.

But the statement hits me in the gut and the heart, twice over, as his words sink in. "Are you thinking about going back to LA?"

He lowers the can, opens his mouth to reply, but before he can say a word, I shake my head.

"No, never mind. I don't want to talk about 'eventually.' We're living in the moment, right?"

"We are," he says.

"Good. Because right now, in this exact moment, I want to make out on your pool table."

A sexy grin slides over his face, his eyes twinkling. "Oh, do you? Well, I can help with that."

When he picks me up and sets me on the edge of the pool table, placing himself between my thighs, the rich yet delicate sandalwood scent of him fills my senses, heady and familiar.

"You're mine all mine, Cupcake," he whispers, his thumbs digging possessively into my thighs.

I shiver, loving it, and I'm thrown back to our first kiss in the kitchen, when I sat on the counter and he touched my thighs. It feels like a lifetime ago already, what with everything that has changed since then— the most important change being myself. I was so embarrassed by my body as he kissed me, then, unable to see past the lumps and rolls to really open up to him.

I'm not by any means as confident as Goldie now, but I embrace the moment and place my hands over his.

"And what do you plan to do to me?" I challenge.

He grins and slides his hands all over my body. "Savor you. Every single inch of you."

With my hands atop his his, I feel him as he feels me. The fire in his eyes burns brighter the longer I allow him to explore. He skims his hands under my shirt, over my stomach and around my breasts. And it feels fucking *good*. When his hands reach my nipples and his breath hitches, I let out a tiny sound.

"Fuck, Win." And then his lips collide with mine.

Our mouths instantly meld together, our tongues entwining. His touch ignites me, warmth trailing everywhere his hands explore. He squeezes, fingers dancing wild patterns along my thighs. He pinches and teases and grabs my flesh.

I try not to think that he's holding on to me like this, and kissing with such intensity, as if to keep me from slipping away.

Well, I'm not going anywhere. I tell him that as best I can with my body and mouth. I lose myself in the intensity, shedding any last concerns about being too much or too anything for him. All that matters is the exquisite sensation of our kiss, just like our kiss weeks ago, but this time with a fresh layer of deliciousness and urgency added to it.

"*Winnie*." His teeth graze my bottom lip, sending shivers down my spine. His thumb, pressing into my skin, teases as he works his way between my legs.

I moan approvingly and tilt my hips toward him.

But as a groan pulls from him, Mason backs up, leaving me perched on the side of the pool table, breathless and wanting, aching for the warmth of his touch to envelop me again.

"What if someone walks in?" he rasps. The line of his cock is long and thick and mouth-watering to look at, even through his jeans.

I groan in frustration. He's being smart. Sensible. I don't want a gossip-mill repeat. Not to mention, the gossip created from us getting it on on a pool table together, would be so much worse than dancing with Theo and Leo. I'm reading get out of here lol

But I don't want to stop now.

"Does the door lock?" I ask, hopefully.

He glances at the door with a rueful expression. "I'm not sure we're allowed to lock it. Safety reasons."

Mason is groaning out his frustration, again, like we're taking turns. He grabs himself, adjusting, as if the fullness of his cock is uncomfortable.

He needs me to set him free.

I squeeze my thighs together, and squeeze my pussy for extra measure, as though that will stop the rush of warmth dampening my panties.

I lick my lips.

He grins. "Fuck me, Cupcake, what are the thoughts in your head making your eyes glow that bright?"

Before I can answer, he's flicking the lock closed and yanking off his shirt in one movement. He locks eyes on mine again, walking toward me slowly as he unbuttons his jeans.

I can't stop the grin on my face as he teases, his stupidly gorgeous body rippling like a panther's as he sheds his clothes down to his tight baby blue boxers.

He reaches me, leaning in for a kiss, but I'm not ready

"All of it," I tell him.

One brow rises. "Is that fair? You haven't taken anything off yet."

I kick off my shoes and smile coyly.

"*That* is definitely not fair."

I mirror his raised brow, and teasingly say, "It's fair, *Cupcake*."

He laughs and drops his boxers, kicking them off. His cock bobs as he moves, teasing me back.

My belly twists with need. I scoot backward onto the pool table, stretching my body out like a pinup girl and batting my eyelashes at him.

Come hither, baby.

His panther-muscles flex, and in a swift motion, he swings himself up onto the table. Before I can blink, I'm on my back, legs spread open so he can nestle his body between them. His cock presses into me and he grins mischievously knowing I feel all of him, even through my pants.

"Now don't you wish you'd gotten yourself naked like me?" he says, hovering over my face, just out of reach of my mouth.

I do. I absolutely definitely do. I grind my hips into him.

He smiles. "I suppose I'll have to fix that, then."

"This is your date, after all." I sound incredibly horny, my voice thick and breathy.

His eyes twinkle as he sits up and reaches for the button of my pants. With a few tugs, my pants are off and on the ground next to his. My panties follow.

He stares at my pussy for a long minute, his hand going back to rub the head of his cock. It's like my pussy is a hypnotist's watch the way the Hammer brothers stare at it. Mason is completely mesmerized, his mouth parted, his eyes glazing over.

He touches me, his thumb skimming over my clit, sliding through my folds, and the sounds he makes is like an animal. He licks my juices off his skin, and his eyes are dark.

"I want so badly to tell you what you do to me. To tell you how much I love the taste of you. *Winnie.*" He says my name like he's desperate, his voice snagging on his emotion, and my heart catches.

"So tell me," I say.

"You've heard it all before, though." His fingers slide into me, at least two, luxuriously slow.

I moan. "Who cares what the others have said?"

Just as slowly as he enters me, his fingers leave, and I want to push against him until he's inside me again, but his eyes pin me in place.

"I just wish I could do something, you know, say *anything* to you, that the others haven't already."

"I think you're too much in your head, Mace," I say as gently as possible, hoping the mood isn't dying.

"Well," he mutters, and then he gives me his fingers again, "It's not like I can tell you what's in my heart. Diesel beat me to…"

His voice trails to a stop and his eyes widen as though he didn't mean to say what he did, at least not out loud. His fingers begin to pump, finding a sweet rhythm.

I moan again, and push my hips in a matching rhythm. But this conversation isn't finished yet.

"Beat you to what, Mace?"

I watch his face carefully, and as I do, I reach for his cock, searching with my hand until I find him. My grip is as solid as he is and his eyes flicker as I stroke him once.

"What did Diesel beat you to, Mace?"

He swallows hard. "I am not saying another word."

I pump his cock again, and he pumps his fingers into me. As we match paces, we stare at each other. And stare and stare. The air is so thick with passion I might actually choke.

"Tell me," I say again, daring him.

And then in a swift motion, he spreads me open wider and settles his body over me, the tip of his cock lining up with my entrance. We still haven't broken eye contact. I don't think I could look away from him if I wanted to. And I don't want to. When he thrusts forward, I gasp, but I relish the thick, deep slide of him.

"I told you I'm not saying another word."

His hips are possessed by some kind of magical spell to make my pussy sing, I'm sure. That's the only explanation for why I completely unravel as he begins to steadily fuck me. I pant, I sweat, and with his molten eyes on me, it doesn't take long before I feel the orgasm rising in me.

"Why not?" I ask, pushing all thoughts of orgasming out of my head. I'm not ready. Not yet.

He sits up, then, shoving my knees toward my chest and grabbing my ass, lifting me higher.

When he thrusts into me again, his cock feels so huge in this new angle that it steals my breath.

"Because," he starts as his hips slam into me. "I've heard it's a bad idea to tell someone that you love them when you're fucking."

My heart isn't beating anymore. My lungs can't take in air. Thank God he's got me on my back, already, because in any other position I'd have collapsed from shock.

"But is it true?" I say.

Well, I try to say it, but he's fucking me harder than before, so my words are sloppy, gasping breaths.

"It's true, Cupcake."

The slam of his cock into me is ten times deeper after he says it. My heart is fully pierced by him.

"I'm going to come," I cry out.

"Let go, baby."

The sounds I make as my body bursts in ecstasy are surely loud enough to be heard throughout the entire building. Mason's sounds are quieter.

"*Winnie*," he says, groaning my name as he shudders into my body. "I love you. I do."

The last words he whispers, but he might as well have shouted them for how my body reacts, tensing even as I've gone boneless. He gathers me close, kissing my shoulders, my neck.

"I really do love you," he says again, his voice slowed down, lazy from his orgasm. "I want you to know it, Winnie. But I don't want you to think it means I expect you'll pick me. It's just something you should know, that's all. So no getting weird about it, okay? You're also the absolute best sex I've ever had. Another truth you should know."

I kiss him again. Again. Again. The more my lips touch his skin the more I crave him. I wrap my legs around him to keep him from sliding out of me, and we kiss until our hips begin to rock, and I can feel him growing hard all over again.

"Damn," Mason swears, pulling out. "If we don't stop soon, I'm going to bury myself in all this sweetness again, and I might not be able to stop."

"Sounds fine by me," I say with a laugh.

"But I already forgot that I planned everything out. You were supposed to be lighting up the recliner just as the sun was setting. There are epic sunsets here and we missed it."

My heart is already full to bursting and then he goes and says that?

"We didn't miss anything, Mason," I say, grabbing his hand, pulling it to my heart. And I hope, even without me saying it, he knows how much I love him, too.

We dress and go back upstairs and I have to hold his hand. I don't ever want to not touch Mason.

It hits me like a wrecking ball that I feel things I haven't felt before. Maybe it was just the catharsis of smashing Gram and Dad's things, combined with that mind-blowing sex, but… yeah. I'm undeniably experiencing a level of emotions, closeness, connection with Mason I haven't felt with any of the others, not even in the tent with the triplets.

Holy shit. Does this mean Mason could be…

But a wave of sadness hits me when I think of Max. And Gavin. And Deezy. Jack.

I could feel good, in this moment, with choosing Mason… if I could just not think that choosing him means not choosing the others.

As much as I never want to let him go, when we get upstairs and I see a door with a bathroom sign above it, I say, "Let me pop into the ladies room before we go, okay?"

I pee and then as I'm washing my hands, I look at myself, really look at myself in the mirror. I don't zone in on my flaws or pick them apart. I just look at the woman standing there. It's probably the first time in my life I confront my reflection and think that I'm beautiful.

Happy tears fill my eyes.

My phone buzzes and I pull it out. Goldie's calling. I would wait until we get home and call her back but I see that there are quite a few notifications from her.

"Hey, girl, hey," I answer. I am giddy. "What's up?"

"Oh, my god, I didn't think I was ever going to get in touch with you. Where are you right now? Are you somewhere you can sit down?"

"Um… well, I'm in a public bathroom, and I don't know if I really want to sit down on one of these toilets, though it is cleaner in here than your average public bathroom. Mason brought me to this place where you smash things. Golds, we had the best time and then we may or may not have just had life-altering sex on a pool table."

She's quiet.

I feel like maybe I should go sit down on one of the toilets.

"Golds?" I prompt.

"You're out with Mason, right now? And you just fucked?"

"Uh… yes?"

She lets out a string of curses.

"Goldie, I think you need to tell me what's wrong. Like, now."

There's a long stretch of silence and I know whatever she's going to tell me is going to be bad.

"Goldie!" I cry.

"I got an offer to be a field producer on another reality show," she says, her voice uncharacteristically somber and quiet.

"Oh. And you're not psyched about it? Did they give you a lowball offer?"

"Winnie, the new show is a 1 Girl, 10 Hammers spinoff."

My knees feel weak. I clearly have heard her wrong. "No, that's not possible. The guys turned it down and we all agreed our Winnie's Favorite Hammer thing is a private thing–"

She's gone silent again.

"Golds."

"The guys turned that show down, yes. But the network wasn't willing to drop it. They came up with another idea called 'Who Wants to Marry A Hammer Brother?' It's going to feature 25 gorgeous–and you and I both know that means skinny and flawless–single women vying for the heart of, and an engagement ring from, a Hammer brother."

"Well, they'll turn that one down, too," I say with a nonchalant shrug.

But part of me feels sick. After I've made my choice, some of them might want to do it. And I'll have to be okay with that.

"Winnie, Season 1 is going to be Max. And Season 2 is going to be Mason. They've already signed on to do it. Filming starts in September."

They've already signed on?

I don't say anything. I can't.

"Winnie, are you there?"

Yes, yes, I'm here. But I feel like the world has just fallen out from under my feet.

Apparently I was wrong when we finished in the smash room. There was something left to break.

My stupid, stupid heart.

CHAPTER 39

Winnie

I don't think I even say goodbye to Goldie before ending our call. And after I do, I stay in the bathroom so long that Mason sends Lindsey to check on me.

Thankfully, I'm locked in a stall and am done throwing up by the time she comes into the bathroom.

I tell her I'm fine.

Has there ever been a bigger lie in the history of time? In the past, I probably would've asked her if there was a back door I could sneak out of. No, I definitely would've done that. But that's not even something I consider today.

I take another five minutes to pull myself together. I realize I should be crying, but the tears haven't started to fall yet. I should be devastated but all I feel is numb.

Dad and Gram are talking louder than ever in my head, judging how oblivious, naive, and just plain stupid I've been.

TEN HAMMERS

I splash water on my face and walk out to where Lindsey and Mason are chatting at check-in. Mason's big-ass grin is dead on arrival when he catches a glimpse of my expression.

He leaves Lindsey and comes over to me. "Hey. You okay?"

I obviously am not. But I can merely assume the worst, or I can get answers.

I deserve answers.

"Before you two leave, don't forget to take a selfie in front of the We Smashed It wall!" calls Lindsey, who is obviously not as fluent in the nuances of my face as Mason is.

"We'll have to catch that next time, Linds," he calls back. "What's wrong? What happened?"

I dodge his touch and fold my arms across my chest. "Is it true, Mason?" I ask and his eyes widen. Before I even give him a chance to breathe, let alone form a response to my question, I ask it again, louder, "Is. It. True?"

Please, God, let Goldie have gotten it wrong. Please let it be a big misunderstanding. Please...

He doesn't have to say a word. The shame in his eyes give him away.

"Let's go home," he says, his voice low, gentle. "We can talk about everything on the way–"

"Mason, you're doing a show called *Who Wants To Marry A Hammer Brother*? You better believe I want to hear how you justify having sex with *me* when *that* is your endgame. But right now, I don't even want to look at you, much less be alone with you."

The numbness has been washed away by an icy cold bucket of dark emotions. Betrayal. Sadness. Rage that tells me despite it all, I am my father's daughter. I swallow all the mean words I want to spew. I'm not going to tear Mason down.

"Winnie, please, if you'll just let me—"

My eyes burn like lava has gotten into them or something. "Did you sign up to do the spin-off before or after we started dating?"

I'm honestly not sure which is worse or why I even need to know. If he signed on before, that means he went into this knowing no matter who I chose, he had other plans.

If he signed on after, though… that means that even if I chose him, he was never planning on choosing me back.

His Adam's apple works as he swallows hard. He at least has the decency to look me in the eye as he says, "After. Win, I am so sorry. Please. I'm begging you, just let me explain."

"Later," I tell him, because I want it to be clear that I am not running away. I am going to face this head on, but right now I want to slap him. I want to go into the smash room and grab the biggest sledgehammer I can pick up and demolish this whole damn building and every building within a three-mile radius.

"I'm going to get a rideshare," I say. "You need to go. Go and tell the others I'm on my way and when I get there, it isn't going to be fucking pretty."

"Win—" he begins, stepping closer.

A wave of nausea hits me. He's *drenched* in the scent of our sex.

I blink away the unshed tears that keep on building, waiting for the dam to burst.

"I have one question. You're doing the second season of the spin-off," I can't even bring myself to say the title again, "and Max is doing the first. What are the other guys doing? Waiting to see who I choose before they make a decision who gets to be the star of Season Three?"

Mason's eyes are downcast. He looks deeply ashamed.

"None of the others know anything about the show, so please don't take this out on any of them," he says. When he looks up, and meets my gaze again, his eyes are wet. "Winnie, please let me–"

"No, just leave. I'll see you back at the house."

"Cupcake, I am *so* sorry. Please let me–"

"I really hate the nickname Cupcake," I say, which isn't at all true, but right now, all the hurt inside me has to go somewhere, so I throw it at him.

And when it hits, it hurts him. His shoulders slump in a way that would be imperceptible to anyone else. I want to throw my arms around him, to hold him, even now. I want to listen to whatever he has to say, to hope beyond hope that somehow, someway, he can justify what he and Max have done.

Whatever he has to say, I can't hear it right now. We were supposed to not have any more secrets. We were supposed to be open and honest with each other.

But then again, how could they tell me that they were never really taking this seriously?

I turn away, because I know he's still staring at me. "Go home, Mason."

Out of the corner of my eye, I see him shake his head. He holds out his keys. "You take my car. I'll wait for a rideshare. I can't just leave you here. I can't just leave, knowing you are hurting."

"Maybe you should've considered that before you hurt me!" I cry, not caring if Lindsey overhears. "Was this just a game to you and Max? Have you just been playing with my heart the whole time?"

My gut screams no, no, a thousand times no. It can't be.

"Winnie. No. *No.* It just... we knew you weren't going to choose us." He rakes his hands through his hair. "You know Max and I loved doing 1 Girl, 10 Hammers. When we were certain you weren't going to choose either of us, we didn't want to pass up the opportunity. Hell, it's not even about the dating aspect of the show. It's just about getting another show. Staying relevant, keeping our careers–"

I hold up a hand to stop him. "The thing is, Mason, you can't possibly know who I was or wasn't going to choose because even I still don't know that! And if you didn't want to do this... you shouldn't be doing this! You should have ended things with me, both of you, before you agreed to do the spin-off. I can't believe you can't see that!"

I feel like I'm being torn in two. Part of me just wants Mason to hold me and make it better. Part of me wants to tell him that first and foremost, he is my friend, and we'll get through this.

But another part of me feels like, even after all we've been through, I suddenly don't know him at all.

Mason… my sweet Mason… he couldn't possibly betray me this way.

And yet, he did.

I'm suddenly exhausted.

I hold out my hand. "I think I'll take you up on the offer to take your car, after all. I just want to go home."

CHAPTER 40

Cruz

I'm alone in the living room when the front door opens and closes.

"You lovebirds are back early. Was the date terrible?" I call.

Joking, obviously. I want every date Winnie has to be amazing, whether it's with me or not. Though… I'm not too humble a guy to admit that Axe, Deez and I set the bar pretty damn high for Mason.

Poor schmuck.

When I hear footsteps, I pull my hand out of my pants, but not fast enough.

"Are you really choking the chicken on Mom's couch, you perv?"

It's Mason. I look behind him, but it's only Mason. No Winnie to be found.

"Where's Win?" I ask.

And, yes, I was choking the chicken on Mom's couch. Is it my fault a commercial for WildVenture Outfitters came on and there was a shot of a tent? Camping will never not turn me on for the rest of my life.

"She's…" he begins, but trails off, looking so damn squirrely and guilt-ridden I almost ask where he buried the body.

"If she went home with another dude, that's a bad sign, bro," I quip.

Obviously I'm kidding. But based on his sigh, I'm guessing he's not amused.

"I need to talk to Max. Know where he is?"

"I am not, as they say, my brother's keeper. But I'm pretty sure he went out with Leo. They said something about tacos or taxis? I wasn't really paying attention. You can talk to me, though. I almost always know where I am."

He narrows his eyes at me, slightly. Then with another giant sigh, he plunks onto the sofa.

"I fucked up bad, man. Max and I both did."

My heart skitters in my chest. I'm a grown-ass man. My heart shouldn't be skittering, but I know their fuck-up has something to do with Win, so skitter my damn heart does.

I click off the TV and put down the remote. Leaning forward, my elbows on my knees, I ask, "What did you do?"

As he tells me, my heart stops skittering and plummets.

"Where is Winnie?" I demand when he's done.

"She drove my car back. I took a rideshare. She left before I did, by like fifteen minutes so she should've been back by now."

And yet she's not.

Shit.

I can tell Mason feels rotten, but that doesn't absolve him in my eyes. He *should* feel rotten. I don't think I've ever been so pissed at one of my brothers. Ever.

"Call Tweedledummer, and call Leo, and tell them to get their asses back here. *Now.*"

I pull out my phone and text Win.

> I need to know you're okay, Darlin'.

I wait for a few seconds but the text doesn't switch to read.

Which is good if she's driving, I guess, but damn it all to hell! What if she just took off?

The vindictive little voice inside me whispers that if she did, at least she made off with Mason's precious Jag. I hope she keys it from hood to bumper.

Too bad that's not Win's style.

I am flooded with relief when my phone pings with a response from her.

> I'm okay, Cruzie. I'll be there soon.

My worry lessens, but my anger does not.

I storm through the house banging on doors, telling everyone to get their asses down to the living room. NOW. When we're all gathered–minus Max and Leo, who are still a couple of minutes out—Jack asks, "What's up with the theatrics, Cruz?"

He's just being a little pissant because normally he's the one that bosses us all around and calls the family meetings.

I glance at Mace and give his dumb ass the tiniest sliver of mercy.

"Let's wait for Max and Leo," I say.

He has an accomplice, after all, and Max needs to get his share of the blame. Besides, it kills two birds with one stone if we kick their asses at the same time.

We don't have to wait long. From the look on Max's face, I can tell that when Mason texted, and told him to come home, he filled him in on what had gone down.

"What the fuck is happening?" Leo asks. "Where's our girl?"

Ah, so Max has not filled him in.

"She's on her way," I say.

Jack glances at me before turning to Mason. "On her way back from where? You two came back from your date and she left to go…?"

"She didn't come back with me." Mason's looking at his hands.

"Why the fuck not?"

"Apparently there's a spin-off of 1 Girl, 10 Hammers in the works," I say flatly, since neither punkass Max nor Mason seem to be racing to confess. "Winnie found out about it somehow and is understandably upset. It's called *Who Wants To Marry A Hammer Brother?*"

Jack looks perplexed. "Is there another set of Hammer brothers I don't know about?"

My eyes flit from one of my brothers to the next. They all appear as clueless as Jack does.

"I mean," Jack goes on. "None of us knew about this, right?" He turns to Mason. "You were with her when she found out? Did you tell her none of us knew shit about this?"

Mason doesn't say anything for a minute, but finally Max speaks up. Maybe the hole I was boring into his forehead with my glare did the trick.

"I'm doing the show," he says defiantly. "I signed up and convinced Mason to do it too. It's only a two-season contract, so I guess they were waiting to see—"

Everyone is speaking at once so it's hard to make out what anybody is saying, but the vibe is impossible to miss. Everyone is angry as hell.

Then Max yells to be heard over us all. "She was never going to choose us!"

We all fall silent.

He repeats, sounding so damn broken-hearted I almost, *almost* feel bad for the little bitch, "She was never going to choose us."

He goes on and it's fucking heart-wrenching to listen to him explain why he felt that way. Then he says again, with more conviction, "She was never going to choose me. Or Mace."

"You're right," a voice says and we all turn to see that Winnie has snuck up on us once again.

She's standing in the doorway between the hall and the living room. "I wouldn't have ever chosen you, Max, or you, Mason."

I swear, we all hold our breath waiting for her next statement.

The identical pain etched on Max and Mason's faces look like she's just taken their dicks and straight ripped them off their bodies. Or maybe their hearts out their chests. On the other hand, several of my brothers can't hide the relief they obviously feel that this means their own personal odds of being Winnie's favorite Hammer have gone up.

"I wouldn't have ever chosen any of you."

Now I feel like she's ripped my heart out of my chest. "Winnie, don't say that. Please don't let what these two have done stop you from–"

She holds up a hand, making my plea die on my lips. Much like the hope that she'll ever be mine is dying inside me.

I glance around. We all look like a bunch of balloons that she's just popped with a single needle.

"Cruzie, this isn't about what they've done. It's about what *I've* done. I've been merrily dating all of you… having sex with most of you… falling more in love with each of you every day… while still somehow trying to convince myself that choosing one of you my favorite is going to be possible at the end. I couldn't when we started this… and I won't ever be able to. So don't be mad at Mason and Max. How they went about it was shitty and shady as fuck, but they did the right thing for them."

We all protest at once like we've fucking rehearsed it. Even Mason and Max.

"Let me finish, please," she continues, and there are tears welling up in her eyes.

I want to go to her and dry them.

She turns her attention to Axel after we've all quieted down. "I know you said I could take all the time I needed to make a decision, that if I wasn't ready to choose once the reno is done, you don't see why I should have to."

We all turn our attention to Axel.

He shrugs. "Meant it when I said it, still mean it now. This isn't something she should have to rush. This isn't something that should have a deadline. And unlike some of you," he shoots eye-daggers at Max and Mason, "I'm perfectly happy with the way things are now."

"Me, too," Gavin and Gunnar say simultaneously. I don't think I've ever heard them say anything in sync before and if circumstances were different, I'd laugh.

But the circumstances are, our girl is crying her eyes out and clearly hurting and we're all sitting around like lumps.

I start to stand, to go to her, and she shakes her head.

"But taking all the time I need isn't fair to any of you. Because I would literally need forever. My favorite Hammer would be the one who died last of old age."

I do laugh at that, because, hell, my girl is funny.

My girl.

How will I ever stop thinking of her that way now that I've started?

"It's not fair for any of you to put your futures on hold for me any longer. I know, without a doubt, I am not going to be able to choose. Letting go of any of you would destroy me. So I have to let go of all of you. You should all sign up for *Who Wants To Marry A Hammer Brother?* I think it's going to be a smash hit," she glances at Mason. "No pun intended."

I can see her lip tremble from across the room as she glances from Mason to Max and back again.

"I can't believe the two of you signed on to do that show while you were dating me. And making me believe you were whole-heartedly in it, too," she says, her voice laced with betrayal. "While I was driving home, it made me question everything. Doubting everything all of you have said to me, done with me. For a split second, I wondered if any of you were taking it seriously. If any of you saw me as an endgame. And I realized… for those of you who haven't broken my trust, I still trust you completely. I will cherish every moment we've had together." She looks around at all of us, her eyes shining with unshed tears. "But I would be foolish to think you haven't all been thinking what comes next for you, if you weren't the one I chose. If you weren't, you should've been. So I can't blame Max or Mason for that. And I don't want any of you to, either. But we were all supposed to be open and honest with each other. And I am so disappointed in you both for doing the exact opposite of that."

Max gets up. "Winnie."

She shakes her head. "We'll be okay, Max. You'll always be one of my best friends. Part of my family. But I need some time alone. I'm not running away from anyone. This is just a loss for me and I need time to grieve it alone."

"Winnie," Max says again. He goes to her and I'm surprised when she lets him hug her. She visibly tenses, but she lets him hug her. When they pull apart, bro is fighting an impending ugly cry so hard it's almost unbearable to watch. "Break up with me. I deserve it. But I pressured Mason into signing on. Don't punish him. And definitely don't punish any of the others."

"I'm not punishing anyone, Max," she says, softly. "I'm doing what's best for you all. Please nobody follow me. I'll be fine. I just need time."

We all watch in silence as she walks out.

As soon as she's out of earshot, Jack says, "Before everyone dog-piles on Max and Mason, I'd like us to all agree that we need to focus on the solution, not the problem. They were dumbasses, obviously, but can any of us say we haven't had the same fears?" he asks. Then he answers his own question before any of us can, "No, we cannot. We need to figure out how to get her back on board."

"Were you not listening to her?" I ask him. "She said she won't ever be able to choose."

"So," Jack says. "Maybe we need to take a page out of Axel's playbook."

"You mean tell her she doesn't have to rush to make her decision?" Gav asks. "I don't think she'll go for that. She seemed pretty adamant about it, actually."

"Yeah, I know," Jack says.

"So...?" Gunnar prompts.

I think I know what Jack is thinking so I'm the one who says it. "So we get her on board by showing her she doesn't *ever* have to choose."

CHAPTER 41

Winnie

I hate sleeping alone, but no one knocked at my door and asked to come in. Deep down, I wanted them to, but I'm glad they have respected my wishes. Besides, cuddling all night would've only made everything harder. The guys must've taken me seriously. Gunnar didn't even serenade me through the wall, something he'd been doing every night, whether I had company or not.

I tell myself it was the right thing to do, but when I woke up, my pillow was still damp from the previous night's tears. This hurts worse than I could have ever imagined.

Still, I get up and I get dressed. There's a reno to finish and I know I'm supposed to stay away so the boys can surprise me with their secret projects, but I just want to get it done and over with.

What I told Max is true. We *will* be alright. Each of those Hammer boys is going to be my friend and found family, forever. They can't lose me that easily. But I need distance to get over them, if that's possible. Lord knows I can't do it while we're in Gram's house, where I'm sure her and Dad's ghosts are laughing their asses off at me from the beyond.

The Hammer home is still and quiet as I creep down the stairs. The sun is barely up. Surely they can't have all left already to get to work. Maybe they're still asleep?

When I open the front door, I gasp at my first glimpse of Gram's house across the street. They must all be asleep because they were clearly working all night long. After I'd had enough of silence, hating the lack of Gunnar's nighttime serenades, I'd put in my earbuds. Otherwise I definitely would've heard some of the noise they had to have made. The scaffolding and tarps are down, revealing that the formerly neglected and rundown exterior now appears brand new, ready for a fresh beginning. The roof has been repaired, the windows have all been replaced. Sad, barely hanging on shutters gone. A brilliant coat of fresh paint.

It's actually lovely. Growing up, I spent so much time dreading going in that front door, I didn't notice what potential it had.

I smile despite everything. That house is going to make a nice little family very, very happy.

I let myself in, and when I see what they've done, all I can do is blink. The walls are finished, all of them, and primed to be painted. But that's not what makes me gasp.

My first assumption is that the place has been vandalized.

Someone has scrawled graffiti all over the fucking walls in the living room. My first inclination is to run back to the Hammer home to get the guys, because what if whoever did that is still in here? Goldie and I once took a self-defense class together but I'm not sure how much I remember, to be honest.

When I step closer, I see the words *My Dearest Winnie* at the top of a block of text.

I take another step closer, and another. When I'm staring at the ruined wall head on, then come the waterworks.

This isn't graffiti.

There was no vandal.

It's letters. From my boys.

My Dearest Winnie, the first begins.

I recognize Gavin's small, blocky handwriting.

> *Words can't express how much I love you. I was honored to be your first lover and I hoped with all my heart I would be your last. That it would be you and me 'til the end. But this process has made me realize something. I don't care if I'm your one and only. I just want to be your forever and always. You know we'll always do whatever you want, but please give us another chance. If you decide not to, I will whole-heartedly respect that. We'll always have the Creepside Manor and you'll always be my Pooh Bear, no matter what.*
>
> *Gav*

I run my fingers across the lines he's written and I can almost feel his soul in the sentences.

I read the next.

> *I wanted to write you a song and sing it to you but Jack, that bossy doucherag, said we had to do it this way. I don't know if anyone else will or not, but*

> *I'll come clean. We made another stupid pact. And yeah, I know. We said no more secrets. But after we started the Winnie's Favorite Hammer thing, we made a pact that none of us would tell us we were in love with you until you'd made your choice. We didn't want to cause you any additional confusion. But Winnie, every song I ever write for you will be a love song. Because I love you. I am in love with you. We all are. You're in love with all of us, too? FAN-FUCKINGTASTIC. I'm okay with it staying that way if you are.*
>
> *Gunnar*
>
> *P.S. Do you know any words that rhyme with orgasm? Y'know. Asking for a friend. Who is writing a song. About making some girl he's head over heels in love with want to orgasm all night long.*

I sob-laugh-sob, covering my mouth with my hand as snot bubbles out of my nose.

> *Winnie, the best day of my life was the day I invited you over to our house for pot roast when we were kids. It was the best decision I ever made. I love everything about you. And I need you to understand that that is never, ever going to change. I'm pretty sure all of my brothers would say the same. Let us keep loving you, darlin'. This isn't about picking your favorite anymore. It's just about choosing to say yes. To all of us.*

I blink rapidly, certain that my tears are distorting the words. What the what?

It looks like I have letters from each of them. As I read the ones written by Leo and Theo, Diesel and Axel, they capture my heart all over again.

Then I get to Mason. I have to draw in a very deep breath before I read his. What he did still cuts so deep. I'll forgive him, obviously. We'll get past it, obviously. But… yeah. It cuts real fucking deep.

> *Winnie, I am sorry for so many things. Small things from calling you Cupcake when you hate that to the worst mistake of my life, signing on for that stupid new show. I am infinitely sorry that I hurt you. When I said I love you, I meant it. I love you more than I ever thought it possible to love anyone, Win. And if you'll give me another chance, if you'll give us another chance, we'll all dedicate every day of the rest of our lives to doing what we're meant to do—protecting your heart. I can't promise I'll never hurt you again, because obviously I can be an idiot of epic proportions. But I will do my damndest to be a better man for you, Win. We all will.*

I move on to Jack's

> *Winifred,*
>
> *You know from our renos through the years that when we all work together, we can turn the worst disasters into masterpieces. I know right now you feel like this experiment was a disaster, but I believe it can still be a masterpiece. We're going to put another layer of primer down over our letters so they won't show through the paint, but they'll always be here. Our love for you, in this house. It'll also be with you wherever you go, Win, with whoever you're with. But I hope like hell you'll say yes to being with us.*
>
> *Jackass*

There are footsteps behind me and I turn.

All of my boys are there.

"I don't understand," I say.

"Winnie. Peach," Diesel says. "If there's one woman on this planet who can wrangle us all, it's you. We talked about it last night, at length, and we want to keep doing this forever."

To say I'm dumbfounded is a vast understatement. My gaze slides to Max and Mason. "All of you?"

"All of us," Mason says.

"We all want to be your man, sweetheart," Axel says. "Not temporarily, not 'til you make a choice. We want to keep things exactly as they are. For as long as you want. Forever if you want."

"But—"

Jack shakes his head. "We realize it's very unconventional. But I mean, look at us. Ten brothers made up of a set of triplets, three sets of twins, and, well, me? We Hammers have always been pretty unconventional."

My heart is beating so fast, I fear it's going to burst from my chest and splatter all over the gorgeous new floors.

"As we used to always say before every reno, *let's make it work!*" Gunnar says, pumping his fist. God, that catchphrase was so cheesy, but the networks insisted. Somewhere in between season 1 and season 8, it stopped being corny and started being a warcry we all took pretty damn seriously.

"Let's make it work," I whisper.

But how?

"We'll figure it out one day at a time, Pooh," Gavin says and I know he knows I'm getting in my head.

"Princess, if there's anyone who deserves the undying devotion and love from ten men, it's you," Max says.

Yep, my heart is definitely going to burst out of my chest.

I look down the line of them, standing before me. "If any of you ever keep anything from me again, I'll kill you. I know where to find a pickaxe."

Cruz groans. "How wrong is it that her threats of violence turn me on?" he asks the others.

He happens to be first in the lineup so I got to him.

"Seriously. I need you all to vow to me, right here and now, that no more secrets. Ever again. And I need you all to keep the damn vow this time. We're open and honest with each other. About everything."

Cruz nods. "Absolutely, darlin'."

I stare at him for a moment and see miles and miles of sincerity in his eyes. I press a soft, sweet kiss to his lips. "Then I choose you, Cruz Hammer."

I move on to Theo. "And I choose you, Theo Hammer." I kiss him just as sweetly.

"Gavin Hammer, I choose you."

"I love you, Pooh," he says, after I give him his kiss.

I move down the line until I get to Jack, who lifts me off my feet when I kiss him.

And when I get to Mason, I tell him the truth. "I actually love it when you call me Cupcake. So please never ever stop."

He smiles. "That's such a relief to hear, Cupcake, because I don't think it's a habit I could break."

"Good. Because I choose you, Mason Hammer."

Then I'm facing Max.

"There was no letter from you," I say, just realizing it's true as I say the words.

"There is. It's just not here. Will you come with me for a few minutes?"

My God, his eyes are glassy with tears.

"Wait. We need to make the rules," Jack says and everyone groans but me. I laugh.

"Honesty, no matter what, and lots of sex," I say. "Those are the only rules we need, I think."

All the guys cheer at that.

I take Max's hand.

"Where are we going, Big Max?"

CHAPTER 42

Winnie

M ax doesn't answer, because Axel interrupts and says, "You're forgetting something, bro."

I watch as the blindfold exchanges hands.

"Can I...?" Max asks with hesitation in his voice and a tentativeness in his beautiful eyes.

I nod.

He covers my eyes with it and fastens it at the back of my head. Then he takes my hand again. Our fingers intertwined, he leads me outside.

"Did you hire one of those planes to skywrite your letter?" I ask.

"Nope, but damn if that isn't a good idea."

I can tell we're in the backyard when he says, "Okay, turn around. I'm going to take the blindfold off but when I do, don't look at anything but me, okay?"

I nod.

When I can see again, I'm confused. He's positioned me facing him, facing the back of the reno house.

"Don't turn around," he says.

"Ahhh," I get it. "What I'm not supposed to see yet is behind me."

"Yep."

"Are you aware of what's behind you?" I ask, because it's the nine others peeking out of various windows.

Max glances back. "Goofballs." But he says it good-naturedly.

Then he takes a deep breath. "Did I completely destroy your trust in me forever?"

There's a fear in his eyes I've never seen before. He's bracing himself for me to say yes, yes he has.

"Max," I gesture for him to come closer and when he does, I hold him tight. He squeezes my body against his. "One really, really, really boneheaded decision couldn't possibly destroy something you've spent most of our lives building."

Am I letting him off the hook too easy? Maybe. But I also probably didn't give enough consideration to what hell it was for him, to watch me with the others, whole-heartedly believing I was going to choose one of them. How it felt for him. One minute I was telling him I wanted him to be my first, and then the next minute, I had nine other offers and everything we had just went away, like he'd been a mere placeholder.

"Okay. For my surprise. Turn around, princess, and behold the castle I built for you with my own two hands. Well, with some woodworking help from Cruz on the final details."

I turn around and nearly inhale all the grass in the backyard with my gasp.

"It's not finished back here so don't judge the landscaping yet, but–"

"Max." Fresh tears flood my eyes again, joyful tears, that blur the most magnificent treehouse I've ever seen in the huge old oak tree. "Holy shit."

"Is that a good holy shit or a bad holy shit?"

"That's… the best holy shit in the history of time."

I turn around again, facing him again, and give him the biggest bear hug in the history of time. "Can we go up?"

"Of course. This is what we wanted to do for you when we were younger. Obviously we didn't have the supplies or the tools or the skills, but…"

I go up, up, up the ladder first with him coming up behind me.

When I get to the top, I laugh and tease, "Max Hammer, you perv, when we were younger you wanted to build me a treehouse with a freaking bed in it?"

This is the most magical place in the world. The bedframe looks like it's made of actual branches, that it just sprouted organically from the tree.

"We didn't have a chance to bring the mattress up, and I wanted to let you choose the bedding. The roof is obviously waterproof."

I look at him in amazement, shaking my head. "This is…"

I don't have words. I spin around, seeing the handwriting on one of the walls.

"We're going to paint that one with black chalkboard paint," he says.

I step forward and read his letter.

> *Winnie,*
>
> *I need you to know that signing on for "Who Wants To Marry A Hammer Brother?" was never about finding a woman I could fall in love with, and definitely not about finding a wife or even a fiance. You know Mason and I loved reality TV and wanted to continue on with it. When the offer was extended, I jumped on it because I thought dating twenty-something women at once would be the distraction I'd need after having my heart thoroughly shattered when you chose one of my brothers over me. It was a real jackass thing to do. But I could date a million women, princess, and I'd never ever find one I'd love even half as much as I love you. There's no woman they could cast who would win my heart, Winnie, because that belongs to you and only you. It's okay with me if you can't say the same to me, that your heart belongs to me and only me. Because you have the biggest heart of anyone I know. And as long as I know you love me, I promise you, nothing else matters. That fact alone will make me the happiest man alive.*

I turn to face him. Then I go to him and hug him again.

"Are you really going to be okay with all of this?" I ask him. "Because I need to know this time, Max. Without a doubt."

"Yeah," he says, pulling away a bit so we can gaze up into each other's eyes, while still have our arms around each other's waists. His fingers stroke my back. "Win, you told me you would call the whole thing off for me, remember?"

"And you told me you didn't want me to! But obviously part of you must have because–"

He moves a hand up to my face and tucks a curl behind my ear. "Like I told you then, it was petty jealousy. Deep down, I never had an issue with you dating all of us, Win. I just couldn't handle the thought of you ending up with someone that wasn't me. Especially not one of my brothers. But now… I just want you, Win. And as long as you want me back…" he drops his voice to a whisper and scrunches up his nose so cutely and says, "Let's make it work, princess."

"Let's make it work, Max."

I stare into his eyes.

"Isn't this the part where you say you choose me?" he stage-whispers.

"No, Maxwell Hammer. This is the part where I say I love you."

He grins the biggest grin ever at me. "I love you, too, Win. So damn much and it feels so damn good to be able to say it."

He lowers his mouth to mine and when he kisses me, I kiss him back with all my heart. Not 1/10th of it. Because he's right. I'm a big girl–and I'm okay with that now–with a big ass heart to match.

"Does this mean you'll take me out on a date now?" I tease, when we break apart.

"Well, um, I haven't actually planned anything but–"

"Good," I beam up at him. "I'll plan it."

I have no idea what we're going to do, but it's going to be public as hell. Let the internet trolls talk. I want Max Hammer to take me out on the town.

"Okaaaaay..." he says, then he pauses then he adds, "Should I be scared? Does it involve the sex dungeon Gunnar wanted to build in the basement that this house thankfully doesn't have?"

"No, no dungeon. It may or may not involve the S-E-X part, though."

"Okay, I'm listening. And when do you want to go on this date that has potential for S-E-X, Miss Wainwright?"

"Tonight?" I ask.

"Can't wait," he says.

After we kiss again... and again... and again, he asks, "Do you want me to get the guys to help me bring the mattress up for the bed now?"

All the light bulbs go off in my head.

Fate, is that you?

"Wait... where is the mattress?" I ask.

"In the back of my truck," he says.

I make him promise to leave it there.

Swoooooooooon.

CHAPTER 43

Winnie

Max looks delicious. He obviously took great care in picking out his outfit.

Too bad all those clothes are coming off as soon as we get to our destination, Big Max, I think.

He's driving, but I'm directing him, hoping I don't get us lost because, if we end up in the wrong place, our first date might wind up with us both getting arrested for public indecency.

"Oooh!" I see the dirt road cutting through the trees. "Turn here, turn here."

He glances sideways at me. "Uh… are you taking me into the woods to clock me over the head with something and roll my body into a river?"

"That was Plan B. I decided to go a different route, but your body will definitely be taken care of," I joke. "Just drive. It will be fine."

"Win," he says after a few minutes. He definitely sounds apprehensive. "We are in the deadass middle of nowhere. In a fucking forest in the deadass middle of nowhere."

"Just keep going."

I'm getting a little nervous myself though, but thankfully, after a few minutes, the trees thin. And after a few more, we arrive.

"Ta da!" I unbuckle my seat belt.

Max raises a brow. "We're in a field."

He doesn't move so I press the release button on his seat belt, too. "Come on."

I hop out of the truck and he follows.

It's a perfect night, clear of clouds, and the moon casts a soft glow on the scrubby land around us. He doesn't look any more impressed once his feet are on the ground. He kicks something, a rock or dirt clump.

"When Gram died," I say, "I found out she owned some land. This—" I gesture around us, "—is it."

At least I hope this is the land.

"Gram owned a field?"

I sidle up to him. His hands find the small of my back, pulling me closer.

"And now," I say, gazing up at him, "it's *my* field."

"Alright," he replies slowly, his brows knitted together. "But what are we doing here?"

"Well," I say. "You know, at one point in time, we'd planned for you to take my V-card. Obviously it's too late for that now. I've had a lot of sex."

"Ah, so you *did* bring me out here to kill me," he deadpans. But even as he says it, he pulls me even closer. The warmth of his touch contrasts deliciously with the cool night air.

"It's too late for you to be the first man I sleep with, Big Max. But I can… no, I *want* you to be the first man I make love to."

Max's expression softens, and I am captivated by the tenderness in his gaze. I have missed the private looks he used to give me, so much more than I realized during these last few weeks.

His grip on my waist tightens ever so slightly as our lips meet. A surge of electricity courses through every fiber of my being. The taste of his kiss is both familiar and new, and it is a heady blend. I'm thrilled to be kissing Max guilt-free. I have missed his passionate kisses just as much as his secret looks. And now we have no secrets in our relationship, no hiding our feelings from the others. He's mine and I'm his, and that gives our kiss an entirely new dimension.

Breaking the kiss much too soon, he looks into my eyes, again, and this time his expression is a mix of desire and curiosity. "But I still don't get why here, Win. You *really* want to make love in the field you inherited from your bitch of a grandma, in the deadass middle of nowhere, on the mattress in the back of my truck?"

I smile, tracing his jawline with my fingertips. "This field is like Gram's house, I think - a part of my past that I didn't want to ever face again. But that's not Gram's house anymore - it's a place with a very bright future."

"Right," he agrees slowly.

"Tonight, just by coming here together, we have already begun to change this field's history. And," I add with a wink, "I think it has a *very* promising future."

He growls softly. "Can't argue with that. Let's make history, baby."

He tilts his hips into mine, pulling me tightly against him.

"I can't think of any better man for the job," I murmur. Then I kiss him basically everywhere that his skin is exposed. He's more gorgeous than ever when bathed in the moonlight.

Max drops the tailgate of his truck and lifts me up to sit at the edge. He parts my thighs and slides his body between them. He pulls me closer, and I respond eagerly, pushing my hips into him, slanting my lips against his. The world fades away until all that exists in my entire universe is Max, Max, Max. The delicious hard lines of him are such a contrast to his soft touch, and I'm intoxicated by him. Intoxicated by the sensation of his lips against mine. The taste of his mouth against mine. The feel of his body growing harder as he nestles into my thighs.

"Too many clothes," I complain against his lips, tugging at his shirt.

He nibbles my pouting bottom lip, and then says, "How about we get naked now?"

After he hops into the truck bed and we end up tangled on the mattress for another lip-locked minute, he begins to kiss every exposed inch of my skin. But before he can remove any of my clothes, I whisper, "My turn."

Stripping each other down in turns, item by item, starting with our shirts we kiss and kiss, worshiping each other, until every piece of clothing has disappeared. His shirt, then mine; his jeans, then my bra; his boxers, my pants, his socks. I tickle his feet, forgoing a toes-kiss and working my way up to his lips for a kiss.

Then his hands are at my panties, and his eyes shine in the moonlight, brighter than stars, as he pulls them down.

"Look at you, sweet girl. Fuck, how I've missed you," he says with a groan as he buries his kiss – a very tongue-heavy kiss – in my pussy. He switches to his finger, and makes out with my clit for a good long time. I start to coil up with an orgasm, but I manage to keep it at bay.

And then, he kisses his way back up my body, covering me with his skin, which is burning hot in the cool of the night.

"You feel feverish," I say, touching his forehead, actually a little bit concerned.

He takes my hand and kisses each of my fingers, even though he definitely has kissed them already. "Of course I do—I have been burning for you for-freaking-*ever*, Win. Now I get you?" he shakes his head in disbelief.

Then his hands cup my face, and he gazes so deeply into my eyes as he slides inside me, as if he's savoring every moment, too important to rush. It takes a good while, because his cock is so freaking long, and when his hips are finally flushed with mine, he feels so incredible my body has the urge to fuck hard and fuck fast.

I try, but with his hips pressing me into the mattress, I'm mostly just squirming, which makes my clit sing, as I slide against him.

Hold out, Winnie, don't let go yet, I think.

"What? No way, Winnie. If you feel the wave, ride it." He rolls his hips, giving me long, luxuriously slow strokes that leave me panting with need.

"I don't want this to end."

"It won't. Because I'm keeping *my* explosion at bay. I plan on making love to you until the sun starts to rise. Or the cows come home. That's fitting for this field."

I laugh and as I do, my clit rubs against him quicker, and there's no way I can hold myself back anymore. I kiss him hard and he slams into me even harder until I burst, clenching around him as I cry out his name. It's a good thing we are in the deadass middle of nowhere, because I've never been louder.

He slows again, moaning as he rocks his hips. I'm sensitive, quivering with aftershocks. He pulls out and we switch spots, him on his back so that I can taste myself on his harder-than-ever cock.

I roll my tongue over him, around him, sucking him deeply, and keeping him going as I give myself time to recuperate.

And when my body is a bit less sensitive, I rise up on my knees, and lock my eyes with his wildly-glazed ones as I sink down on him again.

"Fuuuck, you're so much tighter this way, it feels like you're still sucking on my dick." He laughs and bucks his hips up so that I rise up from the bed, as he fills me completely.

I'm so much more sensitive now, and feeling extra full. But when he reaches out and touches between my legs, and the slam of his hips comes faster and harder, I feel the coil building up inside me, and in a rush that takes me by surprise, I come all over his cock again.

He laughs, but doesn't stop bucking and touching me, and even though I'm more sensitive than before, he grips my hips and grinds into me, and my body begins preparing to explode again.

He rolls to the side, stretching out against me so that my ass is spooned against him. When he slides into my pussy from behind, the different angle gives me a whole new experience. As his hands touch my clit again, he groans against my ear.

"I'm going to come. Think you can come along?"

"I don't know. I've never come more than twice like this."

I can feel him smile as he kisses the curve of shoulder. And while his hips flex and he teases my nipple with the hand that isn't teasing my clit, I wind up tight again, until I start to unravel.

"I'm coming, Max," I say, and his hands go to my hips then.

He slams into me with a quick, steady rhythm that has my body rising into the heavens, it feels like. There's no way we are still in a field, in the middle of nowhere, on a mattress in the bed of his truck. We've transcended space, possibly time.

When I burst for the third time, it skyrockets me straight into the stars.

"*Winnie*, fuck," he shouts as he slams into me one last time. Then whispers, as he shudders around me, "You're perfect. This is perfect."

When he pulls out of me, I swear, we both whimper.

I roll over so I'm facing him.

He gives me the most tender kiss.

"I can't believe I almost blew this."

"Shhh," I say, reaching up to run a hand through his hair.

"I don't want to shhh," he says. "I want to tell you, Winnie Wainwright, that I love you with all my heart and soul and never in my life has anything been so worth the wait."

He pulls me against him holding me close, whispering, "I love you, I love you, I love you."

"I love you, I love you, I love you back," I tell him and never in my life have I been so happy as I am right now.

CHAPTER 44

Winnie

Since I never got to make my pot roast dinner for the boys, the next morning, I'm downstairs early making them all breakfast. It was hard leaving Max sleeping in his bed, where we cuddled all night after getting home. I've decided to do a buffet of each of their favorites.

They filter in one by one and start pitching in even though I try to shoo them away. Axel and Max are setting the table while Theo puts the finishing touches on my fruit place.

"Morning, all," Gav says, sauntering in and looking scrumptiously rumpled. "Can I do anything?"

"No! I want to do this by myself!" I cry, playfully, as Diesel sneaks up behind me nuzzling my neck and palming my butt with both hands.

Cruz, wearing only a towel, bless him, starts getting out glasses and pouring OJ for everyone.

"You have ten boyfriends. You're never going to get to do anything by yourself again, Peach." Diesel nips my earlobe with his lips while giving my buns a squeeze. His cock is hard against my back. My blueberry walnut pancakes aren't the only mouthwatering thing in the kitchen this morning. I press back into him making him groan.

"No time for hanky panky, Easy Deezy. I've got to get these hash browns in the skillet–"

"Mmm," he murmurs into my hair. "How 'bout we forget that and I'll try to put a bun in your oven instead?"

"Oh my god," I laugh, thankful he's obviously just teasing because I am not yet ready for that level of It's Complicated. "You horny, horny man. If you insist on hanging around in here while I cook, please go crack those eggs over there."

"Consider your eggs cracked, Peach."

"Thank you. And please wash your hands first since you just groped my ass."

"What do I look like, some kind of Neanderthal?" he teases.

"Yep," Mason cracks.

"Hey," says Axel. "Since Deez and I are identical I take offense to that."

"Eh," Cruz says. "I don't take offense to anything."

I get a delicious, minty fresh good morning kiss from each of them as we bustle around.

This is my life!!!

"Holy shit, Jack slept in?" Gunnar asks, when he finally wanders in and takes a head count.

"No, he's up," I say. He was up in more ways than one until I made him sit down at the table under which I gave him a blowie when it was just the two of us awake. My cheeks flush thinking about it. Anna is going to kill us if she ever finds out what we've been up to in her kitchen.

"And he's not bitching that there's no coffee?" Gunnar goes to the coffee maker and gets that going.

"I sent him to the market to get some powdered sugar."

"Oh, Darlin', don't you know I can give you all the sugar you need?" Cruz winks at me from the blender.

Everyone but me groans. I blow Cruz a kiss.

Diesel's hands are back on my ass.

"Deez, I need you to resist while I'm holding a hot skillet."

"Oh, baby, but how can I when you're in those little shorts?" He's behind me again, and whispers in my ear. "Especially since I've had my cock buried inside this fine behind–"

"Okay!" I announce. I'm sure I'm beet red. "I'm going to change into something with more coverage."

"Noooo!" at least three or four of them chorus.

"Don't let my bacon burn. I'll be right back."

I get to my room and lock the door behind me before any of them can sneak after me and follow me in for a morning quickie. Not that I'd say no. But I really don't want to wind up permanently bow-legged from too much sex.

I'm in a t-shirt but haven't gotten my overalls on yet when my phone starts ringing.

I glance at the display. It's Lexie our manager.

"Hey, Lex," I answer. Then I say as kindly as possible, "If you are calling to try to get me to do some kind of 1 Girl, 10 Hammer spinoff, please don't."

Max and I talked about it at length last night and eventually, he and Mason do want to do another show, but it'll be some kind of home improvement show. Definitely not anything to do with our personal lives. He and Mace both formally backed out of Who Wants To Marry A Hammer Brother? before even writing their letters to me.

"I'm not calling to try to get you to do anything, Win," Lexie sounds extremely flustered, but I mean, that's kind of on brand for her. "Well, yeah, actually I am. I need you to convince Max and Mason to say they were out of their damn minds and obviously didn't mean it when they decided to back out of the new show!"

Uh, yeah, not happening, babe.

"Max and Mason are big boys, Lexie. They do what they want."

"Well, the consequences are not going to be pretty!" she screeches.

"They are well aware that they're in breach of contract and there's going to be financial–"

"We're not talking about financial shit, Win. We're talking about something money can't fix. The guys are going to be blacklisted from the entertainment industry. They'll be lucky if they can get a gig on a freaking local morning show after this. The project was moving very quickly and both the production company and studio are out for blood over Max and Mason backing out."

I sit down on the bed. "Oh, boy."

"And when I say 'the guys' are going to be blacklisted, Winnie, I want to make it perfectly clear that I mean all of them. I can't stress how dire this is. You could all be ruined, your reputations tarnished beyond repair."

Fuck. Lexie is wound tight, sure, but she's not one for hyperbole or being overdramatic. If she says it it's true.

I run a hand through my hair, wondering what this might mean for the others' careers. For Gunner and Diesel's music even.

Fuck.

I think long and hard for a few minutes. I don't want any of my boys to lose out on their dreams, on their careers, on *anything* that makes them happy for me.

"Do you think it would help if we offered to do another show instead? All of us?" I ask.

"I'm listening," she says. "But it would have to be something really, really special."

I think it will be, but I hope it'll be enough.

After I make my pitch to Lexie, who promises she'll call me back ASAP, I pull on my overalls and go downstairs. Part of me wants to wait until I hear back from her, but that part of me is outvoted by my heart, which loves these boys so, and my conscience, which holds me to the same standards I'm holding them to. I'm not starting out this phase of our relationship with deception.

Jack is back with the powdered sugar and all of the others have finished up the dishes I left in various states of done. We all sit down to eat and I lay out the current state of affairs, including what I proposed to Lexie.

Nobody looks happy about the situation and everyone is picking at their food.

"I'm so fucking sorry," Max says, rubbing his hands over his face. "I wish I had something else to offer, but... yeah. That's it."

"What you and Mason did was really fucking unprofessional, bro," Theo says.

"Don't be a douchebag," Gunnar says.

"Gun, you don't have to defend us. I appreciate it, but it's unnecessary. Theo's right," Mason says.

Theo clears his throat. "What Max and Mason did was really fucking unprofessional but... let's make it work. Hopefully Lexie will get back to us with good news."

Someone nudges my foot under the table and I suspect it's Gavin, who speaks next, "Pooh Bear, you sure if she says it's a go that you'll be okay with it?"

What I pitched to Lexie is a 1 Girl, 10 Hammers special mini-series of three or four episodes–the fans are obviously still clamoring for more after the finale just aired–where we film the rest of the reno on Gram's house. I explained to Lexie how deeply personal it is, and how I'm willing to talk on camera–as many confessionals as they want– about my past and what this house did to me growing up and how the renovation has healed those wounds.

"If we have to, I'm on board for offering them to resurrect 1 Girl, 10 Hammers for a couple more seasons in lieu of that. Winnie shouldn't have to lay her soul bare on national television," Jack says. "Period."

"No way," Max says. "I mean, I agree with you. She shouldn't. But you shouldn't have to go back to the show, either, Jack. You said you were done and we heard you. You want your privacy back, man, and you deserve that."

"Everybody, hear me out," Diesel says.

"No," the rest of us say automatically, because we can all tell he's about to say something none of us like.

"What if they go with the Who Wants To Marry A Hammer Brother thing?" he suggests.

Um, how about hell no?

"Hell no," Mason says.

I fight a smile.

"Just listen. You can fake your way through it and break up with whoever you choose right after it's over."

"Because that's fair to the women?" I ask, quirking an eyebrow at him.

"Okay, you've got a point," he relents.

Gunnar bites his lip, dragging it through his teeth. "It's not the worst idea."

"They're not doing Who Wants To Marry A Hammer Brother," I say. I don't feel right adding that when I'm sleeping with all of them, I don't want to watch Max or Mason kissing dozens of other women, even if it's just for show. But then I remember the whole open, honesty thing. "I don't want to watch either of you kissing other women, even if it's just for show. Sorry if that's hypocritical."

"Wait," Jack says. "What Gun said just gave me an idea–"

My phone buzzes.

Lexie.

We all hold our collective breath. She works quick, but, even for her, to have gotten an answer this fast is astonishing. Rejections tend to come quicker than acceptances, though, so I brace myself.

"Lex, you're on speaker. You've got us all," I tell her when I answer.

"Sorry, Win. It's not enough," she says flatly.

"Damn," mutters Leo, who's been quiet about the whole thing.

"Hey, Lex. It's Jack," he says. "Find out if that no would change to a yes if we could give them the 1 Girl, 10 Hammers romance storyline they've always wanted."

I look at Jack, bug-eyed. All of the guys are gaping at him too.

"Jack, what the hell are you doing?" I whisper, frantically.

Though we all hope there will be a day where I can go to the movies and sit in between Cruz and Axel and hold both their hands… the day when I can go dancing again with Leo, Theo, and whoever else wants to go and make out with them all out in the open… the day where we can take our unconventional love public… the day when we can tell the world we're us and if they don't like it, they can fuck off… none of us are quite ready for that day to be today.

Except maybe Jack?

Jack holds up a finger to shush me.

"If you're talking about some fabricated storyline, Jack, the audience will never buy it."

Then how come we were pushed to do just that for almost all eight full seasons, I wonder.

Jack takes my phone and presses the mute button. "Do you all trust me?"

We all say yes, though some of us are more hesitant in our reply than others. Gunnar, especially, probably because of the Great Nail Gun Accident of Season 3. I don't think he 100% believes it was a total accident on Jack's part.

But Jack is Mr. Man With A Plan.

"Lex, Winnie and Leo are a couple," Jack says, smoothly, after unmuting.

It's nothing short of a miracle if Lexie didn't hear at least one of us gasp.

Before Lexie—or any of the rest of us—can say anything, he goes on smoothly and part of me is wondering what the fuck he's up to, but the rest of me thinks, damn, the way he takes charge is so sexy. I can't wait for him to boss me around in the bed…Okay. Not the time for fantasizing.

"They've been together for a while but wanted to keep their relationship private. That night at the club and that whole picture fiasco… they were on a date. Theo was really just there as a third wheel so no one would suspect anything if they were spotted."

Theo makes a face and gives Jack the middle finger.

"Are you shitting me?" Lexie asks and I have that anxious twist in my stomach. Even Lexie isn't going to buy that Leo would choose me as his girlfriend? I shake my head.

Because what she buys or doesn't won't matter in the long run. He has chosen me as his girlfriend. They all have.

This IS my life!

"No," Jack says. "That's why we were so against doing the Winnie's Favorite Hammer spin-off."

"OH MY GOD," Lexie shouts like she's mid-orgasm. "I knew it. I knew it. I knew one of you had to be banging her. The sexual chemistry amongst you all… Wait, Winnie, Leo, you are willing to go public? On the show?"

Now it's Cruz who lurches forward, snapping up my phone and muting it. "This will make the internet trolls double down on attacking Win," he says, his tone fiercely protective.

"I promise I won't read the comments, Cruzie," I take my phone back from him, unmute again, and say, "Lexie, if it will undo the damage Max and Mason have done," I say, pause to mouth *sorry* at them both, then go on, "Leo and I will do anything on camera you want us, too."

"Yes, love, absolutely anything at all," he agrees, winking at me.

"I just wish there was some way to tie your romance into the storyline about the house and Winnie's past…" Lexie muses. "That would really sell it."

"Well, the lovebirds are planning on moving into the house when it's done," Jack says with a shrug at the WTF expressions on all of our faces.

"Yep," I go with it. "I couldn't be in the house at all without feeling like I was going to puke with this journey started, but now… well, we've turned it into a home."

"Okay. Give me a couple of hours. No, give me one. One hour."

"Live in Gram's house?" I ask Jack incredulously after I end the call.

"It's a really nice little house now," he says. "I wouldn't mind living here."

"Keyword being little. There's two bedrooms. I'm more than down for threesomes but no way am I waking up spooning one of you douches," Diesel says.

"You couldn't have said it was me and Win?" Theo grumbles.

"Leo comes first alphabetically. Besides, it'll only be a couple weeks, tops. In fact, we might have to undo some stuff to give us enough to fill a couple weeks." He's already looking around, planning.

By the end of the day, we have expedited contracts in hand for 1 Girl & Her Favorite Hammer: Renovations & Romance.

CHAPTER 45

Winnie

The superpower of any great reality show producer is getting the cast to cry, but Goldie hasn't even asked me a single question yet, and my eyes are leaky faucets.

"Happy tears," I tell Golds. "They're all happy tears."

"Off the record," she whispers. "Are you going to be able to pull this off? Pretending you're strictly platonic with all the guys except Leo for an entire week?"

During the day, when the cameras and crew are around, I'll sure as hell try. At night, when they're gone and we're back in the Hammer house, just the 11 of us? I wouldn't bet on it.

"Hey, love," Leo comes into the partitioned off confessional area and squeezes my shoulder. "Are you two ready for me?"

"I'm always ready for you, stud," I say, saucily, even though there are no cameras on yet.

"Ooh, redo that and I'll catch it," Goldie says, reaching over to her camera and the red light starts blinking.

Once Leo is sitting next to me, holding my hand, Goldie transforms from Bestie!Goldie to Producer!Goldie and doesn't pull any punches. She knows all about what we need to accomplish here and why.

"So, Winnie, tell me where you were, mentally, when this journey began and where you are now," she says.

I take a deep breath. Leo gives my hand a squeeze.

"This is the house I grew up in. When we first arrived to start the reno…" I swallow hard, thinking about that night with Gavin, when I gave him the grand tour of the disaster this place was, and told him about the disaster I felt like. "My grandmother and father's voices tormented me. They were both cruel. Mostly about my weight, but they were very skilled at making me feel worthless, period."

I glance at Leo and he gives me a nod of encouragement.

"By the time I got out of here, when I was eighteen, my self-esteem was nil. And Grams' and Dad's voices weren't the only ones I let tear me down. I'm sure most of the people watching this saw the picture of me with Leo and Theo out dancing. That was mortifying. People can be cruel. So that's where I was at the beginning. I wanted to take a wrecking ball to this place, the way all those voices took a wrecking ball to my confidence, to my soul."

Goldie nods. "You need a break?"

I shake my head. I'm tearing up, but am surprisingly okay. Leo hands me a tissue and I dab at my eyes with it.

"Awww, honey, it looks like you need a tissue too," I say to him. His eyes are wet.

"The thought of anyone making her feel that way," he swipes at his eyes with his fingertips, "breaks my heart. And really, really fucking pisses me off."

"Beautiful sentiment, but since you seem to have forgotten, the network doesn't like the shows littered with bleeps so anything with an f-bomb in it is likely to end up on the cutting room floor."

"Well," he says. "I definitely want that to end up on the air. So let me say it again in a more family-friendly way."

"And where are you now, Win?" Goldie asks, once she's gotten a take she can use from Leo.

"Well, I'm ridiculously in love for starters," I beam. "But that's nothing new. I've been in love for a very long time. I just wasn't in a place where I could accept that a Hammer brother could love me in return."

"And you can now?"

I nod. "Oh, yeah. This reno didn't just transform this house. It transformed me. Every day, little by little, the voices that tormented me grew quieter. And every day, I learned that those aren't the voices that matter."

"Great," Goldie turns off the camera. "That's almost all I need for now. Just one more thing and this is off the record… who's the best *cunning linguist*, if you know what I mean?"

"Me, obviously," Leo says, then he laughs. "We gotta find you ten men of your own, Golds."

"I wish!" she laughs. "Can one of you send Jack in next?"

Though Leo and my relationship is a major storyline in the show, obviously it's about the reno, too, and the fans are going to want plenty of the boys, so that's what they're going to get.

"Lordy, Winnie, you are *flushed!*" Sam, here to make sure we're always camera-ready, is coming at me with her powder puff of doom.

I'm flushed because Diesel's at the staircase, caressing the banister in a fairly obscene way, going on about how they were his favorite part of the house. "You can really get a workout on these stairs," he says into the camera with a matter-of-fact nod.

"Oh, how I've missed you, Sammie," I say and I realize that I have. I've missed this. I'm glad we're doing this.

As she de-flushes me, I give a little squeal when I catch sight of Jonesy, the cameraman who overheard and filmed me lamenting to Goldie that I wanted to lose my virginity to a Hammer brother but they would never see me as more than a friend. And that didn't happen that long ago at all. Yikes. He could totally blow our cover and confirm that Leo and I have not, in fact, been together for awhile a la the story Jack sold to Lexie.

Dammit.

I'm about to rush over to him and… do what? I have no idea when I'm summoned upstairs.

Axel and Diesel are flanking the outside of the door to the room that used to be my dad's. I haven't been allowed inside it almost since the very beginning of the reno, but the padlock is gone now. I notice cameras at either end of the hall, so I know that whatever is happening here, it's important. They don't want to chance missing my reaction from any angle.

"As I was saying," Axel says. "This is a room we've already completely finished but Winnie hasn't seen it since demo day."

"This used to be her father's room so we wanted to turn it into something really special," Diesel takes over, with that natural charisma that all the boys have and all the fans adore.

"Damn," Axel snaps his fingers, "We should've brought a blindfold for this."

And all the work Sam did on my cheeks is completely undone. They grow hot at his words, the insinuation in his eyes as he glances at me, and I hope to God the camera doesn't catch it.

"I'll close my eyes," I say, doing so.

I don't hear the door open–it no longer creaks–but Axel, no, it's Diesel, guides me into the room.

"You can open those baby blues, love," Leo says. So he's here too.

I open my eyes and draw in a breath. "This is so…"

I can't find words. Not even one. The room where my dad spent his nights doing God only knows what after days making me miserable is completely transformed. It's not even a bedroom anymore. There are floor-to-ceiling mahogany bookshelves on the two side walls, complete with a ladder. On the back wall, surrounding the huge window, are built-ins, with what look like endless drawers. In the center of the room is a large round table.

"It's a library-slash-gameroom," Cruz, who is also present now, tells me, although the library part is pretty evident.

TEN HAMMERS

"The built-ins are storage for games so that the room won't get cluttered. It's unfinished because we wanted to let you pick out the chairs for the table and the furniture for the reading nook, which will go in that corner."

"I lobbied for a pool table, but these fools, apparently, don't know how much fun a pool table can be," Mason says, with no innuendo in his voice. But there's definitely a secret just the two of us share in the smile he gives me.

"What do you think, darlin'? I mean, Winnie. I mean…"

Bring on that powder puff, Sam, my Cruzie is flushed.

Leo laughs, good-naturedly, "You've always called her darlin', Cruz. It's fine."

"It's… amazing. You all are amazing." I glance around at each of my guys, who are all present and accounted for. I give them each a big, friendly hug. But I want to give them each a big, sexy kiss, of course.

I walk around, skimming my fingertips over the woodwork, taking it all in. I glance up. "I love the chandelier. It looks familiar…? Have I seen it before?"

"We used an identical one on the Tanner reno," Cruz says. "Season five. You loved it then, too."

I grin. "Right, we used it in their dining room."

"Yep," he grins.

"Okay," Jack says. "Everybody back to it. This reno ain't gonna finish itself. Everyone not in the kitchen needs to head out to the backyard and help Axel so we can stay on schedule."

"Winnie's not allowed in the backyard," Axel says.

"Another surprise?" My cheeks ache from grinning already.

"Jack," says Marcus, our director, who mostly just makes sure we've got all the footage we need and the right confessionals to turn it into a cohesive story but has always given us plenty of leeway. "Do you think I can steal our happy couple to get some B-roll of them being a happy couple?"

"No problem," Jack says.

So I spend the morning sitting on the porch with Leo, walking up the street with Leo, holding hands, kissing Leo in my childhood bedroom…

"Thankfully you had the forethought to take the before-and-after pictures," Marcus says. "We can use inserts of those before we show the afters. By the way… Don't want to be nosy, but… this is meant to be a young girl's room, right? Are we thinking about little Hammers pitter-pattering around?"

"When we designed this room, we hadn't decided we would be living here yet," Leo says, smoothly. "My girl was going to give the house away to a family who needed it. But now that we've decided to stay here… Well. We'll just use this as a guest room for now."

"Okay," Marcus says. "I think that'll do for now. Since craft services won't be here 'til tomorrow, what's good to eat in this town? Let's break a couple hours for lunch."

"Tino's Bistro is Win's favorite," Leo says. "But I love the Sub Emporium."

Once Marcus calls it, everyone clears out fast.

Jonesy was the one who was filming the B-roll so I ask him to wait a minute. Leo shoots me a questioning look but when I tell him it's okay, he says he'll be out in the backyard seeing if Axel needs anything.

"Jonesy, I need to ask you a favor…" I begin.

"You don't need to ask me anything, Winnie. Your private business is your private business."

Huh. I guess I'm not the only one who has been transformed recently.

"Oh. Okay. Thanks. I mean it."

He gives me a nod and says, "That Tino's got good lasagna?"

"The best lasagna."

I go downstairs and try to find Goldie but she doesn't seem to be around. So I head across the street, planning to lie down for a few minutes and rest my eyes. I'd forgotten how exhausting shoot days were.

I've barely gotten into my room when the door opens again and Jack slips in.

"We don't knock anymore?" I tease.

"This isn't a visit, it's an ambush," he says.

I laugh and raise my eyebrows. "Excuse me?"

And then my mouth goes dry when I see he's holding bungee cords.

CHAPTER 46

Winnie

"Jackfruit, what have you got there?"

"A way to restrain you, Winifred."

I swear my clit reacts like he's just held a damn vibrator to it. Which, please, oh please, let that be something he's actually planning to do.

"You see, my dear. You've been a very, very naughty lady. Torturing me all morning, so much PDA with Leo while your poor, poor Jackfruit gets no love."

"Well, this was *your* grand plan, sir."

"Doesn't matter." He shakes his head slowly.

I cock an eyebrow. "It doesn't?"

"No, baby, it doesn't. I'm afraid I'm going to have to punish you for being so very, very bad."

He closes the distance between us like he's a predator and I'm the prey, dropping the bungee cords to the floor so he can gently take my face in his hands. He kisses me, passionate and sweet, til we're both breathless. When we pull away, all the sweetness is gone and there's only raw passion in his voice when he says, "Now, I want you to take everything off but your panties and go lay on your back on the bed."

"Jack, I really don't think–"

"I wasn't asking if it was something you wanted to do, baby," he says gruffly. "Because I *know* you want to."

I know, of course, that I can say no if I want to. But he's right. I'm already eager to do exactly what he tells me to.

I pull my shirt over my head and let it fall to the floor. I unzip and shuck off my jeans. And then I unfasten my bra and fling it over my shoulder, really not caring where the hell it lands.

"Do you know how long I've been waiting to fuck you, Winifred?"

"Too damn long, Jackie Boo Boo."

He laughs but raises an eyebrow. "Jackie Boo Boo?"

"I'm too horny to think straight. Are you really going to tie me to the bed with bungee cords?"

"I am. Then–"

Before he can say anything else, there's a light knock on the door. I instinctively cover my chest with my arms the best I can.

"Win? It's me."

Gavin.

"Should I tell him to piss off or invite him in?" Jack asks.

Ooooh, good question! "Do you mind if we—"

Jack shakes his head. "If he wants to watch me fuck you, far be it from me to stop him, baby."

"Well, well, well," Gavin says, surveying the scene. "Jackie boy, looks like you had the same idea I did. But you beat me to it." His eyes drop to the bungee cords. "And brought accessories. Mind if I stay and play or you two want private time?"

"You can stay," Jack says.

Gavin locks the door.

Five minutes later, I'm staring up at the ceiling, spread-eagle on the bed, bound to the bedposts by my ankles and wrists. "I kind of like Fifty Shades of Hammer."

"You do, huh?" Jack grins. "Before you got here, Gav, I was telling Winnie she needs to be punished for being such a naughty girl, giving us blue balls while making out all over the damn place with Leo."

Gavin winks at me. "You have a point," he says to Jack, seriously.

"We were just going to fuck, but maybe…

"Maybe a fitting punishment would be to make her squirm a little, first?"

"Where are your infamous dildos, baby?" Jack asks.

"W-what?" I ask.

"You heard me."

"Um, second drawer. Underneath my pajamas."

He walks over. "Mmm-hmmm," he murmurs after a second. "Which one is the Jack?"

I blush. "The biggest."

"I should probably check and see if you're wet enough to take it, huh?" Gavin asks.

My nipples are rock hard and I think every ounce of blood in my body has rushed to my clit. And, yes, I'm wet enough to take a baseball bat at this point in time. Gavin rubs me through the thin fabric of my damp panties and I whimper.

"Hmm," he says. "Can't tell."

I instinctively lift my hips off the bed as he slides a hand down my belly and underneath the elastic waistband of my panties.

"Oh, she's wet as fuck, man."

He pulls my panties down to my knees.

Then sits on the edge of the bed and I moan as his fingers find my clit.

Jack comes towards us holding my Jack dildo and a wicked smile.

"I would ask you to show me what you do with it, but obviously, your hands are tied…" he says. I close my eyes, remembering how all my senses were heightened while wearing the blindfold.

His hands brush my thighs then the head of the dildo is at my opening. Gavin picks up the pace working my clit as Jack penetrates me with the dildo with agonizing slowness.

"Can you take it all, baby?"

I'm squirming trying to get away from Gavin's touch, trying to get more of it, I don't know. Holy fuck these boys.

Then the door opens again.

"Oh my god. I am *so* fucking sorry!" It's Samantha and she's covering her eyes with her hands. There isn't a powder puff in the world big enough to hide my full body flush. "Axel asked me to come get his soil pH tester probe from off his dresser and this… isn't his room."

It isn't. And it's not his soil pH tester Jack has buried inside me either.

Holy shit.

She's still covering her eyes. "I am so sorry. I am so embarrassed. I will not say a word to anyone. I swear. Oh, my God. Oh, my God."

She turns around and runs out.

I don't know why *she's* embarrassed. "Can one of you untie me? Please?"

"I don't understand," Gav says. "I locked the door."

"Obviously we need to put fixing that on our honey-do lists," Jack says, as he unties me. "I am so sorry, baby. Are you okay? I'll talk to Sam and make sure she doesn't say anything."

"Yes, please do that. But please make me come first, unless you did intend for this to be punishment."

I'm probably going to die of humiliation but if I do, I want to go out satisfied.

CHAPTER 47

Winnie

"Ohhhhh, Cinderella," Cruz sing-songs, "Your chariot awaits, Darlin'."

It's our last weekend in the Hammer house before Anna and Popsy come home from their trip. I come out of my bedroom to see Jack standing there, holding out one arm. I shoot him a questioning look which gets no response as I loop my arm through his.

"More like a truck than a chariot," he says to me as he leads me down the stairs, "but it'll do the same job and deliver you to your final surprise.

"A truck. Well, that's good," I say as I glance down at my usual overalls, "because I forgot to wear my ball gown."

He walks me to the front door where he transfers me to Gavin, who is waiting. But not without giving me a kiss.

After being busted by Sam, who as far as I know kept her word and kept our secrets after Jack explained that I was not cheating on Leo, we all agreed that we needed to be more careful in case of cameras.

And, with cameras around, we'd had to keep it strictly platonic, except for me and Leo, for the rest of the week.

But now we are done. The crew are all gone and it's just us again.

"What's going on?" I figured I'd be meeting Axel, who is one of the few Hammers whose final surprise still isn't present and accounted for.

"I think we're supposed to be your fairy godmothers." Max has come up behind me and whispers, "Stand still, please."

Then he's putting a blindfold over my eyes.

I don't remember this part happening in any Cinderella fairy-tale version, but I'm one million times for it. "Um…"

"Be *still*, Princess."

"Okay, but what in the fresh once-upon-a-time hell is going on, guys?"

I don't know whether to be perturbed or intrigued or ashamed of myself for hoping it's something real damn kinky.

This princess wants *all* the balls. Ha.

"I can't see anything," I protest as Max ties the blindfold.

"That's why I'm here," Gavin says.

I hear the front door open and he ushers me out.

"Be home by midnight or you turn into a pumpkin!" Gunnar's voice comes from somewhere behind me.

"Watch your step," Gavin says as he leads me off the porch.

How? I'm blindfolded. Also, there's nothing romantic about being in traction. Also, please-oh-please let this surprise be kinky.

"Gav," I say. "What is up with all the pomp and circumstance?"

"That," he says. "You will have to ask your Prince Charmings."

"Charmings?"

Axel and…?

"Treat her well," Gavin calls. I can hear the distinct sound of Diesel's truck's motor.

"Diesel?" I ask. My ass clenches and I shiver with delight. But as much as my inner nympho is screeching *kinky kinky kinky!*, my heart is quietly protesting that I'm focusing on the wrong thing - the secret gifts are all about *love*, not sex.

"I'm going to help you into the truck, if that's okay?" Diesel asks, sounding oddly stiff and formal. He walks me around to the passenger's side.

Once on the road, we talk and laugh and listen to music from our high school days, and I lose complete track of the time.

When he pulls onto a dirt road, I feel a confusing familiarity. And then he stops the car, parks, and says, "We're here. Wait a moment, and your next Prince Charming will be here to escort you the rest of the way."

I'm still blindfolded when Axel opens my door and takes my hand. He takes the blindfold off as soon as my feet hit the ground.

I blink into his gorgeous face, unable to hide my curiosity when I realize where we are.

As twilight descends, a soft palette of purples and pinks paints both the sky and the field where Max and I made love.

I can't believe my eyes. It's like the glamping site where the triplets took me, but a million times better. There's a fire pit, a gazebo, what looks like it could be a dance floor, surrounded by pots overflowing with flowers. The gazebo itself is a simple metal structure, but draped in gorgeous fabrics that ruffle in the soft breeze. Twinkling fairy lights are woven through the gazebo's canopy, creating a magical night-scape.

My heart is caught in my throat as I take it all in, disbelief rolling through me that this part of the field has been transformed into something truly beautiful. It is the kind of magical place where time stands still, and the world outside ceases to exist, just as I hoped it would become the night I spent here with Max.

I turn to Axel, my heart swelling with gratitude and love, and find him watching me with a quiet intensity. "You like it, Win?"

I run into his arms. "I love it."

He kisses me, pulling me tighter against him, and I melt in his arms, molding myself to his body.

"I haven't stopped thinking about our camping trip date, Sweetheart. We have so many memories together, you and I, but fuck me, Win. That night was something else. *You're* something else."

I'm smiling so hard. My heart is absolutely filled to the brim with love.

He kisses me gently, and whispers against my lips, "We never had a chance to have another foursome before you chose your final Hammer, though."

My thighs clench, automatically. "Ye-es," I agree, slowly. "That's true, but our time never ran out because I never had to choose."

"And if you were to choose, perhaps this time from among all of us, who might you want to have your next foursome with?"

I swallow hard. "Do you mean… tonight?"

"If you like."

My cheeks heat as my mind scrolls through all ten of my gorgeous men.

"I have to pick only…how many?"

He laughs as he drops kisses along my jawline. "How many of us are you ready to handle, sweetheart?"

I scoff, but my stomach flips over. "All of you."

He raises a brow. "Is that so?"

I raise a brow back at him, as if in a challenge.

He smirks. "You really think so?"

I roll my eyes, as if to say, *obviously,* but it's really because I can't speak. Because oh, my God, what is happening right now? Are we really having this conversation? And what does it mean?

I glance around for Diesel, and only then do I notice that he's gone, and so is his truck.

"Where's Deez?"

"He's on call tonight. All you have to do is beckon and he'll race right back over." He gives me a wink. "They all will."

I glance over at the gazebo, bright with fairy lights, and I can see the bed inside. It takes up the entire space from what I can see.

They're all on call. For me.

"All of them?"

"Now, is that a question, or an answer?" he asks.

My brain, my heart, my loins all explode with one giant, silent OH, MY GOD just at the very thought of all of them. Tonight.

"I… I…" I'm too dead to respond.

Axel chuckles and pulls away. "Go inside the gazebo. Go see if you like it. And leave all the rest up to me."

I swallow, and head straight for the gazebo. It is truly beautiful from the outside, all lit up with fairy lights. The canopy softly rustles as I pull it back and peek inside.

It looks like I imagine the inside of a cloud, floating through heaven, and the fairy lights through the fabric, are an entire galaxy of magical stars.

The bed is vast, making the gazebo look so much larger inside than out. The bed looks so soft, too, and I can't wait to climb in. It's not the only thing in the space, there's a gorgeous wooden bar built along the banquet-style bench seats. On top is an overstuffed gift basket of snacks and drinks.

It's incredible.

"It'll be easy to take down, and move, so don't be sorry if you hate the location," Axel says from the entrance of the gazebo.

"No, it's gorgeous. But I love that it's portable. I want to take it with us wherever we go."

He grins and joins me by the bar.

"Are you hungry? Thirsty? The gift basket of snacks was Mason's idea. He wanted there to be a pool table, too. Always going on and on about a damn pool table…"

I smile and rise up on my toes to kiss him. "I'm hungry. But not for just any snack." I nip at his shoulder and he laughs. "I want *this* snack."

He scoops me up and tosses me, fully clothed, into bed. My heart skitters and my stomach drops and I giggle as I sink into the soft bed and am enveloped by pillows.

And then I am enveloped by his body as he covers me, kisses me deeply. And as he kisses me, he rolls his hips, pressing his cock into me, knowing I'll be washed in desire.

Yup, my panties grow wetter than ever. I clench my pussy in an effort to keep my horniness at bay, but I'm not sure it helps.

"Fuck, Winnie," Axel says with a groan as he suddenly rolls off me, and off the bed.

I watch as he begins to strip, first his pants, unbuttoned then off. His shirt is slower to remove until he yanks it off, ripping it. A few buttons go flying.

When he drops his boxers my mouth goes dry. It doesn't matter that I've seen all of him before, I react to him – to *all* of them – like I'm seeing them for the first time. Mouthwatering.

He is back in bed with me in an instant, his hands at the waistband of my pants. "I want time to have you all to myself for just a bit longer," he says as he undoes the button.

"Do you mind sharing me with the others tonight?"

He shakes his head. "No. You've got a lot of love to give, sweetheart. I know that. I admire that."

His finger gently traces the crease of my lips and I respond by sucking it into my mouth.

Axel responds to that by stripping me naked. It takes longer for me to get undressed than him, but I can't stop kissing him, or reaching for his hard cock, wanting to touch his naked body as much as he wants to touch mine.

Once I'm fully naked, he sits between my spread legs. With one of his hands, he caresses my belly. I fucking love the feel of that. His other hand moves between my thighs. I moan as he thumbs my clit.

"You're very, very wet, Winnie." He draws lazy circles, and I whimper. "You want something in your pussy, now, sweetheart?"

"Please."

"Get on your hands and knees," he commands.

I do what he says without delay, and am rewarded as two of Axel's fingers press into me. It doesn't take more than a moment before I'm pushing back on him, trying to fuck myself with him, wanting more more more. He gives my ass a tiny slap and drops a kiss on the skin. I wiggle my ass back at him. He grips my hips and slams his cock inside.

Once he builds up a hard, steady rhythm, he reaches around and circles my clit again, and it doesn't take long before I'm making sexed-up squeals every time he slams to the hilt, dropping onto my elbows because I'm so full, so gloriously everything.

"I bet the others would like to watch you come," Axel says, as I squirm against his hand, wanting even more. "Should we let someone else join in on the fun?"

It's mostly a growl, low in my ear.

"*Yes*," I pant. "Yes, please, but…."

Oh, my God, I'm coming apart. The entire world has ceased to exist and it's just our bodies and fucking and my heart pounding with love and lust for these boys.

"But they're not here," I finally say with a pout.

Really, it's not fair.

He laughs. "Shout out for someone, baby."

I stop, surprised. "For whom?"

"Whomever you want."

I furrow my brows. "Gunnar."

I pick him because I have been salivating to reciprocate that delicious afternoon on the stairs, and still haven't had a chance, with all the cameras around.

"Hey, Gun. Get your lucky ass in here," Axel says.

I am genuinely perplexed, and my movements slow.

"You really didn't hear any of their trucks, did you, Win?" he says with a chuckle. He tightens his grip on my hips and slams into me again. My moan is probably loud enough to resound through every inch of wide open space around our gazebo.

"Yeah," he says with a laugh. "You were a bit loud. So were their trucks, but…"

He slams into me again and my deliriously happy moan nearly drowns out the sound of Gunnar's voice as he says, "Holy fucking hell, *yum*."

"Where do you want Gunnar?" Axel asks me, slowing his slide in and out. "Do you want him in your mouth?"

I nod and Gunnar's big frame moves into my eye range. His hypnotic blue eyes lock on mine as Axel flicks my clit just right and it's like I've been hit by a lightning bolt.

FORTUNE FAVORS THE BOLD. I lick my lips as he strips off his shirt, exposing that tattoo of his that I love so much. And then he's unzipping his jeans, and pulling out that cock I love so much, too.

He slips it between my lips and I latch on, loving being able to suck him and make him feel as good as Axel is making me feel. For a long while, I get lost in the taste of him and the moans I pull out of him, and rhythmic sounds of Axel's skin slapping mine as he thrusts into me.

"Does it feel good, Sweetheart?"

I moan with appreciation, swirling my tongue around the head of Gunnar's cock. "Except for my ass... My ass feels so... empty."

Axel laughs, low and rumbly. "I think I know a remedy for that. I hear Leo and Theo have been thinking about a Winnie sandwich–"

"A what?" I stop moving completely.

Axel gives my ass a little slap and resumes pumping his hips, but this time, he wets his finger and pokes the tip into my ass. I squirm and moan, sucking Gunnar deeper into my mouth.

"Is that what you want?" Axel says. "A Winnie sandwich? They'd be pretty good at it–they've been hugging you like that for years, anyway."

"Hey, Theo," Gunnar calls. "Did you hear what our girl wants?"

He cradles the crown of my head as I hear Theo's reply. "No."

Axel's hips gyrate, and the slide of his cock out and then in again is too good. He slaps my ass cheek again, and presses his finger in a tiny bit deeper, wiggling it. "Tell Theo what you told me, Winnie."

Holy shit.

"My ass feels empty."

It comes out as a near whine. My cheeks burn from how desperate I sound.

"Well, we can't have that," Theo murmurs from a few feet away.

"Alright, five more seconds, tops," Gunnar says, and Axel begins fucking me in a way that ensure we've all got five more seconds, tops.

But then Axel pulls away, just a moment before Gunnar's cock explodes in my mouth, filling my mouth with his warm, saltiness.

As soon as Gunnar's cock is free of my mouth, Axel slams into me again, so deep, so deliciously, and I feel him spasm in me as he shouts out my name.

I haven't come yet, but Axel kisses my shoulder before pulling out of me, and whispers, "Don't worry, Sweetheart. Your fun is only just getting started. And I brought plenty of lube."

CHAPTER 48

Winnie

I remain in the middle of the bed, sitting on my knees, still panting and wanting and needing. I glance over to the entrance to the gazebo to see Theo and Leo moving in. They're still fully clothed. *Boo.*

As if reading my mind, they yank their shirts over their heads.

"Axel told us to go quick so you wouldn't be left growing cold," Theo says.

"Want us to warm you up, love?"

They know I do. Theo joins me first, pulling me against his gorgeous body and kissing me deeply. He touches between my legs and growls. Then he slides his thick cock inside me.

"Oh, yeah. She feels so fucking good, dude," Theo says. He thrusts and I cry out.

I hear the pop of the lube bottle and my whole body quivers. The mattress moves and Leo climbs in, too. My nipples grow hard at Leo's touch when his hand goes to my ass.

Theo is giving me sweet kisses, teasing my tongue and keeping me smiling, but I expect him to stop, and help me onto my knees. But he doesn't. He holds me tenderly but tightly, against his chest as Leo crawls over our tangled legs.

Leo grips my hips in his large hands, and parts my ass cheeks with his thumbs. "Mmm…"

The air feels cool against my skin. But not for long. Theo slides out of my pussy, but keeping me pressed against him, kissing so deliciously. But as soon as I'm empty, Leo lines his cock up with my ass and pushes inside.

There's a moment of pain as I stretch around Leo, but before anything grows worse than uncomfortable Theo is sliding into my pussy and then they're fucking me at the same time, both wrapping me in their arms.

I'm so full. Oh, fuck. My eyes close in sheer contentment as they gently stroke me with their cocks, finding the perfect spot to elicit pure bliss.

"You like that, huh, love?" Leo chuckles, kissing my neck as he pumps into me.

Theo groans. "So fucking tight."

Leo matches his groan. "So fucking *sweet*."

So fucking perfect.

Then Theo nuzzles my mouth with his, whispering sweet words of love against my lips as he fucks me. Leo does the same along my spine, kissing, licking, and whispering. I can feel their cocks all the way through me, both of them spearing my heart and soul. It's as if Leo and Theo are a well-oiled ecstasy machine, thrusting in unison.

"Oh my God," I cry.

I hope Leo is enjoying my ass-wriggling because I can't be still. I whimper as they both prepare to come, ready as well. And as they buckle and thrust, we unravel together.

I have about four-point-two seconds to recover after Theo and Leo pull out, before Cruz and Gavin pop their heads inside the gazebo. And I realize it's not 'recovery' that I need. I might be rolling in the waves of orgasmic pleasure, but I'm far from sated.

The grin on Cruz's face shows his dimples, and the wash of excitement that rushes between my legs hits even before he pulls out his bungee cords.

My eyes widen when I see them. I might have moaned. Ever since Gavin and Jack restrained me with them, my fondness for bungee cords has only grown.

"I had this thought to fill your bungee-fuck fantasy, but I'll need Gav's help," he says.

Gavin gives me a wink as meanders over to the side of the bed, where I realize I'm perched eagerly. I watch as Cruz hooks the bungees around the frame of the gazebo, and after a moment, realize that Gunnar and Axel have slipped away.

Oh. Should I feel bad that I didn't notice? Should I have said goodbye?

I think I need an Official Hammer Orgy list of rules. I'm sure Jack will be more than happy to oblige.

I don't worry for more than a second before Gav's mouth lands on my shoulder and his teeth find my neck and his pierced tongue trails a long, sensuous line behind my ear. In a matter of moments, he pulls me up from the bed and over to the contraption Cruz miraculously put together, what looks like a giant swing.

I am going to die. Not because it looks dangerous, which it kind of does, but because it looks like FUN. And the boys are holding their giant dick-missiles between their legs, which I can see through their jeans already look ready to blast the fuck off. Well, I am, too.

Gav picks me up and I link my arms around his neck, and wrap my legs around his waist. He grips the globes of my ass cheeks while I lick his nipple rings. We kiss as he brings me over to the Bungee Web of Pleasure or Pain (or Both?). I carry on kissing him, stopping only to kiss Cruz, as the two of them set me on the cords like I'm sitting on a swing. Cruz has that gorgeous, mischievous grin on, again and they each take turns keeping me from falling from the bungee swing and kissing me while the other undresses.

My fantasy comes true, only it's with a delightful twist. As Cruz fucks me, bouncing me up and down in long, fast strokes, I grip Gav's cock, stroking in the same rhythm. I'm so sensitive, having already come once, and it makes me shiver as I kiss Cruz and he thrusts up into me. I moan and cry and forget I'm even holding on to Gav until he and Cruz both come. Cruz grips me tight and jams his eyes closed, moaning as he shakes. Gav makes a hissing sound, and then his cock surges in my fist and spills over.

They're both loose-limbed and for a moment I worry that I'll be dropped, but another set of strong arms comes around me from behind.

"I got you, Peach."

Diesel shoos the others away as he untangles me from the bungee contraption.

And his smile stretches into one that is much more wicked than Cruz's. My heart begins to slam when he turns me around and bends me forward, using the bungees to give me something to hold on to. Something to keep me upright rather than face first into the ground from weak knees as Diesel runs his fingers over my fully exposed ass.

He whistles. "Look at this sweet pink bottom." He spreads my ass cheeks and touches me once, whistling. "Nice and ready for me. You're so fucking hot, Win."

I cry out when he snaps open the bottle of lube, and quiver when the cool gel touches my sore skin. It feels good. And surprisingly, it feels even better when Diesel runs his finger through the gel and then into my ass. "Like that, dirty girl? Yeah I know you do." Then he slides into me, in one easy thrust.

I cry out for him, and cry out for Mason.

Diesel laughs. "You're a ball of energy, tonight, aren't you? But, baby, you have got me wrapped around your finger, tighter than these bungee cords were squeezing your ass cheeks and leaving all these pink stripes." He gathers my hair in his hands, taming the wild red curls, and uses it to hold on to as he begins to bounce me on his cock. "Where do you want Mason, Peach?"

My mouth.

I long to say it. But I can't tell him that. I am too breathless.

"Mason! Get in here, quick!"

Mason comes in and begins dropping his pants as soon as he sees that I'm licking my lips, parting them for him.

"Hey, Cupcake."

He bends before me, lining our faces up and kissing me quickly on the lips before giving me his cock. He looks into my eyes as I take him into my mouth, and gently touches my face, watching the changes my expression goes through as Diesel pulls out and thrusts back in, faster this time.

"So beautiful," Mace whispers, as if to himself.

His cock is the perfect taste and texture, thickness and length to distract me from my impending orgasm as he begins to fuck my mouth and match Diesel's tempo. I moan onto Mason's cock, which causes him to moan in turn, as Diesel slowly pulls in and out.

I don't know how long Diesel can keep fucking my ass or how he has such incredible staying power, but odds are I will not be sitting down tomorrow without a donut pillow.

I don't care. I don't ever want him to stop.

But even as I think that, he comes hard, with a wild and sexy shout. I think he says my name, but it's mostly an incoherent babble.

After Diesel withdraws, I'm ready to give sucking Mason off my full attention. Then I hear Max say, "Can I give that pussy the fucking it deserves, now, princess?"

I am the textbook definition – if there is one – of sex-drunk. Fuck, I want Big Max inside me.

"Ye-ee-eess." I moan around Mason's cock.

Max settles into the space Diesel stood, and takes me quickly from behind. My pussy clenches from the tightness as he pushes in. We both make similar sounds of satisfaction deep in our throat. It makes us laugh, and as we do, he pushes deep inside me. And as I gasp with pleasure, I pull Mason deeper into my mouth, the head of his cock pushing into my throat.

His groan sounds tortured.

"Fuck, Win," he hisses, carressing the top of my head. "Deep throat me once more like that and I'll be filling your throat with my cum, like, now."

So I do, and as he comes, he shouts, a sound like pure joy, as he pours himself into my throat.

Max bounces me on his cock harder once my mouth is free.

"*Winnie.*" He gathers me against his chest and buries his nose into my neck. He kisses my shoulder, and lets me fuck him like that, at my own pace, for what feels like hours.

This time when the orgasm hits me, it destroys me. I might have blacked out. I'm not sure. When I come to, I find myself out of the bungee contraption and nestled in Jack's strong arms as he carries me back to the bed.

"Hi, Jackhammer."

"Hi, Winifred."

He gives me one of his famous smiles, the kind of smile I can *feel*. Swooooon.

"Your turn," I whisper excitedly.

His reaction is all wrong. He barks out a laugh. "Absolutely not. Are you crazy? Your body needs to rest–"

"My body needs *you*, Jack."

He shakes his impossibly stubborn head as he climbs into bed beside me. "You need–"

I push him down onto his back and climb on top of him.

"Win," he protests.

But he doesn't protest too hard. He's a zillion times stronger and could stop me from undressing him. Because he's fully dressed, unfortunately, but I undo the button of his jeans and tug them down enough to spring his cock free.

"Win," he protests again, even weaker than before.

But then he's rolling out of bed and scooping me up. He tosses me over his shoulder and stalks off toward the entrance of the gazebo.

"Jack, put me down, right now!"

He listens, slowly lowering me down the front of him. But as I meet him face to face, I hook my arms around his neck and wrap my legs around him.

He's hard. I squirm against him.

"You want me," I point out to him, proudly. "You're hard."

"Of course I fucking want you," he growls, shaking his head at me. "I *always* want you, you know that."

I catch his eyes and hold them. And as I do, I reach between us for his cock. His eyes widen and he lets out a soft sound, then his gaze drops down between us.

He stares at my pussy, pink and glistening. He licks his lips and then his eyes are back on mine, but now it's like the pupils, brimming with desire, have swallowed Jack's irises up.

I've won, but I can't gloat. I can't manage to do anything other than tip my chin up so that he captures my lips in a kiss, and wrap my fist around his cock.

We moan in unison. He shifts me in his arms, maintaining his balance easily, and then he's sliding his cock into me.

We moan again, longer and louder. I thought the torture was over, but Jack has other ideas, and by the time he's done plunging into me until I see an entire galaxy of stars, I've been rocked by an orgasm that melts every single one of my bones. We drop into bed and he pulls my limp body alongside his, gathering me into his arms. He drops kisses on my eyelids, which I didn't even know could feel this heavy just from sex.

"Hey, Win, by the way," I hear Cruz say from the entrance of the gazebo, "I could be hard again instantly if you—"

I laugh. "Sorry, Cruzie. Every part of me needs downtime. Like a week's downtime."

"Fair enough," I hear him agree, and then I'm drifting off to sleep, nestled in Jack's arms. Wrapped up tight in all of their love.

EPILOGUE

Winnie

Several Months Later

"It's time for turkeys, you turkeys!" Jack shouts.

While no one else laughs, I do.

"Thank you for the pity giggle, Winifred," he says, pulling me into his big, strong arms for a deeply satisfying kiss.

"Aww, it wasn't out of pity. And anytime, Jack-of-all-trades," I say. "I love you, baby."

"Mmm, not as much as I love you."

Of course, Diesel takes the sweetness out of the moment by giving my ass a ridiculously hard squeeze as he passes us by. I squeal in protest but I've found that I like it when he occasionally digs those fingertips in just enough to leave a mark. "Happy Thanksgiving, Peach."

As always, Thanksgiving dinner is set up buffet-style so everyone can fill up their plates before heading to the table.

But what's different is that for the first time since the boys gifted me my cottage in Whispering Glen, we're celebrating the holiday in Smithville, not there. We're celebrating the holiday at home.

"What a feast," Cruz remarks.

"Yeah, I kind of went overboard this year, but–"

"Oh, honey, baby, darlin', I wasn't talking about the food, I was talking about the cook." He squeezes both of my shoulders and presses a kiss to the side of my neck.

"Could one of you guys run across the street and tell your Mom and Popsy we're ready for them, that would be great," I say.

"I got it, Pooh," Gavin volunteers.

As he heads out, I double check everything.

Sweet potato casserole, green bean casserole, macaroni and cheese, dressing, homemade cranberry sauce, mashed potatoes, two turkeys (one fried), a ham, brussel sprouts, cornbread, dinner rolls, five pies…

"The only thing we're missing is Max and Mason," I remark.

1 Girl & Her Favorite Hammer: Renovations & Romance was such a hit, Max and Mason were immediately offered another show. Nothing to do with dating this time. Max & Mason Make It Work is strictly about swooping in and fixing up a family's home on a shoestring budget… while shirtless, of course. While they've been away filming for the last month, the three of us have become experts in the art of phone sex and x-rated video chats. I think of last night, when Max told me exactly how he wanted me to touch myself and made me make myself come several times. Then

he turned me over to Mason whose dirty talk reached all new levels of panty-melting hotness. Unfortunately, they won't be back until Christmas.

Then I glance around. "And Axel. Where's Axel?"

I've been so busy I haven't realized he hasn't been around for a couple of hours.

"He was picking us up from the airport, princess," a voice I know all too well says and I swear I get chills as I spin around and see Max standing in the doorway to the kitchen. I run to him and he lifts me off my feet, giving me a kiss to make up for four weeks of missed kisses. Then he puts me down and steps aside so I can get the same treatment from Mason.

"How's my favorite cupcake?" he asks as I breathe in the sandalwood scent of him.

"Pissed!" I swat at him. "You weasels made me think you weren't going to be here!"

"Only because we know you love surprises," Axel says.

Theo pulls me away from the others. "Speaking of surprises, I was emptying the trash," he whispers. "And I happened to see a positive preg–"

"Shh," I place my finger to my lips but it doesn't hide my smile. With all the sex, all the condomless sex, with all my virile boys, one of their supersperm was bound to break through the barrier of my birth control.

"Hey," Max calls, coming over to us and tugging me back, towards him, away from Theo, who gives me a grin and a wink. "Ma isn't here yet, is she? I need to see that tat in person, Win."

I turn around and lift up the back of my shirt. I jump, getting insta-shivers as he runs his fingers along the 10 hammers all in a row I've had tattooed on the small of my back.

"Well, that's sexy as fuck," Mason says.

Max pulls me in for another quick cuddle. "Room for both of us in your bed tonight?" his whisper is low and husky and I nod but my clit is practically shouting YES! YES! YES!

"The execs loved the demo!" Gunnar bursts into the kitchen. He's referring to the five song EP he and Diesel recorded at a local studio. He beelines towards Diesel, tackling him. "We're making an album, you douchecanoe!"

"Oh my god! Congratulations!" I race over to them and get swept into the bro-hug. We're jumping up and down and screaming like idiots when Popsy and Anna come in. Gavin is carrying Melody.

"I've never been greeted with such enthusiasm," Popsy jokes.

"I left Monkey Monkey," Melody says.

"Oh, no," Anna, who has gone straight to Max and Mason to give them welcome home hugs, says.

"I'll go get him," I volunteer.

"No way," Jack shakes his head, "You've done enough. You need to set down and let us—"

"I don't mind," I say. "Really."

I like going to the house that used to be Gram's and my father's now.

As I walk across the street, I hear no voices. It's quiet and peaceful and still.

No, we didn't move into the reno house, as we told the world on television. If the plan had just been for me and Leo, yeah, that would've worked. But the house is way too small for all eleven of us and I'm not living anywhere without all of my boys.

But, serendipitously, when Anna and Popsy returned from their 40th anniversary trip, they broke the news to the boys and me that they were planning on selling the Hammer house. The ginormous Victorian, which used to be a bed-and-breakfast–the only house big enough to raise their brood of sons in and give everyone their own room–has been simply too much for them and now that everyone is grown, they've wanted to downsize for a while.

But their plans to move out of the neighborhood and into a townhome were dashed when they saw the finished product of Gram's house after our renovation. Anna fell instantly in love… especially after she saw the treehouse and my former room, perfect for a little girl.

I run in and grab Monkey Monkey. They haven't formally adopted four-year-old Melody yet, but they're fostering her and I don't see any other outcome.

They'd questioned whether or not they were too old to start over with another child that needs a home filled with stability and love, but when we'd told them they'd have all of us, right across the street, to help out… it was a no-brainer. Yeah, obviously we weren't going to let the Hammer house go on the market. It's home.

As for my cottage, I did give that away, to a fan, a young woman much like myself who grew up in a house where she wasn't valued or taught to love herself, who needed to get out on her own, have a fresh start, have the oasis the boys gave me. I don't need it any more.

I pause on the porch to straighten the pillows on the swing–Jack's surprise for me–and then start back across the street.

Leo pokes his head out the front door and yells, "Come on, Winnie Hammer, love, we can't start without you!"

No–we're not married. As much as there have been many a joke about how the world is not yet ready for 1 Bride, 10 Grooms, I don't think the world is quite ready for that televised wedding. Truth is, I don't know what the future looks like for us. Except there will be lots of honesty, lots of sex, and lots and lots of love.

But I did legally change my last name from Wainwright, my father's surname I was born with, to Hammer, the family I found and will always be a part of.

THE END

Dear precious reader, thank you for reading Ten Hammers!

When I finished writing the book, I couldn't put down my pen yet… not until I wrote a little something extra special just for you. If you want more of Winnie & her ten gorgeous best friends, scan here to get your bonus epilogue.

P.S. If you enjoyed Ten Hammers, then I think you'll enjoy Ten Mountain Men too! It's Book 2 in the Ten of a Kind Series, featuring the one & only Goldie.

Turn to the next page for a sneak peek...

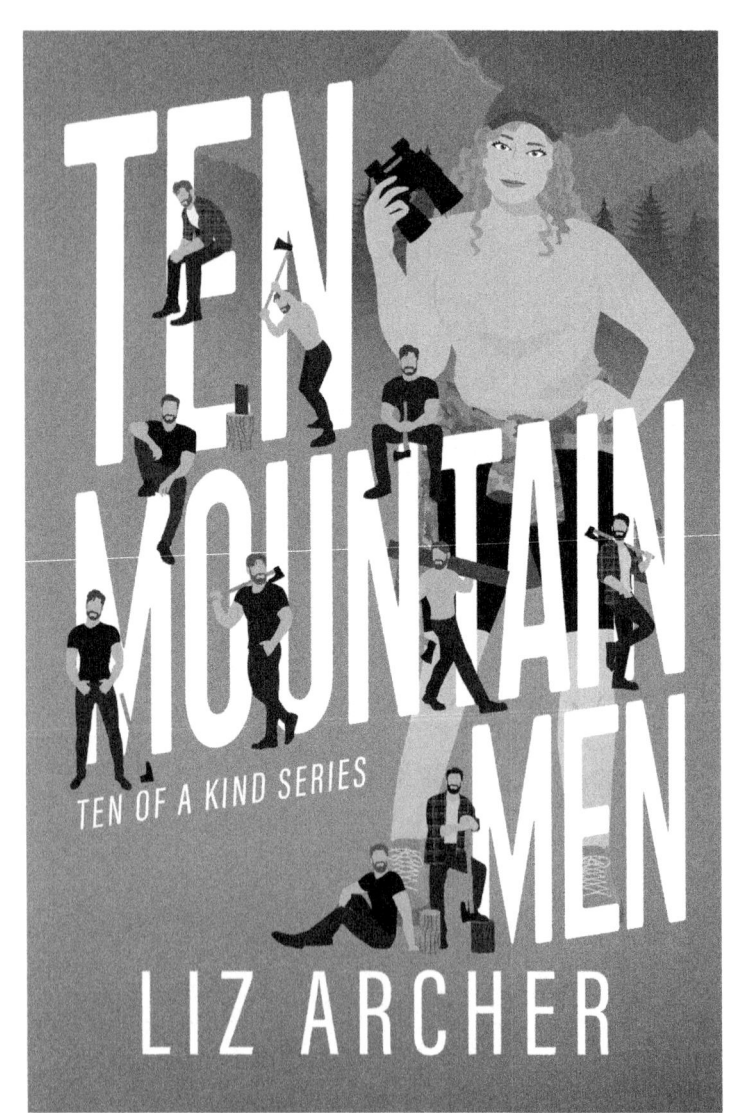

TEN MOUNTAIN MEN

TEN OF A KIND SERIES

LIZ ARCHER

Breaking news: Bigfoot ain't real.
But the ten big, burly mountain men bathing in the river are…

I met the Björnsson brothers when I broke my ankles hiking in the mountain wilderness.

Okay, so I panicked when I saw them naked in the river, convinced they were a pack of grizzly bears, and ran like the wind.

But when they offer to carry me back to their cabin and nurse me back to health, I can't say no.

The ten brothers take turns feeding me, healing my wounds, and taking care of my every need.

I don't ever want to leave their cabin.

But even if I did…

I don't think these ten possessive bearded alphas will let me.

CHAPTER 1

Goldie

Whenever I need to take my mind off something that's bugging me, I recite quotes. It's something one of my mother's old boyfriends did, and it does the trick, oddly enough. Working as a field producer in reality television for most of my twenties, I've rarely been alone, so I got in the practice of reciting in my head. But it's just me now. Me and the open road.

Me and the open road and no bathroom in my near past, present, or future, oh God.

"Perfection is not the absence of flaws, but rather the embrace of imperfections in the colorful threads that weave the unique fabric of our existence," I say, loud enough to be heard outside of my BMW—who I named Petunia.

Good thing only trees are around to hear me. That one's a mouthful. Way too flowery and, in my opinion, completely untrue. Bullshit, is what it is. But my mother's third husband, Roy—another ex-husband now, of course, but my favorite of them all—was the one who added that quote by the prolific Anonymous to my repertoire, so I keep it in rotation.

I prefer the shorter, sweeter, and more spot-on, *Perfection is everything.*

Perfection is my snazzy little convertible which still looks as shiny and new, inside and out, as it did when I drove it off the lot two years ago in all its Thundernight Metallic glory—only the most gorgeous shade of purple known to man.

Perfection is my pink Dior sunglasses with the darling tiny pair of gold stars on either side of the frames, my favorite nude lipstick, and the brand-new, high-speed, shockproof, waterproof action camera with wireless microphone that hangs on a cord around my neck, ready to go.

"Perfection is not," I say, wrinkling my nose, "pulling over and squatting behind a tree to pee."

I glance at the gas gauge and bite my lip. I may not have a choice about the whole squatting behind a tree to pee thing, because even if my painfully full bladder can hold out until I hit a rest stop, I don't think the fuel situation is going to.

"Dammit, dammit, dammit!"

The demanding ache in my lower abdomen insists I do something already.

Focus on the foliage. The leaves are an explosion of colors. Gorgeous. Stunning. Golden amber. Flame orange. Saffron yellow. Crimson red.

Ugh. I could name all the colors in the world's largest Crayola box, but that's not going to help me hold it. No distraction will. I'm one-hundred-percent going to wet myself.

Then I see it.

Up ahead.

A break in the endless line of trees. And there's a sign.

Piney Grove Trading Post and General Store.

My pulse accelerates and so does my car. Pedal to the metal, baby.

I yank the steering wheel just in time to bulldoze into the tiny gravel lot, my tires kicking up all kinds of grit and debris. I apologize to Petunia, hoping I haven't caused any damage to her pristine exterior. I'd be so upset with myself if I nicked the paint. Normally I take great care with everything I do, and I pride myself on never being the person who parks like an entitled jackhole, but I'm desperate now. I skid to a stop, coughing on my own dust clouds as I scramble out.

The cozy log cabin, nestled between the towering pines, doesn't look like a shop. Aside from the creaky old sign swaying in the breeze, it looks like someone's charmingly rustic home. The scattering of colorful flowerpots on the railing of the wraparound porch, and the painted rocking chairs, add a burst of color to the rugged wilderness.

After working on the wildly popular home renovation show *1 Girl, 10 Hammers* for eight seasons, it's hard not to assess and admire a well-built home. Even when spontaneous urination is imminent, toilet or no.

I race up the steps and a bell jingles as I burst through the doors.

Thank God, I made it!

I let out a sigh of immense relief.

And then I recoil immediately, stopping in my tracks as horror floods my veins.

I am *surrounded* by useless knickknacks, worthless doodads, and gaudy baubles. Clutter, clutter, clutter, everywhere I look. This is not a trading post and general store—it's my own personal hell. I *despise* clutter.

I take a step back and bump into something. It teeters, then topples, crashing to the floor.

A freaking garden gnome, garishly painted with a grotesque grin. Hideous thing. But dammit, I hope I haven't broken it. I don't think—

"May I help you?" a sharp voice asks.

I glance up, and it takes me a moment before I see her behind the counter. Not just because there's so much clutter surrounding her, but because she's so small her head barely clears the countertop. She studies me with lips tightly pressed together. Even from a distance, I notice the shrewdness in her clear blue eyes and it unsettles me.

"I knocked over this gnome." I gesture toward it. I swear his creepy-ass smile widens, as if he enjoyed the pain. Masochist little fucker.

"I see that." The woman marches over, scoops up the gnome, cradling it in her arms for a moment like it's a baby, glancing at it with clear love. She then sets it back down, upright, patting it on its head.

Okaaaaaaaaaay.

"I didn't mean to—"

"He's fine. And the Wilderness Haven Retreat and Lodge"—she makes a face like she's tasted something city we filmed in. I once slept over at her townhouse, and I swear I had nightmares for weeks about being attacked by anthropomorphic snow globes and *I Heart Wherever* pens.

There's *nothing* in my apartment that isn't necessary. If it doesn't serve a purpose—have a function, and perform that function exactly as expected—I have no room for it. I don't even have art on the walls, but that's mostly because I could never find a single painting that felt just right.

"Do you have any paintings?" I ask the woman.

"No," she replies. Physically, she's behind the counter again, but her eyes follow my every step. "Passing through, then?"

My brows draw together. "Excuse me?"

The woman harrumphs. "If you're not going to the Wilderness Haven Retreat and Lodge, what are you doing in this neck of the woods?"

"Oh!" I say, excited to get to tell someone, though her question wasn't exactly issued with warmth or friendly interest. There was a hint of *You don't belong here* in her voice. "I'm camping up on the mountain!"

"On the mountain?"

"Yes!"

"Alone?"

"Yep. Just me."

Which is disappointing, actually. I should have a whole crew with me. However, absolutely no one has shown any interest in my passion project.

Yet.

All the networks think they want something salacious. Not the wholesome tale of how a plucky plus-sized filmmaker sets out on a quest to find—

"Terrible idea. Very dangerous up the mountain," the proprietor of this overstocked tacky trinket emporium warns. "You could fall. There are often rockslides. You should go to Wilderness Haven. They have safe trails there. With professional guides."

She looks me up and down again, with more disdain this time, though my outfit is on point. The wardrobe department at the studio let me take some nature-loving fashionista outfits from a pilot that never got picked up, called *Heidi Goes Hiking While Glenda Goes Glamping!*

Yes, I'm roughing it, but that doesn't mean I can't look cute as hell. And a little sparkle never hurt anyone, right? Camouflage is camouflage even if it's pink with strategically placed sequins.

I shake my head as I try to decide whether I want an ashtray—does anyone smoke cigarettes anymore?—or a coaster.

"I'm actually here to make a documentary," I explain.

Her gaze sharpens into a laser-pointer glare. "On the mountain?"

"Yep!" I can't stop my story from spilling forth. "When I was younger, I came camping here and I was attacked by a bobcat. Well, almost attacked by a bobcat. I narrowly escaped, because at the last minute, I was saved!"

Her stare is unnerving. Shocked, and a little angry. "You were nearly killed by a bobcat and you came back? Why? Why would you do that?"

Even though we're alone, I lower my voice, because everyone I've ever told the truth to questions my sanity immediately. But I'm going to show them. I confide, "I was saved by Bigfoot. And now I plan to find him again."

And film the whole thing!

Prove, once and for all, that Bigfoot is real.

It's my life's work. It's what I was put on this planet to do. I feel it in my soul.

The woman suddenly darts from behind the counter and dashes over to me. She grabs my upper arms, her fingers digging in. "You cannot do this thing. There is no such thing as Bigfoot, and you *will* get killed by a bobcat this time. Or a bear. This is a very treacherous place for a young lady to be by herself. Go to the Wilderness Haven Retreat and Lodge. You will love it there. I promise. You can get a massage."

"Um…" I say.

"You must," she insists. "I foresee your demise if you go up the mountain. Yes. The spirit of death hovers around you. I hear the bobcat's breath. Do you feel it, hot on your neck?"

What the actual fuck? The only thing I feel is this woman's bony-ass hands bruising my arms.

I free myself from her grip. "Are you psychic?"

"Yes," she says quickly, but I know when people are lying. I've made a bloody career out of pulling the truth from people. "And I've foreseen it. You will be eaten."

Now it's my turn for my eyes to narrow, skeptical. She knows something, but it has nothing to do with the spirit of death hovering around me. She knows about Bigfoot. She doesn't want me to expose him to the world. That's got to be it. But wouldn't proof of a mythical creature actually existing nearby be good for her business?

Still, there's no reasoning with some people, and I don't have all day to stand here letting her try to talk me out of my plan.

I attempt to look very afraid. "Maybe I will go to the Wilderness Haven Retreat and Lodge after all."

She nods. "Smart girl."

"Now, just let me figure out which of your lovely items I want to purchase and I'll be on my merry way!"

"To the Wilderness Haven Retreat and Lodge," she adds, pushing. Then, "I hear their mud masks are heavenly."

I shudder, because I hate mud, but say, "To the Wilderness Haven Retreat and Lodge!"

"Go right now," she says. "You don't have to buy anything. Just go."

But the display of wooden sculptures in the corner has caught my eye.

I walk over, stooping down to get a closer look at the intricate carvings. I've never felt the tug to own something just because looking at it made me feel a spark of joy, but…

I smile and pick up a carved bear. It won't fit in my glove compartment, but it's too beautiful to be hidden away.

I'm tempted to tell her I want it, to take it to the cash register and have her wrap up my new treasure with care. But I'm not going to start collecting stuff that doesn't serve a purpose. She said I didn't have to buy anything, so I'm not buying anything.

"Thanks for letting me use your restroom," I say.

"Enjoy your stay at the Wilderness Haven Retreat and Lodge."

I nod, smile, but my destiny is calling. And it's up on that mountain.

Bobcats and rockslides and lack of running water be damned. I've got Bigfoot to find.

CHAPTER 2

Goldie

My memory doesn't fail me, though my footwear is letting me down. The blisters forming on my toes are screaming as I trudge up the narrow, nearly invisible pathway through the woods. These boots are not, in fact, made for walking. But I had to leave my car all alone at the bottom of the mountain when the road ended in a muddy parking lot, and for the past two hours I've ventured forth, my camping gear strapped to my back as I crunch through fallen leaves, a determined smile on my face despite my blisters.

"A smile is a frown wearing its Sunday best," I even said to myself at one point—a quote by my mother, which is why it's kind of a confusing one. She's a bit of a mess. And we never even went to church.

But now my smile has widened—not just wearing its Sunday best, but a red carpet–worthy ball gown. Because I'm on the right trail, I know it!

My hands start to shake as I grab the camera cord around my neck. This is the spot. This is where it all happened. I can hear the river, the exact roar and hush of the rushing water, just as I hear it in every memory of that terrifying day.

I had wandered off, away from my friends, trying to find a little privacy—because my small bladder was just as much of a curse when I was a kid as it is now. I'd just found the perfect bush to squat behind when I found myself face-to-face with the bobcat.

Like any sane person, I'd turned to run, and in classic Goldie style, I lost all balance and tripped. Falling, falling, falling, but before I could face-plant into the ground and become bobcat breakfast, I was scooped up by a massive pair of strong, shaggy arms.

And the funny thing is, I was never afraid, not of the Sasquatch—because that's what I realized held me in those massive and massively hairy arms. A Sasquatch. The real Bigfoot. And he wasn't a monster, not at all.

He had the kindest eyes.

Now, twenty years later, I'm close to where he saved me, I can feel it in my bones.

There's a sharp cramp building in my left shoulder because my gear is heavy as hell, but I press on. Onward and upward! I forgot to fill up my canteen, so I'm parched. But water is near! Water, and my hero.

Since they don't exist—ha! Yeah, right—no one knows the life expectancy of a Sasquatch. But my Bigfoot *has* to still be here. It's more than just the documentary—I never got a chance to thank him.

The bobcat, Bigfoot, looking death in the face, and then being carried to safety. What happened between being rescued by the Bigfoot and then arriving back to my friends is kind of a blur, though they swear when I got back to them I was all alone. They saw nothing, except that I had wet pants. Worse, they thought I was making up the encounters! Both encounters—the one with the bobcat and the one with Bigfoot. They thought I was just embarrassed that I'd peed myself and trying to make excuses to save face.

But I've never questioned my own experience. I know what happened.

Up ahead, there's a clearing. Sunlight filters through the foliage, shadows dappling the forest floor. The perfect campsite. I hurry forward, my arms spaghetti noodles as I finally set down the tent I've been lugging, and the backpack, and the small cooler. The relief instantly spreads through my whole back.

The crisp air carries the earthy scent of pine needles and freshly fallen leaves, and I take a deep breath, inhaling it all.

Okay, it's more like a wheeze. That hike was way more strenuous than the spin classes I took back when I used to worry about my less-than-petite size. And that's saying a lot, because Jason was a fierce body coach.

Looking around, I shake out my hands, trying to get some feeling back in my fingers, the chilly breeze reminding me of the coming winter season. I'm so glad I waited until fall was in full swing. It's gorgeous.

Pulling out my phone, I'm not surprised there's no service. But I am disappointed. I've been working hard on my social media presence, and a stretch of not posting is likely to cause a significant dip in new followers and mess up the algorithms. I'll just have to make sure I have loads of content for when I get back to civilization, in case I don't ever get a signal up here.

Sometimes you have to sacrifice for your art.

I take some photographs, which I'll edit later, and after touching up my makeup, I shoot a couple of quick videos to establish both the setting and my plans. I do several takes of each, so I can decide later whether I look better with or without the safari hat. Either way, my waist-length blonde curls look amazing highlighted by the sun. Unfortunately, the same sun makes me squint, so even though I'm a firm believer in making eye contact with my audience, my sunnies are necessary.

I'm using my phone camera now, but I have professional videography equipment—the very best—including my small, high-action camera (no blurry Bigfoot footage for this professional), and a slew of tricked-out hidden cameras that I plan to distribute throughout the area later. They're tiny and disguised as things like snails. So clever. Even if I don't spot Bigfoot with my own two eyes—though I plan to—I'm going to get evidence of his existence one way or another.

"Look at this scenery!" I say, holding my phone up and swinging it around slowly. "It's breathtaking, isn't it? Autumn has always been my favorite season, but up here, it is truly something else. I'm going to pitch my tent and then I'll be back…"

My voice trails off because I hear something in the near distance. I put a finger to my lips, even though there's no one but me to make a sound, anyway.

A series of deep grunts rumbles through the trees!

My eyes fly open, and my heart skips a beat. Is it possible? Could it be my Bigfoot? Hope and exhilaration replace fear as I imagine the possibility of encountering the legendary cryptid, again, not more than two minutes after arriving at my campsite.

I hear something else mixed in with the grunts. Laughter?

I spin around, excitement coursing through me. But there are so many trees…something or someone could be hiding behind any one of them.

My heartbeat quickens. Could it be another bobcat? Or maybe a playful raccoon? Didn't I hear somewhere that coyotes' calls sound like creepy laughter?

Hopefully not a coyote.

Hopefully not a bear.

I hold my breath and listen. It's definitely laughter, but not the kind that belongs to wild animals.

I eagerly head in the direction of the sounds, keeping my phone up in front of me, set to record so I don't miss anything. But I'm also grabbing for the high-speed camera at my neck, searching for the power button and pressing it on with my shaky fingers.

Suddenly, I'm caught in a tangle of fine, sticky near-invisible strands. It takes me far too long to realize I've walked face-first into a spiderweb.

A shriek of revulsion pops out of me. Holy shit, I really hope that spider isn't in my hair! Shuddering at the thought, I swipe at my face, wiping away the clingy, nasty threads with trembling fingers.

But I have to get a grip, so I take a deep, shaky breath and right my phone, which is still on record. It's a good thing I don't have reception and therefore couldn't go live, because that probably would have gone viral for the wrong reasons.

The grumbling, grunting, laughing noises are still going on, along with splashes—lots of splashes. Deep echoing ones, and I remember a swimming hole in the river…

Excitement builds in me again as I hurry toward the sounds, and then catch sight of movement—lots of movement through the trees. But my joy is dashed when I see the line of trees thinning 'til they're basically gone. Well, shit. I won't be able to hide in the wide open!

Creeping as close to the tree line as possible without totally exposing myself, I pocket my phone and switch to my high-speed, shockproof, waterproof action camera, zooming in as much as possible and holding my arm out, watching the screen as I center on the figures.

I stand, unblinking. Holy smokes. Holy shit. Their constant movement in the water makes it hard to focus, but even so, their big, burly, hairy bodies are right there on the screen.

Holy moly shitballs! I move out from behind my scrawny tree and inch forward, watching with more care now. I duck down behind a bush, so what I'm seeing doesn't see me.

That damn spider *was* in my hair, and it bit me and injected me with some sort of hallucinogenic venom, obviously. Otherwise, I would not be seeing what I am seeing. Not two, not three, but…a whole heck of a lot of them. Bigfoot! Bigfoots? Bigfeet?

I don't know, whatever, it's a whole lot of Sasquatches. A whole crew of them splashing in the water like children.

Ginormous, joyful children.

"You guys," I whisper, hoping the microphone will pick up my voice. "Are you seeing what I'm seeing? I cannot believe my luck!"

I squint at the screen, counting. Seven, eight of them?

I want to whoop and holler, like they're doing. I want to do a celebratory dance. I want to march right down there and introduce myself because—

Suddenly, the opening notes of the old Hall & Oates song, "Maneater," begins blasting. Mom's ringtone. Shit! Apparently there *is* service up here. That fact should make me happy, but as I frantically wrench my phone out of my pocket and scrabble at the buttons to shut it up with one hand while keeping the camera steady with the other, I glance in the direction of my newfound discovery and see that the Sasquatches, too, have made a discovery.

They're all looking in my direction. And, despite the majority of their faces being covered by hair—fur?—it's apparent that they are not happy with my presence.

And they do not look like a crowd you'd want to march right down and introduce yourself to, so I'm glad I didn't go that route. Especially not when "Maneater" won't stop blaring from my phone. The song choice seemed funny when my mom was marrying her eighth husband—her love life is one of those you either laugh or cry situations—but it's not at all humorous when one burly Sasquatch points in my direction and starts making snarly noises.

Surely I stopped the ringing already. Is she calling me back? Yes, there's her smiling face, popping back up on my phone.

Oh God, and they're all swimming toward the land. They're fast swimmers. They're clambering out of the water, lumbering toward the tree line. Toward me.

My brain is shrieking RUN!!! But my legs are not listening.

"ROSE-GOLD, ARE YOU THERE?" my mother's voice is squawking from my hand.

Oops. Did I accept the call?

"Mom, I'll call you back!" I hiss, my eyes glued on the approaching figures.

I'm going to die. The *Piney Grove Trading Post and General Store* lady totally predicted it. The breath of death or whatever is on my neck.

They're coming toward me and they look pissed. Maybe I don't remember things so clearly, because my Bigfoot did not look pissed. He had the kindest eyes ever!

And these guys are ginormous, did I mention that?

"Rose-Gold, it's over! Clive and I—"

"MOTHER! Holy shit, I've got to run."

Like, literally run.

"Rose-Gold Amber Locke, do not say *holy shit* to your mother!" Mother chastises. I can see her mauve-lined lips, which match the current dye job in her short-cropped hair, twisting with disappointment. "I need you right now. My marriage is ending. I cannot handle another divorce. I simply cannot—"

"MOTHER!" I shriek.

They're shouting. There are seven or eight or nine of them. What's a group of Sasquatches called? A gang? A murder? I don't know. But a flock of birds erupt with squawks of terror, flying off as the thundering mass of shouting, pissed-off Sasquatches chase me. Arms are pumping, their hair is flying behind them like streamers, and they are coming for me.

I'm going to die.

"Rose-Gold, are you listening to me? You better not hang up on me in my time of need. You're my only child. I can't go through another…"

Mother's words, words I've heard before—words I could recite like quotes, I've heard them so many times—blur together as my legs finally obey my brain and I take off running, questioning all of my life decisions.

The gift shop lady said the spirit of death was hovering around me!

Why didn't I listen?

You know how you always see women running through the woods in movies and they do it like they're gazelles or something, effortlessly bounding and darting over roots and fallen limbs?

Yeah, that's not real life.

Real life is tripping and stumbling and branches to the face. And I have to keep looking over my shoulder to see if they're gaining ground. Which is stupid and impossible, because in real life, there are stumps and roots that seem to pop up out of nowhere like nature's booby traps, bound and determined to send me flying onto my ass.

Dead meat.

TEN MOUNTAIN MEN

I am dead meat.

"Rose-Gold, I can hear you gasping for breath. Baby, are you okay? Did you go back to that spin class?"

"Not okay. I'm dead meat. I have to call you back later. Sorry about Clive!"

The grunts and snarls are getting closer, and then, to my astonishment, one shouts, "Get her!" in perfect English.

My Sasquatches speak English!

So, I could stop and explain to them that, you know, as far as I know, we're still in the United States where murder is illegal.

I glance back in a moment of contemplation, just to see if the English-speaking Bigfoot could—

BAM!

Pain catches me in the forehead and radiates all the way down to my blistered toes, and I lose all the wind in my lungs from the impact. Even my scream gets caught in my chest as my body ricochets off what must be an enormous tree and my feet fly out from under me, my ankle doing something I'm pretty sure is not normal for an ankle to do, as I'm knocked on my ass.

CHAPTER 3

Luke

"Damn every last one of my brothers," I mutter under my breath, frustration building with every one of my steps as I trudge along the path into the forest. "Damn them all."

"Be back by lunch," I told them, my tone letting them know just how damn serious I was. *"If you aren't back by lunch, I'm eating without you and I'm eating your food. All of it!"*

And yet here we are on the same damn hamster wheel. Every day, we do this, following the same frustrating routine. Every day—even though I swear I won't—I retrieve them from wherever they're off dillydallying, completely oblivious that it's noon. Then it's a mad dash back home to hopefully get them to the table so we can eat before our meal is cold.

I hate cold food, a trait I remember sharing with Dad. And I hate dillydallying, a trait I know comes from Ma. But seriously, we eat at the same time every day. It's not that hard to keep track of the time, now is it? It's not like they're children. The youngest of us, Rusty, is twenty now. Grown-ass men, the lot of them, and I shouldn't have to—

I stop in my tracks as I hear a feminine shriek, followed by a hell of a lot of shouting.

"What the hell?" I mutter.

Then she bursts through the trees, a vision of wild beauty.

I blink, stupefied for a second. Part of me thinks, *Holy shit, she's gorgeous,* and the rest of me thinks, *Who is this woman and what the actual fuck is she doing on my mountain?*

She's running toward me, looking back over her shoulder. I follow her fearful, desperate gaze and watch as one, two, three, four, five, six, seven—*seven* of my dumbass brothers stumble and lurch out onto the path behind her.

All of them are naked as the day they were born, hauling ass after her, their hollering breaking through the trees with a discordant echo.

No wonder she's running. The sight and sound is truly terrifying. It makes me want to turn around and haul ass too, to be honest.

But I stand, frozen, watching the scene in front of me play out, as if it's not damn obvious I'm unfortunately about to become a part of it. Before I can even step out of the way, she closes in, picking up speed, glancing backward, not noticing either me or the sloppy patch of mud on the path between us.

"Watch out!" one of the guys—Hunter, I think—calls to her or to me or maybe the pair of us.

She doesn't notice. In a burst, she hurtles toward me, her ridiculously impractical boots skidding in the mud. Something hard gets me right in the knees, and then she's falling backward. My eyes water as if I took a direct hit to the nuts. She flails. She reaches out, presumably trying to catch hold of something to steady herself. I don't have the good sense to move, so what she catches hold of is me, grabbing onto my shins. It's just enough to make me off-balance, and down I go, into the mud, right along with her.

Damn.

"I'm wearing my good pants," is what I say to this woman, who somehow managed to fall so that she's on top of me.

"You're wearing pants," she says, amazed.

Why the fuck wouldn't I be? Oh, maybe because my brothers gave the impression that we're one big nudist colony up here.

I'm covered in mud, she's covered in mud. She reaches up, wiggling her body until she's straddling my hips, and my breath catches in my chest as she attempts to wipe the mud off my cheeks with her even muddier fingers—smearing it into my beard, I'm sure.

I'm on my back and she's on top of me, this woman, this total stranger, tenderly touching my face. She peers down at me, amazed.

I just wanted a damn sandwich and some damn stew.

"Could you not?" I demand, swatting her tiny little hands away like they're a hoard of damn mosquitoes.

Then those hands are on my chest.

Well, fuck. I'm not old enough for a heart attack, surely. But I'm not exactly a young buck anymore, either.

"God, your pecs," she murmurs, raking her fingers through my chest hair, making me wish I was wearing my good shirt with my good pants. Or any shirt, actually. *What. The. Fuck.* "I can't believe how close I am…"

Her thumb grazes my left nipple and…oh no, not now. My cock is more than happy to remind me that forty-two isn't very old, that my body still has a lot of life in it, the way it hardens underneath her perfect, plump, squeezable ass.

The way her eyes fill with more intrigue by the second makes me want to push up against her, return her caresses.

Which really pisses me the fuck off.

"Would you kindly get off of me?"

I do not say it kindly, but I do not fucking care, because this woman needs to fucking go.

Instead of listening, her lips part and she licks them with her pretty pink tongue. So goddamn pink. Fucking glistening to boot. "I…I think I hit my head, or maybe it was the spider's venom but…are you real? You can't be."

Her eyes are so big, so blue. So…lovely, actually. A lot of us have blue eyes, but I've never seen blue eyes in a shade quite this bright before. Her pupils are a bit dilated, giving her a slightly dazed look. She has a knot forming on her forehead. From the way my right kneecap is throbbing, I think I can figure out what she knocked that noggin on.

But even though she looks like she's about to sprout a horn, she's incredibly attractive, this woman, which makes me like her being here even less.

"Your pecs are so…wow. You're not as furry as I remember, though. But chiseled. You're so chiseled."

She pets my shoulders, my biceps, like I'm a damn dog. Her touch sends heat sparking through my blood.

All of which seems to be filling my cock now. It's never felt this engorged, this fucking hard.

And my cheeks. I'm blushing like a fucking teenager— what the hell? I'm thankful for my beard, which will at least keep anyone from seeing the pinkened flesh beneath.

"How did I manage to find so many glorious specimens of Bigfoot right away?"

Her voice is like a sexy purr, but her words hit me like someone's tossed a bucket of ice-cold water over my head.

"But not a full colony," she continues, quizzically. She sucks her lip in between her teeth for a second. "Just the males. How fascinating. Perhaps there are females back at their… cave? Nest?"

I have no idea who she's talking to, but she's so beautiful that I can't manage to do more than glare at her intrusion, though my mind does catch on the word *Bigfoot*. Fucking fuck.

I can't have heard her correctly. I can't have—

"Unless," she says, wrinkling her brow, "I'm hallucinating all of this. Maybe I bumped my head too hard."

"You did crack it pretty good," I tell her.

"I did?" She touches her forehead, smearing mud across her creamy skin, pushing too hard on the lump. "*Ow*. Oh."

"But I'm also real," I add. "Not a hallucination."

"How do I know you're not just a hallucination telling me you're not a hallucination just to mess with me?" she asks.

She fingers a strand of my hair. "A silver fox is what you are. Unless you're prematurely gray. You must be the patriarch."

With ease, I finally free myself, getting up and pretty much letting her slide off my body into the mud puddle with a splash.

Which gives me mixed feelings. While her reaction—shocked expression and an accompanying screech—to sliding into more cold mud is satisfying, my reaction to her body sliding along mine was a little too strong for comfort. With the way my erection is tenting them, not only are my good pants caked in mud, they're in serious danger of ripping open right at the crotch.

"I'm not a silver fox, and I'm not a damn Bigfoot," I say, "because Bigfoot is not real. You're not hallucinating, but you are trespassing, so I'd appreciate it if you'd go back the way you came and get off my damn mountain."

"Oh," she says, looking around at the faces of the others who've gathered around us, her mouth falling open. "This is…your mountain? I didn't know it belonged to anyone, I…"

And she looks down with a shocked, curious gaze that slides, staring, one by one, to each and every bare dick, all pointed straight at her like cannons ready to fire.

So my brothers have noticed she's attractive too, but at least a couple of them have the good sense to hide it when they finally notice all the ogling she's doing.

"Why the hell are you all naked?" I demand.

"We were bathing in the swimming hole. She was spying on us!" Ash says. Then he hastily adds, "But I'm sure she didn't mean any harm."

He smiles at her then, and she looks up at him, stunned. I'm stunned too, because Ash is usually way too cynical to take a stranger at face value, just assuming they don't mean any harm.

"I didn't mean…I thought you were…but then you were chasing me. One of you yelled, 'Get her.' I thought you were going to kill me and eat me." The blonde pouts. "Oh God, are you going to kill me and eat me?"

So first we're Bigfoots, and now we're damn cannibals?

My eyes stray to her bottom lip as it pokes out, pretty pink and glistening wet. I glance away.

"We're sorry if we scared you, ma'am," Ash says. "We just wanted to talk to you, find out what you were up to. You took us by surprise."

I roll my eyes. The Ash I know would've wanted to tie her to a tree and interrogate her, making damn sure she's not a threat before setting her free.

Just wanted to talk to her, my ass.

"That's okay," she says, nearly a whisper. "I'm sorry I interrupted your…your…your, um…privacy?" she says questioningly, as if she's not sure she's using the right word. "I didn't realize you were all…" She looks down at Ash's now semi-erect dick and blushes prettily.

"Lunch is ready," I say, not quite ready to acknowledge that every shred of normalcy has gone out the window and there's no way I'll be eating lunch any time soon.

All I want is a nice quiet meal—while it's still hot. Is that too much for a man to ask for?

"Are you okay?" Clay asks suddenly. I can't get over how serious he sounds. Normally Clay would make some wisecrack, poking fun at me for getting knocked on my ass.

"No, I am not okay," I grouse. "My good pants are covered in mud and I'm covered in mud and I'm going to have to take a damn shower before we can eat and I'm hungry as hell."

"Clay wasn't talking to you, Luke," Nash says. He rushes closer and, both he and Clay, cocks still out, kneel down next to this woman.

This woman who shouldn't be here. Who cares if she's okay? She's got to go. Already the chaos she's causing is too much.

"May I help you up, ma'am?" Clay asks her, offering his arm. His thick, muscled arm, which she stares at before placing her palm atop almost reverently. She shifts her position and then her big baby blues are suddenly welled up with tears and her plump lower lip quivers.

Oh, damn. Not the waterworks.

"I'm hurt," she says, a tremor in her voice. "Oh, the pain. The...why is everything spinning?"

At that, they all predictably race to her, jockeying to be the one to help her up.

"She probably doesn't want all your cocks in her face, nimrods."

"Oh, shit," Brooks says. "We forgot to put our clothes on."

A few of them have the decency to look embarrassed. Even fewer cover themselves with their hands.

"I swear they aren't stupid," I tell her, though why am I telling her anything? I don't care if she thinks my brothers are stupid.

I stomp over and hold out a hand, hoisting her up. She cries out in agony and I have to grab her to keep her from going down again as her ankle buckles.

"Your ankle. It might be broken," Lynx says. "Don't put any weight on it."

I groan, but it's drowned out by the commotion as Buck races onto the path, carrying everyone's pants. He distributes them to the others, brushing his hair out of his eyes so he can better see the lady. He greets me with a chin nod, then he turns his full attention back to her, eyes like damn saucers.

"She's injured," Lynx tells him. "Possibly a broken ankle."

"Who is she?" Buck asks. He sounds awestruck, like it's a unicorn not some meddlesome lady who does not belong here. "What is she doing here?"

She's clinging to me like I'm her damn life raft, that's what she's doing here.

"She's a vision," Brooks breathes, sounding like a teenager with a crush rather than a man in his late-thirties.

"Shut up, Brooks," I say. Then I ask the lady, "Do you have amnesia?"

She giggles, like she, too, is a teenager with a crush. This is bad on so many levels. I have to get her gone. Now.

"I don't think so," she says. She blinks. "But my head doesn't quite feel right. So…maybe?"

"You know your name, your address, where you came from, and how to get back there?"

She nods. "My name is Gold—"

"I don't care." I transfer her to Clay and Lynx, who are the closest to us, getting them both muddy too, but when I said I don't care, I meant it.

We don't like outsiders, and they aren't welcome here. Even the pretty ones. My eyes flick over her curves.

Especially the pretty ones. Damn.

"You drove here? To the mountain?" I ask. "In a car?"

She nods. "It's the prettiest shade of purple known to—"

"Escort her back to wherever she's parked," I tell Lynx. "Then come right back. Lunch is getting cold."

"Luke, she's hurt," Nash protests.

"Not our problem. This is private property, ma'am. My brother, Lynx, will get you safely back to your vehicle. He can give you directions to the nearest hospital. But you have to go. Now."

I turn to leave, but catch my brothers shooting meaningful looks at each other.

"No," I say. I know what those meaningful looks mean.

"She's hurt," Clay insists. "We have to take her back to the cabin and let her clean up and tend to her wounds. It's the right thing to do."

His face is as serious as his voice. What the hell? Clay ain't acting like Clay.

"Then I'll take her to her car," Lynx says. "After I've tended to her and let her rest up a bit. We can't let her drive if she has a concussion, Luke."

Dammit. He probably has a valid point, but I said no. Didn't I say no?

"I SAID NO."

More meaningful glances.

"Don't I get a say in this?" Gold asks in a small voice.

"No, ma'am, you do not," I reply. "You have to—"

"Luke's right. You don't get a say. We caused you to fall and injure yourself, so we insist that you stay and let us make sure you're alright. And feed you lunch," Hunter tells her.

I can't help myself. I groan a groan that rises from deep within my soul. If I know Hunter, and I do, he isn't going to take a no from her or me.

They're all making lovesick cow eyes at her, like they've never seen a woman before. All at once they're yammering, each vocalizing their desire to be the one to carry her to the cabin as all of them but Hunter scramble to get dressed, falling all over themselves to be the one to save the damsel in distress.

Smitten, every damn one of them, and I want to smack them all on the back of the head, one at a time, and remind them that love at first sight is bullshit. Love is bullshit. This is bullshit.

I don't like it.

And I don't like that I'm outnumbered. I'm always outnumbered. You'd think being the oldest, what I say would go, but nope.

"Do not bring her back to the cabin," I tell them.

But I know they won't listen. *We're not a Lukeocracy*, they'll say. *Everyone gets a vote, everyone's vote is equal.*

They're too blinded by her beauty to see it, but I know this woman, whoever she is, is nothing but a headful of blonde hair, curves for days, and a whole heap of trouble.

End of Preview. Continue reading
Ten Mountain Men here.

Printed in Great Britain
by Amazon